SOME JUSTICE

A GHAZI AMMAR MEDIEVAL MYSTERY

LAURY SILVERS

CONTENT NOTICES ARE SPOILERS

Violence of all types is the bread and butter of mysteries and thrillers. I do not describe any violent acts in detail, but they may still prove disturbing. For more detailed content notices, please turn to the last page in this novel, as content notices are spoilers.

This novel includes frank and extended discussions of **suicide**. If you have experienced loss or thoughts of self-harm, support is available through local services, or you can reach out to:

• In the U.S.: National Suicide Prevention Lifeline—call or text **988**
• In Canada: Talk Suicide Canada—1-833-456-4566 (24/7)
• If outside North America, visit **findahelpline.com** for international resources.

Ghazi Ammar's
Baghdad

This map is "Ghazi Ammar's Baghdad," not "Baghdad," because it is a fictional reconstruction for my story's needs. Readers interested in the historical scholarship can visit my blog, Baghdad Maps, on my website: www.llsilvers.com.

LEGEND

1. Samir's body
2. Clothier's Market, Suq at-Tarrazun, and Samir's home
3. Old embellishment shop
4. Bint Afshin
5. Abu Sa'id and Khalil
6. Ibn Suwayd
7. Salma
8. Ibn Hisham
9. Stationer's Market
10. Brothel
11. Buratha Market Gate

Map by Jess Tat

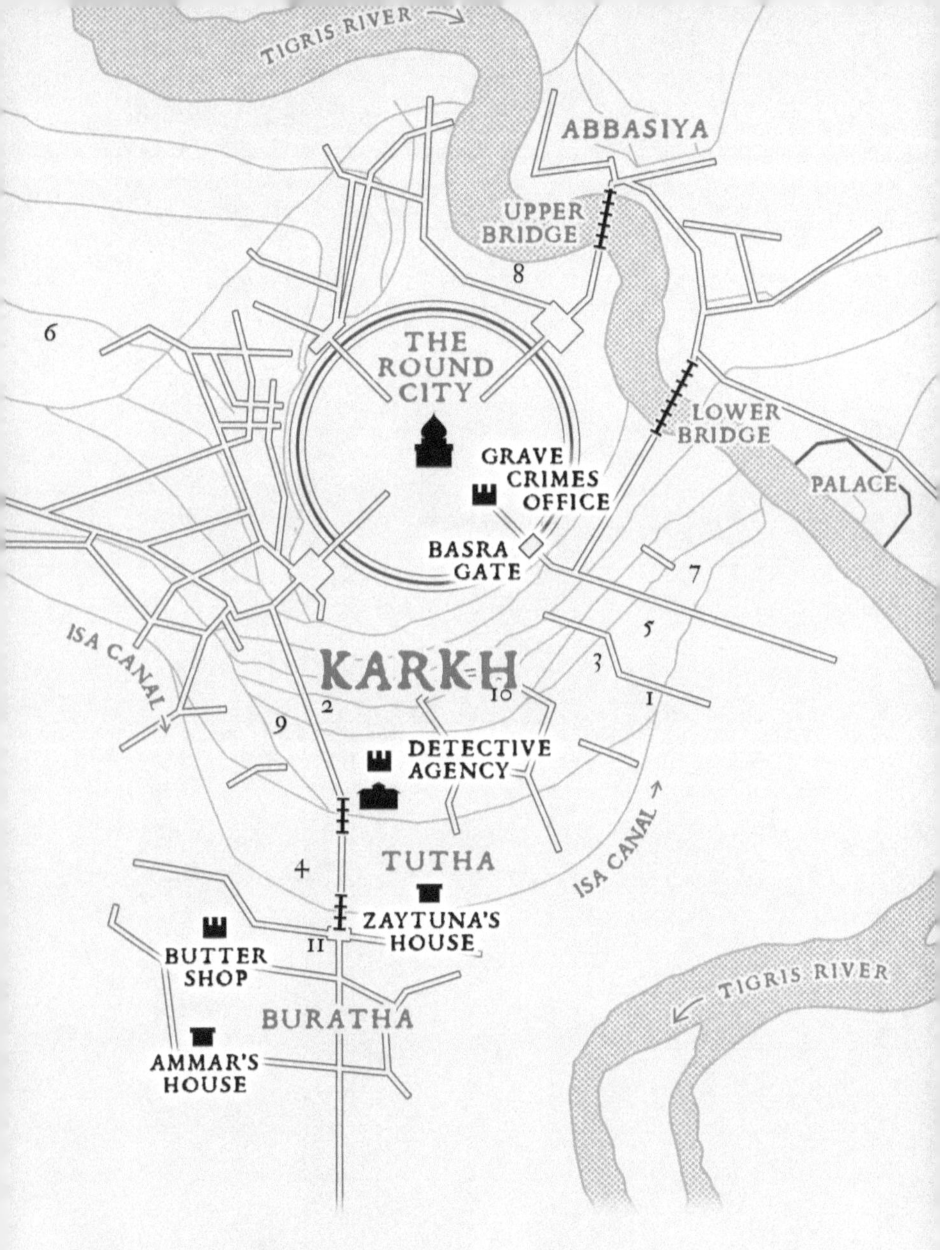

TIGRIS RIVER
ABBASIYA
UPPER BRIDGE
8
6
THE ROUND CITY
GRAVE CRIMES OFFICE
LOWER BRIDGE
PALACE
BASRA GATE
7
5
KARKH
3
10
1
ISA CANAL
9
2
ISA CANAL
DETECTIVE AGENCY
TUTHA
4
ZAYTUNA'S HOUSE
II
BUTTER SHOP
BURATHA
TIGRIS RIVER
AMMAR'S HOUSE
Ghazi Ammar's Baghdad
Mosque
Canal
Hospital
River
Building
Road
House
Bridge

HELPFUL TERMS, NOTES ON BAGHDAD, AND SUICIDE

Readers may find the following helpful, although all terms and historical events are clear within the context of the story.

Quran [qoo-RAHN]: Understood by Muslims to be the word of God revealed in Arabic to the Prophet Muhammad [moo-HAHM-mad] through the angel Gabriel. The Quran occupies a central place in Muslim life: it is recited in daily prayers, memorized in whole or in part, studied for guidance, heard in public life, woven into conversation, and treated as a sacred object. Passages from the Quran appear in italics throughout the novel and are introduced by "recited" or "God said," etc.

    Recommended reading: *The Qur'an*, translated by M. A. S. Abdel Haleem. Ingrid Mattson, *The Story of the Qur'an: Its History and Place in Muslim Life*, 2nd edition (accessible).

Ghazi [GHAH-zee]: A title given to those who fought along the frontiers of the Islamic world, whether in campaigns of expansion or in defence against incursions—most famously along the borderlands facing Byzantium. The title evokes the memory of those who fought alongside the Prophet Muhammad and the early leaders of the Muslim community. It was considered a hard-won honour and conferred considerable respect.

Shia [SHEE-ah]: Muslims who hold that the Prophet and God —as expressed in certain Quranic verses—designated 'Ali [ah-LEE], the Prophet Muhammad's cousin and son-in-law, as his rightful successor rather than Abu Bakr [ah-boo BAH-kr]. This early dispute was not only political; it led to the development of distinct Shia theological teachings and ritual practices. Central among these was the expectation that legitimate political and religious leadership should remain within the Prophet's direct family line. People in this period may not always have used the term "Shia," but I use it here for clarity. Personal names that trace back to the heroes of Karbala remain common among the Shia, and characters will recognize each other by them. Shia communities were a significant presence in the neighbourhoods of Karkh and Buratha, where my novels are set.

Recommended reading: Lesley Hazleton, *After the Prophet: The Epic Story of the Shia-Sunni Split in Islam* (accessible).

Sunni [SOO-nee]: Muslims who hold that the Prophet and God —as expressed in certain Quranic verses—entrusted the Prophet's companions, beginning with Abu Bakr [ah-boo BAH-kr], to lead the community after Muhammad's death. Distinct Sunni theological teachings and ritual practices developed from this understanding, including the expectation that political and religious leaders should be chosen from among the community's qualified members. In practice, however, about thirty years after Muhammad's death, the caliphate shifted toward hereditary succession for political leadership (beginning with the Umayyads), while religious authority increasingly came to rest with scholars rather than rulers.

Recommended reading: Lesley Hazleton, *After the Prophet: The Epic Story of the Shia-Sunni Split in Islam* (accessible).

Karbala [KAR-bah-lah]: The site of the battle in which caliphal forces killed the Prophet Muhammad's grandson Husayn [hoo-SAYN], along with his family members and followers. Husayn had set out at the urging of supporters in the city of Kufa who rejected Umayyad rule and looked to him as the only morally legitimate alternative. His death—and Zaynab's [ZAY-nab] powerful condemnation of the Umayyad ruler Yazid [yah-ZEED] in the days that followed—turned a political crisis into a defining moral reckoning.

For Shia Muslims, Karbala marks a pivotal moment of martyrdom, justice, and faith. For Sunnis, it stands as a profound tragedy in the history of the community. The conflict over legitimate leadership that set these events in motion remains central to how Muslims remember this period. The courage of those who faced the caliphal army deeply influences devotional memory—and inspires our protagonists, Ammar and his wife, Nasifa.

Recommended reading: Omid Safi, *Memories of Muhammad* (accessible)

Sufi [SOO-fee]: Sufism is the principal mystical path within Sunni Islam, seeking direct knowledge of God through disciplined practices of worship, reflection, and meditation in addition to the daily devotional life. Baghdad was an early centre of Sufi thought and practice. During the era depicted here, women had public and private roles as teachers and students in mixed-gender gatherings. Women's leadership continued in later centuries, though increasingly within private or domestic spheres.

Recommended reading: A. Helwa, *The Secrets of Divine Love* (theological, accessible); Carl Ernst, *Sufism: An Introduction to the Mystical Tradition of Islam* (historical, accessible); for more in-depth but accessible historical detail of early Sufism, see my fictional series *The Sufi Mysteries Quartet*.

Ghuraba [ghoo-rah-BAH]: A term used in medieval Islamic sources for groups we associate with the diverse communities known today as the Roma or Travellers. These communities have their own names for themselves and were never culturally uniform. The Ghuraba of the Islamic world made notable contributions to the societies in which they lived, including skilled craftsmanship, performance traditions, and—most intriguingly—developments in early forms of printing, including pre-Gutenberg movable type. They were also known for the production and sales of talismans, fortune telling, and small criminal activities. Their compounds were called "mastabas."

Recommended reading: Kristina Richardson, *The Roma in the Medieval Islamic World* (scholarly).

———

Baghdad [bahg-DAHD]: Medieval Baghdad was one of the world's most cosmopolitan cities, renowned for its intellectual, artistic, and scientific achievements. The novel's mix of cultures, languages, and faiths reflects historical reality—if anything, the city was even more diverse and remained into the present. Administratively and socially, Baghdad is best understood not as a single urban centre but as a vast metropolitan region made up of interconnected districts, markets, and suburbs, each with its own character.

Recommended reading: Emily Selove (ed.), *Baghdad at the Centre of a World, 8th–13th Century* (accessible); Scheiner & Toral (eds.), *Baghdad: From its Beginnings to the Fourteenth Century* (scholarly).

The Round City: Founded in 762 CE as the fortress-capital of the Abbasid caliphs, the Round City served as the administrative and ceremonial heart of imperial power. Over time, Baghdad expanded far beyond its circular walls into surrounding districts such as Karkh, forming a vast metropolitan region. Long before the time of this novel, the caliph moved to the other side of the city, across the Tigris, and the Round City became used mainly for military, police, and other administrative activities as well as devotion, as it boasted the greatest mosque in the city. The original Round City did not survive intact; repeated floods, fires, political decline, and ultimately the Mongol invasion contributed to its destruction. Modern maps are reconstructions based on medieval descriptions and archaeological findings.

Karkh [kahrkh]: Older than Baghdad itself, Karkh was eventually absorbed into the expanding city and became its great market district—so dense with trades and shops that medieval writers called it the "Grand Market." It was also a centre of Shia life, home to many notable Shia families, scholars, and communal institutions.

Buratha [boo-RAH-thah]: A suburb south of Baghdad (sometimes spelled Baratha) with a strong concentration of Shia families and scholars. In the novel, Ammar and his household live on Buratha's southern edge, near the goat-grazing lands that open toward the distant plain of Karbala.

Tutha [TOO-thah]: A neighbourhood in Karkh known for its Sufi community and its cemetery, where significant early Sufi masters are buried. Zaytuna and her family live near the site of the original Baghdad Sufi circle, centred on the home of al-Junayd al-Baghdadi [al-joo-NAYD], who died shortly before the year in which this novel is set.

Hospitals: Medieval Baghdad was renowned for its hospitals, though historians continue to debate their exact chronology, locations, and functions. Their social role, however, is well attested: they offered medical care, teaching, and public service to the city's diverse population. Although the famous Barmakid Hospital [bar-MAH-kid] may not have survived into the period of this novel, I use it as a setting because of its convenient location near my protagonists' homes. Likewise, the physician al-Rāzī [ar-RAH-zee] (Rhazes) may have directed a hospital across the Tigris River at another site. The depiction of medical practice and public service in the novel is faithful to surviving period sources.

Recommended reading: Peter E. Pormann & Emilie Savage-Smith, *Medieval Islamic Medicine* (accessible).

———

Suicide: Medieval Muslims generally regarded suicide as both sinful and socially shameful, and some refrained from performing public funeral prayers for the deceased. Legal and theological positions, however, turned on the person's intention and capacity, and scholars debated what counted as moral or diminished responsibility. The novel reflects both the historical spectrum of opinion and attempts to frame this difficult subject with contemporary compassion. Ibn Ali, the novel's pharmacist, philosopher, and free thinker, gives an account that is rooted in classical perspectives and leans into my personal view: most cases may be considered the tragic end of a terminal mental illness, abandonment by community, or unaddressed physical suffering.

The Hadith Zaytuna quotes as an opportunity for compassion and the right to pray over the deceased is as follows:

Jabir narrated:

Tufayl bin 'Amr went to the Prophet (God bless him and give him peace) and he said: "O Messenger of God, do you have a secure fortress?" The tribe of Daws had a fortress in the days of Jahiliyya. The Prophet (God bless him and give him peace) refused that offer, as God had reserved it for the Ansar. When the Messenger of God (God bless him and give him peace) performed the Hijra to Medina, Tufayl made the Hijra with a man from his tribe. They reached Medina and he became sick, and felt anxiety. He took iron arrowheads and cut through his finger joints, and his hands gushed out until he died. Then Tufayl saw him in a dream. His condition was good, but his hands were bandaged.

Tufayl asked him, "What did your lord arrange with you?" He said, "He pardoned me with my Hijra to his prophet, God bless him and give him peace." Tufayl asked, him, "Why do I see your hands wrapped?" He said, "It was said to me, 'We do not repair what you damaged.'"

Tufayl told the story to the Messenger of God (God bless him and give him peace)."

"The Messenger of God (God bless him and give him peace) said, "O God, forgive his hands too."

In: Muslim, *Sahih*, "Kitab al-iman," #17

Recommended reading: For a helpful discussion of this

report, see Michael Muhammad Knight, *Muhammad: Forty Introductions* (accessible); for medieval perspectives on suicide, see Emily Silkaitis, "Suicide: A Study of the Tafsīr," *Der Islam* 99 (1), 2022 (scholarly) and Franz Rosenthal, "Suicide in Islam" (scholarly); for a contemporary understanding of suicide prevention in Islam from a therapeutic perspective, see Awaad et al., "Islam and Suicide: An Interdisciplinary Scoping Review," Spirituality in Clinical Practice, 2023 (scholarly).

CHARACTERS AND PRONUNCIATION

Recurring Characters

Most recurring characters first appeared in The Sufi Mysteries Quartet. The events of this novel take place some three years after the close of that series.

Ammar [ah-MAHR]: Shia Arab, former frontier fighter—*ghazi* —and principal investigator for Grave Crimes in the Baghdad police. After leaving the force, Ammar established his own investigations agency: *Ghazi Ammar's Agency of Investigation and Implementation*. He lives in Buratha with his wife, **Nasifa [nah-SEE-fah]**, and his son, **Husayn [hoo-SAYN]**, as well as his extended family (father, mother, and his brother **Muhsin [MUH-sin]**), who would prefer he herd goats.

Zaytuna [zay-TOON-ah]: Nubian mother and Arab father. A Sufi and former clothes washer, she is the daughter of a famed female mystic known as *al-Ashiqa al-Sawda*, "the Black Lover of God." Zaytuna is married to **Kamal Ali [kah-MAHL ah-LEE]**, a producer of the finest butter in Baghdad. She lives in Tutha with her husband; their daughters, **Nura [NOO-rah]** and Layla; her twin brother, Tein; his wife, Saliha; and their chosen-family aunt and uncle, Yulduz and Qambar.

Tein [TEEN]: Nubian mother and Arab father. He is Zaytuna's twin and a former frontier fighter and investigator alongside Ammar in Grave Crimes. He is husband to Saliha, churns butter for Kamal Ali, enjoys being a homebody, and talks philosophy with Ibn Ali, **Baraqan [bah-RAH-gan]**, and others.

Saliha [SAH-lee-hah]: Arab Sunni, Zaytuna's best friend, wife of Tein, and a corpse washer at the Barmakid Hospital with Shatha **[SHAT-ha]**, her senior, and the men's washer, Taha **[TAH-ha]**. She serves as a junior forensic specialist under Ibn Ali.

Layla [LAY-luh]: Arab, a former child servant indentured by her parents at a young age, later fostered by Zaytuna and her family to become Zaytuna and Kamal Ali's chosen daughter. Special friend to **Abdulghafur [ab-dool-gha-FOOR]**, a cook in the kitchen at the Sufi gathering house, who shares her painful past.

Yulduz [YOOL-dooz] and Qambar [KAHM-bar]: Turkmen and Persian, Sunni and Shia, the elderly married couple are Zaytuna and Saliha's neighbours who moved with them when Kamal Ali raised the entire household's fortunes.

Firdaws Ibn Ali [feer-DAOUS ibn ah-LEE]: East African mother and Persian father; imagined as the child of the famed Persian pharmacist Ali ibn Sahl Rabban al-Tabari (c. 838–870 CE), who wrote *Firdaws al-Hikma* (*Paradise of Wisdom*) and taught the great physician al-Razi (Rhazes). Firdaws Ibn Ali, named for that compendium, is the senior forensic specialist.

Auntie Hakima [hah-KEE-mah]: An elder female mystic, a composite character based on several early Sufi women.

YingYue [yeeng-yweh] and Abu YingYue [ah-boo yeeng-yweh]: A Chinese mystical prodigy from Taraz, a city on the eastern edge of the Muslim empire. She married Zaytuna's childhood love, **Mustafa [moos-TAH-fah]**, but ultimately chose a life of celibacy and worship. The two are married in name only, and Mustafa now lives in Medina. Her father, known as **Abu YingYue [ah-boo yeeng-yweh]**, a former paper manufacturer in Taraz, owns a copyist and print shop in Karkh.

Shabib [sha-BEEB] and Ahab [AH-hab]: Arab Shia watchmen whom Ibn Marwan hired as Ammar and Tein's replacements as Grave Crimes investigators for Karkh on Ammar's recommendation.

Khalil [kha-LEEL]: Arab Sunni, a former *ghazi* who now works as an enforcer for the debt collector **Abu Sa'id [ah-boo sah-EED]**.

Razba ibn Salim [RAZ-bah ibn sah-LEEM]: A Ghuraba [ghoo-rah-BAH] (Roma) leader and powerful figure in the Baghdad underworld. An intellectual, he is interested in developing movable-type printing with Abu YingYue and in discussing philosophy with Tein, Ibn Ali, and Baraqan.

Girgis [GEER-gis]: A Marsh Arab and Mandaean who has had to seek his fortune on the streets of Baghdad, most recently as a boat hand on the Isa [EE-sah] Canal.

Mazal [mah-ZAHL]: A Jewish apothecary with a penchant for writing bad poetry.

———

Major Characters in this Novel

Samir Abu Bashir [sah-MEER ah-boo bah-SHEER]
Bashir [bah-SHEER]
Basma [BAHS-mah]

———

Ibn Hisham [ibn hee-SHAHM]
Sitara [see-TAH-rah]
Keyvan [KAY-vahn]

———

Bint Afshin [bint ahf-SHEEN]
Adnan [ahd-NAHN]
Gul [gool]
Yasmin [yas-MEEN]

———

Abu Fidda [ah-boo FID-dah]
Abduljabbar ibn Fadi [ab-dool-jab-BAHR ibn FAH-dee]
Abdussamad [ab-doo-sah-MAHD]
Bilge al-Attar [BEEL-geh al-aht-TAHR]
Hamza [HAM-zah]
Ibn Malik [ibn MAH-lik]
Ibn Salim [ibn sah-LEEM]
Miqdad [MEEK-dahd]
Muhammad ibn Shams al-Ghassal [moo-HAHM-mad ibn
shahms al-GHAS-sahl]

Rejep [REH-jep]
Umm al-Yatama [umm al-yah-TAHM- ah]
Umm al-Hurayra [umm al-hoo-RAY-rah]
Suwayd ibn Wardan [soo-WAYD ibn war- DAHN]
Taha [TAH-hah]
Yusuf al-Multani [YOO-soof al-mool-TAH- nee]
Ibn Shams al-Ghassal [ibn shams al-ghas-SAL]

SOME JUSTICE

PROLOGUE
BAGHDAD (912 CE)

Girgis shielded his eyes to sight an incoming boat. The canal waters twisted around his ankles, hollowing channels in the sandy mud. He had taken off everything but his sirwal, hiking them up to his knees, but the loose pants had become soaked. His tanned, muscular body was all but naked; he exulted, knowing the girl on the hill was watching.

Ahmad teased, "She's not even hiding!"

Salman slapped the back of a porter as he waited to unload goods from the next skiff. "Avert your eyes. Our young friend here is putting on a show."

The man only grunted, exhausted from hauling sacks to and from the market.

Of course his friends were jealous but also eager to see the girl come down to him. It was the third day she stood in the swaying knee-high grasses looking out at the water as if she were there to watch the skiffs and round, reed boats running swiftly along the canal.

The men had challenged Girgis to go get her already and lead her through the marshy reeds to the soft clearing where they took their naps. He preferred to wait for her invitation.

Born a beauty, Girgis used to dance in the street for his family's dinner, easily drawing the attention of women from behind their veils. He knew the sign that she was ready for him had already come.

Before, when he had glanced at her, she would turn away, playfully hiding her face with the edge of her wrap. Yesterday, the wind caught it and it fluttered open, exposing the curve of her breasts and hips through her gown. She held his eye and laughed brightly as she covered herself, her hands quick and dark against the honey-yellow cloth. He would bet the world that today was the day.

Birds, great and small, burst out of the reed bed, screaming and breaking left and right into the sky, as if to clear their way.

"Boy!"

It was her.

"Boy!"

He turned slowly, forming a curious expression to disguise the pleasure of the moment having come to him.

"There!" She pointed toward the clearing in the reed bed where he had been anticipating uncovering her.

"Go!" She was not smiling, and there was something odd about her voice.

Salman and Ahmad cheered as he left for the narrow path to the clearing. The old man who walked the canal road every day pointed and waved him on to hurry.

The fertile scent of the soft marsh bed invited them. Except for the reeds brushing against each other, it was silent; even the toads held their tongues. He did not need to look to see if she had followed. The small, quick steps of her sandals slapping the moist earth were just behind him. As she drew near, he pushed aside the reeds to widen the path. A few moments more, then he could turn, and she would give herself to him. One last step and the reeds parted completely.

She screamed.

An elderly man lay contorted on the ground. His tongue was blackened and lolling. His turban was flung aside, exposing his shorn head. His long, bright robe was splayed open as if he had torn it in the panic of his last moments. The stench of feces and vomit hit Girgis, and he spun around. The girl fell into his arms with a sob, then violently pushed him off. For only a moment, he felt the curve of her waist as she twisted away to run back and up to the road, calling for a watchman.

1

DAY ONE

"Tein did a job for you?"

Zaytuna sucked her teeth. "He's my brother."

"He's my friend," Ammar retorted, knowing he sounded like a child.

A delivery boy arrived, balancing a fire-blackened clay pot on a hanging tray in one hand and a slab of bread in the other.

Zaytuna took it from him with thanks and placed the pot and bread on a small table in front of Ammar, saying, "What were you doing sitting in the dark?"

"Light comes through the slats in the door."

When she had intruded, Zaytuna had found him slumped on the low couch, door shut, stomach growling, and contemplating the shabby office where he, Ghazi Ammar at-Tabbani—the once storied frontier fighter and respected police investigator—now chased down errant husbands instead of Byzantine soldiers and murderers. It had been three years since his last big case. The sign over the door—*Ghazi Ammar's Agency of Investigation and Implementation*—once installed with pride, mocked him.

"I'll see to the door," she said. "Oil for the lamp, too."

There were no pretensions between them, but her constant

managing and that she was the only one bringing in cases did little to endear her to him.

"To your health," she said, handing him a wooden spoon from the cabinet nearby.

He broke hunks of the bread she paid for into the broth she paid for. "May God replenish your stores," he muttered and dug into the mutton stew like a starving man.

If his family knew how much he relied on her cases to keep the office open, they would accuse Ammar of having no shame. If he would only quit this fantasy of being a private investigator and get back to herding goats. If only, then he would be the one keeping the fat on his wife and son instead of his father and brother. He would be the one giving charity instead of receiving it.

But hadn't he been the one who gave Zaytuna her chance at solving crimes? Hadn't he fed her brother when he was desperate? When Ammar had found his old comrade a drunk, ruined from their life of battle, hadn't he helped Tein clean up and given him a job alongside him in the police? Wasn't Ammar owed some loyalty from those two now he had nothing? When Tein had walked out on the job with Grave Crimes, Ammar went with him. Yet Tein did not return the loyalty by joining the investigations office—and instead of his friend, Ammar got Tein's sister, a partner in the business by her wiles, certainly not in name.

She stood over him, watching him eat. "I can't find any evidence the husband is cheating, but there's something going on."

"Mmmph," Ammar replied, swallowing hard.

"I've followed him as far as I can go. Yulduz has been sitting with her old women, listening at corners for gossip. I've talked with the family's washing girl. The husband goes to work, goes home for the midday meal, then returns to his job. He sits with his friends on stools in the square. He goes to the mosque. Back and forth."

She would not move until he answered her. "Remind me. Why is the wife suspicious?"

"Money missing."

Ammar pushed the bowl away. "And the washing girl isn't taking it?"

"The wife checks the jar after the girl leaves."

"A tight hold on the house purse, then."

Zaytuna sat on the couch opposite him, arranging her plain wrap around her as if it were one of her brightly coloured silks. She got airs since marrying the man producing the most sought-after butter in Baghdad. "The husband brings his pay home from the brick pit and puts it into her hand. So, yes, Tein asked about the work and the pay for me. The husband isn't lying—"

"For you." Ammar cut her off. "Tein asked around—for you."

"He won't do a job for you because you want him back in the game. I don't."

"How often?" He gritted his teeth. "None of the men at the butter shop could have done it for you? Your husband could have made them. Kamal Ali would do anything for you."

"It is between Tein and me."

Ammar pulled the bowl closer and spooned a chunk of broth-soaked bread in his mouth to keep from speaking. The resentment had got hold of him, but he could only direct it at the client. "What did her husband do to make her suspicious? Go to work. See his friends. Pray at the mosque. Nothing but jealousy and greed."

"Aren't you at least interested in the puzzle of where the money goes?"

"Why can't a man have a little money without his family having a right over every fals!"

Zaytuna did not react, not even offering a glance of understanding that would have pushed him into a worse temper. "So the husband gives her everything," she carried on. "She figures in the dark of the dawn prayer, he reaches in and takes some out again."

"You aren't watching him constantly." He drank the last of the broth, wiping his mouth and beard with his sleeve. "You can't report accurately what he's doing."

"Exactly." She gave him a hard look. "I could use some help."

"Get your brother."

But he got nothing from her but a firm expression that he knew too well.

"Fine. You tell my wife I'm not coming home at night for the handful of change this woman is paying." Ammar stood to give the impression of a last word, despite there being no last word with Zaytuna.

"Skirting night watchmen and thugs in the dark is not a job for a woman."

Ammar stared longingly at his old battle cuirass and sword hanging on the wall and tried to imagine Seyyedina Husayn—the grandson of the Prophet Muhammad, the hero who sacrificed his life for the people at the battle of Karbala—following a poor man around at night to see where he spent his coin. He sighed with resignation. "Where do they live?"

"It's not far for you."

"At least tell me he's a bad man?"

"I wish I could." She stood alongside him. "Worse, there's no love for him in her eyes."

He nearly whined. "When do we ever get a decent person who needs help? It's always some petty relative or a jealous woman."

"That's overstating."

"Not by much." He wiped his spoon and returned it to the cabinet.

She said to his back. "You have a wife and child to support. A business to build. You're not fighting at Karbala with our honoured ancestors."

He turned on her, ready to spit back that she had no right to speak of that day. Only the Shia—those who had kept their loyalty to the rule of the Prophet's family—knew the meaning of the Battle of Karbala, where so much had been lost. But one look at her standing there, observing his temper, unperturbed by a cursed thing, and he gave up.

Where was the old Zaytuna, the tortured mystic, the wretchedly skinny washerwoman with calloused hands who combatted him with a tongue as sharp as his sword? Justice used to mean something to her. Yet here she was, fattened by love and childbirth, well married, working these useless cases to entertain herself, and handing over all the money to support Ammar's investigations office. Her happiness did not suit him at all.

She stood in the open door, back to him, midday light streaming in behind her.

"So that's it? You're leaving? You going to tell me where this hounded man lives?"

Zaytuna didn't answer. "Assalamu alaykum," she said, looking out into the square.

He waved off her farewell, half-grumbling his reply, "wa alaykum assalam," when he realized she was not leaving but greeting someone outside.

He quickly put aside the pot and straightened the rough linen pillows on the sagging couch.

"Ahlan wa sahlan, welcome," she said, gesturing inside.

A man's shadow withdrew from sight.

Had the man changed his mind? Ammar tugged his belt and robe straight, adjusted his turban, and, hoping there was no grease on his sleeve, went to convince him to stay.

A handsome young man with two women stood together as a family. Ammar guessed them to be a son, his mother, and his sister. This was no poor family in clothes washed thin, like their regular clients. The son wore a striped robe of tissue-thin wool with densely embroidered edges, a matching turban, and a brown shawl in the same fabric tossed over one shoulder. The two women wore silk wraps in vibrant patterns over layered gowns whose embellished edges could be seen pooling at their feet. The mother only showed one eye, but it was swollen and red from tears. The younger woman's face was exposed, defiant yet grieving.

"Ahlan, please." Zaytuna urged them inside again.

The son took a step in and glanced around worriedly until his eyes rested on Ammar's battle-scarred leather cuirass and the Yemeni sword in its scabbard. He nodded to his mother, then addressed Ammar. "I am Bashir ibn Samir az-Zarduzi. My father has been murdered, but the investigators at Grave Crimes will not investigate. A watchman sent us. He said you were the best in your day. We demand justice."

2

———

Zaytuna waved over a sharp-faced boy lingering at the corner for small jobs.

"Yes, Lady," he said, running over.

"Assalamu alaykum. I haven't seen you around here. Are you working?"

"Wa alaykum assalam. Yes, Lady."

"First, bring me a pitcher of basil seed juice with five glasses. Do you know the juice stand in the square beyond that alley?" She pointed down a street so narrow the houses leaned in on each other on the upper floors.

He nodded vigorously.

"Glasses, not clay cups. Tell Farhang that Ghazi Ammar at-Tabbani is requesting it. You got that?"

"Yes, Lady."

"While Farhang is preparing the juice, go to the dried fruit and nut stand next to it and get a mix of the best nuts for three people. Tell Arslan to put it in one of his copper bowls." She handed him five dirhams and warned, "I'll pay you based on the quality of what you bring back, so no skimping to keep the difference in change."

"Yes, Lady." He ran off through the alley and disappeared.

She returned to find the family sitting awkwardly on one of the sagging couches and that Ammar had already started the interview.

He leaned in. "What makes you believe he was murdered?"

"His tongue was black," Bashir said.

She nearly interjected that alone was hardly evidence.

"Why won't Grave Crimes investigate?" Ammar asked.

The son looked out the door to see if anyone was listening. "We suspect they think he took his own life," he whispered. "But they were unwilling to say it aloud to save our father from going unaccompanied to the grave and to protect our family's reputation."

"You suspect?" Ammar asked.

"They only told us that he died of a convulsion. They had seen it before."

"I've seen men's tongues turn black from strangulation. I don't know about the rest. What about the state of his body?"

Umm Bashir whimpered. "There's no need for this. My children."

Why would they want to raise the spectre of suicide at all? To go through an investigation to prove Samir was murdered would only inspire gossip. And the mother obviously did not want them exposed. Their insistence made little sense to Zaytuna.

An uncomfortable silence settled into the room.

The daughter broke it. Her cheeks were flushed, and her tone was defensive. "Father would not kill himself. My brother is to be married soon. Even if—"

Zaytuna suddenly understood and finished for her. "Even if he had wanted to take his own life, he would not have done it prior to the wedding but waited until a reasonable time afterwards. Otherwise, the bride's family would break off the engagement."

Umm Bashir pulled her wrap over her face completely and began to sob softly. "Please, stop."

The daughter put an arm around her, saying, "His life was to see his children married well."

Hands out to slow them down, Ammar said, "If that was his life, consider that if he died by his own hand or another's, or even if it was a natural death, the investigation could jeopardize Bashir's marriage and maybe even the marital prospects of other family members. You, Basma. Your cousins. Their reputation is on the line here, too." He sat back, hands on his knees. "It probably was a convulsion, like they said."

It was kindly done and would let the family walk away with dignity but also lose him the investigation fee. Ammar was a good man, through and through, reminding Zaytuna why she worked with him, despite his complaints adding to the small, ongoing fires she had to tend everywhere.

Umm Bashir glanced at her children hopefully, but they treated Ammar's suggestion as an affront.

"People are already talking." Basma said, jutting her chin. "You worry about our cousins. They are among those gossiping! They have no fear of their reputations. Why should we?"

Bashir nearly shot out of his seat. His mother tugged at his sleeve, begging him to calm down, but he could not be stopped. "I have held men, my fist in their faces, demanding to know who said he took his own life, but everyone denies it."

With that, Ammar had a case and a glint in his eye she had not seen in a long time. But they needed one more chance to let it go—at least for their mother's sake—before Ammar got his teeth into it.

"If this is about the shame of suicide," Zaytuna said, "it is a tragedy, not a shame. The Prophet Muhammad, God bless him and peace, prayed for a man who had taken his own life. More, he was informed that God rewarded the man for his good deeds like any other."

Ammar glanced at her, irritated.

They were caught off guard. Umm Bashir's face softened, more tears fell, and she whispered, "God is the Merciful, the Forgiving. May He bless our gentle Prophet."

But she did not pray for her husband's soul. Zaytuna suspected that she believed her husband had taken his own life. Basma kissed her hand to comfort her but clearly would not accept the possibility of suicide no matter the harm it would do. Bashir sat straighter, staring at Zaytuna in a way that was more than resistance to her suggestion. There was something behind it, and she would pay attention to see where it led.

He said precisely, "My father did not take his own life."

There was a moment of silence, and Zaytuna hoped that at least Basma would come to her senses.

Ammar gave Zaytuna a quick look to say that line of concern was finished and said, "I have to warn you that we will need to ask some uncomfortable questions, and we'll need you to answer honestly. You cannot hide anything from us. More than that, we will have to ask questions of your friends and colleagues that you may not like."

Zaytuna added, "No one comes out of these investigations unscathed."

Was that hesitation on Basma's face? Had it finally dawned on her that she might find herself without friends, let alone unmarried, because of the choices her family was making right now? Or did she finally care what their insistence was doing to her mother?

"Ask," Bashir said.

Zaytuna could not help feeling this was a mistake, but they had been warned.

He began, "Your father is named az-Zarduzi. Is he the embellisher, or is that an old family name?"

"My father and I. We own a shop in the Suq at-Tarrazun in the Karkh Grand Market."

The son's eyes shone with pride. It was in the Clothier's market district that sold the most luxurious fabrics and employed only the finest tailors and embellishers. Ammar would be well-paid if this case lasted long enough.

"We are sought out by the highest society. My father's reputation was known across the city, and"—he blushed uncomfortably—"mine, by virtue of training under him."

"Did Samir have any difficulty with other shop owners or customers?" Ammar asked.

"He recently retired. He came into the shop to keep busy, but," Bashir repeated, "his only interest was to see his children married and to see my mother happy."

"That wasn't my question. Was there any trouble tied to the business?"

Bashir paused for a moment too long, then waved off the question. "The business is very successful. There are no concerns, none at all."

In other words, there was trouble. Zaytuna withheld a sigh. Why did clients lie only to have it be exposed later?

"Our father was well-loved by all," Basma insisted. "His funeral prayer filled the hall. So many men walked with him to the grave. They continue to mourn with us."

If there was trouble at the shop, perhaps it was Bashir's problem, not his father's, and one he did not want to share in front of his mother and sister. But his problem could have led to his father's death whether he thought so or not.

"How long ago was this?"

"They found him early last week."

"Who found him?" Ammar asked.

"A boat hand."

"Where?"

"On the Isa Canal. In a marshy landing east of its confluence with the Tabiq."

The boy returned, face screwed up from balancing a tray holding a long-necked pitcher of juice, glasses, and a bowl of nuts.

"On the table, just there," Zaytuna said.

Although there was no need, he slipped off his sandals before stepping on the reed mats, placing the tray in front of the family.

"Please," Zaytuna said, then nodded to Ammar.

He started, realizing she meant him to pour, and stood to take the pitcher.

Zaytuna followed the boy outside. He gave her the change; it was what she had expected. "You did well. May God bless you and your family." She picked several coins out and placed them in his hand. He grinned and ran back through the alley.

Inside, Ammar was asking, "That spot is a long way from the Suq at-Tarrazun. Do you live nearby?"

Bashir gave him directions to their home near the Clothiers' market.

Zaytuna pressed, "Is there any reason why he would have been there?"

A long pause expressed their discomfort with the question. Umm Bashir turned her head to the side. Was there a second wife living near the canal?

Bashir put his glass on the table with a firm clink. "No."

"I sense your discomfort," Zaytuna said. "We would never want to bring any—"

But Ammar interrupted her line of questioning. "What did he talk about that morning? The night before? Or even the week before he died?"

The family was relieved at the change in direction. That in itself was informative, making her less irritated by Ammar's interference.

"Only his joy at the coming wedding." Bashir's eyes filled with tears. "He oversaw it all with my mother. His eyes were weak, but he wanted to guide every thread sewn for Sitara's trousseau."

Umm Bashir touched her son's cheek, smiling softly.

Zaytuna said, "I would love to hear about your betrothed."

His eyes brightened. "We never expected her parents to agree."

"You were garments for one another from the first look, body and soul." His mother sniffed and patted his hand.

"Why would anyone object to such a match?" Zaytuna asked.

Bashir admitted, "We were not introduced properly. Her father—"

He paused for just a moment too long, and his sister finished, "Ibn Hisham had someone else in mind for her."

Zaytuna asked with surprise, "Was that in discussion, or was there an engagement?"

"Discussion," Bashir said.

There was something off in what he said. She asked, "Was there a falling out between the families?"

"Of sorts," Bashir said with a clear undercurrent of anger.

She could only guess that Sitara and her family were paying the price. "She took a risk for you."

His face filled with wonder. "Yes, and I will raise up her name and the name of our children."

Ammar finally grasped the implication. "Did the other family blame your father for the falling out?"

Zaytuna restrained herself from raising an eyebrow in his direction.

"Ibn Hisham and my father both struggled with the engagement on account of our disobedience. But," Bashir said, "Sitara's father came to love mine as his own brother."

Again, that was not what Ammar had asked; she took a sip of her juice, barely tasting it in the excitement of the moment.

"We can take your case," Ammar said definitively.

Bashir reached into his robe and brought out a small purse bursting with coins.

"Not the entire fee now." Ammar was gawking but answered them professionally. "I charge five dirhams a day to cover daily expenses. The fee and additional costs will come later."

It was fairly costed, but only covering the bare necessities; there would be nothing to bring home to his family yet. She smiled. Ammar was not just a good man but an ethical one, even when his complaints begged him to be otherwise.

"Will a week be sufficient to begin?"

"Please." Ammar finally picked up his glass and gulped the juice down as Bashir counted the coins in front of them.

Zaytuna gathered the coins and put them in the cabinet.

"First," Ammar said, "we'll need to speak to the corpse washer at the Barmakid Hospital and our consultants there."

"He was not washed there. The police had no way to identify him, so they took him to the one nearest. They did not find us until that night, but we still don't know how."

The reminder brought tears to his mother's eyes again. Of course, it was unthinkable for Samir to be washed without family nearby or her son in the room.

"He was not alone." Zaytuna reached out to Umm Bashir. "A dear friend is a washer of the dead. I assure you they treat each person as if they were their own family."

Umm Bashir heaved and fell against her son.

Ammar was frowning, and not at the heartbreak. She understood completely. When Ammar and Tein worked grave crimes in the Baghdad Police, they started the practice of bringing suspected victims to the Barmakid Hospital, where a doctor and the pharmacist could examine the body and give their opinion on the cause of death. Bashir was right to suspect that the investigators must have been convinced it was suicide and wanted to avoid an official opinion that would obligate them to inform the family. A kindness, surely, but any evidence on the body was now lost and buried. She only prayed the washer was an observant man.

3

Ammar said, "Up there on the right."

But Zaytuna paused by the path leading down to the landing where the body was found. "Not question the boat hands?"

"I want to hear from the corpse washer first," Ammar said.

"That makes no sense," she said, wiping her brow.

Ammar wished he had not brought her along. It was unusually hot and humid, and her interference was making him more uncomfortable.

They stepped aside for a donkey cart laden with sacks. The driver had been prodding the animal with hups and clucks instead of his stick, but it maintained a plodding gait.

She continued, "If we have an account of the body, how they found it, and the scene, then we'll be in a better position to ask questions of the washer."

The donkey screeched in complaint. The driver had finally taken the stick to it.

"Or the other way around," he insisted. "I'm the lead on this case, Zaytuna."

The donkey carried on, but at the same pace.

Ammar walked ahead to end the conversation, getting in behind the cart.

Catching up, she said, "It was wrong of them to bring the body here."

"If you were Grave Crimes, wouldn't you?"

"If I were trying to cover up a suicide, yes."

He nodded sharply. "Exactly."

The road ran alongside high-walled estates. Densely patterned curtains obscured narrow balconies. A woman held the edge of a curtain across her body as she watched the boats on the water, but her chestnut hair was loose and gleaming in the sun. He quickly looked away, then asked, "How wealthy do you think the family is? Could Samir have had a wife or mistress here? You saw their clothes."

"I think a servant is more likely."

"Their clothes struck me as wealthy," Ammar said.

"They are mercantile class. More to the point, their manners did not match the quality of their clothing."

He quipped, "You an expert now that you're a lady of high standing?"

"Indeed." She gestured comically with her hand as if servants walked before them. "But seriously, the last case you worked with Tein—you remember the women."

He only remembered how uncomfortable she had been navigating the circles of women closest to the caliphal harem.

The cart stopped just before the lane, blocking their way. The donkey brayed.

"What were they like?"

The driver stood up, swinging his stick in the air. "Your mother was a demon!"

"They moved like dancers and spoke like poets, confident they could get away with anything."

Bashir and Basma did not seem like that. "Servant, then," he said.

The cart moved, but more slowly this time, and the driver sat down grumbling.

They were finally free to turn down the lane. They headed for the blue-tiled arch at the end. It opened onto a market street cooled by reed awnings and smelling of clean earth and spices. An older servant laughed as she haggled with the shopkeeper, gesturing at him with a long slice of dried melon. Around the corner and onto the main street, grain and legume merchants called to passersby, while clerks attended to customers inspecting goods displayed in sacks with their edges rolled down. Lanes branched out left and right. He turned back, choosing the one closest to the market entrance. "This one."

Zaytuna did not answer, and only then did he notice she was not with him.

He found her, hand over her heart, thanking an elderly man in a bright red turban.

"What was that?" he asked as she joined him.

"I got directions to the washer. Man by the name of Muhammad ibn Shams al-Ghassal." She struck out ahead, returning the way they had come and down the lane he had just suggested.

Ammar followed, bristling.

"Here!" She waved him over and was through the wide door before he could join her.

The reception room was empty except for two long benches where family would sit as their loved one was washed. Women's low voices carried through to them from the room on the right. He whispered, "What did you not understand about me being the lead?"

"Women are working in that one," she said, ignoring his question.

"I knew that already."

He knocked on the door to the left. A serious-faced man with a closely trimmed grizzled beard answered. He wore a neat turban and a spotlessly clean apron over his plain, short robe and loose pants. His sleeves were rolled up, and Ammar hoped they did not disturb him. "Assalamu alaykum," said Ammar. "Muhammad ibn Shams al-Ghassal?"

"Wa alaykum assalam." He looked beyond them, expecting porters with a body.

"I am Ghazi Ammar at-Tabbani. This is my associate, Zaytuna bint al-Ashiqa as-Sawda. I am following up on the death of an unnamed man you washed. The police would have brought him to you last week."

"Ghazi, sir." He bowed his head.

Ammar stood straighter for his respect.

Then his eyes narrowed. "Are you with the police?"

"I was the lead investigator for Grave Crimes. Now, I take on cases for families who want more than the police can offer."

The answer softened his expression, but only slightly. "You mean the embellisher, God rest his soul."

They answered his prayer together, "Amin."

Ammar wiped his face with the prayer, then asked, "How did you know his trade?"

Instead of answering, the washer took up a defensive posture. He was short but muscular from lifting and turning bodies, giving the impression he would not be moved, even if pushed.

Zaytuna quietly handed Ammar the note from Bashir instructing the washer to speak freely with them, took a few steps back, and sat on the bench out of view.

"The police miss things," Ammar said, "but you didn't."

The washer seemed to appreciate the compliment. "I will say this, but only because it is no secret." He glared at Ammar to drive the point home. "I found a small pair of expensive scissors in the pocket of his sleeve and gold thread for embellishment. It had been knotted beautifully. Very fine work. But it was his hands—he had the callouses of a man who works with needle and thread." He paused, taking a breath as if to control his temper. "The police interviewed me in the street. I was forced to reveal the private details of his body so that anyone could hear."

"The street?"

Ibn Shams frowned in disgust.

"God knows your intention. I know it would have been a helpful observation."

"They did use it to find his family. Porters came to get him by the end of the day."

"Just porters? No family?"

"If someone in the family was with the porters, they did not introduce themselves to me."

Was he implying that Bashir had not introduced himself directly? Or did he not come at all? Bashir did not mention coming to get his father's body, but it would be the rare son who would not. More, all of them would have been there, cousins and neighbours included.

"You noticed his callouses," Ammar said. "Sharp eye. Was there anything else about the body that seemed unusual to you?"

There was something he wanted to say, but his mouth was shut tight.

Zaytuna coughed to get Ammar's attention, then gestured to the paper in his hand. As if he had forgotten it. He nearly coughed back at her.

"The tailor's name is Samir az-Zarduzi," Ammar said. "His son, Bashir ibn Samir, asked us to come to you." He handed over the note. "They do not accept the verdict of a natural death by the police."

Ibn Shams gripped the paper tightly. The man looked like he was ready to burst at the seams. Even his cheeks turned bright above the edge of his beard, but he kept his mouth shut.

"In your hand," Ammar prompted.

"I can't read. How do I know what's on this?"

"I'll get someone who can. Someone you trust. Just tell me."

"Out there? Those backbiters? Bring the family to me. Or come back with the police." At the last word, the red in his cheeks deepened, making him look like a child holding his breath to make a point.

"Do you know the corpse washers at the Barmakid Hospital?" Ammar asked.

"I know the police bring them suspicious deaths."

"Then why did the police bring the body to you and not to them?"

His eyes darted to the outside door as if local gossips were listening. "Is it for me to ask the police why they do a thing?"

"Would you speak to the washers at the Barmakid?"

He crossed his arms. "Without the family, how can I be sure you speak for them?"

"The note."

He threw it to the floor.

"Come to the hospital now. A doctor could read it to you."

"I am here alone." He looked at the outer door again. "My assistant is ill."

Zaytuna spoke up from the bench. "We could bring a nearby washer to read it to you."

His eyes lit up with the purity of his purpose. "Why would a washer need to know how to read when everything we have learned is in our hearts and hands?"

They were hardly illiterate as a profession. The man would not give any ground, but neither would Ammar. "Meet us at the hospital in the morning."

Ibn Shams gave it thought before answering, "Would the embellisher's family be there?"

Ammar took the only opening he could and lied, "Certainly."

"Then, inshallah. I will meet you at the hospital. But at sunrise, I must be here immediately afterward."

Ammar thanked him and left, half expecting to find a neighbour listening at the door, but the lane was empty.

Zaytuna joined him a moment later.

"What was that?" Ammar asked.

"Other than you lying?"

He rolled his eyes at her moralizing when she, herself, had lied on cases.

"You know they can't speak about the bodies they wash," she went on. "This is sacred work, Ammar. He was careful to say that noticing the callouses and thread was no secret."

"That's not what I was asking. I meant what he wouldn't say."

Zaytuna responded as if she had not just done her best to irritate him, "Those cheeks. There is something important he is holding back."

"Listen"—he started for the market street—"I've got to get Bashir there in the morning."

"A message?" She came up beside him and opened her hand. The note was in it. "If Bashir cannot come, find someone he trusts to read it to him."

He grabbed the note out of her hand. "Did he see you?"

She shook her head.

"He wouldn't have brought it with him tomorrow."

"I didn't think so either."

"Good work," he said grudgingly.

Out on the main market street, Ammar looked for a boy to send a message to the embellishment shop. But Zaytuna already had one by the wrist and was bent over speaking to him.

"Say the name back to me, and the message."

The boy's voice was high and thin but certain. "Bashir ibn Samir az-Zarduzi in the Suq at-Tarrazun. Come to the Barmakid Hospital at sunrise. Ammar at-Tabbani."

She looked up at Ammar. "Yes?"

What could he do? Send the boy on his way and start over again just so she was not in charge of every last thing?

Zaytuna handed the boy a coin. He ran off, dodging passersby.

"That should have come out of expenses, not your pocket."

"Give it to me, then." She held out her hand.

But Ammar only patted the coin purse under his robe. "Let me know what I owe you at the end of the week, but only essentials." He intended to be frugal, giving anything left over to his wife. There could be no more displays of the most expensive nuts and basil seed juice in glasses costing a day's allowance.

The boy turned a corner and was gone. "I hope he doesn't run off with it."

"It is in God's hands," she said. "To the canal?"

But Ammar doubted the boy. "Tomorrow. I should go myself to tell Bashir to meet us, just in case."

Hands on her hips, she said, "Anything to keep from doing the interviews my way?"

Ammar nearly snapped at her, then noticed her eyes. There was a laugh behind them, and it only frustrated him more.

"Come," she said, warmly. "I should pick up Nura from Kamal Ali. I'll walk with you as far as the Hospital Bridge."

4

―――――

"Look!" Zaytuna pointed.

The boy she had grabbed was running toward them from the market, grinning at the good fortune of finding them. He stopped hard, kicking up a bit of dust, and smoothed his robe before breathlessly assuring, "I met the man and gave the message, and he told a woman there he would meet you!"

Zaytuna pressed a coin into his slim hand. "Well done, thank you."

More out of expenses. Ammar glared at her. If she had her way, there would be nothing for him to give his wife but good news of the case.

"If you are going home, walk with me as far as the Buratha market?"

He would rather not, but Ammar fell in beside her anyway.

The afternoon sun was hotter than midday, and he could taste the dust kicked up by carts and riders. At least the bridges were mercifully uncrowded, and they crossed the canals quickly. She chatted with him about their children, and he spoke with pride about Husayn and chuckled at Nura's antics. Stories of the children wore him down, and he found himself enjoying her company. But there was no doubt she would irritate him again and insinuate herself into the investigation where she was not needed. He longed for Tein's company. There would have been talk about family, certainly—but it would be more about the case and the city, and where they disagreed, it would be men locking horns, not her feminine intrusion.

"Come with me," she said, as the Buratha Market Gate came into view. "Stop for some buttermilk. We can send you home with a jug and butter for your family."

Tein would be there. Ammar knew what she was trying to do; his irritation with her returned, but she was also right to do it. How long had they gone on like this? No one speaking about the two of them barely speaking? He wanted to force Tein to argue it out with him, and this was as good a chance as any. Get it over with and get him back working cases. But before he could answer, Zaytuna went ahead through the grand gate, weaving her way through porters, old women offering clutches of fresh herbs, and sellers of curses and magical squares for love and success.

Ammar watched a Ghuraba woman hawking talismans. She wore a multicoloured apron over a gown of bright red, her hair tied back with a kerchief that exposed her ears. He wondered if she was one of Razba's community. Their bands moved through the city each year, but Razba and his people had stayed, and the man's influence in Baghdad had become wide and deep. But before he could ask her, she had moved on to a customer, an old woman in tears, and Ammar joined the streams of people entering the market.

Zaytuna was long gone, but he knew the way. He found her watching the men close out the butter shop for the day from across a small square. The workers were cleaning the churns and polishing large copper trays. The day's butter would be already in the back, cooling in sealed amphora, ready for delivery in the morning. But Tein was still standing over a churn, Nura on his hip, leaning into the staff as she tried to lift it. Tein guided the staff up and down with his free hand.

They could hear her small, commanding voice even from a distance. "I do it!" He moved his hand out of sight as Nura focused on her work. Tein lifted the staff slowly this time. She yelled again, "I do it! I do it!" But this time, in celebration.

Kamal Ali emerged from the office and caught Zaytuna's eye, smiling at her like the besotted fool he was the day he met her. Ammar had to admit that Zaytuna's looks had grown on him, especially after she gained weight. But this man had taken one glance at her when she was at her worst and declared he had met the living embodiment of a Nubian queen he had seen painted on a monument in Egypt. She was more a long-faced Arab than African, like her brother, but Ammar had to give Kamal Ali credit for a gift for romance.

Zaytuna finally approached, calling out, "Nura! Light of my eye!"

Tein turned at the sound of her voice. His face was soft with the expression he saved for children, then he saw Ammar and it hardened. Tein took the staff out of Nura's hands and put her down to go to Zaytuna.

"No!" She reached for the staff.

Tein picked her up without a word, moved her far enough away from the churns, and turned her to face Zaytuna. Kamal Ali met them, took hold of Nura's hand, and crossed the square.

"Azizati! I missed you!" Zaytuna touched her cheek.

Staff forgotten, Nura buried her face in her mother's wrap. Zaytuna picked up her daughter and kissed her cheeks until she giggled. Nura was the image of her father with her wide face and big eyes but had inherited her uncle's russet complexion and Zaytuna's stubbornness.

"Assalamu alaykum, ya, Kamal Ali."

"Wa alaykum assalam, Ammar. Good to see you. We have missed you."

Tein stayed just outside the shop, staring at them and tugging at the few hairs on his chin he called a beard.

"Uff," Ammar answered, staring back at Tein.

"Now, now," Zaytuna said, presenting Ammar with Nura to kiss.

He lightly pinched her cheek, but Nura glared at him, making everyone laugh and him want to leave.

Kamal Ali asked, "How is your family?"

"Alhamdulillah, well," Ammar said. "I'm just on my way home."

"You cannot visit without stopping for buttermilk."

Tein stayed in place, observing the scene, and Ammar's temper got the better of him. "Not with him staring at me like that."

"Oh, posh," Zaytuna said. "Come."

Tein disappeared into the back, returning with a jug and tray of clay cups. He placed it on the table harshly, such that one cup turned over, then sat rudely, not waiting for the others.

Ammar sat across the table, back straight, readying himself for the fight.

Tein said, "It's been a long time."

"My mother says the same about you when you don't join us for lunch."

Kamal Ali frowned at them and took Nura over to the churns, while Zaytuna sat, eyeing them like a mother demanding her sons make up but unsure if there were still a few blows left in them. Ammar wanted to assure her that blows remained at the ready.

But at the mention of Ammar's mother, Tein's shoulders softened. "God forgive me," he said. "I should have visited her long before this, even if I can no longer come regularly."

No longer come regularly. What did he do but churn butter, watch Nura, and meet Ibn Ali at Baraqan's once a week to talk about things Ammar did not understand?

"Please offer my apologies to your mother until I can give them in person."

Tein's remorse only made Ammar want to come back at him harder. Instead, he got up, knocking his stool back in a clatter, and stormed across the square.

There were heavy footsteps following him, but he did not turn around.

"Ammar!" Tein called out.

But he kept walking, and the sound of Tein's footsteps fell away.

He carried on, eyes ahead and anger barely in check. Once home, Ammar paused at the gate and laid his forehead against it, listening for the life beyond it. He could hear his mother's voice and his son; then she said, "Husayn, habibi, take this to your mother."

Husayn was named after the hero and martyr of the battle of Karbala, but also Tein's infant boy, who had been killed during a Byzantine raid, along with his wife, so many years ago. When Ammar's son was born, he had imagined Tein loving him as his own, playing battle with him as he grew. When Nura was born, he dreamed of the two children growing up as cousins and someday falling in love. The worst part was that Husayn had all this, but without him. The first time he came home with his mother, excited about visiting Auntie Zaytuna's house and wrestling with Uncle Tein, it was all he could do to keep from breaking the boy's heart with harsh words.

Head still pressed against the gate, he took a few deep breaths to cool off. One look, and his mother would demand to know what was troubling him.

The gate opened, and Ammar stumbled in.

"My child, what's wrong?" his mother asked. Her eyes were still bright despite her years, and her wrap, wound around her like an apron, was spotted with soil from tending their garden.

"Ummi." He took her weathered hands, kissed them, then kissed her soft cheeks. "I have a new case. Rich people. I want to tell Nasifa."

"Then why are you sad?"

"A father died. The family is worried."

"It's not like you."

He forced a smile. "Where is my son?"

"I had him only a moment ago."

"Husayn!" He called out, then regretted it, hoping his father had not heard him and would not come out—kerchief draped over his head instead of a skullcap, wine belly straining at his qamis—and blame him for not working for the family.

Instead, Husayn came running from the rear courtyard, barefoot, bareheaded, and covered in dust. The boy had a bullface like him and was short and barrel-chested, too. Even at three, he looked as if he could knock his way through a wall and had the determination to try. His son was not going to stand for raising goats anymore than he could. Ammar grabbed him and swung him into the air, then held him close, kissing his fat, sticky cheek. If he could build up the agency, Husayn could come and work with him. He would have the sign repainted: *Ghazi Ammar and Son's Agency of Investigation and Implementation.*

Nasifa followed, holding a jug of water at her waist and a cup crooked in her finger. "Assalamu alaykum, husband." Her long black hair spilled out from her kerchief, loosely braided with strips of colourful cloth. She tilted the jug on her hip and handed him a cup of water. It was cool and tasted of mint from their garden.

"Come and sit out back."

He followed with Husayn in his arms and settled on a bench

in the outdoor kitchen. Husayn squirmed out of his hands and began an attack on his leg. Ammar shook and kicked while his son tried to subdue him, grunting and red-faced. Finally, Ammar began making sounds of submission, then declared, "You have me!" as his leg died a slow but honourable death. Husayn jumped back and pounded his chest. Ammar grinned but wondered if Tein had shown him that, imagining him, head thrown back, thumping his fists and declaring victory.

"That's new," he said to his wife.

"His cousins were wrestling with him before they went out with the goats," she said with displeasure. "They did not give him a chance to win. And them, so much older. Qasim pounded his chest when he let Husayn go."

At least Husayn did not seem bothered. Ammar had been the same as a boy. Losing never bothered him, either. He memorized the other boys' attacks and devised countermoves in his sleep.

The wall in the back courtyard was low, built so his mother could imagine seeing the plain of Karbala in the distance, but it also allowed them to keep an eye out for the boys and the goats. His nephews were like specks in the low grass as they followed the growing herd.

Nasifa pulled up a small table in front of him. It was no more than a stool used for every purpose, marked by knives and burns. She placed freshly baked bread in front of him, smothered with butter made from their own goats and drizzled with honey from the hives of a neighbour.

Husayn abandoned his victory to hold out his hands. "Ummi, please."

The boy settled at his father's feet and licked all the butter and honey off first. Ammar tore off a bit of his own bread and held it up to Nasifa. She tried to take it from him, but he shook his head. As graceful as an egret at the edge of the water, she bowed, and he placed it in her mouth.

"I got a good case," he said. "Rich family."

"Oh, my love," she said. "Alhamdulillah."

He saw her pleasure—but relief, too, and was sorry he had put her in a position to feel it. "If it goes well, they'll tell their rich friends. That'll mean more good cases."

"Inshallah. This is what you've been waiting for."

"Ammar!"

Nasifa put on the smile she reserved for his father.

He did not turn to greet his father immediately but touched his son's shoulder.

"You should be out there with the men," his father bellowed as he came out to them.

"Father-in-law." Nasifa hurried over. "I have some cool water for you."

Husayn squirmed in between Ammar's legs, and he draped one around him in protection. Nasifa said his father was gentle with the boy, but nothing could hide the man's nature, and Husayn already feared him.

"I got a well-paying case, Father. When it's complete, let's discuss it."

His mother hurried around the corner with a clutch of herbs and waved at her husband. "Sit, sit. I can make mint tea if you like. There is bread with butter and honey."

Ammar stood to give his father his spot. Husayn scrambled up and stayed close.

His mother took the cup of water out of Nasifa's hand and gave it to her husband.

Drinking deeply, he smacked his lips and then turned to Ammar. "I'll believe you've got business when I feel the coin in my hand."

5

____

"*Flower of my heart, Allah huv. Rose of my cheek, Allah huv.*" Zaytuna shifted Nura to a more comfortable position on her hip and whispered in her ear. "*Sleep, my moonlit dove, Allah huv, Allah huv, Allah huv.*"

She hoped the walk home and Yulduz's lullaby would calm Nura enough to sleep easily, but she was kicking her long legs with the kind of exhausted energy that promised a tantrum.

"*Flower of my heart—*"

Nura dug her hand under Zaytuna's wrap for the large bead she kept threaded through a thick braid. She had done the same as a child, strapped to her mother, grasping at her locs and the beads threaded through them. All she had from her mother now was that one bead and the drum, binding her and her daughter to the woman who had died when Zaytuna was still a girl. Turning the bead round and round in her little fingers, Nura demanded, "Crane song!"

Zaytuna hummed it the best she could, but the song was in Chinese, and Zaytuna could not even approximate the words. "Ask Auntie YingYue to sing it when we see her."

They turned the corner to their alley and saw Layla walking

hand in hand with Farhana. The girls kissed cheeks in farewell, and Layla hurried to meet them by the gate. "Ummi! Nura!"

She ran as if she were still little, her long hair falling out of her kerchief for all to see. But she was fourteen now, and Layla was becoming a beauty. The neighbours were already gossiping. Aliyah had even spoken to Yulduz about it. But Yulduz, as she put it, had "shut her trap for her." Layla's youth had been stolen from her in hardship. As far as she and the rest of the girl's foster family were concerned, they would not curtail any childlike indulgence. She was as true a daughter to Zaytuna as Nura, and she would protect the girl with her life. Zaytuna's only concern was her friendship with Abdulghafur. They were getting too old to spend so much time together. Something would have to be done soon.

Yulduz and Maryam were chatting in the courtyard, comfortably seated on a rug in the shade of the pomegranate tree. Its blooms had fallen, the tiny fruits had budded, and its full leaves showered them with dappled sunlight. The sturdy old women's legs were stuck out, and they sat shoulder to shoulder, their wrinkled faces bright with whatever gossip they were sharing. Qambar had a pile of tufted wool before him and was restuffing the linen pillowcases. His hands were swollen and twisted from a life of cutting reeds, and she wished he did not have to do any work at all now they were all comfortable under Kamal Ali's care, but rest was not the old man's way.

"Good afternoon, everyone."

They returned her greetings, and Yulduz patted the space in front of her. "Come, girl."

Zaytuna put Nura down. She scampered into the old woman's arms and kissed her on the cheek. Then she kissed her Auntie Maryam, then her Uncle Qambar. When she thought no one was watching, she ran for the kitchen.

The girl was fast, but not as fast as her mother.

"The brazier's cool!" Yulduz yelled after her.

The door should always be shut, but Yulduz refused, huffing that "back in her day" children learned how to behave around a fire. Zaytuna closed it, making sure the high latch was firmly in place.

"There's food 'ere, Nura!" Yulduz called to her, and she obliged.

Layla settled next to Qambar with her sewing box.

"You did a good job cleaning the wool, Layla." He handed her a stuffed pillow adorned with her own simple embroidery, and she began the work of closing it.

Small plates were laid out with bread, honey, butter, dried fruit, and, of course, a jug of buttermilk.

Maryam was cooing at Nura and placed a bit of dried apricot in her mouth.

"Did you tell Ammar we've got nothing for all the work we've done?" Yulduz took the jug and poured buttermilk for everyone. She tipped her chin at Maryam. "Us following that man, and there's no sign 'e's done a thing wrong."

Maryam leaned forward and helped herself to bread and butter and drizzled honey on it.

"I make budder," Nura declared.

"She did," Zaytuna said. "Tein could not get the butter staff out of her hands. She'll have her uncle's job when he retires."

Nura shot up, dashing to the other side of the courtyard for her doll, then ran around in circles. She finally slowed, carrying her doll like a baby and singing the Crane song. She knew the words. If the people who loved Nura had their way, she would speak Arabic, Turkmen, Persian, Chinese, and, she hoped, some of her mother's Nubian.

"I told him," Zaytuna said to Yulduz, returning her attention to her case. "He may or may not have agreed to watch the house himself at night. He has to ask Nasifa."

Yulduz pressed, "And what has Nasifa been saying to you?"

She was not going to share Nasifa's confidences, no matter how much Yulduz guessed.

The old woman answered her own question. "Tired of that man sulking, I'm sure. All 'is talk of Seyyedina Husayn. As if that great man ever sulked at a struggle thrown at 'im by God."

Zaytuna ignored her, unwilling to give Yulduz the confirmation she sought.

"So what now?" Yulduz glanced uneasily at her husband.

"I could help," Qambar protested, slapping his leg. "As long as I don't have to chase him."

"You might have to, or run to avoid the night watchmen," Zaytuna said.

Qambar shrugged but stuffed the next pillow with greater vigour.

Maryam squeezed Yulduz's hand and said, "I think Qambar could help. Just sit outside the house. He could at least tell us when the man leaves."

Yulduz nodded, head tipping toward Qambar, begging Zaytuna to agree. But she did not need to beg. Zaytuna would do anything to protect the old man from the grief of being good for nothing but stuffing pillows. She remembered how he had ruined his body cutting reeds. How he had cared for Layla when she first came to them, lost, defiant, and sorely needing love. The night he gave Tein an ultimatum to do right by Saliha. He had stood strong for Zaytuna, too, when she felt so few cared. He had no reason to feel unmanned by age, but reason was beside the point.

Maryam offered, "My brother's jealous. He wants me to ask you for a job."

"You never said," Zaytuna answered, wishing Yulduz had kept the discussion of the case for when her old friend had left for home.

Maryam laughed. "He's jealous? I'm jealous of my job! Why would I share it with him?"

"Why bother?" Yulduz chuckled. "What're men good for but being out at night?"

"They can't even do that if they run into a watchman," Maryam said.

Qambar answered a little sharply. "Pay a watchman to do it, then."

Hiring watchmen was tricky business and not worth it for this job. Zaytuna answered instead, "It's not in the budget."

"And we're in the budget?" Yulduz asked.

"You're cheap," Zaytuna quipped.

Qambar frowned. "Such a fine woman you are to use the word 'cheap'!" He would take jokes at his expense, but not his wife's.

"I'm sorry, Qambar."

He nodded, accepting her apology.

"Qambar," Zaytuna asked, "would you be willing to watch the house?"

Before he could answer, Maryam said, "My brother'll come, and he won't need any pay. He'll do it for bragging rights."

"He can't brag, Maryam." Zaytuna said sharply, "You can't brag, Maryam."

"I only ever shared my stories with my brother. I never give names, never say nothing," she countered, then added, "We live so far! Across the river!"

"It's all right, just please, no more." Zaytuna went into her room to get some change to pay Maryam. Forget hiring her brother; knowing Maryam gossiped about the cases meant she could not be used again. Yulduz would put up a fight, of course. She lifted the lid of the trunk where she kept her clothes and a few dear things, thinking she might give Maryam meaningless jobs to keep the peace.

The trunk was against the far wall, next to her side of the bed and set between her mother's drum and the jug and cup she had bought to replace the one Mustafa had made for her. Change in hand, she sat on the bed a moment longer. What Mustafa had made for her with enduring love, she had put into the street. She had made her choice but still worried about him and prayed he was happy in Medina. Zaytuna reminded herself to ask YingYue if she had a letter from him recently.

The gate made its signature rattle, but it was too early for Tein and Kamal Ali to be home, and certainly not Saliha. Coins in hand, she returned to the courtyard.

Maryam was gone.

"You insulted her," Yulduz said with a laugh. "Her pride. She'll be back."

She wished she had been more careful with her words. "Did she say anything about her brother?"

"That he'll never work for you."

"Just as well," she said, relieved. "I'm not sure there is anything more to be done on this case."

"Nothing more to be done?" Yulduz asked, unbelieving.

Layla was sewing near Qambar but had been listening. Zaytuna worried that her burst of frustration with Maryam would be taken as a model for Layla's own behaviour. Ignoring Yulduz's question, she asked, "Are you sure she'll be back? I want to apologize for how I spoke to her."

Qambar said, "She'll accept it. You were right, and she'll have to accept that, too."

"I asked about the case, woman." Yulduz demanded.

But Nura had slowed down and was whining in a way that meant trouble. It was too early for her to sleep, but the only choice was trouble now or trouble too early in the morning. She said to Yulduz, "Come with me tomorrow to see Bint Afshin. We'll talk on the way."

Zaytuna picked Nura up gently and brought her into their room, laying her down on their bed. Her eyes were closing as Zaytuna changed her into her nightdress. She tucked her in, then picked up her mother's drum and thumped it lightly to the beating of her heart, and sang softly, "*Allah huv—*"

6

DAY TWO

Ammar ran across the hospital bridge. He was late to meet the corpse washer. He prayed Bashir was already there, permission had been given, and Ibn Shams was ready to talk.

Husayn had a rare morning of sleeping late, and he and Nasifa had lain on either side of him, half-asleep from the first thread of light into the grey dawn. His son's arm was thrown over his head, and his round cheeks were flushed. Nothing existed in that half-light other than his beautiful wife and child.

She gazed at them dreamily, whispering, "My loves."

Ammar remembered the day he devoted his life to her. He took her hand, kissed it, and then brought it to his forehead, vowing again to protect her and make her proud.

Nasifa glanced at the door over his shoulder; her eyes widened in shock. His body shot through with readiness to fight, and he was up, grasping the dagger from his belt on the floor.

"Ammar! Your case!"

Husayn woke with a cry.

She got up right behind him, handing him his clothes. He washed quickly at the basin. Dressed and boots on, he buckled his dagger belt as he ran down the street.

Now he stood panting before a belligerent guard in the arched foyer of the Barmakid Hospital. "Did a corpse washer come here looking for me?"

The guard crossed his arms over an ill-fitting leather cuirass that had never seen action. "Who are you that he should be asking?"

"Ghazi Ammar at-Tabbani. He is waiting for me."

"A man asked for you, then." He shrugged. "I told him I don't know you."

Ammar nearly grabbed him. "Did he leave?"

"I sent him back to the washers."

Ammar hurried through the courtyard, trying not to startle the patients sitting beside the fountain and on benches under the bitter orange trees. Past the bonesetters, the wide doors to Ibn Ali's pharmacy were open, and he stopped to ask him along.

The elder African was dressed in finely wrought clothes; his robe had narrow sleeves not to get in the way of his work, but he would not look out of place if he were called to administer his medicines in the homes of Baghdad's most powerful, as he sometimes was. He was leaning over a table, working a mortar and pestle and instructing an assistant in the back. Ammar knew better than to disturb his work and went back to the corpse washers.

Around the corner, he found Saliha standing in front of Ibn Shams and Taha. She turned at the sound of his footsteps, and he stopped short. The woman was too bold. Her brightly patterned wrap was arranged so her heavy breasts and the curve of her hips were on display for the men behind her. Ammar lowered his gaze, not wanting to stray from Nasifa even by a look. He was glad he was not Tein; he could not bear the jealousy over a wife so reckless with the treasures God had given her.

"Good morning, Ammar." She left the men to meet him.

He looked past her to greet the men at the end of the hall, but they were deep in conversation.

"Zaytuna couldn't come," Saliha said. "She asked me to keep an eye out for Ibn Shams and help if needed."

He had not even thought of Zaytuna until that moment. She might have something to contribute. But what help could Saliha give him? The corpse washer was a scrupulous man. He would not speak to her, washer or not, while she displayed her body in such an unprofessional manner.

Ammar asked, "Is Bashir Ibn Samir here yet?"

"No, but I told that oaf out front to direct him here when he does." Saliha led him out of the hall. "Zaytuna said I might need to vouch for you if Bashir doesn't come in time."

"I worked with the men's washer when I was with the police." He moved to go around her. "Taha can vouch for me."

"It's done already. You scoff at me, but because of this"—she lightly slapped her hip—"Ibn Shams will talk."

Ammar pulled back. "But the man refused yesterday on the sacred honour of corpse washers!"

She raised one of her perfectly arched eyebrows. "If Zaytuna would only eat more, she could have done the same yesterday and saved you the time."

The thought was so absurd, he nearly laughed.

"You can thank me later," she said. "They're waiting for you."

"Ibn Ali?"

"I already spoke to him. I'll get him as soon as I introduce you, and then I have to go. There's a body waiting for me. He can assist and judge if we need to bring in a doctor."

A tray of exotic dried fruit and a small pitcher of juice was in front of Ibn Shams and Taha. Ibn Shams was nodding to Taha as he chewed a mouthful, two slices of fiery-orange persimmon in his hand.

She had thought of everything.

Saliha said, "Ibn Shams, sir, Ghazi Ammar at-Tabbani is here."

He looked up, but his eyes were only for Saliha as he addressed Ammar. "I have been assured by this gentle lady I can speak to you about the body. I am more than happy. Taha and I have refrained from discussing it until you could be here."

Saliha said, "I will ask Firdaws Ibn Ali, our pharmacist, to join us. He may decide to bring in a doctor." She smiled deferentially to the men. "Although I am sure we may rely on your opinion independently."

Ammar nearly rolled his eyes. The Saliha he knew was more likely to curse you to your face than feign like this to get what she wanted. But it had worked, and he would thank her for it later. Ammar sat down as the two men watched her go.

Ibn Shams began, "Let me give you an account of the body. The deceased had suffered a terrible injury to his hip in the last few years of his life. It would have been painful, and he would have walked with a significant limp."

"How do you get that timing?" Ammar sat forward.

"The condition of the scarring."

"He could have been unsteady on his feet. Did he slip and fall?"

"The body showed signs of a convulsion—certainly he fell then."

Ibn Ali arrived, striking an imposing presence, and bowed his head to the men with his hand over his heart. "Assalamu alaykum."

"Wa alaykum assalam wa rahmatulallhi wa barakatuhu," Ibn Shams replied.

"Did you say convulsion?" Ibn Ali asked.

"Yes, the body was brought to me shortly after he died. There was no time for rigour, but his frame was twisted. We see it if someone dies from the falling disease or in an accident.

They are held fast in the moment of death. There were no injuries to his head. His turban, of course, gave him some protection, and I was told he died in a soft area of the marsh bed by the canal." He glanced down the hall to look for Saliha. "The police intimated it was a place where men and women meet."

A place where men and women meet. Had Samir gone there for an assignation? He was an old man, but God knows there were those who were virile to the last. Not a family among the servants of the nearby estates, then, but a woman sought out for the thrill?

Taha asked, "Was there any sign of what caused the convulsion?"

"This is what we should discuss," Ibn Shams answered, slapping his thighs.

Ibn Ali asked Ammar, "Did his family indicate if he had the falling disease?"

"No. If he had that, wouldn't they assume he died of it?"

The corpse washer asked, "His blackened tongue no doubt made them suspicious."

"Yes, that was their reasoning."

Ibn Ali remarked, "I believe Dr. ar-Razi argues that the falling sickness originates in the brain itself, generated by the corrupting influence of black bile, which darkens the organs it infects." He looked behind him. "I would have to consult one of the doctors."

"Strangling can turn the tongue black," Ammar said. "Did he have bruises on his neck?"

Ibn Ali sat down.

"No bruising."

"Any other signs on the body we should know about?"

"No."

The man was observant, but he may have missed something important all the same.

Ibn Shams asked, "Maybe he choked during the convulsion. Would that be like a strangulation?"

"If so, then a natural death," Taha said.

Ibn Ali added, "He could have choked on a morsel of food as well."

The four men were quiet for a moment, and Ibn Shams filled his mouth with more persimmon.

Taha perked up. "Would pain medication cause a convulsion?"

"Was he in pain?" Ibn Ali asked.

"Yes!" Ibn Shams grasped Taha's shoulder in agreement, swallowing hard. "I said before you joined us that he had a broken hip that healed badly."

Ibn Ali said, "Opium, mandrake, and henbane, singly or combined, may have been prescribed by an apothecary, to be taken internally or applied as a poultice or salve to ease pain. These are powerful combinations that could cause the body to seize. Conversely, they are used to treat convulsive disorders. Also, consider that we use these substances to blunt pain or even make a patient unconscious for surgery. He could have taken more than prescribed. But in that case, it would be more likely he took his medication at home, not by the canal."

Ammar said, "If he were dependent on the painkillers, he might have been taking more than he should without their knowledge. That might put him on the canal."

"Unfortunately, that should be considered," said Ibn Ali. "You must have seen such dependencies and the behaviour that follows when you were police."

Ammar nodded.

"We consider dependency when prescribing medicine for pain, but not all apothecaries are as scrupulous."

"I'll ask the family what he was taking," Ammar said.

Taha said, "Whatever the reason, we seem to have come to

the determination that he convulsed and choked, causing his black tongue, at least."

"Do you not want to consider jinn possession?" Ibn Shams asked.

Ibn Ali said firmly, "I suggest we exhaust the mundane possibilities and leave the jinn to their world for the time being."

Ammar silently thanked Ibn Ali for redirecting that question, then asked Ibn Shams, "What did you tell the police?"

The man's face flushed, just like yesterday. "I told them to bring the body to the Barmakid. But the next thing I know, the porters from the family were there."

So this is why he was angry. The police ignored his professional advice. Ammar still wanted to know if Bashir or a cousin, anyone in the family, had come for the body. "Did the porters come alone?"

"Yes." Ibn Shams flushed again at this inexcusable behaviour.

They had allowed their father's body to be transported without them, and now Bashir did not show up as promised.

Ibn Ali said, "Ammar, I would suggest you ask the family if he had any symptoms such as stomach cramps or loss of appetite."

Taha asked, leaning forward. "Arsenic?"

Ibn Shams asked, "It causes convulsions and a black tongue?"

"If he took a very large dose at once, certainly," Ibn Ali said. "If given slowly over time, perhaps."

He leaned back, shocked. "I have never seen such a case."

"Here at the Barmakid," Ibn Ali said, "we have had the opportunity to see a wide range of cases, giving us a breadth of knowledge and experience. Ghazi Ammar and Ghazi Tein were right to ask us to examine the bodies of those who died under suspicious circumstances."

"Exactly why I told the police to bring him to you," Ibn Shams said. "How could I even offer an opinion?"

"The question remains, why would Grave Crimes bring the body to you at all?" Ibn Ali asked.

"I hesitate to bring it up," Ammar continued, "but the family says there is gossip that he took his own life. If the police suspected suicide, they might have thought to spare the family by bringing him to the nearest corpse washer and closing the matter quickly."

Ibn Shams nodded slowly. "I can forgive them if that was the case. God covers sins when we cover sins."

His conclusion raised Ibn Ali's temper. A kind of furious precision came over him—somehow his back became straighter —and Ammar almost felt for Ibn Shams, who could not be prepared for whatever was coming.

"Sin?" Ibn Ali asked. "God prohibits it harshly to bar the way for those who can stop themselves. For those who cannot, God forgives. I deem suicide the end of a terminal illness, not a lapse of trust in God's will."

Ibn Shams flushed again, but this time with a posture of righteous indignation. "Are you suggesting that God burdens a soul beyond what it can bear?"

"Do you think that God wills a person to bear their suffering alone? What of the verses compelling us to support one another with compassion and generosity? Family and neighbours bear their burdens with them. And when they can no longer help, we care for them here." He gestured sharply down the hall. "Would you like a tour of the wards?"

The corpse washer crossed his arms and looked away.

But Ibn Ali did not relent. "Let us return to your original claim of sin. To whom are these divine statements directed? As you are no doubt aware, acts are judged by capacity and intention. An illness of the body or mind can rob a person of the capacity to make decisions with sound intention. Those without capacity are not held responsible for their intentions or the actions that follow." He leaned in, saying with finality, "There is no sin, except for those who have the capacity to help and do not."

Were these the kinds of questions Ibn Ali, Tein, Baraqan, and other men argued at their weekly gatherings? As much as Ammar appreciated this view, he was relieved he was not called on to debate them.

But Ibn Shams did not appreciate it. He rose violently, as if shaking off Ibn Ali's offending opinion, and addressed Ammar. "I would advise the family to give up this foolish desire for justice where there is none to be had but in accepting God's will."

As Ibn Shams left, Ibn Ali said, "Keep all possibilities open."

Ammar was going to have to if he wanted more than a day's pay out of the case because this meeting had done nothing but point away from murder.

7

———

Nura was squirming in Zaytuna's arms. "Down!"

She did put her down, but Nura tugged the wrap off Zaytuna's head as she slipped away, nearly dragging the kerchief underneath, too.

"You go!" Nura scowled, pushing her toward the door.

Adjusting her veils, she said to Yulduz, "I need to explain to Bint Afshin that we haven't found anything and are not likely to without a man to watch her husband at night."

"That's right," Yulduz said with a swift nod.

"But, too," Zaytuna said. "I'm thinking of something Ammar said yesterday. She's a hard woman. What's wrong with leaving her husband in peace?"

"Is that for you to decide?" Qambar said.

They took money for jobs that ended in heartbreak. Often their clients wished they had never hired them at all. It always felt like everything was for her to decide.

"Yulduz, I could use your judgment. Please, come."

The old woman gestured furtively at Nura, then at Qambar.

Tein and Kamal Ali had already left for the butter shop. Layla would be off to school. And Qambar could not take care of Nura with his bad leg, but they could not say so in front of him.

"Nura, you don't want to help me?"

The girl lit up and tried to push Zaytuna toward the door again. "Nura help."

"First, help Layla clean up."

Small plates were scattered across the cloth. Nothing was left of the fresh cheese, walnuts, and honey. Only a piece of barley bread remained next to a small pile of date pits. Layla put the bread in her pocket before collecting the plates. Was she off to feed the birds with Abdulghafur?

Nura tugged at the cloth, pulling it away from the reed mat underneath and onto the ground, scattering the pits. Layla took the cloth from her, saying, "Thank you, Nura," but her voice held a note of irritation.

"Here." Zaytuna held out her hand to take the cloth from her and went out to the lane. She waited for two girls with buckets to pass before shaking it out. It would need a quick rinse, but she would do it later so Layla need not bother.

When she returned, Yulduz was adjusting her wrap over a Turkmen cap and instructing Nura in picking up the date pits. "You missed one there." Nura had only succeeded in pushing them into different places, and when Layla came out of the kitchen and saw the mess and Yulduz smiling proudly, she stalked back to her room.

"Yulduz, would you get Nura ready to go?"

Zaytuna had the courtyard clean by the time Nura pranced out, dressed in a bright red qamis and sirwal, an embroidered Turkmen apron-dress over them, and tiny sandals on her feet. Yulduz had even let her wear the embroidered cap. There was no time for the matching braids she would demand when wearing it, and Zaytuna braced herself for the complaint, but she only said again, "Nura help Ummi."

Layla emerged wearing her plain wrap for school, but underneath she wore the floral qamis and sirwal from Sind meant for special occasions.

"Can I come with you?" Layla asked.

Zaytuna tucked her head back. "It's been a long time since you've come on an investigation."

"You go with your friends." Yulduz joked, "Maybe one of 'em wants help with a problem. There's always something to stick your nose in."

"Yulduz!"

Layla mock whispered to the old woman. "I stick my nose in plenty."

"You'll have a case in no time."

"Layla," Zaytuna interjected. "Keep your nose in your books. We don't want your teacher to complain again."

"'Makes jokes out of poetry. Handwriting sloppy. Cannot sit still'." Layla rolled her eyes.

"I know you got a late start, but you'll catch up."

The sound of girls chattering came over the courtyard wall.

"Your friends are waiting. Go."

Layla kissed Nura on the cheek and rushed out.

"The fine clothes were for 'er friends, then."

"You see everything." Zaytuna wanted to hug the old woman. "Does she see much of Abdulghafur?"

"Nothing that causes me any worry."

The women in this family kept Layla's secrets now that her life had changed and, Zaytuna was relieved to see, kept an eye out, too.

"Where are you off to?" Qambar asked.

They had just said. Was the old man forgetting already? She said a prayer for him, for all of their sakes, not wanting to lose him in bits and pieces. Not wanting to lose him at all.

"To see our client," Yulduz said proudly.

"I'll watch our little one." He winced as he settled down on the reed mat. A basket with the blocks he had made for Nura was nearby. "Come now."

"I need Nura for cover," Zaytuna lied.

Nura ran over to him, crawled into his lap to give him a kiss on the cheek, then scrambled up and grabbed a handful of Zaytuna's wrap.

"Do you want to argue with this one?" Zaytuna asked.

"Never with Bint Zaytuna," Qambar said.

She chuckled. Whenever Nura was strong-willed or making trouble, she was Zaytuna's daughter, but when she was placid and helpful, she was Bint Kamal Ali.

Once the gate was closed behind them, Nura twisted free of Zaytuna's hold and ran into the middle of the lane. A cluster of women in faded wraps caught her, clucking with pleasure as they returned her to her mother.

Zaytuna picked her up, and they carried on, pointing out small distractions. There were horses and donkeys, barefoot boys dodging carts as they ran errands, and women and men in brightly coloured wraps and robes. "Yellow!" "Blue!" "Green!" Nura clapped with glee when they turned onto a main road and two camels draped with colourful tassels sauntered ahead.

She was getting heavy, and Zaytuna wanted to put her down, but not here, and not if they were to get there quickly. She shifted Nura onto the other hip, remarking, "I should have worn her on my back."

"She'd only pretend you were a camel," Yulduz quipped.

"Am I your camel, azizati?" Zaytuna asked.

"Hup! Hup!" Nura yelled loud enough to turn heads.

Zaytuna shushed her as they turned the corner to Bint Afshin's home.

An elderly villager woman sat hunched over a pile of kittens in her lap. She eyed them and nodded, holding her finger up to silence any greetings they might offer, pointing to the kittens' poor mother asleep at her feet.

But Nura had seen them and was rapt. "Ummi, Ummi, Ummi," she said in a tiny voice. They were already feeding the street cats at home. There was no need for one of their own. But Zaytuna knew better than to say anything, so she simply kissed her and went to the gate.

They had barely knocked when Bint Afshin opened it. She was a sturdy woman fuelled by bitterness, the kind who would carry on long after her husband passed, no matter her joints and complaints.

"Assalamu alaykum," they said.

The woman grunted in reply and let them into her courtyard. It reminded her of their home before she married Kamal Ali, with its reed mats, two narrow pillows for their backs, and a brazier made from bricks, likely fuelled by dried dung cakes. Proud Yulduz in those days, boiling the same bone over and over, always claiming that there was a bit of flavour left.

"Sit," she gestured indifferently to the reed mat.

They settled, but Nura, tired of being restrained in her mother's arms, ran circles in the courtyard while singing a made-up song.

Bint Afshin did not approve. "Imagine bringing your child on an investigation."

"Imagine how it looks on the street," Zaytuna responded. "No one will think we are here for anything other than a social visit."

But the old woman snapped at Nura. "Stop that, you!"

At that moment, the case was over for Zaytuna. She shifted to stand, but Yulduz pulled her back, directing her attention to Nura, who was giving Bint Afshin a look more expressive than anything Zaytuna might have said, even in her less circumspect past. But the old woman scolding her daughter was the sign she needed to let the case go. She would explain what they had done, return what money was due her, and then leave.

Bint Afshin clacked her mouth shut as Nura strode back to sit in her mother's lap.

Yulduz whispered, "Bint Zaytuna."

A loud snort erupted from the room across the courtyard, and then a low rumble followed.

"Your husband is here?" Zaytuna asked quietly.

"Adnan can sleep through anything."

"We'll only stay for a moment, then."

"Then I'll not bring out anything for you," she said.

As if the woman had planned on doing even the least required. Better to get it over with. Zaytuna gestured to Yulduz. "I've brought my associate with me, so you can see we have done our best."

"Your best. That's the start of telling me you cannot solve the simple matter of where Adnan spends my coin. He probably saw you following."

Yulduz interjected defensively, "No one suspects an old woman."

She huffed. "He takes my money. Now you take my money and nothing to show for it."

"These women have created a pattern of what he does. Where he goes," Zaytuna said. "I've followed up at the locations they identified and asked about him. A man has queried at his work. There is no indication of another woman or gambling."

The woman's back got up. "You're missing something."

"Perhaps he is giving the money in charity."

"Without me knowing?"

Zaytuna repeated the Prophet's dictum: "The right hand should give so the left hand does not see."

"All 'e does is sit with friends." Yulduz leaned in. "Not even a game of dice."

"Does he go out at night?" Zaytuna asked.

Bint Afshin said, "Listen to that."

The snoring had gotten louder.

"He slept through the morning prayer."

"You sleep heavy?" Yulduz asked.

"I try to stay awake." She glanced at their room, and, for the first time, there was sincere worry on her face, rather than a desire to control her husband. "I can't bear it anymore."

The sincerity pulled Zaytuna back from the edge of quitting. "He spends no money during the day. We're going to hire a man to watch the house at night and follow him, if necessary."

"Hire," she said harshly.

Nura stiffened in her lap, but Zaytuna touched her cheek with the back of her hand. "Your original payment covers it if we do not have to watch him more than two nights."

"Right, then."

Zaytuna got up, lifting Nura onto her hip, and glanced at the room. She stopped for a moment, unsure of herself. A feeling swept through her that she did not recognize, but there was an uncomfortable thread in it that quivered through her heart. She wished she had quit the case, after all.

Back on the road, she asked Yulduz, "What do you think?"

"If 'e's got another woman, good on 'im."

Zaytuna agreed, but the thread she felt concerned something other than an unhappy marriage.

Can you watch Nura today? I need to discuss this with Ammar."

8

———

"How did it go?" Zaytuna asked Ammar from the office doorway.

He was pacing and stopped only to glance at her, then went back to it. "I won't have more than a day's pay out of it."

She went to the cabinet to get the lamp.

"You forgot the oil," he grumbled.

She sat down on the couch facing the door. "All right. Why only a day?"

"Probably choked during a convulsion." Ammar remained standing, shifting from one foot to another. "That's what turned his tongue black."

"So, natural causes?"

"Samir had a broken hip that healed badly and caused him a lot of pain. Maybe the pain medication caused him to seize, or he took too much of it. So not quite natural, but not murder."

"Will you tell the family today?"

"Ibn Ali has some questions he wants me to ask." Ammar added before he could stop himself, "There's still some hope."

She held out a hand. "Ammar. It's fine."

"God forgive me. I need this."

"If it makes you feel better, I think his children would only be happy if you kept going."

"I think I can drag it out a day or two." He stood before his sword and cuirass hanging on the wall, asking how he came to this: making something out of nothing for pay.

"Even if it ends there," she said, "they'll refer you to others. You've given them more than the police were able to do."

He faced her. "Willing to do, maybe."

"Is there more?" Zaytuna asked, perking up.

"Remember Ibn Shams' bursting red face? He told the police there was reason for suspicion and expected them to take the body to the Barmakid."

"Did nothing at the crime scene suggest murder?"

Whether it did or did not, he and Tein would never have given up until they were certain. He paced again. "Maybe I need to ask Grave Crimes that myself."

"You should." She sat forward. "What did Ibn Ali want you to ask?"

"He said it could have been poisoning. I mean, medicine taken in too high a dose makes it a poison. But he meant it intentionally. Maybe even arsenic. He wants me to ask about physical symptoms. His behaviour."

"Why didn't you say that first?" She threw out a hand in frustration. "That doesn't sound like it's over."

Ammar stared at her hopefully. "There's also something strange about the family. Ibn Shams confirmed no one went with the porters to collect the body. And Bashir did not show up this morning."

"No? You must find out why. Was Saliha there?"

"Yes, but she was called away."

Zaytuna frowned. "She'll be sore at being left out."

Ammar did not mind. He doubted Ibn Shams could have

focused while she was there. "You can let her know the corpse washer only spoke to us because of her."

"I don't understand."

"She sweet-talked him into trusting us, even though the family and the police were not there."

"Saliha's more than a pretty face, Ammar. She can help."

There was ire behind that statement, and he pushed back. "If a woman ends up dead or if a man needs help changing his mind. Fine."

"That's no better," she added dryly.

"I know she's smart."

"She works closely with Ibn Ali. He's been teaching her the signs to watch out for so she knows whether to call him or a doctor when a body reaches her. You can ask her first when you have questions about a body. She'll go to Ibn Ali if she does not know."

"If Tein doesn't mind."

Zaytuna sucked her teeth. "Poor Ammar."

"What's that supposed to mean?"

"You think Tein would tell her what to do?"

There was no understanding their men. Kamal Ali, Tein, and Qambar had married women who did not listen to their husbands, let alone consult with them before acting. Thank God Nasifa was not like that. Having to work with Zaytuna was enough. But coming home to it?

As if she read his mind, she said, "Are you forgetting when Nasifa helped with a case, and on her own initiative?"

"Are you forgetting Nasifa put herself in danger?" He snapped back, "She's a wife now. A mother."

Zaytuna raised her eyebrows.

"You're different," he added lamely, then changed the subject to get her off his back. "Tell me about your case."

She gave a deep sigh before allowing it. "Yulduz and I visited

Bint Afshin this morning. We have to hire a man to watch her husband at night."

There it was. "You need men for something!"

She burst out laughing. "We have found your purpose!"

But Ammar did not laugh, wanting to tell her to ask Tein for help, even though it would dig him in deeper.

There was an uncomfortable pause before she asked, "Did you speak to Nasifa about letting you out at night?"

"No. I did not speak to Nasifa. I am not going to either. Not until it's necessary."

Zaytuna went on as if she were not trying his patience with every word. "I just told you it was necessary."

"Give me a day on this before I do an errand for you."

"My cases are errands. I see."

"I didn't mean that!"

She held a hand up in truce. "Fine, what's next for you, then?"

Ammar sat down and put himself in order before saying, "First the canal to speak to the boat hands and see about other witnesses. Then, interview the family again, but at home. See them in a different light. I'll put Ibn Ali's questions in front of them, and my own."

"I need to go home." She stood, arranging her wrap to leave. "I sent Nura back with Yulduz. I cannot leave her with them too long. She's a demon, that daughter of mine." She gave him a wry smile. "I have a better appreciation of what my mother went through."

"With twins."

"Indeed." She stood at the door, hand on the jamb, and looked out into the street.

Ammar said to her back, "Your mother was a formidable woman."

"All mothers are formidable."

He thought of his own mother and Nasifa. Strong women. But still, he made things harder on them at home by refusing to join the family business.

"Your mother and wife want you to be happy," she said, her back still to him. "They know this makes you happy."

How did she always know what he was thinking?

"I cannot read your mind." She turned to face him.

"How did you cursed-well know I was thinking that!"

Zaytuna shrugged. "You, like most men, are obvious."

But there was a strange cast to her face, like when she was in prayer. She turned back to look out at the street.

"What is it?"

"I should drop my case. There's something in it I don't understand, and I don't want to touch."

"Is this because men are obvious?"

She looked back at him from the door and smiled, but the smile came from a peaceful place within her. He didn't like this either—her hunches and when her face got that deep inside look. There was nothing to be done with her, especially when she was like this. Nothing to do but get on with the case and start making enough money so he could run the office without her. He got up to leave. "I'm off to the canal."

"Not so fast. Bashir is coming."

Zaytuna stepped out into the square.

"Assalamu alaykum, I was just leaving," Zaytuna said, "but Ghazi Ammar is inside."

Ammar adjusted his turban and tugged at his robe. The room was still too dark without a lamp, and he went to meet him in the square. "Well met! I have some questions."

"Have you found anything?"

"I was at the Barmakid today. We expected you."

He frowned. "My mother. She held me back."

"We were able to get what we needed without you, but it was

close. The washer who took care of your father refused to speak without you at first."

"Our mothers have rights over us," he said firmly. "I could not join you."

Ammar prodded, "The washer found it surprising you did not come for your father."

"As I said."

"I mean, he mentioned no one came with the porters."

Bashir's eyes flashed with anger, but only for a moment. "My mother collapsed and would not let me or my sister out of her sight."

It would be the rare son who would blame his mother, even if she were in the wrong; a lie would have more of a ring of truth. He left it for the time being. "Do you want to come with me? I was on my way to the canal to speak to the boat hands. You can hear for yourself what they have to say."

"I must return to work. Tell me what was said at the Barmakid."

Ammar filled him in, recounting their analysis, ending in death by choking during a convulsion, then asked Bashir about stomach pains or any other strange symptoms.

"He was not ill before he died. Certainly not the falling sickness! Father never had a seizure. Only his injuries bothered him, but he bore up under the pain."

Ammar hid his disappointment that there were no signs of slow arsenic poisoning and turned to the accident. "How did it happen?"

"A donkey bolted. He pushed a man out of the cart's way and was run over."

"It never healed?"

"The bonesetter said they could only do so much."

He wished they would have taken him to the bonesetters at the Barmakid. "Was he taking any pain medicine?"

"Not that I know. We should ask my mother."

Ammar hated to say it, but he could not deceive them. "I have to advise you. I doubt the convulsion was due to murder. We can end this matter here."

"No!" He grabbed Ammar's arm. "You mentioned arsenic?"

"You said he had no stomach pains, but," Ammar added hopefully, "if he was poisoned right before he died, it's possible."

"You must go on."

"And if I spend days, maybe weeks, investigating and it turns out to be a natural death or suicide?"

He let go of Ammar. "I appreciate your honesty, but we will only be satisfied when you have asked every question."

Ammar's chest expanded with purpose, and he clasped his shoulder. "I will do everything in my power."

"Come to us after you have been at the canal to give us your news." Bashir put his hand on Ammar's shoulder. "Ghazi, sir. I will be home at midday. Eat with us. Do not wait until the afternoon."

"I will, inshallah." Ammar wanted to pull him into an embrace but let him go.

He watched Bashir head toward the market and went back to retrieve his cuirass and sword. "Ghazi, sir," Bashir had said. Ammar felt more like himself and wanted the feel of the leather armour against his chest and the hilt of his sword in his hand.

As he was closing the door, a boy appeared with a small jar of lamp oil in hand. He opened his hand slightly to show a coin. Zaytuna must have given it to him as she left. The boy handed over the oil, bowed, and ran off.

9

———

The humidity was thick by the canal, and with the heat, Ammar could barely breathe. His leather cuirass had become tight from disuse. He'd had to adjust the buckles as if he had borrowed it from another man, his body no longer its home. The sun bore down, and he wiped his brow, wishing he could strip like the boat hands and get into the water, but there was nothing he could do.

The round reed boats and skiffs laden with goods and people lined up, one by one, to stop at the landing. Other boats carried on in the centre of the current, heading into the Tigris. The men worked efficiently, guiding the boats in and out, making space for the porters to do their job. A small clearing in the reeds opened off to the left. Ammar fell in beside the sweating, sun-burnished porters trudging down the hill.

He stood to the side, waiting for a break. Half-dressed, the young men waded in and out of the water to catch the boats or push them off. All wore sun-faded turbans to protect their heads, except for one whose long black curls obscured his face. They pushed out the last skiff, then stood back to catch their breath. One broke off, heading for a sweating jug of water jammed into the silty ground.

"Assalamu alaykum!" Ammar called out as he went to meet him.

He grunted his reply as he bent over to pour himself a cup of water. He was wiry and sharp-nosed and drank the water so greedily it poured down his face onto his chest.

"Were any of you here when that man died a few days ago? God have mercy on him."

He took another drink, then said the customary phrase, "We belong to God and return to Him," as he poured a third cup. The other young men joined them, curious about him but more eager to get some water before this one emptied the jug.

The wiry one pointed at the one with the long hair. He had pulled it up, winding his curls into a loose knot on top of his head, revealing a face so beautiful, he could have passed for a young woman at the height of her promise. Ammar wondered if he had ever been forced to do so. He waited for the beautiful one to take a drink, then asked him about the body.

"You with the police?" The young man asked it casually, but in a way that meant he had not witnessed anything.

"Not anymore."

"What does that mean?"

Ammar liked his attitude. "Which part?"

"'Not anymore'."

"I quit."

"Why?"

Ammar deflected. "I'm helping the family understand what happened to their father."

"Does it pay?"

"You looking for work?"

"Always."

Ammar sized him up, wondering if he should hire him to do

odd jobs instead of a watchman. He could do the same for less and probably be better at it. There were honest men, but many watchmen were unreliable, violent, or corrupt. Running into them patrolling the streets at night could just as likely get a man beaten or robbed as released or sent to jail for good reason.

Ammar asked, "Can you get around the watchmen at night without being noticed?"

The beautiful young man slapped the back of the one next to him. "He asks can I outsmart the watchmen?"

That one wiped the water from his mouth and shook his head with a small laugh.

"You still friendly with the police?" The young man asked.

"I left on good terms, if that's what you mean. They'd have me back, but I don't want to go back." But Ammar understood what he wanted to know. "I never put my boot on the neck of any man to solve a case."

He gave Ammar a brisk nod. "I will work for you then."

"Oh, you will?"

One of the others teased, "Careful. You are falling for his talk like the girls."

A skiff with passengers to drop off sailed in.

"Wait there." Girgis gestured behind him to a shady spot.

Instead, Ammar took the break in the reeds. Birds burst out left and right in a clamour of wings and cries, forcing Ammar to step back. His boots sucked up silt in the first few steps, but then the path dried out and he came to a small clearing. The air was still and smelled of mud and living things. A reed mat was rolled up to one side, and beside it sat another jug of water and a cup laid over the top. Shade from the swaying reeds drifted slowly along one edge, making him strangely drowsy, and he was tempted to lie down.

But another path opened on the far side. It was less used than the one he came by, narrowed by encroaching reeds. He followed it and went up the embankment to the canal road. The shaded alley that he and Zaytuna had taken into the local market to the corpse washer was just across. He looked down from the embankment. From there, the clearing was exposed. There might have been a witness: one of the camel drivers, a donkey cart driver, or a passerby. He went back down, pushing through undergrowth and reeds into the clearing. The young man was there.

"It was here that I found the man." He said it confidently, not in his previous street-tough tone, but as if he were mimicking the voice of a religious scholar.

"What did you see?"

"He was an older man, perhaps fifty years old or more. He used to sit on the embankment sometimes, but I never spoke to him. He was in expensive clothes, but of the sort not meant to seem so. The cloth was fine, and the embellishment on the cuffs of his robe must have cost a great deal of money. He was twisted up as if he had died in pain. His turban had come off. His tongue was out and had turned purple. There was vomit down the side of his face and on the ground. There was a small jug here, too," he added, "but that could have belonged to any of us boat hands."

"Where's that jug now?"

Girgis shook his head.

The vomit was new. Ibn Shams had not mentioned it. The young man did not need to mimic a scholar for Ammar to take him seriously. He was good.

"Did you clean up the vomit?"

"The police did that."

"The watchmen?"

"No. The two men who came after. They said they were investigators for Grave Crimes."

So Shabib and Ahab cleaned up the vomit and took him to a

local corpse washer. If the jug were his, it could have been poison. A window onto the case opened, and the old excitement gripped him. "His clothes were intact? No signs of a struggle?"

"Not that I saw."

Ammar gestured to the secondary path behind him. "Do you know which way he came?"

"I was working. If he had come down the main path, we would have noticed him. He did not dress like a porter."

"Could he have been a passenger for a skiff?"

"Yes, but why come this way, through the brush, in those clothes?"

Ammar grinned at his reasoning. "You found him when you were going for a nap?"

"We sleep here when we get a chance."

The young man was not telling the whole story.

"Tell me what happened from when you decided to take your break."

"I walked through the reeds and found him."

Still something missing.

"Don't leave anything out. I can tell."

An expression crossed his face, maybe worry that Ammar could see. Then his eyes widened, as if he were remembering something. "Ibn Malik was up by the wall. He walks here daily. Sometimes he comes down and chats with us. He lives in one of those estates. He was waving at me and pointing at the clearing. I thought it was a greeting."

"Pointing?"

"Now I realize, Ibn Malik must have seen the man."

"Pointing doesn't sound like a greeting. You didn't think anything of it?"

He hesitated.

"If you want to work for me, you can't hide anything."

"I was meeting a friend."

Ammar understood and put his hand out to reassure him. "You thought he was cheering on your tryst. You know, anyone can watch you from up there."

The young man shrugged, but he could not hide his embarrassment.

"Do you know her name? I'll have to talk to her."

"She stood on the hill, watching me. I would have spoken to her for the first time that day."

"Does that happen a lot?"

His expression changed. "No."

"Really?"

"Not here."

Ammar understood. Before he came back to his religion, he had been a player himself. He had never been beautiful like this young man, but on the frontier, the strut of a ghazi could charm even a married woman into an indiscretion. It made Ammar want to hire the young man—if only to give him guidance—but beauty could be a liability on the job. Then he remembered how Saliha had gotten the corpse washer to trust him by hugging her wrap around her curves and considered that this young man could get something out of women, and some men, where he or Zaytuna could not.

"You good in a fight?"

"I'd rather run."

Ammar laughed. He had the muscles for it but the wisdom to avoid it, and that spoke well of him. "What's your name?"

"Girgis Asqalonaya."

"Grew up on the marshes?"

Girgis gave him a sharp look to see if it was an accusation or an honest question. Ammar cut off the suspicion with the offer of a job. "I need an old man watched." He gestured to the landing. "You'd have to be back here the next day with no sleep."

He slapped his chest. "I am at your service."

"You'll be working for my colleague, Zaytuna bint al-Ashiqa as-Sawda."

"The Black Lover of God!"

Ammar enjoyed his surprise at Zaytuna's mother's name. "Her mother was a great saint. Wandered the empire alone, if you can imagine. Could crush the pride of the greatest man and return him to faith. Zaytuna's got a bit of her mother in her, so no funny business. She'll have a word with God, then what will you do?"

Girgis became serious, threw back his shoulders, and took on the scholar's tone again. "I will respect the work. God and the lady will have no complaints. Where do I go?"

He nearly burst out laughing but held it back and told him the location of the old couple's home, then the location of the office. "I'll send for you when I need you."

"I am here every day," Girgis said.

"Listen. I want to talk to Ibn Malik. You know which of these estates?"

"No. But I saw him earlier. I don't think he has circled back yet. If you wait—"

Ammar could not wait. He had to get to the family's home for the midday meal.

A worker called out, "Girgis! A boat!" He turned to run back to the landing, then gestured to the road. "That's him there!"

Ibn Malik was observing them. Ammar hailed him to wait as he followed Girgis out to the landing, then went up the embankment.

Ibn Malik was deeply tanned and dressed in a tissue-thin wool gown and robe in stark white shot through with threads of every hue. The embroidery along the edges and in the sash of his robe was in tiny repeating patterns of green and blue, and he wore a turban to match. His sandals were equally fine. He smelled of mint and citrus and seemed cool, as if the heat and humidity did not bother him, while Ammar was soaked through and, no doubt, stinking.

"Assalamu alaykum. I'm working for the family of Samir az-Zarduzi. The man who passed away here. I understand you were a witness."

"Passed away? Such a euphemism for what he did. It is better left alone."

"What are you saying?"

Ibn Malik frowned deeply. "At times, Samir came here to watch the boats."

"The young man I spoke to said he did not know him."

"He wouldn't. Samir kept away from everyone."

"But you knew him," Ammar asked.

"Only to speak briefly. He tended to avoid me. Samir was troubled. It was easy to see. I offered to listen or just sit beside him so he was not alone, but he refused."

"What do you mean, troubled?"

Ibn Malik said, "Meaning, I am not surprised to find him dead."

"How do you think he did it?"

"I saw the vomit. The state of him. Poison. I witnessed it once in my youth." The pall of a terrible memory was cast over his features. "It is not a good way to die."

"Did you see him take it?"

"No," Ibn Malik said. "Just his body after. God forgive him."

Shabib and Ahab felt the same. That was why they wiped the vomit off of him and took him to the local corpse washer instead of the Barmakid. That was why they insisted on natural causes. Despite their efforts, everyone suspected suicide, leading the family to hire Ammar to prove otherwise.

"Did you see if he brought any food or a jug with him, anything like that?"

"As I said, I only saw him after."

"Did he usually bring anything with him?"

"At times. I believe I saw him eating nuts." He mimicked dropping nuts into his mouth from his fist. "A small jug. God knows what was in it, but I never smelled alcohol on him the few times we did speak."

If someone wanted to poison him, it would only take spiking the jug he took with him or the food. That would put the killer in his household, whoever prepared the food, or whoever paid off the person who prepared the food.

"Were there any other witnesses up here on the road?"

"The young woman Girgis was planning on using so grievously. God's planning is perfect. She had been waiting here for several days, posing for him, begging to give up her virtue. He is beautiful, I understand. She is a Christian, and he a Mandaean; it is not my business as a Muslim. But I doubt her family and God would approve."

"Maybe she was a working girl?"

"No. She did not have the look."

Ammar wanted to jab at him—ask how he knew the look with such certainty and whether God would approve—but he asked instead, "What did you see?"

"As I said, she had been standing in the grasses by the road. She could have seen Samir from there. She followed Girgis through the reeds. She screamed and fainted when she saw the body. I pray she understands it as a presage of what she will suffer in the next life if she does not repent of her whoring ways. Girgis would leave her no better than a prostitute."

Ammar did not like him, but the man had a point. Sex with Girgis would likely lead to nothing but harm for her and no consequences for him. "Has she returned?"

"I have not seen her since that day. The police questioned her, though."

"If I have to speak to you again, may I come to your home?"

"I walk here regularly. You can find me on the path." He bowed his head and left.

He watched Ibn Malik go—probably taking the long way around so Ammar could not follow him home—then Ammar turned toward the breeze, hoping it would dry him off enough to meet Bashir and his family. First, he returned to the landing to press Girgis on the identity of the young woman. If he really did not know her, the investigators for Grave Crimes did.

10

———

Zaytuna nodded to the elderly woman on her stool, then knocked on Bint Afshin's gate. It was God's will whether or not she answered, but Zaytuna needed a sign. If Bint Afshin answered, then she would carry on. If not, Zaytuna would come back next week and apologize for finding nothing. There was no answer, but she waited a bit longer, praying under her breath to make the sign perfectly clear, "God, if you want me to continue, then let her open the door."

"What do you want? She's out."

Mewling kittens were squirming in the old woman's lap as their mother rubbed against her leg. With her eye on Zaytuna, she leaned down to give the mother a morsel of food from a cup on the stool beside her. She had crescent moons tattooed across her knuckles, and her kerchief was tied under her chin. There was a light on the old woman's face revealing a soft heart, exactly the sort to care for a mother cat and her babies.

"Do you know when she's coming back?"

"You that investigator she hired?"

"Yes," Zaytuna answered. "Are you two close?"

"Once. Before her daughter ran off and broke her heart."

She had never considered there was a child. Bint Afshin never mentioned one and used her patronymic, the daughter of her father, Afshin, rather than calling herself the mother of her daughter.

"Come 'n sit." The old woman took the cup off the stool and patted it. "What are you called?"

"Zaytuna."

"I am Umm Hurayra: The Mother of Kittens." She giggled.

Sitting beside her, Zaytuna caught the sharp, clean scent of orange flower water. The lane was quiet and shaded from the sun on that side. A welcome breeze rustled through trees set behind courtyard walls. Birds flitted through and perched in branches, singing despite the unusual heat. She handed Zaytuna the cup of food. No sooner had her hand touched it than the mother had her dusty black paws on Zaytuna's knee. The green-eyed cat begged with the chirping reserved for calling birds from the sky, and Zaytuna could not resist her either. She held out the milk-soaked crust. The cat politely took it between her teeth, then settled down again to eat.

They sat in silence for a bit longer. When the moment felt right, Zaytuna asked, "Why did her daughter leave?"

"Pregnant. Gul wouldn't name him who did it, but we all knew."

"How long ago?"

"The child would be four by now."

"How did you know the identity of the father?"

Umm Hurayra's face darkened. Zaytuna guessed what had happened and understood the thread that connected her to this case.

"Went past me dragging her wrap in the lane. Her face beaten, and her clothes torn. I called to her, but getting up was not easy for me even then, and she ran into her house."

"Her mother?"

"Nursed her like a baby. Begged to know who did it."

"Did Gul say?"

"No. But like I said, we all knew." Tears rolled down the old woman's cheeks. "We suspected."

"How?"

She wiped her face with a kerchief, then said. "A young man in the neighbourhood. He had his eye on her, but she had nothing for him. He even came to her parents asking to marry her. They turned him away, saying she was already promised."

"Was that true?"

"Of course not, and he guessed as much. After, he taunted her about the man she was to marry, asking why he did not come and get her."

"Did her father intervene?"

"It didn't do any good," Umm Hurayra said. "Have you met Adnan?"

"Not to speak," Zaytuna hedged.

"He's a gentle man, soft-spoken. That vile one wouldn't listen to the likes of him."

"Everyone in the neighbourhood knew at that point?"

She nodded slowly. "My husband, God have mercy on his soul, would not help. Said it would shame Adnan if he took the young man down. But I spoke to that ugly soul when he crossed by me here. I never saw such evil."

Zaytuna touched her knee, saying, "God protect us."

"He threatened I'd find my cats in his stew if I did not get my nose out of his business. I was just grateful my girls were long married and out of the house."

"You live here alone? Not with one of your daughters?"

"And leave my cats?"

This brave woman. How she reminded Zaytuna of all those in her life who stood up for her at home and in the street. But the story of Gul's rape also raised a mother's fear for her daughters, and her heart turned to stone. She prayed for Layla and Nura, breathing slowly into it until her heart came back to life.

"Everyone knew that Adnan could not protect his family. How did Bint Afshin feel about that?"

"There was a lot of talk. She lost some respect for him."

"Then one day Gul is pregnant."

"When it showed, we all knew how."

Zaytuna's heart spilled open for the girl and her child; she knew too well what it took for a woman to raise the children of rape on her own. They fell silent, and Zaytuna touched the cheek of the mother cat.

Her own mother was first raped under an olive tree. Zaytuna had always imagined it from above. Her view was obscured by the silver-grey leaves and black fruit drawing her eye away, while her mother's cries to God were lost beneath the rattling leaves. But she had also conjured memories of the women who fed her mother as she wandered, heavy with twins; who midwifed her as she chanted into the pain; and who cared for her and Tein when they were as helpless as kittens.

Who was with Gul?

The second time her mother was raped, she and Tein were just children. Tein was forced to protect her, and Zaytuna could only watch, clutching her mother's arm. Her mother told her and Tein that night, "I have fixed what is between God and me." But that did not fix what her mother's wandering had done to them, especially her brother.

Who was with Gul's child?

Her own pain healed by love and trust, she prayed for Tein and what he still carried. She prayed for Gul's child and all the children borne of violence. She prayed for Gul and all the mothers with the burdens they carry.

The woman brought a kitten to her cheek, delighting in its

softness. She whispered to it and placed it back into the wriggling pile in her lap.

Zaytuna broke the silence, asking, "Did the man demand to marry her?"

"After all that. No. Neither did her family. You know there's them here who wanted the problem of her pregnancy ended in marriage and were not shy with their opinion. But her parents were already getting old when they had her. She was their blessing, and they stood by her."

She felt a moment of empathy for Bint Afshin. It could not have been easy, yet she chose her daughter over shame. "So why did their daughter leave?"

"That man was still there, taunting her every day."

Zaytuna wished they had been able to grasp what it was doing to Gul and had moved to another neighbourhood.

"There was so much grief when Gul disappeared. I was there with her mother for all of it. Adnan looked the city up and down. My husband helped him. But it's no trick to disappear in Baghdad. They gave up, and their door was shut to the rest of us."

"This is terribly sad." But now Zaytuna knew where the money was going. "She hired me to follow her husband."

"We've heard her nagging him over the wall these past few weeks. There's no secrets in that woman's mouth. But there's nothing new in her taunting him, either. She blamed Adnan for not killing the man who raped their daughter. Maybe he's had enough." The old woman looked at her apologetically. "No insult intended, but you aren't needed for her to know he must have found a woman who speaks to him kindly."

"None taken." But Umm Hurayra was wrong. It was not another woman. He had found his daughter, and maybe the grandchild, if the child lived. But why did he not tell his wife? Perhaps Gul swore him to secrecy? Or did Gul not want to see him either? The thread warning her about the case tightened. She asked Umm Hurayra, "Do you think I should keep following her husband or let it go?"

The mother cat reached up. Zaytuna gave her another morsel.

"What kind of answer could help a mother without her daughter?"

"What if it brought her daughter back to her?"

"You think he's found her! And the baby?" Umm Hurayra sighed and held out her hands in prayer. "Ya, Allah!"

"Hearing your story," Zaytuna said, "I think he is either spending the money trying to find her, and she's gone. Or he's found her, and she won't return."

The thread connecting her to the case was clear enough, and it was three: her mother, herself and her brother, and her daughters—all twisted around each other into one. Bint Afshin had not opened her door, but Zaytuna had her sign. She would be there to support Gul and her child—just as women had been there for her own mother—and, God willing, follow the thread through to face old worries and new.

11

Samir's family home stood on a wide street lined with fired-brick buildings, two and three stories high, boasting intricately carved window screens. It was close to their shop but too far from the landing on the canal to explain why Samir would go there regularly. With the pain he suffered, he must have taken a cart. Still, there were closer access points, and Ammar had to ask, why would he go that far at all?

A couple in fine clothing emerged from the house as he arrived. They stopped short seeing him. The woman gasped, clutched her wrap, and moved behind her husband. Had they never seen a ghazi before? A woman and her young daughter followed. The woman pulled her daughter along, giving Ammar a wide berth. Then he heard it. The girl, now running to keep up with her mother, said, "That ugly man stinks!"

Ammar flushed with embarrassment. Of course he must stink after the heat and humidity by the canal, then the long walk to the family's home. There was nothing to be done now. They were going to have to decide if they wanted a ghazi investigating their case or one of their own, smelling sweet but having no idea what he was doing.

The gate led directly into a central courtyard through an arched vestibule. Mourners mingled in the courtyard. Low couches, luxuriously upholstered with bolsters to lean on, lined the walls. Potted flowers circled a small central pool. A jasmine vine climbed one arcade pillar and clung to the upper balustrade. Arched doorways opened to private rooms above and below. Downstairs, servants hurried in and out of the kitchen, carrying trays. Curtains were drawn over a room from which he heard the quiet wailing of women grieving with the widow. At least he was clear on one thing: they had the money to pay him. Ammar hoped they would remain devoted to taking the case wherever it led, for as long as it took. Bashir was speaking to two men when he noticed Ammar's arrival and excused himself.

"Alhamdulillah. Please, come." Bashir looked harried as he showed Ammar to a small room with couches and small tables set here and there. The upholstery in this room was not as fine as he expected given the wealth displayed in the courtyard, and there was no rug underfoot, just freshly woven mats still smelling sharply of grass. This must be where they stick the help.

"Please, sit. I'll get my mother and sister. I tried to get my cousins to stay and speak to you. They will return in the evening," he said with an apologetic look as he left.

An older male servant came in and laid out numerous small plates of food for him. There was halva, chopped salads, a mound of tender roasted lamb, cut fruit, olives, and soft, white bread, but only enough for one. He guessed he was not meant to share their midday meal with them, after all. Still, he hesitated before reaching for the food.

The servant noticed and said, "Ibn Samir asks that you begin."

It was all he needed. The lamb was served over flatbread

soaking up its juices with a side of roasted garlic and chopped herbs in olive oil. He started with a large piece of the tender roasted lamb and bread, dredging it through the oil. He had barely chewed in his hurry to stave off his hunger before he heard the son's voice carrying through from the courtyard. Ammar stood, swallowing hard.

Umm Bashir and Basma entered first. The mother looked like she needed to rest, not be part of this conversation, but her daughter had a firm hold on her.

"May God give you ease," Ammar said, bowing his head slightly.

Bashir followed them in as they murmured, "Amin," and sat on the couch furthest from him.

At least they were polite enough not to openly complain about his stench. They looked at him expectantly.

"I have some questions and some news," Ammar said, "but I am glad to find you with so many mourners. They must give you solace."

Basma burst out, "Solace!" Her mother grasped her hand, but she could not be controlled. "Every last one of them told us to drop the case, to let his death go."

"My daughter, stop."

But she would not be stopped. "That horrible Umm Afiya recited God's word at me: *Every soul will taste death, and we test you with the bad and the good.* Yes, it's a test. A test to hold on to the truth and to fight for our father."

The mother broke down in tears and drew her wrap over her face.

Basma put an arm around her mother, but it seemed like little comfort.

"When I insisted he had been murdered," Bashir said, "they recited, *Forgiveness is better for you.* They misunderstand our desire for justice."

"Do you know why?"

The sister started to speak, but her brother held out his hand. "They say Father died of an illness, but they mean something else. Ahmad said our father had been acting strangely. A neighbour said the same, revealing he had seen him weeping at an apothecary not far from here. We had no idea."

How could Bashir not know his father was seeking help for his pain? At least now Ammar could find out if the medicine prescribed could have caused a convulsion or if he could have been poisoned by it. He addressed Umm Bashir, "How did he manage the pain from his hip?"

She did not answer, only saying, "Why must any of this be said at all?"

It wasn't his place, but Ammar had no choice. "Maybe your mother would like to rest?"

Bashir suddenly became aware of the effect the conversation was having on his mother and took her hand, whispering to her. But she jerked it back, saying with surprising force, "I will not leave."

A servant came in with a tray with a pitcher and glasses. They waited to speak while he served them. Ammar shook his head at them. If they thought the servants did not know every one of their secrets, they were fooling themselves.

Bashir reached for the glass but nearly knocked it over. His hand was trembling. "Our father refused medicine, seeing it as a salve for his sins. I don't understand why he would be at an apothecary. He would have told us."

"Do you mind my asking what sin?"

"No sin at all," Basma objected. "The man whose life he saved did not escape without injury, and he never forgave himself."

Ammar understood the guilt. Working Grave Crimes, how many lives had he ruined by righting their wrongs? He said, for the mother's sake more than anything, "It sounds like he finally decided to do something for the pain. Maybe he forgave himself."

Bashir ignored the comment and asked, "You said he might have died from pain medication?"

"It is possible that he took too much, or that he was prescribed the wrong dosage"—he paused—"or that he was poisoned. I have heard more evidence this morning that supports these theories. I need to interview the apothecary. Do you know which one?"

"Only that it was the square nearest to us," Bashir answered. "But what is the evidence?"

"He had vomited, but the police cleaned it up before they took him to the corpse washer."

"They are covering over the murder," Basma snapped.

Ammar cautioned, "There may be a good reason for cleaning him up, but I promise you I will look into it."

"They'll lie," Basma said.

"I know these men. They'll tell me the truth." He did not add, "They'd tell me, assuming I'd not tell you," but asked instead, "Can you tell me more about the accident?"

"Is it related?" His mother asked, her voice weak again.

"Unrelated matters can come to have great significance as a case moves forward."

She nodded, tried to explain, and then gave up.

Bashir stepped in. "It was several years ago. A donkey bolted. The cart it pulled was about to hit a young man. Father was able to push him out of the way. The man was only glanced, but Father was hit square on. His hip was broken and his thigh. He was bruised from head to foot and also took a knock to his head. We were afraid he might not recover. He did, but the pain was terrible."

"The young man must have been in his debt," Ammar said.

"As anyone would," Bashir answered. "He was visiting from Jerusalem and returned not long after. Before leaving, he promised he would perform the pilgrimage for our father, as he would no longer be able."

"Your cousin said he had been acting strangely. It may have been from the knock on the head. The symptoms can be long term."

"What would it have looked like?" Bashir asked.

"Confusion. Headaches. Difficulty with his eyesight." He added quickly so as not to put undue emphasis on it, "Uncontrollable sadness or anger."

Bashir answered, "He had difficulty seeing the embellishment work and had to give it up. His work was very fine, and he was famous for it. But loss of eyesight is typical for those in our profession. I did not think much of it. Recently, I had to take over the day-to-day business. He could barely see what was written in front of him."

"A man at the canal said your father went there often to watch the boats."

They glanced at each other. This was the first they heard of it.

"He said your father was inconsolable."

There was silence in the room for a moment. Bashir frowned, and Basma turned red, but Umm Bashir was nodding ever so slightly. His wife knew his state of mind, even if his children chose to look the other way.

Ammar took a few bites of food to give them time, but he could not taste any of it.

Finally Bashir asked quietly, "Are you suggesting suicide?"

"People who are sad can be murdered just like anyone else."

"All right," Bashir said. "Please, continue."

"When he gave up control of the business, did he have any

suppliers, clients, or potential clients who might resent him? The other embellishers in the market?"

Bashir was irritated by the question. "I told you. There is the usual jealousy and goodwill."

"What about the jealousy?"

"You must know that shopkeepers look sideways if they believe you have better clients or are making more money than they are. It is to be expected, for God's sake."

Ammar ignored his tone. "How long has this business been in the family?"

"It is an expansion of the embellishment work we did under our former employer."

A simple statement of fact, but there was something he was not saying. Whatever it was, it was driving Bashir's heightened tension. "Is your former employer unhappy that you left?"

"He was sorry to lose us," he said. "We were the reason clients of a certain quality frequented his shop."

"When you left, you left with his clients," Ammar said.

"Your tone suggests we were in the wrong to take this opportunity, and I do not like it."

But his sister shot at him, "He's trying to find out who might have wanted Father dead!"

Bashir still did not like it, but Ammar silently thanked her. He went on, hoping Bashir could be tripped into admitting there was animosity. "I'll ask them about it at the old shop."

"Will you speak like this to the owner?" Bashir stood, trembling. "Will you stir up trouble between us?"

He poked at Bashir's fine sensibilities. "I know I can be rough around the edges from my days in Grave Crimes, but if you want the truth, this is how we get it."

"Rough? Yes!" Bashir exclaimed. "And you smell like it. Do you not think to wash first when you work with your clients?

Who would even speak to you in this state? We only do so because we are desperate."

At the insult, Ammar lost his composure and stood, glaring, half wanting to walk out and half wanting to tell him that this rough-hewn ghazi was the only man who could help him.

But Basma got between them. "Brother, please. I am angry. I am offended. I am grieving. But this disgusting little man is asking questions no one else did."

Her insult hit him in a way that Bashir's had not. Ammar felt small, as if he were a child again and his father was standing over him recounting his inadequacies one by one.

Basma continued, "He will find out who killed our father, and if you cannot stand the smell of a working man now that our circumstances have changed, then you have changed beyond what I would like to imagine."

Their circumstances had changed.

With difficulty, Ammar got himself under control to find out what she meant. He ignored her though, not even able to look at her, and went at Bashir. But not with the resentment he felt towards them both. Instead, he forced himself to apologize, using all his power to keep his voice even. "I am sorry for the state I am in. I came directly from questioning the men at the canal. I had no time to go to the baths or back home to Buratha to change."

"Yes, yes." Bashir shook his head and returned to sit next to his mother.

His mother lightly slapped his hand, then kissed it and held it tight.

Ammar forced himself to face Basma. "What did you mean by 'circumstances changed'?"

"Our father and my brother were embellishers, as you know. Their former employer is Abduljabbar ibn Fadi. His shop is in the Little Tanners District."

Talk about stench. He nearly huffed with vindication. That was not a neighbourhood frequented by the wealthy. He had imagined them working in a lesser area of the Clothiers' market before making their big move. But there? They could only be making clothes for the working poor in a neighbourhood that stunk of rawhide soaking in piss and salt. They were well used to the sight and smell of working folk who only had basins to wash in at home and made it to the baths when they could.

Their accents held no trace of the old neighbourhood. They'd come a long way, but not far enough, and this was the reason for Bashir's offence. No doubt Bashir smelled the same just a few months ago, and he was ashamed.

He tried to keep the smugness out of his voice as he asked, "So how did the 'quality clientele' find you there?"

Bashir answered, "My father was embellishing a garment in the sunlight. A man who had business with the tanners walked by and admired it. He was back soon, making an order. It followed from there."

"And you made enough money to leave and win a bid on a store in the Suq at-Tarrazun?"

Basma answered, "Father inherited a sum of money. Bashir would have the chance to master a business, carry on the family name, make his own reputation."

"I'm sorry, but I have to speak to people in both locations."

Bashir looked stricken again.

Ammar threw him a bone, hoping for a revelation. "Is there something I should avoid asking?"

But Bashir only responded, "Who am I to tell you your job? I am sure you will be professional in every respect."

It was not a note of confidence.

Ammar said, "I will ask if anyone wished your father ill."

The sister and brother shared a quick look.

"That there. I cannot help you if you do not tell me everything."

"Tell him," Basma said.

"The business we purchased. A cousin of the owner wanted to buy it, but we outbid him. A son of the previous owner told me privately his father was glad to sell it to us, as he hated the cousin. He had difficult relations with everyone in the family. Apparently, there is no one he does not despise. But the cousin would hold as much of a grudge against the family who sold the business as he would against my father."

Ammar nearly came at them for not telling him this before, saying instead, "That's quite a family secret to share."

"I, too, was shocked, but I encouraged him to give us every detail. I felt it was important to know if this cousin was going to create problems for us or not. He assured us that the man failed at everything he touched, as if he were cursed, and hated everyone for it but was incapable of action."

"He never hurt anyone or lashed out over it?"

"Grumbling only. He despises everyone for their success and glories when they fail."

"If you are serious about this investigation, you cannot hold back anything. You thought he would not hurt your father because he is unwilling to kill anyone in his family. Your father is not his family."

Basma nodded briskly, understanding.

The servant returned. "Abu Keyvan Karim ibn Hisham al-Baghdadi is here with his family."

The brother's face flushed again, but brightly this time. "My betrothed, Sitara, and her family."

They all stood, but Bashir held Ammar back. "Please, I am sorry to mention it again, but I would prefer not to introduce you while you are, uh, in this state."

"Of course." He held back from taunting them to take the

family to the real sitting room, not this place where they stick the help and stinking friends from the old neighbourhood.

Basma left last, pausing to hold out her hands in prayer. For what, he did not know. A good marriage for her brother? Finding her father's killer? That Ammar be less repulsive?

Alone, Ammar peeked through the curtains. He nearly gasped at the family's wealth. These were not people of the estates. They would be comfortable in the caliph's circles, and the humiliation he felt at Basma's blithe insult redoubled. How could he work a case involving people like this? If he were police, he could force them to admit him, to show him respect. But who was he now but a disgusting little man?

The father and son were tall and handsome, strong men wearing clothes worthy of court. Both had long swords at their belts; the beautifully worked sheaths were matched only by the craftsmanship on the handles. The mother and daughter were draped in silk wraps so delicate even the softest hands would tear them. Layers of gowns and robes pooled at their feet. The mother touched the edge of her wrap, revealing a sleeve embellished with tiny pearls. Their faces were uncovered, revealing their beauty.

Nothing could have prepared him for Sitara. She was the woman of a poet's longing. Her complexion was the colour of summer wheat. Her round cheeks blushed prettily. Her forehead was low and broad. Her arched eyebrows met delicately at the centre. A small mole was set on her lower cheek near the curve of a shy smile. But unlike a poet's unattainable lover, she only had eyes for Bashir. When she stole glances at him, her eyes glittered with adoration. Ammar felt ashamed to be in her presence.

He lowered his gaze, forcing his attention to the rest of the family. Ibn Hisham had the bearing of a man used to commanding others, but it was clear he had not commanded his daughter to marry Bashir. He greeted his future family as if they were servants. The son mimicked his father, as if practicing to take his place. And while Sitara got her beauty from her mother, her mother's face was marred by her distaste for having to breathe the air in this home.

Now he understood why the couple was surprised that her parents agreed but also doubted Bashir's account that Ibn Hisham had loved Samir like a brother. Treated Samir well in a display of noble generosity, as expected, but never love.

He dropped the edge of the curtain and waited for them to move to the main salon, then left quietly to find the apothecary. But first, the baths.

12

Ammar waited for the apothecary stalls to open in a small square sheltered by an ancient fig tree. He settled near a man sprawled out, sleeping off his midday meal on one of the thick reed mats laid out around the tree's massive trunk. Insects buzzed from the heat, and birds chirped as they pecked at the budding fruit, as the man snored lightly. Relaxed from the bath, his mind drowsily turned over the puzzle of Bashir and Sitara.

There was nothing strange about love matches—his own brother had found his wife in a chance encounter—the strangeness was in the parents respecting her choice. There would be no trouble marrying Sitara into the greatest families of the empire, if not into the caliphal family itself. Had she threatened to run off with Bashir or hurt herself? He tried to imagine her tearing at her hair, but she did not have the look of a bold or dramatic girl. Even that, though, would not compel any family who had control over their daughter. And there was no world he could imagine in which the commander did not have control over Sitara.

One by one, the apothecaries returned. Ammar got up as an elderly woman passed, appraising him with caring eyes. She wore a honey-yellow and blue striped turban with sprigs of dried flowers sticking out of the folds and a long robe of the same colour with floral embroidery along the hem.

Ammar watched as she unlocked her door, got up onto the platform behind the narrow counter, and pushed open the shutters. A small man with a stooped back arrived from the other side of the square with a slip of paper in his hand. She set out two stools in front of the shop, and he sat, waiting for her to finish opening. Customers arrived for the others, and the apothecaries leaned out over their narrow counters, handing over medicine in small jars or linen-wrapped packages.

The old woman's customer lingered at her counter, sharing a laugh, and finally left, offering her warm farewells. She liked to take her time with her customers and enjoy a bit of chat. Ammar decided to try her first.

She watched him approach, smiling broadly. "Welcome!"

The shelves of her shop sagged with carefully labelled jars in a script he recognized as Hebrew from his old days on the job in a Jewish neighbourhood of Baghdad. There was a room behind the shelves that he could just see. Mortars and pestles sat on a wide counter. She even had one of those round-bottomed glass jars over a custom-made brazier, as he had seen in Ibn Ali's pharmacy.

"Good afternoon. My name is Ghazi Ammar at-Tabbani."

"And I am Mazal. How can I help you?"

"I am looking into the death of Samir az-Zarduzi for his family. They told me he had visited an apothecary here."

"Blessed is the True Judge. What a sad affair. I plan on closing early today to share their grief."

"How close were you to the family?"

"Samir was my client, no more."

Ammar held back a smile. He had found her on the first try.

She gestured to the stools and came to sit beside him. "He

was new to the neighbourhood, and we had only started to build a relationship."

"Customers seem to come and go quickly, but not you. Your last customer stayed a while."

"Unless I am taking written direction from a doctor from the Barmakid or a healer I respect, I only prescribe to those whose lives I come to know." Mazal looked out at the other shops with concern. "It's too easy to make mistakes without knowing their history and habits."

"You felt like you knew him well enough to prescribe?"

"Yes," she said with a sad, small laugh. "We enjoyed talking to one another. He would bring me candy, and we would pull up stools and chat."

Ammar liked her and thought if she were anywhere near his own home, he would entrust his family's health to her. "It was a big change for him, moving to this neighbourhood. I'm glad he found you."

"I am a simple woman. Samir was a simple man. We got along just fine."

"Did he miss his old life?"

"Oh yes. He loved his embellishment work, but his sight was going, as is typical in that work. He felt he had to make this change for his son's sake."

"It worked out well for the son." Ammar pressed, "He met his betrothed at the new shop."

"Sitara? No. It was at the old place. Love at first sight."

"What would she be doing in that neighbourhood? Wouldn't they bring craftsmen to the house?"

"It had become a trend to go there, especially because of the stench of the small tannery. Sitara's mother is a woman of great style, I hear. She brought her daughter and—."

Ammar guessed she rued the day.

"—*One glance, and fate between them twined.*"

"That sounds like a line from a poem."

"It is about them. I wrote it." She beamed.

Ammar warmed to her even more. "Romantic gossip inspired your poem!"

"You scoff," she giggled. "But you have not heard it."

"I met Sitara's mother and father today. Their daughter and a man from the mercantile class? They must be scandalized."

"In the poem, the girl sneaks out of their estate." She closed her eyes and recited:

A gazelle became the hunter kind.

Her eyebrow arched into a bow,

her lips the quiver's crimson glow,

and in his heart her arrow shined.

It was awful, but she was pleased with herself, and he nodded in appreciation.

She asked, "What choice did the family have but to make it good?"

The family had a choice—to lock up Sitara. "And Bashir, what did he do?"

"In my poem, he acts with the utmost propriety. But his father affirmed it. She came day after day searching for him, but Bashir would arrive before dawn and work out of view. The gossip was more than the shopkeeper could bear. Customers who knew her family were talking and accusing the shopkeeper of encouraging her. Finally, the owner of the shop had to beg her to go home. She declared she would only leave if Bashir promised to approach her family."

So the girl was bold and dramatic, after all. He said, "Quite the scandal." But more than tarnishing the families, he did not see how the shop could rise above the gossip. What respectable family would allow its women to visit after that? Not only did they lose their famed embellishers, but also their reputation.

"Perhaps my poem will help the couple outpace the scandal

to become a romance for the ages." She recited, "*Hands brushed over silken knots.*"

"You are a romantic."

"Is there an Arab who is not?"

He had not been until he met Nasifa. "All this, and her parents did nothing?"

"Of course not. When the girl told them to expect her suitor, the father sent a fierce guard to tell them to stay away and ignore the girl if she returned, or steps would be taken. There was no need. Samir assured them Bashir had no intention of courting her."

"Had Bashir fallen in love, too?"

She repeated the line from her poem. "*And in his heart her arrow shined.*"

"So what brought the parents around?"

"It seemed over. Sitara never returned. Without her knowledge, the father and son started their new business in a new neighbourhood. But then one day, there she is, standing before the new shop. The girl fainted at the sight of Bashir and refused to eat until her father agreed to admit him."

"And Bashir?"

"He left it in Samir's hands. Now that their situation was improved, Samir agreed to speak to Sitara's father on behalf of his son."

"Did Samir tell you about his inheritance?"

"A relative with no family left him a bequest."

"Perfect timing," Ammar said skeptically.

"*To everything there is a season and a time to every purpose under the heaven.*"

"What's that?"

"A verse from our Kohelet."

"Meaning, everything happens at the right moment?"

She smiled.

Clearer than the sun, Bashir sneaked out of the old shop to meet the girl, and then she found him again when she realized she was pregnant. But why had Sitara's father not sent her away to have the baby and give it up? And, after all that, why would Bashir's family invite more scandal by insisting their father was murdered? No wonder everyone they knew was encouraging them to drop it.

"Do you mind if I ask about the father's treatment?"

"The family sent you?"

"Yes."

She took a long look at him before answering. "You lie."

"I know he never told them he came to you."

"How did you find me, then?"

"A cousin saw him here."

This answer satisfied her. "How will my answer help you?"

"Maybe if the family knew more about his health, they could let it go." He decided to tell her. "He was found twisted up by a convulsion. His tongue had turned black, and he had vomited."

Her eyes widened. "He came to me with severe pain from an old accident. Bones healed badly. He had trouble walking. I gave him a low dose of opium as well as poultices. With time, he begged me for more, but I would not give it to him. I have seen what happens to those who take too much. Opium rarely causes convulsions, and what I gave him would not do it."

"And his emotional state?"

"Physical pain begets emotional pain. At first the opium lifted the pain and his spirits. But lately, he was suffering and unhappy."

"Do you think he would have taken his own life?"

"Never."

"What makes you so sure?"

"He was looking forward to the marriage. Sitara's father had promised to take Bashir on, setting him up in a business venture that would be more suitable to their status. Eventually, Samir could let go of the tailor shop and retire. The whole family would be lifted up."

That, at least, answered the question of status, but the marriage still made no sense. And he was no closer to knowing how the father had died. "Do you have any thoughts about his death, given what I told you?"

"I will not offer an opinion. But I cannot understand it from anything I gave him. I would suggest you visit the doctors at the Barmakid or their esteemed pharmacist, Firdaws Ibn Ali."

Ammar thanked her, placing his hand over his heart. He scanned the other apothecaries, wondering if he should ask at each of them, too, just in case. Instead, he turned back to the old woman. "Did he ever speak to any of the others here?"

"One." She frowned. "I would have said so, but I didn't think it mattered."

"Who? When?"

She gestured to a man across the small square. Ammar looked over to find a tall man scowling at them. "Bilge al-Attar. I saw him there, but only for a moment. Not long enough for Bilge to suggest a treatment, let alone prepare one for him."

But the man's scowl meant something. Ammar bowed his head in thanks.

13

———

Bilge al-Attar looked ready to argue with Ammar before he even reached him. Instead of the scientific orderliness of Mazal's pharmacy, dried birds, bits of bone, snippets of hide, and fur swung in net bags from the ceiling. It was heavy with the scent of dried roots and herbs and felt more like where one went to get potions for love and protection than medicine. There were medicines in labelled jars on the other side of the shop, but it all seemed like simple remedies to him.

The apothecary asked brusquely, "Did my colleague not have what you needed?"

He ignored the question and said, "My name is Ghazi Ammar at-Tabbani. I'm a private investigator looking into the death of Samir az-Zarduzi. I understand he was a client of yours."

"The witch told you he came to me?"

Ammar nearly smiled. If anyone misdiagnosed Samir or gave him the wrong medicine, it was this man. Ammar sized him up, judging how best to approach the interview. In his experience, insults and flattery worked with men like this. Ammar began with an insult. "Absurd, I know. I see your shop, and I have to agree you would not know of any medicine to help him."

"As if you are educated in such matters to form an opinion."

Ammar gave him an appraising once over. "And you know what you're doing?"

Bilge smiled smugly.

"So, did you prescribe for him?"

"Why would I speak to you?"

Ammar pivoted, giving him the chance to feel superior to a dead man. "I think he took his own life."

"He was the weak sort who would do it." Bilge shrugged. "It would not be on account of the pain, though. I changed out his poultice."

He gestured behind him. "But Mazal says he did not stop here long enough for you to treat him."

The man rolled his eyes. "Samir did not want to hurt her feelings. We would meet when she was away for her midday meal and nap, and he continued to buy her medicines and throw them away."

Or maybe keep both, Ammar thought, and die by overdose. He asked, "Why would your poultice make such a difference?"

"Because I know medicine the fools in this square do not know."

"You want to explain?"

"I studied in the tradition of Sun Simiao." He pointed to a paper scroll hanging behind him in letters he could not read but that looked like Chinese to him. "That is my certificate of completing my education and permission to dispense."

Ammar turned to flattery. "I'm surprised you do not work at the Barmakid. I know the pharmacist there personally, and he would be interested. Do you know Firdaws Ibn Ali?"

"Ibn Ali," Bilge scoffed. "He loves his Greek texts and his experiments but has no curiosity about Chinese wisdom."

If Ibn Ali turned him away, the man was a charlatan. "I can see why Samir came to you, then. Only you could help."

"I only treated him for a few weeks." Bilge glared across the square. "He suffered unnecessarily until then."

"What was in the poultice?"

"A small amount of opium, henbane, and toad venom. Together, they numb the skin and then travel down to the muscle and bone. The relief was profound."

Toad venom. Ammar knew enough about toads in the marshes to know you did not touch them. He needed to talk to Ibn Ali.

"Do you know how he died?" Ammar asked.

"I heard a convulsion."

Ammar took a chance. "Your poultice may have caused it."

His face paled as he objected, "It is impossible. Not in the dose I gave him. Perhaps a dog or a child, but not a man."

Not if Samir doubled up his medication. If Samir did not tell him, Bilge was not guilty of anything other than being an ass. He would have to discuss it with Ibn Ali. Until then, Ammar assured him. "Good to know. The family will be relieved to hear it. I appreciate your time."

The man caught himself, his colour returning, and with that, his arrogance. "Only a fool would believe this medicine could kill a man. Their family raised in station. They are ungrateful! Making these accusations!"

"To be clear, no one has accused you of anything."

Ammar turned to leave, but the man called him back, his voice menacing. "That family is a scandal. Unworthy of my knowledge. I guess you know that Bashir manipulated his way into the heart of their perfect daughter?"

"Yes." Ammar faced him.

"Well, what do you think about it?" Bilge taunted.

"More like I want to know what you think about it."

"Ibn Hisham is a gracious man to admit them to his presence."

The reputation of any man hinged on his generosity. No doubt Samir had spoken well of him. But Ibn Hisham could turn any situation to his advantage, and the marriage, on the surface, was not it.

But Ammar had found the most immediate explanation for Samir's death. He was taking the opium prescribed by Mazal and had added Bilge's poultice to hers. Ibn Ali would confirm, but it was probably enough to kill him.

A few more leads to follow—interview the cousin and at the shops, find the Christian girl from the canal—then, if there was nothing, Samir had died of an overdose.

14

———————

DAY THREE

"I don't believe it," Zaytuna said to Ammar. He was in some sort of pique, looking like a lost boy, putting two children on her hands.

Nura was hanging onto her leg and begging to be lifted up. "Ummi, Ummi, Ummi, Ummi, Ummi, Ummi. Upsies!"

She could not answer the needs of both Nura and Ammar. Zaytuna caught Saliha's eye, asking her to take the girl so she could focus on what Ammar was saying.

But Saliha only gestured at Layla. "I'm getting ready for work."

"Up!" Zaytuna yanked Nura onto her hip. The girl kicked and arched back against her arm, squealing. She wondered what would happen if Saliha did get pregnant with Tein's child. Her friend had little maternal interest, but Zaytuna consoled herself that Tein had enough for the two of them.

She hadn't heard half of what Ammar was saying but caught, "—pointing to his dying of an overdose."

"Come here, you," Layla said, reaching for Nura.

Zaytuna gratefully handed her over.

"That makes sense, although—" She paused before finishing, wanting a moment to let her judgment come together in a way she could not with all the busyness at home. "We need to go see Ibn Ali."

"That's why I'm here so early."

"I'll come with you. I want to hear what he says, but let's wait for Saliha."

"Wait, what you said before. What don't you believe?"

"The nonsense about the romance." Her tone was sharper than she liked. It wasn't just that Ammar and Nura were both demanding her attention; the greater distraction was Tein. If he came out while Ammar was still here, she would have to manage Ammar's testiness all day. "I agree she must be pregnant, and that's why the marriage is going ahead. But I don't understand why a family like that would not have just sent her away to have the baby in secret, provided for it to be raised, and brought Sitara back to society, well-chastened."

"Maybe he thinks he is above gossip. Ibn Hisham has the look of a man who commands armies."

"Then he just commanded an army to an embarrassing defeat."

Yulduz lumbered out bleary-eyed and caught sight of Ammar. "You're 'ere early. Sit. I'll get breakfast."

She left Ammar to Yulduz and went to dress.

Kamal Ali was tying the sash on his robe. "I heard Ammar."

"I'm in a temper," she said.

"What can I do?"

"Keep me here until the storm passes?"

The morning was still cool, and soft blue-grey light shone through the small window high on the wall. Kamal Ali had folded back the light quilt so the mattress could air out. She sat down on the edge of the bed and admired her husband. His broad forehead, the wave of his auburn beard, the nobility of his aquiline nose, and the tenderness of his brown eyes bore a close resemblance to descriptions of the Prophet Muhammad. In the past, for her, no man had been worth loving when compared to the Prophet, but then God sent her one who not only shared his countenance but also his character. She said longingly, "Remember when we used to linger in bed on mornings like this?"

He sat beside her and took her hand, intertwining his fingers in hers, then kissed hers one by one. "I remember. Such mornings gave us our beauty, Nura. God protect her."

"Amin."

"Is Tein awake?"

"He must be. I'm afraid of what will happen if he comes out," she said.

"They will face each other."

"They miss each other. That's all it is, and both are too stubborn to say it."

"It's more than that, I think," Kamal Ali said.

She gave his opinion weight. He rarely shared his thoughts, and when he did, she knew they were well-considered, and she waited for him to continue.

"There was a case when they were police. Tein told me about it. He had a difficult conversation with Ammar, and their friendship has never been the same."

"The case of the jinn and the talisman writer." She remembered too well. Ammar had taken a wrong turn in his character and had paid for it, with Tein and with himself. But she thought they had repaired it, especially when Ammar agreed to give up policing, more for Tein's sake than his own. "What do you think Ammar wants?"

"From Tein? I don't know. But I think Ammar still feels guilty."

It fell into place. "He believes Tein refusing to work with him means Tein has not forgiven him. And when Tein does a small job for me, it feels like proof. I won't ask Tein for help again until they work it out."

He kissed her on the cheek. "I'll go eat with Ammar and keep the peace if necessary."

When she joined them, Tein was on the rug, Nura placidly settled in his lap, and Layla was leaning up against him. He was putting bits of bread and cheese into Nura's mouth while talking to Layla about her day ahead. It was always like this with him and the girls, but Tein was using them to avoid Ammar's eye. And Ammar was ignoring him by trying to have a conversation with Yulduz about Bint Afshin, but she was having none of it.

"Talk to Zaytuna. She came back with one of those looks to 'er face."

"Look to my face?" She sat down next to Kamal Ali and asked, "Where is Saliha?"

"Gone already," said Layla.

She had hoped they could all walk together and talk about Ammar's case. Saliha could demonstrate that she could be relied upon. Not everything had to go through Ibn Ali. Maybe if they left now, they could catch Saliha before work. Only a moment out of the sanctuary of their room and everything felt rushed again. Zaytuna turned to Ammar. "If you've had enough, let's go." She forced a smile. "I can explain what that look is on my face."

"As long as all that news reaches me in the end," Yulduz said, then popped a date into her mouth.

Nura crawled out of Tein's lap and into her father's, reaching for the food in his hands.

He was stuffing a thick piece of barley bread with soft cheese and pitted dates. "It's for your mother, azizati." He kissed her head, then handed it off to Zaytuna. "Eat on the way, or you won't eat at all."

"Love for my loves." She kissed her fingers, touched Kamal

Ali's cheek, and tickled Nura's chin. Nura stood up on her father's lap, reaching for her. "Upsies."

Those big eyes, so much like her father's. How could such all-consuming love exist? In that moment, all she wanted was to tell Ammar to head on without her and leave her to her husband and child. But she said, "I have to go, baby."

Ammar shifted to get up, but Tein stopped him. "Your cup is empty." He filled it in a clear gesture of friendship. Zaytuna could have kissed him, and Layla did, a loud smack on the cheek that made everyone laugh, except Ammar, who at least drank the buttermilk and then went to join Zaytuna.

She asked, "Who has Nura today?"

Qambar answered, "We've got her. You all go."

But Zaytuna shot Kamal Ali a look, asking him to take her if Yulduz and Qambar seemed tired.

Outside, a light fog was still clinging to the corners and alcoves of the narrow lanes, making the city feel quiet. Sleepy girls lined up with buckets to fill at the local fountain while workmen shuffled off to their jobs. Ammar kept his thoughts to himself, and she was glad of it. Her own thoughts felt crowded, leaving her irritated. But once on the main road, they fell in beside a cart, and Ammar repeated his earlier opinion.

"It's hard to consider anything but an overdose."

"Accidental or otherwise," she said.

"Yes."

"But?"

"The family won't simply accept the conclusion that he overdosed. I have to track down every lead." He began counting them out on his fingers. "I don't know how to find her, but there is that witness to question—"

"The police interviewed her. Ask them."

"I want more before I go to them. They'll think I'm interfering if I don't have a wider case to present." He finished his list:

"They took business from their old boss, affecting his reputation. The bequest seems too convenient. Then there is jealousy at the new market. And a cousin who wanted to buy the business and lost his chance."

The news of the overdose was compelling, and the witness could probably close the case. He was dragging it out. "One more day to tie up these loose ends, then?"

"Maybe someone drove him to suicide to ruin the new business?" He tugged on his beard.

"This is spinning tales," she said curtly. "Maybe another shopkeeper did want Samir dead, maybe their old boss, and even had some plan to drive the son out of business. But it's a lot of effort to make it look like suicide. Just kill him. This is Baghdad. You and Tein said when you were on the job if the murderer wasn't seen, didn't stick around, and didn't talk, that he was not likely to be caught."

He reacted defensively. "There were only two of us working those cases for all of Karkh."

"That's exactly my point."

"All right. All right." He stopped for a moment. "What if the commander killed him to stop the marriage?"

She stepped back as a boy in a scrap of turban came rushing past, with a girl in chase behind him. "Kill the son, Ammar. Not the father. Are you trying to drag this out?"

He started to answer her but bit it back with a small frown.

Zaytuna considered him. His face had that strange flush men had before they broke out into tears. At some point, he would tell her what was wrong, but for now she just wanted to get to the hospital, hear the news, and get back home.

They crossed the busy street to the hospital, and he paused in the arched vestibule. The breeze tunnelled through, and Zaytuna had to hold on to her wrap to keep it from blowing open.

"I wouldn't drag it out," he said, sounding hurt.

There it was; he was conflicted about the case, worried about pushing it past its limits. But that was nothing to inspire this emotion. He might be tempted, but Ammar would not in the end. She regretted saying it not just because she was wrong, but also because a petulant Ammar was even more frustrating. Hand on her heart, she said, "Forgive me," hoping her tone was sincere.

Saliha called to them. Her hair was carefully bound under a white kerchief, and she was wearing her plain work wrap wound around her waist with the long end loose to toss over her head when she left the corpse washing room. "Ibn Ali is here; hurry."

"Is he busy?"

"No, I am. I got word a woman's body will be here soon. I want in on the conversation before she arrives."

Ibn Ali was ready to meet them. They joined him at the benches near the fountain. The hush of the morning fog suffused the courtyard, and they kept their voices low. A wide arched door to the men's ward was cracked open, and she could see a patient still asleep within. The sound of the flowing water and the scent of the few sweet blossoms left on the bitter orange and lemon trees soothed her.

It was not until that moment that she realized she had been having trouble listening and was being short with Ammar because she had left Nura before she was ready to let her go. She said a prayer for her baby and whoever had her in hand to take good care of her until she could get back.

Ammar had already shared the outline of his interviews with the pharmacist and was waiting for Ibn Ali to give his opinion.

As always, Ibn Ali's expression was engaged. "I met this apothecary you mention."

"Yes, he said so. He did not think much of you," Ammar said.

"He accused me of not being interested in Chinese medicine.

Nothing could be further from the truth. Our prophet commanded us to seek knowledge as far as China. In fact, we have purchased various substances from a Chinese importer, but we will not prescribe them until they are studied. I personally asked the importer to bring us Chinese pharmacological texts similar to my father's, more precisely like Sabur ibn Sahl's *Formulary*, but he has not returned with one." He waved the apothecary's objections off. "We are interested in scientific knowledge from every source."

"He has a certificate of having studied under a famous Chinese pharmacist. I don't remember the name, though."

"I have been assured that it is a few lines of Chinese poetry."

God forbid he prescribed for children. Zaytuna hoped Ibn Ali could get him shut down.

Saliha asked Ibn Ali, "Did the apothecary mention any substances that were new to you?"

"Everything he offered is locally available." Ibn Ali addressed Ammar. "I still do not understand why he came to me, knowing himself to be a charlatan."

"To me, it makes sense," Saliha said. "He gets his authority by saying he confronted you and you rejected him. He can say he has secret knowledge that the great pharmacist at the Barmakid is withholding from the common folk."

This is exactly the kind of observation Zaytuna knew Saliha could offer, and she hoped Ammar had heard it.

"I will contact the Marketplace Inspector," Ibn Ali said. "That is, if we find that Samir died as a result of his use of toad venom. Toad venom is a dangerous substance. In very small doses, it would cause numbing. High doses would cause vomiting, drooling, hallucinations, weakness, erratic heartbeat, and, yes, convulsions and death. Mixed with henbane and opium, it would be a strong painkiller but an even more potent poison. This is a dangerous combination."

"And you say his first apothecary was still prescribing until the end?" Saliha asked.

"Yes," Ammar said.

"Double-dosing with toad venom in the mix—it would have been fatal," she said.

Ibn Ali asked, "Did his family report any change in his behaviour? The effects of that would have been noticeable."

"They said no change at all," Ammar said.

"This suggests that although he continued to buy the original prescription, he did not use it," Ibn Ali said.

Ammar responded, "Bilge said so, but I assumed Samir was lying to him or he was covering over his own malpractice."

"Why did Samir seek out a second apothecary?" Saliha asked.

"Mazal refused to give him more opium when he wanted it," Ammar said.

"Good woman," Ibn Ali said, "but—"

Saliha interjected, "Did she prescribe anything else to address his pain?"

"No."

She addressed Ibn Ali. "That must be what drove him to the other apothecary. One must make sure the patient is comfortable within safe means."

Ibn Ali nodded, a small smile of pride on his lips, but Zaytuna could not restrain her own. Her friend had come a long way from a penniless woman escaping a deadly husband. They had washed clothes together for chinks of coin and slept on thin reed mats with barely a blanket between them. Now, here Saliha was, happily married to Tein, a respected corpse washer, and learning from one of the empire's great practitioners and scholars.

He asked Saliha, "If the toad venom poultice were given in a safe dose, why might there still be a risk of poison?"

"It is absorbed into the skin through the muscle. The effect could build over time."

Ibn Ali nodded.

"But he was only being treated for a few weeks or so," Ammar said.

"Then only if the poultice was in a high dose," Ibn Ali said. "But the effect would have been noticeable, and as you said, there was no change."

"Correct," Ammar said.

"The toad venom poultice was not too strong then, offering better relief, but not enough to affect him. I doubt that is what caused the convulsion. I will still speak to the Marketplace Inspector, though. There may be other complaints about this man."

"Patients don't buy poultices ready-made, only the liquid vehicle or paste to apply at home. He may have been stockpiling it to take his own life. Have you ruled that out?" Saliha asked.

It was an excellent point, Zaytuna thought, but Ammar did not answer it directly.

"Even Mazal said his mood was low but that he was looking forward to the wedding. It seems impossible any father would kill himself before his son's wedding, even if the compulsion consumed him."

Saliha said, "Impossible for us who don't suffer, who don't know what it is like to feel so alone. I knew someone who attempted to take her own life because she was certain her family would be relieved to be rid of her."

It was an important observation, one that Zaytuna had not considered.

But it seemed as if Ammar had dismissed it. "If not the poultice or double-dosing, then we still don't know what killed him."

Saliha started to speak but held back.

"What?" Ibn Ali asked.

She cocked her head. "It is possible to have a convulsion without any previous history or obvious external cause, correct?"

"That is true," Ibn Ali said, "but because we were not permitted to examine the body, we will never know."

Ammar did not seem dissuaded, though. First ignoring that Samir may have stockpiled the poultice medication, now that the death could have been natural. If anything, he was confident where he had not been this morning, saying, "I may come up with an answer yet."

Zaytuna nearly sucked her teeth at him, ready to get back to Nura.

Two watchmen were coming through the entrance to the hospital with a body on a pallet covered by a worn blanket. Saliha followed the men to the back, and the three of them raised their hands to pray for the dead.

15

───────

Ammar stood outside the hospital with Zaytuna, hand on the hilt of his dagger, feeling like a fool. Zaytuna had been only half-listening and short with him from the start. Tein's gesture of friendship had confused him, and then she insulted him with her comment that he was "dragging it out." Her careless apology only topped it off.

"Like Saliha said, people sometimes make choices that seem impossible to us," she said. "Who among us could imagine a parent killing themselves before a wedding? But he may have thought they would be glad to be rid of him."

"I didn't say it back there, but a man who walks the canal road every day told me Samir went there regularly to watch the boats. To be alone. He said Samir seemed troubled and was not surprised to find him dead." He gave her a hard look. "I'm not ruling out suicide."

"Good. Even if the family does not want to hear it."

"But I won't put aside anything that leads to a better explanation."

She sucked her teeth, as if he were not advising simply good investigative practice.

He shot back, "Am I putting you out?"

"I'm sorry."

The apology was as insincere as the last, and he could not see what he had done wrong.

Then she waved her hand, urging him on. "What is next?"

"We can talk on the way to the office."

"No. I must go home."

"What's wrong?" He thought back to the morning; everyone seemed well.

"I want to be with my daughter today."

"You gave up your case, after all?"

She ignored the question. "Before I leave, if the commander dotes on the daughter—if she is spoiled and is used to getting everything she wants—then he might permit the marriage, no matter the scandal. Like you said, wrong or not, he may consider himself above it."

"So now you are interested in the romance?"

"Look, if you are not going to write the case off as suicide, then don't discount the romance being connected to the death of the father."

He tucked his head back. "Before I was spinning tales, now you're all in for alternative theories?"

She became even more impatient with him. "Did Samir get in the way of lifting up Bashir in social class? You said the father was a simple man, uncomfortable in his new position."

"The apothecary said so. He opened up to her."

"I've been in these circles. I know what they are like. Bashir's mother knew how to carry herself in her beautiful clothes. That's all that's required for her to sit with the commander's women. If she can say very little, she will be fine. But Sitara's father? No matter how noble it would look, do you imagine Ibn Hisham including a simple man from the lower classes among his friends?"

This was new social territory for him. Even when he dealt with the rich in the past, he had the authority of Grave Crimes and had the right to answers. If he wanted the money that came with cases from people of this class, he needed to understand them. He needed to move comfortably among them, but Basma's humiliating insult pricked at him, souring his gut and making it seem impossible. By God, he needed to know how to walk across Baghdad without needing a bath! All this time she had been insisting she wants to be a partner, and now that he needs her, she wants to get home.

Ammar did the one thing he knew would keep her there: ask her advice. "How do I investigate it?"

She took the bait and became suddenly thoughtful, then said, "You cannot say straight out to Bashir that Ibn Hisham had his father killed so he would be more suitable for his foolish daughter."

"Walk with me to the office, then turn back. I won't keep you long."

She sighed but followed. "Ask around that query. Make the questions seem as if they are about another matter. You need to speak to Ibn Hisham, though."

Ammar gestured for her to continue.

"You want to know how he felt about Samir. Come at that by working the conversation around to the families and their social engagements. How soon is the wedding? Maybe some of the pre-wedding festivities have begun? Find out if Ibn Hisham has even had them over to their home. If so, were other family members there? Observe their discomfort when he describes the event. You'll find something to ask."

Her tone had shifted from impatience to confidence in him, but he did not feel up to this job and quipped, "Maybe I'll pretend I'm you."

"You can do it."

He did not feel it.

They turned onto the alley behind the hospital wall. The office was just around the corner, and she slowed down, ready to turn back.

He repeated the tasks ahead, "I need to go to the market where they keep their shop, too."

"Yes. That should be next."

"The old tailor shop and the angry cousin."

They turned the corner.

"And—" He unlocked the door to the office.

She sighed. "Okay, inside. But I'm not sitting down."

The sun was still too low, and the room was dark. The pounded earth floor was damp. The reed mats were worn. He was comforted by the scent of cool earth and dried grass but guessed rich clients would not be. Worse, the upholstery on the couches was shabby, and their cushions were thin, stuffed with straw instead of wool. His chest tightened, remembering Bashir's first reaction, then imagining someone like Ibn Hisham coming there.

Ammar asked, "Should I start using incense?"

She looked at him strangely. "What does that have to do with the case?"

"These rich people. They don't like the way I smell."

"Oh, to cover up body odour in your clothes?" She laughed lightly. "Ammar, no. The rich wear freshly washed clothes every day. Infused with perfume, yes, but not for that reason. They even change during the day."

He would have to buy more undershirts and another qamis. Probably needed a better quality robe, too. He should have asked for more in expenses. "How come you don't smell even when we walk a long way?"

"I use an alum stone and florals. Even so, I still smell. We're used to it. They aren't."

Is that why Nasifa always smelled sweet? Did she think he stank but never told him? Basma's insult transformed into Nasifa's secret thought, and his eyes stung with tears.

What had he been thinking, opening this agency? He was a goat herder, a grunt of a soldier, made into an investigator only because he was foisted onto Grave Crimes by his troop sergeant for solving a crime in the barracks that absolutely no one wanted answered. Three years with his own agency and nothing to show for it but this one case, and he could not even do that. His wife at home, ashamed of him. His chest tightened more, and his breathing became shallow as if his cuirass had suddenly grown tight, and he panicked, reaching for the buckles, only to find he wasn't wearing it. A squeak of air escaped his throat.

"Take a deep breath."

The room began to spin.

"Sit." She put her hand on his shoulder. "Breathe with me."

He sat hard on the couch, barely hearing her guiding breaths over his own panting, then his ears began to ring.

Zaytuna sat beside him, then pushed his shoulder so his back was to her. She cupped her hands over his back and spoke softly into them. Ammar knew she was praying directly into his heart. He could not hear it, but slowly, the band around his chest loosened, his breaths reached deeper, and the ringing in his ears subsided. He bent over, head in hands.

"Don't tell Nasifa."

"Tell her what?" She asked as she moved to sit at a more respectable distance.

The sun had reached just over the edge of the hospital, and a patch of light fell in through the door.

"Let me tell you about my case," she said. "The missing money."

He could barely listen, but she went on slowly, taking her time describing the old woman with the kittens. How she fed the mother so she had enough milk for her babies, how polite the mother cat was in taking the morsel, and finally the stillness of her prayer settled fully in his heart. He took a deep breath, raised his head, and saw an impossible light on her face and knew he could do it.

"She told me the daughter ran away," Zaytuna continued in the same soothing tone. "She was pregnant with their grandchild. The daughter and grandchild are out there, and Adnan must be looking for them."

Ammar got up and went outside for some air. His wife was always telling their son to take one thing at a time, that he could do anything if he took slower steps. Husayn rushed all the same, but Ammar wondered if the lesson was meant for him. He touched the coin purse under his arm and went back inside, ready to work.

"Another pregnant girl, then?" he asked, hoping his voice sounded firm. "Did her parents shun her?"

"The parents wanted her, but she felt she couldn't stay."

"Why didn't her mother tell you this?"

"Maybe that's what she was truly after." She looked at him curiously. "Why did I only realize this now? She does not suspect her husband of cheating at all. It would explain her insistence that I carry on despite our inability to find anything."

"Why not just ask the husband?"

"They've fallen to pieces since the daughter ran off. She's driven the husband off with her bitterness, but it's over the loss of their daughter and grandchild." Zaytuna got up and went to him, touching his sleeve. "Thank you."

"But you still don't want to pursue it? Talk to him?"

"After sitting with their neighbour, I decided I would."

"Following the husband may not lead you to the daughter."

"True," she said. "He may be looking in the wrong places. Where would any girl end up if she were pregnant with no husband? Before the baby is born, if she could wash clothes, she could share a room somewhere. Hopefully, she found her way. But that makes her harder to find."

"She might be begging, cutting reeds—" He did not say the obvious.

"You can say it. She may be in a brothel now."

"So you'll search there?"

"Maybe I should ask Tein's old friend, Khalil. He could help me inquire."

Ammar balked. "The debt collectors are rough men. You shouldn't be involved with them."

"A last resort, then."

But he could see she was thinking of Tein as the only alternative to check the brothels. He did not want to get in her way, especially after Tein's gesture with the buttermilk. The words came out before he could stop them. "Why will Tein help you but not me?"

She hesitated, then said, "He misses you."

The old resentment reared up. "Funny way of showing it, then."

She moved to leave. "I shouldn't have said anything."

"All right. All right." He put his hands out.

"I have to go to Nura. I did not mean to stay, only—"

"Only I needed your help."

"Alhamdulillah."

He searched for something to keep her there just a little longer. "I still need your help," he said, looking around. "I'm not going to make enough money on this case. Could I ask you for a loan to fix this place up? If we're going to get rich clients, you know?"

She nodded. "An investment."

"A loan."

"I don't want my name over the door," she said plainly.

Ammar was not willing to concede she should be considered for a partnership. After everything that just happened—how could she, who understood so much, not know that a man needed something of his own first, a bit of pride to take home to his wife? He responded firmly, "A loan."

"Fine," she said as if it did not matter one way or another, although he knew it did. But she added, "I pick everything out."

"As you like, my lady." He bowed his head. "Give my greetings to Nura."

She was halfway out the door but had paused to look around, clearly making plans.

"If I am going to stay on my case," she said, looking at him meaningfully, "I'll need help watching the father at night."

Suddenly he remembered—Girgis. "I have the perfect person for you."

16

———————

The new shop was in a quarter of the market that catered to the wealthy. Ammar passed jewellers displaying heavy gold necklaces, earrings, and bracelets set with stones in every colour, and cobblers selling slippers meant only for women carried in litters when they left the house. Nasifa wore the same small pieces of jewellry from her trousseau at every holiday and wedding, and he imagined bringing her home a bracelet.

He turned the corner onto a street of narrow shops, their walls lined floor to ceiling with bolts of colourful fabrics in the best wool, cotton, and silk. Customers lingered over them as clerks brought down one bolt after another, while their servants waited nearby. If Nasifa even stood near these people, they would take her for a beggar. He felt sick at the thought, wanting more for her than he knew he could give.

The Suq al-Tarrazun was in a small square just beyond the lane of tailors. Diamond-shaped boxes filled with spindles of thread in every imaginable hue lined their walls. Shopkeepers talked to customers over counters, examining sample patterns, while the embellishers sat in the back, legs crossed and hunched over, tugging tiny stitches. Two boys were in the square twisting colourful threads into the delicate rope that would be sewn into patterns along the edges of garments.

Bashir's shop was shuttered. The others were busy, except one. The proprietor was sour-faced and wore a colourful turban, so elaborately wrapped that Ammar wondered how the man held up his head as he leaned over his counter, observing the business of the square. His establishment was too narrow for anything but spindles. But here, the gold and silver thread was out in view rather than locked away. There was also a shelf holding perfumes in delicate glass jars, each set inside a polished box decorated with bone inlay. He wished he could bring one home to Nasifa, but the cost of the box alone would be more than he could hope to make on this case.

"Assalamu alaykum."

The man grunted in reply, then returned to spying on his neighbours.

Ammar opted for a jab in return. "An embellishment shop with no workers and selling perfume?"

"Ha!" He flashed a smile and stood straight, giving Ammar his attention. His voice bellowed across the square. "You are not here to have that robe embellished. What do you want?"

Ammar gestured toward Bashir's shop. "It's shut."

"Mourning."

"They've hired me to look into Samir az-Zarduzi's death."

"Then you already knew why it's shut."

"I think you are a man who sees a lot."

"I do," he replied, laying his thick-fingered hands on the counter and giving Ammar a look that said: "And I see you."

Ammar settled in, casually leaning against the counter. "The family thinks it was murder."

"With good reason."

"And what is that?"

The man frowned deeply. "The watchman told us all."

"What would a watchman know?"

The shopkeeper stood up, his frown exuding the confidence of a man who has secured valuable information. "He heard the investigators from Grave Crimes talking."

Ammar gave him a moment to continue, but the man simply crossed his arms. Getting this self-important ass to talk was like pulling teeth. "I give," he finally said. "What did he say he heard?"

"Aren't you careful with words? You think he was lying?"

"All right. What did the investigators from Grave Crimes say?"

"That they were going to take the man to a corpse washer who would not create any trouble for them, rather than the Barmakid Hospital."

"Was the watchman at the canal with them?"

"How else would he have heard it?"

"So how was it he came here?"

"As the watchman told it"—he winked—"they were sent out to the markets to find which shop was missing a tailor."

That jibed with the corpse washer's account. "So he was one of many watchmen sent out to the tailor and embellishment shops."

He bellowed, "Isn't that what I said?"

"First, it's a mighty coincidence that the watchman who over-heard the investigators ends up being the one to find the right shop. Second, I'm trying to understand why they would admit they were covering up a murder to a watchman."

"Coincidence is an unbeliever's word for God's will." He cocked an eyebrow. "As for the second, don't you think I asked that?"

"And?"

"The police did not know he heard them. To return to the first question, he helped carry the body to the corpse washer and was in the street when they questioned the man. He gathered that Samir was an embellisher dealing with upmarket clients; thus, he volunteered to come to this market."

"That doesn't sound like a coincidence at all now, but good police work."

The shopkeeper said, "Nothing occurs except by God's permission. The watchman pulled Bashir out of the shop and told him right there in front of everyone."

Ammar glanced back at the small square. "Customers watching? A bit dramatic."

"So the watchman had no manners." The shopkeeper shrugged. "More reason to trust that he would say what he shouldn't."

"Fair reasoning."

He leaned in. "Your name is Ammar at-Tabbani?"

"How did you know?"

"The watchman told the son to get you. Right there, as the man is in shock, he grabs him by the arms." The shopkeeper reenacted the moment, holding out both his arms, and mimicked the urgency of the watchman's voice. "'The police are going to lie to you. Your father was murdered. Find Ammar at-Tabbani. Behind the Barmakid Hospital. He'll find out who killed him'."

The first thing he felt was a wash of pride. Three years and his reputation still held. What Bashir had reported, Ammar now recalled as a backhanded compliment—the way he had added "best in your day," meaning, it seemed, perhaps no longer—whereas in this man's telling, Ammar felt remembered as a man of justice. He put his hand on his dagger, ready for battle.

The second thing was that that kind of insistence did not sound like supposition. Ammar's bile rose. It wasn't a cover up of suicide out of compassion, but murder. If so, it could only be a political favour or a payoff. He had difficulty believing it of

Shabib and Ahab. Guilty of being too good, naïve even, but not corrupt. When he was the lead investigator, they followed a case to its end no matter the result, even if their sergeant had to clean up the political mess they left behind. No matter the reason, Grave Crimes had covered up the cause of death, and they would hear about it from him when he had the case in hand.

Given the shopkeeper's bellowing, the others had to know what they were discussing. He turned around to see what they thought of it. They shot glances at him when they could. One seemed to be hurrying along a customer, and Ammar expected him to join them any moment.

"Do you mind my asking your name?"

"I am Abu Fidda Zayd al-Karkhi."

A fellow Shia, and one whose family traced back to days before the founding of Baghdad. He would care more about justice than preserving the status quo. Ammar nodded, hand over his heart, giving his opinion greater weight. "What did the others think of Samir and Bashir?"

"Good people. But everyone knew Samir was not much of a businessman."

"Meaning, what?"

"He would have run that business into the ground if Bashir had not taken over."

"Oh, and he's the one who is bad with business?" Ammar quipped, waving his arm dramatically at the lack of customers.

He barked out a laugh. "I don't work with clients here."

"No?"

Abu Fidda glanced at the nearby shops with disdain. "My son brings samples to the great estates. My clients do not lower themselves to browse in shops in the marketplace."

There was always someone above someone else in this life, and Abu Fidda was paying attention. "What kind of mistake was the father making?"

"They were embellishment men. Never had their own shop. What would they know?"

"But the son is doing better?"

"He took advice from us."

"I'm looking for a reason someone might want the father dead."

"Any number of reasons. You should look at them all."

"Odd. Samir's family thought there were none."

"And one right there in front of them, too."

"You want to help me out here?"

"The man who sold to Samir chose wealth over family."

"Tell me more."

"A cousin wanted to buy the business, but Samir and his son came in with an offer so high he could not refuse."

This was the cousin who always failed. "His offer?"

"Reasonable. Exactly what the business was worth."

"How did the cousin feel about losing the bid?"

"As you would expect."

"Why did the owner sell in the first place?"

He nodded sagely. "They didn't need the money. He had tired of the trade, and his sons had no interest. Then the perfect buyer appears."

"Wait. I'm confused. Did Samir approach them to buy it, or was it publicly on offer?"

His eyes widened. "We all knew he wanted to sell, but I was only aware of the bids as they happened."

"Were there many?"

"One from here, but not serious. The cousin. Samir's family."

"That doesn't sound like a public sale."

"I never said it was."

"You know why Samir's family paid so much for it?"

"We heard there is a father of a pretty girl whom Bashir needed to impress."

This was new. As the apothecary told it, the young lovers had lost touch until Sitara discovered Bashir in the new market. This lent more weight to the idea of her being pregnant. "You sure that's why they wanted to buy it?"

"If you know the family, then you know if it is true or not."

"The story I heard and the one you tell are a bit different."

"All in a day's work for you, then." The man looked past Ammar and sighed. "It seems an esteemed colleague would like a word."

Ammar turned around. The shopkeeper he had seen shooing off a customer had broken free.

"What's the name of the cousin?" Ammar asked Abu Fidda quickly before the other shopkeeper could shut the conversation down.

"He wouldn't have done it. I know the man."

"But you just suggested him as a suspect."

He smiled playfully. "Did I?"

Ammar was ready to take back giving the man's opinion weight. "Tell me what you know."

"The cousin blames everyone for his failures."

Ammar scoffed. "You make him sound guilty!"

"No, he's a weak man. Too weak to kill."

Where did he get the idea that only people of strong character kill? In his experience, it was the weak, more than others. Those who cannot control their emotions and those who let a suspicion go round and round in their head until they get someone's neck in their hands. Ammar said, "I'll still need to meet him. He might know something helpful."

The other shopkeeper approached, elegantly dressed in a long robe and sash of fine, natural wool with embellished edges meant to show off the skill of his workers. "Assalamu alaykum. How can we help you?"

"Wa alaykum assalam, I'm Ammar at-Tabbani. Samir az-Zarduzi's family has hired me to investigate his murder."

"Murder? Grave Crimes has declared it to be a natural death."

"You don't agree with the family?"

"Or the watchman?" Abu Fidda shot back.

The man gave Abu Fidda a scolding glance and pulled Ammar away and out of earshot. "The watchman must have misheard, and now this one here is spreading gossip that can only bring more suffering to the family."

"I am here on the family's behalf," Ammar assured him.

"The family are grieving and not in their right minds. They should put their heads back in their business if they have any hope of succeeding."

"Not doing well?"

He realized too late what he had given away. "I said no such thing."

"Give me something. How else will the family let it go?"

"Samir took his own life." He glanced around him. "God forgive him. The police are covering it up for the sake of the family."

"What makes you think he killed himself if the police said it was a natural death?"

"Everyone knows. It is not a secret."

"What everyone knows could be gossip."

"Suit yourself, but you harm the family by carrying on with these questions."

"I understood you all walked with the bier to the graveyard and even visited the family at home. If you thought he killed himself, why would you do that?"

"Because we were given the blessing of pretending it was not. You must understand that we saw him day to day, becoming more and more despondent, driving the business into the ground." He rudely pointed at Abu Fidda. "No one was surprised except him there, who loves trouble."

"How does he do business with the rich houses if he gossips like that?"

"Abu Fidda would never say a word about his clients. We don't even know who they are. He has some discretion when it comes to protecting his business, but none otherwise."

Was Abu Fidda playing with him? Maybe not. He may have heard something in the circles he serves that he could not say outright.

Ammar returned his attention to the shopkeeper. "Why did the family pay so much for the shop?"

"I am sure Abu Fidda told you there is a wealthy girl involved. Samir needed to raise his family's station for the son's sake. Of course, it is not enough for that family, but it is enough to allow the marriage to go forward."

Even more confirmation that Sitara and Bashir never lost touch. "Is that true?"

"The family did not tell you?"

"No one said anything about it."

"Why would they?" He opened his mouth to say more, then closed it.

Ammar pushed on. "If Samir was trying to raise the family up, then why would he take his own life and destroy it all?"

"Fine. I will tell you so that you stop this. His son mentioned he would sell the shop as soon as he turned the losses around."

"Bashir said nothing about that to me either."

"Ask yourself why the people who hired you are lying to you. They are not in their right minds."

Ammar was planning on it.

The shopkeeper looked around to make sure they could not be overheard, then said, "The business was meant to lift the father's social status. The girl's father was taking Bashir into his business. I am certain Samir felt that he would benefit his son best by simply no longer being a problem that needed solving."

Saliha's point rang true. The father might have thought they were better off without him.

"Listen to me," the shopkeeper said. "Samir could barely walk. He was in so much pain some days, he could hardly speak to clients. He was losing his eyesight, as one does in this work. What did he have left but losing his son to a wealthy man who would have resented calling him brother?"

Samir saw himself as a burden. Ammar extended a reassuring hand. "I need to go back and get some information from Abu Fidda, just to tie up some loose ends, but I hear you."

"Good." He said with a swift nod and left without a farewell.

"What did he tell you?" Abu Fidda asked when he rejoined him.

"You don't know already?"

"The son will sell the shop now, I imagine."

"He'd never make back the money they put into it," Ammar said.

"Considering the family he is marrying into, it seems to be money well spent." His expression became serious, and he touched Ammar's sleeve. "I will tell everyone to the end of my days Samir was murdered. We are brothers, you and I. I will not cover it up to make society more comfortable."

This vow—how could Ammar ignore it? It was more convincing than anything the other shopkeeper had said. Samir's state of mind did not mean he was not a victim of a crime.

Ammar grasped his hand. "I will work this case to the end."

"Good man." He stood back, satisfied.

"I would still like to talk to that cousin you mentioned."

"Suwayd ibn Wardan. I heard he lives in Tulayha these days. Ask at a tavern there."

If that is where the cousin lived, then he was not far off from sleeping in the cemetery. If he had the money to bid on the shop, then why was he out in the flood basin?

Abu Fidda said, "I imagine he will welcome the opportunity to share his side of it. He never failed to express his complaints."

Ammar was giving his farewell when a question came to him. "Before I go. You said Samir nearly ran the business into the ground. They'd only have the business for a short time. How do you run a business into the ground that quickly?"

The call to prayer rang out from the small mosques in the surrounding market.

Abu Fidda smiled broadly. "My brother! You got there in the end. They were busy all the time. They had all the clientele that came with the new business and those they brought with them. Yet they were losing money, a lot of it. Where was it going?"

It was the most important question he would be asking. Ammar put his hand over his heart again to thank him, but the man stopped him, reached for one of the inlay boxes of perfume, closed it, and handed it to Ammar.

"Musk and saffron, for your honoured wife or mother." Abu Fidda's expression softened. "Go. I trust you. But do not worry if the killer remains out of your grasp. I am certain of God's justice. The killer will taste it, if not by your hand, then another's."

17

Ammar headed north in the market, holding the perfume box against his chest, afraid he might drop the precious gift for his wife. He tucked it into his robe, tightening his belt around it, almost giving up on interviewing the cousin to get the perfume home safe to Nasifa. He imagined handing it to her when they were alone, breaking the seal to discover the scent, and placing a drop on her slim neck. His heart beat faster, and he shook himself free of the thought, knowing he would not be able to pray otherwise. A small mosque was just up ahead, and he hurried toward it.

He washed quickly alongside several men, then went through a dark passage to a large room covered by a plastered reed roof. The centre was open to the sky and let in a pillar of light so bright that the men formed their prayer lines around it. The call to stand in prayer came, and he tried to let his mind wander away from the case and to God, but that only led to him thinking about what God wanted from him.

He followed the imam in prayer, prostrating with the congregation, and questioned his decision not to work with his family herding goats. It was one thing when he was young and wild to run off to war, then to work for a pittance for the police, but now he was married, a father.

The only good money he ever made was churning butter for Kamal Ali.Forehead down in prostration, he huffed into the prayer mat. Herding goats would be less mind-numbing. If he could pull himself around and help his family, he could buy Nasifa the little things she deserved. But she deserved more than the riches of a poor woman. Nasifa deserved elevation, and he prayed to give it to her. Men still remembered him as a man of justice. This work was his to do.

Getting up from prostration, he let out a deep sigh, trying to accept Zaytuna's insistence that the women in his life wanted him to be happy, not things like fine perfumes and expensive jewellery, but she did not understand he would only be a man when he could provide both. If he could bring this case to a satisfactory end—one the clients would accept in the face of its thoroughness—maybe he could be that man.

Confession of murder aside, the cousin might give him something that would move the case forward. The walk to the flood basin took longer than he expected, and, as he used to before battle, he let his mind rest by observing his surroundings. Back then, it might have been comparing Byzantine waterways to Baghdad's canals, watching how farmers coaxed water across stony fields, or appreciating how the Byzantines built on stone laid by Romans and Greeks.

Leaving Karkh, he took note of how the planned roads gave way to narrow lanes and curving alleys where the poor had built their homes shoulder to shoulder. Everywhere, flood marks scarred the walls, sun-dried brick patched again and again, soft as clay against the inevitably rising waters. If the city had used stone, he could have imagined the city lasting the centuries. As it was, there would be a day when this Baghdad would be washed away and another would take its place.

The neighbourhood was like any other. Children ran through the dusty streets, sweating as they carried baskets and sacks or chased their friends, but their worn clothes were scrubbed clean by proud women. Old men sat on stools in small pockets where the alleys widened enough for a square to take shape. Shops were no more than a setback in a wall, selling fruits and vegetables, cooked meals, tinder for fire, or bread piled high. The scent of meat searing on a grill with rosemary and garlic made his stomach growl. But he thought of the undershirt he would have to buy and stopped at a corner for bread.

Herbed flatbread brushed with olive oil was piled high next to stacks of round barley bread and seeded wheat. It was midday, but it smelled as inviting as it would have that morning. He gestured to the herbed bread, pulling out a chink of coin from his sleeve. As he paid, he asked, "How far until Tulayha? I was told to turn at a tavern."

"Nearly there. You'll see the tavern, for shame, and go left there."

There was no shame in the tavern as far as Ammar was concerned. The cousin had to be a regular, and he might get exact directions to Suwayd's house—maybe even find him there. As he walked, he tore off a large piece of the bread and chewed. The warmth of the oil, herbs, and its charred edges made the bread as close to meat as he was going to get, and it satisfied him. The tavern was not far off, as the man said. He ate the last of the bread, then stopped at a fountain set into a wall and washed the sweat and dust from his face before drinking from the cup hanging from the tap.

The tavern was a hole in the wall crammed with large amphorae and shelves lined with jugs and cups. Three empty tables waited outside under a reed awning. The proprietor was half dozing in shade along the wall but lifted his head as Ammar approached.

"Assalamu alaykum. I'm looking for Suwayd ibn Wardan."

The man put his hand over his heart as he returned his greetings, then said, "Stop for a while first, my brother."

"Just where he lives, please. I've got to get back to Buratha before dark."

He frowned as if his greatest friend had disappointed him but gestured around the corner. "I've had to carry him home, so I know it well. Pass the square, then three doors down on the right."

A stepped acacia stood in the centre of the small square. Reed mats had been laid out underneath, and two old men sat in its shade, chatting. Hand over his heart, he greeted the men as he passed, and they wished him peace with warm smiles.

Ammar called out at the doorway before crossing the short passage. A woman's gravelly voice answered, "Come ahead." The house was small, nothing more than a sliver of courtyard with two rooms opening onto it, but tidy. The floor was swept, the basin brimmed with clean water, and rough curtains hung freshly washed. In the courtyard's only shade, an old woman sat next to a brick brazier, chopping greens into a pot. Her swollen legs were thrust out, greens mounded on her lap.

"I won't get up." She tapped her leg. "What can I do from here?"

"Assalamu alaykum, Auntie. I am looking for Suwayd ibn Wardan."

She gestured with her small knife. "Wa alaykum assalam, son. He's in there."

As if Ammar had woken him, a grumbling voice came from the room.

"Go in." She waved him on.

The reed and plaster roof was in such good condition that no light peeked through. It took a moment for his sight to adjust, but then he saw an impossibly thin man curled up on a thick mattress staring at him with beady eyes.

He moaned, "Who are you to intrude on my grief?"

"I am Ammar at-Tabbani. I was hired by the Samir az-Zarduzi's family to look into the death of their father."

"That old thief is dead?"

"If you mean Samir az-Zarduzi? Yes, he is dead."

"May God ruin his children and never grant him peace."

Ammar was taken aback. It was a curse one could not come back from without a recompense of charity this man could not afford or a fast he could not survive.

"You bid on the shop," Ammar said.

"It was mine. He stole it from me."

Ammar looked around the room. There was a good tamarisk wood chest, and he caught the scent of cedar shavings. A decent rug underfoot, too. But nothing that would indicate he could bid on a shop in that market. "Do you mind my asking how you could afford it?"

"You think this is where I lived before they ruined me? I was a capable embellisher. I kept my wife and children clothed, fed, and in a neighbourhood better than this." A look of pride touched his face, lifting the awful bitterness from his expression for a moment. "My son is a student in Dar al-Silsilla."

The neighbourhood was known for its Shia scholars. Ammar felt for him having pride in his son, even if he no longer had any pride in himself. Without asking permission, Ammar sat across from him.

Suwayd threw his arm over his face and wept. "My wife and my little ones were forced to go back to her parents. I am alone. I have shamed my family."

Ammar took his hand. "My brother, tell me."

"I asked my cousin to sell the shop to me in stages. He did

not need the money up front, but he refused me. The selfish beast told me to bring all the money at once or there would be no bid."

"What happened?"

"I borrowed money! I borrowed only for him to turn me down, and I could not pay it back."

"I don't understand. Why didn't you just return the money when you lost your bid?"

He moaned. "The terms! Usury. No one trusted me." He wailed again. "They were right! Look at me. Why trust a man like me?"

Ammar prayed to God to forgive him. Even a good man could be driven to curse in the grip of an illegal loan.

"My sin is longing for what my cousin had. I wanted my wife and children to be clothed like his family. To have servants place food in their mouths. So I borrowed."

Ammar squeezed his hand, understanding too well.

"The interest was daily, doubling, tripling, compounding. The sale dragged on for months. He dithered and dithered. I begged my cousin. He said I must wait, then he sold it out from under me." He jerked his hand away. "May his children die!"

"God protect them," Ammar said under his breath. It was a curse worse than the last. But this was new information. He had thought the shop had been up for sale only briefly before Samir stepped in with their bid. He asked, "Why did the sale drag on?"

"One day my cousin wanted to sell. Another day he had changed his mind. He was waiting for more offers. Dangling mine to get a better one! May he sleep on the ragged carpet of poverty!"

God help him, the man was making his bed in hell. Ammar asked, "Did he know what kind of loan you had taken?"

"No," he turned over and wailed. "He should have known.

He should have known I did not have it! Who would trust me? May rats eat the bowels of my enemies!"

Suwayd was the man Abu Jidda described—a weak man who failed at everything he touched. Ammar could only guess that his cousin did not want to entrust a business to someone who would run it into the ground. Then came the high bid, and he sold it to Samir, not knowing he would ruin it all the same.

"How much did you owe in the end?"

"Enough that I had to sell everything." He moaned again.

Ammar was becoming afraid of the curses and growing tired of the moaning but still felt some sympathy for a man getting so far in over his head. He was curious if it had been Khalil who had come to collect. He was the size of a mountain and known in his soldiering days for terrifying even his allies. "Who came to get the money from you?"

"A small, nasty man. May sixty thousand diseases strike him! His hand was on the hilt of a dagger the whole time he threatened to kill me."

They did not kill debtors, but they did injure them. In the hands of some, death might be better. Suwayd did the only thing he could: sell everything to pay, even if it ended in his debasement.

"And that wretch!" He shot straight up, indignant. "A man who should have no right to wealth winning the bid! It was my right!"

There it was. This man's failure came from feeling owed, not owing money. Men like this kill easily. He asked, "Did you confront Samir?"

Suwayd's beady eyes narrowed. "You ask if I killed him?" He pointed to the heavens as if he were about to swear on God's name. "I would have killed him if I had not been so busy losing everything that mattered to me. But it seems that God has answered my curses with the blessing of his death!"

Yes, men like this kill easily—Ammar whispered a prayer of protection—by calling in jinn and demons.

Ammar held out his hands, praying, "May God restore you," silently intending a restoration of faith, not wealth.

"Restore me?" He fell into a ramble of complaints and curses against his enemies.

Ammar stood, keeping his head bowed so as not to rile a curse against him or his family, and stepped eagerly into the harsh sunlight.

"Come, come." The old woman called to him. "See this pot?"

Ammar only wanted to leave, but he went to her.

"There's meat in this stew. His son pays for it. Pays for everything. Me to care for him. The poor boy comes every week to check on his father, but that wasted soul pushes him away."

"He was going on about how no one would trust him. Did the son say why?"

"What's to say why? He would bring down the heavens. A spiteful man he is, but the son is an angel. His own wife came once, and he turned her away. She and the other children are safer without him—I can tell you that."

"Aren't you afraid with all those curses?"

She pulled at the leather thong around her neck. A talisman was tied at the end.

Ammar hurried away from the house, touching the perfume box safely tucked into his robe, fearful that his own brooding could lead him to such a place. He wished Zaytuna were with him. She would know what to say. But he straightened his back, thinking she would only remind him of what he already knew: stone or mud, all this will be gone one day, leaving only the justice they had stood for in the soil to feed the generations to come.

18

———

The door was open to the gathering place of the Sufis of Baghdad for their weekly ritual. Men and women streamed in ahead of Zaytuna and Kamal Ali, some in fine but simple clothes, others in worn, patched robes and cloaks. Layla walked hand in hand with Zaytuna, swinging her arm. Kamal Ali carried Nura, who was staring raptly at the entrance. In this place, her untameable baby girl was how Zaytuna imagined her own mother as a child, fierce but governed by God's presence and love. Layla saw a gap at the door, let go of Zaytuna's hand, and ran ahead.

"I forgot," Kamal Ali said as they entered. "A man came by today asking for donations for an orphanage."

"Alhamdulillah, I am sure you left him happy," she said.

"I did."

Zaytuna squeezed his hand.

"He made me think of something."

"Yes?"

"The young woman in your case, Gul. She was pregnant and ran away?"

She followed him immediately. "You think Gul gave up her child to an orphanage?"

"Perhaps."

"I will ask at the orphanages if they've seen Gul's father. Thank you."

The reception hall was crowded with friends catching up on news. Kamal Ali went ahead, taking Nura into the courtyard to find Abu Bakr ash-Shibli. The elder mystic was fond of the girl, and she would fuss if he was not there, running to YingYue for solace.

As always, Zaytuna checked the stairs to see if a young seeker was tucked underneath, deep in contemplation. It was empty, and she longed to sit there for a moment and feel the peace she had known as a child when she would crawl into the nook and mimic the movements and words of her elders. Instead, she stood among her people, enjoying their closeness, the warmth of their chatter, and the scent of roses and orange flower water.

YingYue waved to her from beside a courtyard pillar. Nura was already clinging to her leg. Shibli must not be there. Zaytuna wound her way through the crowd to them.

"I've had a letter from Mustafa," YingYue said, round cheeks bright and grasping her hand.

"Oh," Zaytuna said, "I was only just thinking of him."

"He has asked for my permission to marry again." She smiled, her eyes glistening with tears.

Zaytuna's heart broke open with happiness, and she knew what YingYue would say before she asked, "What will be your answer?"

"His wife is to be Imam Abu Abdurrahman's niece, after all. He gains a wife and a son. I gain a sister and a stepson. Even if they never visit Baghdad, they will be my family now, too."

"A blessing for everyone. Maybe once they are settled, they'll come."

YingYue, ever insightful, assured her, "If they come, we will be there for him and, more importantly, for her. She will know that she is his most true love. Your love, a memory, and me a wife to my worship alone. He will see we have honoured her and her son."

Zaytuna took shelter in her words, "your love, a memory," and embraced her. "Mustafa will be happy now."

"Yes, I will pray it is so," she whispered in her ear.

They joined the people taking their places for the evening's ceremony. Long reed mats covered with sheepskins were laid out in a circle, leaving a space in the centre, open to the sky. Zaytuna longed for the drums and recitations of love for God to begin, when ecstasy would overcome the worshippers, and some would rise to sway and turn there. Lanterns were set into niches and hung from the archways, sending flickering light across the courtyard. Once the sun had truly set, elaborate patterns would move along the walls with the slightest breeze, as if they, too, were remembering God and swaying with love as the ritual overcame them, and she would join them.

She took a moment to breathe, wanting to feel the release of Mustafa's happiness for her own life and her own lingering guilt assuaged. But she knew she would only feel free when she saw him happy for herself.

Nura was still holding onto YingYue as they went to join the women. She touched her daughter's chin so that she looked up at her. "Will you sit with your Baba? Me? Auntie YingYue?"

Surprising her, she answered, "Baba." She let go of YingYue and ran to Kamal Ali.

YingYue asked with a small laugh, "Should I be hurt?"

She left YingYue to find Layla, suspecting the girl was near the kitchen, either with Auntie Hakima or Abdulghafur.

Auntie Hakima was with a few of the elder women, deep in conversation. Fatima was next to her, sitting thigh to thigh, reminding her of herself. Fatima was plump where Zaytuna was slim, short where Zaytuna towered, and her clothes spoke of her family's wealth where she had been poor, but a familiar anger marred her face. Fatima had wandered in not long ago, and Auntie Hakima had asked both YingYue and Zaytuna not to advise her for the time being, no matter what she said. YingYue agreed out of duty and wisdom, and Zaytuna out of experience, remembering there was not a word anyone could have said back then to subdue her incandescent rage.

Zaytuna ducked into the kitchen to find Layla. Looking past the old cook, she saw Layla on a stool in the corner, smiling up at Abdulghafur. But the smile was a different sort than she expected, and it stopped Zaytuna cold. Her daughter was gazing brightly at the broad-shouldered young man from beneath her lashes. While Abdulghafur leaned against the wall next to her, staring at her like a puppy.

"Assalamu alaykum." Zaytuna said firmly, breaking their spell.

They turned with a start, embarrassed, and Hilal tried to cover up his harbouring the young lovers with a joke, "This one is coming to work in the kitchen with us now."

"If only she knew how to stir a pot," Zaytuna retorted and left the kitchen before her tone grew worse.

Hilal had been with them, but that was not good enough. The old cook needed scolding for allowing it to happen at all.

Drums in hand, Dawud passed her to sound their skins by the kitchen fire. The little room could not hold them all. Layla would be out in a moment.

She grasped the girl's hand as she hurried past. "Sit with me."

Layla's expression flashed between guilt and defiance as she tried to pull her hand away, but Zaytuna held it firmly.

"We love Abdulghafur," Zaytuna said, "but none of this sneaking around. This is a decision you will make with your family."

"There is no decision." She jerked her hand back and ran through the circular lines of seated men to the reception room. Kamal Ali saw, nodded to Zaytuna, and got up to follow her, leaving Nura in the hands of a friend.

Auntie Hakima called Zaytuna over. Fatima had moved to sit against the wall and had pulled her red silk wrap over her face. Zaytuna was bursting to tell the old woman about Layla. But before she could, Layla returned, hopefully chastened, yet avoiding her eye. Auntie Hakima asked the elder woman next to her to make space for the girl, then directed Zaytuna to sit on the other side. The old woman pressed her thigh against Zaytuna and took Layla under her arm.

The dafs now in the hands of the drummers, Zaytuna was eager for the sama to begin. The drums and poetry would send her into that exquisite joy of being at peace with God that would last for days, nourishing her and making every hard choice that much easier. She held out the problem of Layla to God, then her case, praying the ritual would pull on the thread that connected the lost girl and herself.

A drum sounded, low and steady, then another. Chanting voices swelled around her, lifting her until her breaths moved with them, their hearts circling like the stars wheeling in the sky or the believers around the Kaaba. The lanterns flickered and blurred. A voice rose up, "Ya, Allah, Ya, Muhammad," and she felt herself slip into the stream of ecstasy. But instead of the floating expansiveness of her soul that she desired, a vision opened up before her.

She was in a passage. Light streamed behind her, illuminating a solid door at the end. Ammar was on the other side, arguing with someone. She tried to push the door open, but it thudded against her. He was throwing himself against it. She yelled, "Move back!" He thudded against it again, and she was jarred by the force. There was nothing she could do. Then a female voice came from the passage behind her: "I am Gul," and then, "Listen." But the rest of her words were lost beneath shuddering cries, and as Zaytuna turned to find her, Gul was lost, obscured by shadows. Zaytuna ran back through the passage toward her, but it opened onto the courtyard of the Sufis, and she came out of the vision, having failed to release Ammar or find Gul.

Returning, she was out of place, far from the peace she expected. Zaytuna focused on the press of Auntie Hakima's thigh against her and the swaying of bodies around her. The warm scent of roses and coolness of orange flowers was mixed with the sharpness of sweat. Her tongue was dry and thick from reciting poetry and prayers with the rest. She touched the sheep-skin beneath her, rolling threads of the compacted wool between her fingers, and slowly returned to this world.

Returned, she held the two failures before her.

In one hand, she held her failure to release Ammar. He would push when he should pull, or he would, through his own stubbornness, find himself stuck. The warning for Ammar came to her unbidden, making it all the more significant, but there was no raising the alarm with him when she did not fully understand.

In the other hand, she held her inability to find Gul or hear her words. In memory, she returned to the passage to listen. She entered into the shadows. She hushed the shuddering cries. She listened, then gasped. The words, an echo of her own mother's voice—Gul begged, "Fix what is between God and me."

Zaytuna's prayer that the ritual pull the thread connecting

the girl and herself was answered, and it was not what she wanted after all. Her mother had said after she was attacked the second time, "I fixed what is between God and me," but Gul was asking Zaytuna to fix it for her. Zaytuna wept with Gul. She could no more help Gul come to terms with God's will than she could fathom her mother's trust in that moment. She had vowed to help Gul the way women had done for her mother, to face her fears, not this.

The vision could only be a warning, not a calling. A warning for Ammar and a warning for her not to get involved in Gul's case.

The ritual over, she felt Auntie Hakima's care surround her before the old woman reached out to take her hand. "I have you, girl," the old woman said, then tipped her chin toward Layla. Zaytuna reached out to her, but Layla shot up to join Kamal Ali and Nura before she could speak to her.

Walking home, Nura slept against her chest. Her sweet one's warm cheek was heavy against her shoulder, while Layla walked quietly beside Kamal Ali. If there was anything she could fix, it was the trouble between her and her daughter. She and Layla would talk in the morning and set things straight. While there was nothing she could do about Ammar until she understood the warning, there was one thing she could settle tonight. She whispered to Kamal Ali, "Tomorrow I will tell Bint Afshin I cannot solve their troubles for them."

"Is that wise?"

Surprised at his questioning her decision, she assured him for now, "I have reason."

To his credit, he did not push, and she used the walk home in silence to recover from the vision's aftermath, soothed by Nura's warm cheek against her chest and her even, sleepy breaths.

At home, the lamp in Tein and Saliha's room illuminated the

courtyard. Within, Tein was singing softly. Kamal Ali went into the kitchen to light two more lamps, then went ahead with Nura to their room, while Layla went to her own. Zaytuna waited in the courtyard, listening to Tein sing a little longer. But then he stopped, and Saliha came out a moment later.

"I love to hear him sing." She took Saliha's hand.

"Sister, you shouldn't listen. It's me who makes him sing like that."

The playful comment pulled Zaytuna out of her worries. She chuckled, lightly slapping Saliha's hand. It would soothe her even more to sing with Kamal Ali tonight, but Layla was in no mood to take Nura in with her, so Zaytuna would have to do with her husband's arms around her, or she would not sleep at all.

"We were waiting up for you," Saliha said. "Bint Afshin sent a message asking you to go to her in the morning. Her husband left the house tonight."

"And no one there to follow him," Zaytuna said. Alhamdulillah. It was for the best.

19

DAY FOUR

Morning chatter lifted Zaytuna out of a deep sleep in Kamal Ali's arms. Nura was splayed at the end of the bed. She had fallen asleep between them, but she had woken up in the middle of the night and crawled around pretending to be a kitten, making mewling noises, until she had fallen back to sleep at the end of the bed. Now, Zaytuna could feel her firm, chubby back against her foot. She got up quietly not to disturb Nura or her husband but found he was already awake. By the time Zaytuna had pulled her wrap around her nightdress and tied up her hair, Nura popped up, wide-eyed.

"I hungry!"

Before Zaytuna could pull open the door, Nura was already at it, trying to push it open and demanding to be let out. As Zaytuna gently moved her out of the way, her vision of Ammar pushing the wrong way against a door was before her.

Nura ran to the family already gathered for breakfast under the pomegranate tree.

"Were you like this?" Kamal Ali asked, smiling.

"She's your fault as much as mine." She sat beside him and

touched his cheek. "I had a vision of Ammar last night. I think he's going to get himself into some trouble."

"What will you do?" He sat up and took her in his arms.

"I don't know."

"I'm not sure you should get involved."

Zaytuna was unused to his sharing his thoughts this way. He questioned her wisdom in quitting the case last night, and now this. Kamal Ali always trusted her visions and dreams. She responded testily, "The question is understanding the meaning of the vision. Is this about trouble with his family? His relationship with Tein? Or the case? There is a risk in speaking to him until I know with certainty." She stood and briskly rearranged her wrap to go out for breakfast.

Kamal Ali grunted as he got out of bed and pulled on a robe. "I agree that telling Ammar is a risk. He might take it the wrong way."

She turned toward him. "You think he'll take it as interfering."

"Mmm."

"Mmm," she answered back, irritated and wanting to cut the conversation off before she said something she regretted. Putting her hand on the latch, she added, "I nearly forgot. We have to talk about Layla and Abdulghafur. They've become sweet on each other."

His eyes widened in mock surprise. "And you, an investigator of crimes?"

"But—"

"Hilal told me. Layla visits sometimes. Abdulghafur is a gentleman. They are never alone. I find it hard to believe Auntie Hakima has not said anything to you."

"Her too?" This was a betrayal at the hands of people she trusted. "Why didn't you say anything?"

"Because I knew you would want to rush a discussion, and there is no rush."

"No rush!"

"Abdulghafur is a fine young man, but knowing Layla, she will grow bored."

What else was he not sharing because he had imagined how she might react? She put her back to the door, fighting the impulse to argue with him. Especially because in this matter, she could not make her case. How could she tell her husband that she feared the two were drawn to each other just as she and Mustafa were—two children bonded by a shared history of heartbreak but not meant for each other? He knew very well how that ended, and it was not by growing bored with one another.

Kamal Ali stood back calmly, waiting for her temper to pass and for her to reconsider the situation.

But he was in the wrong here. They all were. Did he think she was wrong to force the conversation with Layla? Should she have pretended not to see the two gawping at each other? It had to be done. She remembered the embarrassment on their faces. They should be embarrassed, for God's sake. It might keep them apart. With that thought, the first touch of a nauseating self-awareness pressed into her gut. She had embarrassed them at a vulnerable moment. Instead of defending herself, as she would have in the past, she allowed the sickening truth to lead her to the rest—her insult to Layla—and she sank to the floor. She had done more than embarrass them; she had made them feel ashamed to love.

Kamal Ali joined her. "She told me what you said."

"I have to apologize."

"Layla forgives quickly, but it will take more than words."

"What?"

"Invite Abdulghafur here."

This was too much. There had to be a different resolution.

"Let's eat." He got up, relieving her of having to agree at that moment, and held out his hand to her.

Breakfast plates were laid out, nearly empty. Yulduz and Qambar were entertaining Nura with the blocks. Only Layla was missing.

Before she could ask, Saliha said, "She's in her room."

Zaytuna started to go to her, but Kamal Ali tugged her to sit beside him. "Not now."

But she wanted the apology over, and his direction made her feel like arguing again. Instead of snapping at Kamal Ali, she turned her ire on Saliha. Her hair was loose around her shoulders, and she still wore her nightshirt with a wrap carelessly thrown around her. Saliha would be late for work, but it was none of her business.

Saliha caught her eye and shook her head. "I see that look, woman. Don't start with me."

"I wasn't," she started, then stopped.

"Oh, that look on your face!" Saliha ordered, "Sit!"

"Everyone seems to know the looks on my face." She did not intend it, but it came out sounding childish.

Saliha just laughed at her.

Where Kamal Ali waited her out, Saliha charged at her with loving mockery, and with it her temper passed. She glanced at Layla's room but let it go, squeezing Saliha's shoulder as she went to sit next to Kamal Ali. He brushed her cheek, reassuring her of their love.

Tein slapped his gut, sighing. "After we got the old woman's message, I wasn't sure if I should have gone out and looked for him last night."

"No need."

Saliha leaned into him. "Only the butter needs you these days, my man. And me."

"Me!" Nura let out.

Tein held his arms out to her, and she left Yulduz and Qambar to sit in his lap. He kissed her on the head, then handed her off to Zaytuna. "I'm going into the shop to check on things." He got up, saying to Kamal Ali, "Nothing to worry about, boss."

He did this every so often, going in on Fridays when the shop was closed to be alone with his thoughts, and no one questioned his excuse.

Kamal Ali nodded in thanks and continued eating.

"Who are you with today, Lady Nura?" Saliha asked.

Qambar said, "Me, if she'll agree to it."

"No." Zaytuna broke off a piece of bread. "I've quit my case. I'll be home. Yulduz and I can take her with us to distribute bread and butter after the Friday prayers."

Yulduz gave her a questioning look, but Zaytuna did not feel like explaining, and there was no need. The father would find Gul, and they would solve it themselves.

Tein returned, dressed for work, and gave his farewells. Moments after closing the gate, they heard him greeting someone in the street. Raised voices followed, then silence. She looked to Kamal Ali, but he held his hand out to wait. A loud knock on the door made them jump. Kamal Ali got up to answer it.

Ammar was there, cheeks flushed and looking uncomfortable. He must have been arguing with Tein. Was this the meaning of the vision? His stubbornness when it came to Tein? If so, that was fine. Let them sort it out. That could be solved without her, too.

"Ahlan," Kamal Ali said, holding open the door.

"Any news?" She asked, taking a bite of cheese.

He stood in the open gate, speechless.

Layla came out of her room dressed for school.

"I—," Zaytuna got up to go after her, but Layla ran past them, past Ammar, and disappeared into the street.

"I came to catch you up," he said distractedly.

"Eat." Yulduz gestured to the food.

Instead of going after Layla like she wanted, Zaytuna went to the kitchen to get him a clean cup for the buttermilk. When she returned, Yulduz had offered him bread and pushed the last of the cheese, honey, and dates in front of him.

"I went to the embellishment shops yesterday." He sounded tense, and Nura looked at him worriedly.

Zaytuna nearly told him to change his tone in front of her daughter, but Qambar had seen it and intervened.

"Let's get your doll." He braced himself on one knee and got up, grunting. Nura was already running to the other side of the courtyard.

"A watchman gave birth to the idea Samir had been murdered. He told the family not to accept what the police say."

She sat across from him. "Why?"

"He says he overheard Grave Crimes covering it up."

"Ya Rabb!" exclaimed Yulduz.

Zaytuna felt the same. The watchman daring to expose the investigators was a risk that could lose him his job. He must have heard something. Was this the vision? Ammar pushing up against Grave Crimes?

"The other embellishers are split."

"Split on what, suicide or murder?"

He went on without clarifying. "Samir bought the business at an inflated price to raise their status for the marriage."

"Wait," Zaytuna said. "The timing is off."

"Exactly. Mazal, the apothecary, got it wrong, or Samir lied to her. They did not meet again by chance at the new market. They were together all along and needed the business to make the marriage less socially awkward."

"So she is pregnant."

"Ya Rabb!" Yulduz exclaimed again, eyes wide, eager for more.

"Samir tried to make a go of the business and failed. Bashir had to sideline him and get it running again. But here's the thing. One of the shopkeepers said Samir had so many customers, it would be next to impossible to lose as much money as he did."

"That matters," Zaytuna said.

Yulduz pushed a plate of dates toward Ammar again, but he did not acknowledge her.

Zaytuna continued, "Who thinks it was murder?"

"Just one man, Abu Fidda, the one who mentioned the business losses to me. He also pointed me to the cousin of the original owners. The one who was cut out of the sale."

"He was helpful. Why?"

"Abu Fidda believes Samir was murdered and wants the killer found."

"Does he? And the cousin?"

Ammar answered, "Suwayd. He took out a usurious loan to buy it and lost everything."

"He has a motive to kill Samir."

"I saw him. Suwayd didn't do it," Ammar said with strange finality.

Zaytuna trusted him but still wanted to know why. That could wait, especially while he was agitated. "So what's next?"

"I need to find out how he could lose all that money."

"Gambling? A woman?"

"We'll see," he said with a grimace.

She wanted to know about the other embellishment men. If they disagreed on murder, did they think it was a natural death or suicide, and why? Was suicide the door he was refusing to open? No, now she was spinning tales. Her vision had to be about his relationship with Tein.

"One of the shopkeepers said everyone assumed he had taken his own life."

She nodded to him as she glanced at Nura. She was still busy with Qambar, but she would grow bored with the quiet play soon.

"I'm still keeping suicide open, just so you know."

His comment came out like a criticism, and she answered him more sharply than she intended, "I'm not suggesting you were."

Ammar bristled and was about to object when Kamal Ali stood. "It sounds like the case is moving forward."

"It is. One step at a time," he said, then turned to Zaytuna. "So what about you?"

His last comment came out as a criticism, and now his question came at her like a taunt. Kamal Ali gave her a questioning glance to see if he should intervene, but she shook her head and answered Ammar. "The old woman sent a note here last night saying that her husband went out, but we didn't have anyone watching the house."

"I should have sent a message to Girgis." His voice was thick with self-recrimination.

Zaytuna reassured him, "No need. I'm quitting the case."

But he took it the wrong way, raising his voice. "You want me to rush to suicide because you think you can't fix your case. You who thinks she can fix everything."

Fix? Her mother's word. Gul's word. She pulled back, demanding, "What do you mean by that?"

Ammar shook his head at her and stood to go.

When the gate was shut behind him, she turned to everyone. "What just happened?"

Kamal Ali said, "It's not about you. It's whatever happened between him and Tein."

"As for fixing, you shouldn't quit that case," Yulduz said as she and Kamal Ali cleared the plates. "You can fix what's wrong in that family."

"Mmm," said Kamal Ali.

Zaytuna stared at them.

"I'll watch our Nura while you go tell that woman to her face that you won't help," Yulduz finished. "We'll see what happens next."

Nura ran by, and Zaytuna picked her up, swinging her around, simply to keep from telling the two of them to stay out of her business.

20

____

It was barely midmorning, and Ammar's temper was already on edge.

Nasifa had refused again to wear the perfume. Last night, he had brushed back her hair, expecting the scent and stain of the musk and saffron perfume on her neck, but she had protested, "Not yet." He went to get the bottle for her. She protested again. Then came sunrise, and she refused with some excuse that it would only be washed off in the baths. His anger flared. Ammar went looking for the box, thinking Husayn might have broken it, but it was not where he expected. She was holding something back, and it was unlike her.

Then he had met Tein outside the house.

Zaytuna had said the day before, "He misses you." Ammar tried to discuss it with Nasifa that night, but she was tired and murmured as if she were listening, but she fell asleep as he asked what Tein's gesture of friendship meant if he refused to work with him. Her silence forced him to answer it himself: Tein refused his friendship except on his own terms. Ammar knew what he wanted to say to Tein. He had played out all the possibilities in his head as Nasifa slept beside him. But in all that he had imagined, Tein had fought back. Not this morning's bowed head when confronted in the street. Nor this hand-over-the-heart promise to come see his mother. Tein felt guilt for his mother, not guilt for him. But how could any man say, "Me! Not my mother!"

Then breakfast with Zaytuna and seeing her silent accusation that he was not giving suicide enough weight.

The gate to Zaytuna's house shut firmly behind him, he stormed off to Samir's old shop. He had to go deep into a neighbourhood that could get dangerous if one did not know which streets to avoid. But Ammar chose those streets, despite being without his cuirass and sword, daring the young toughs swaggering with toothsticks in their mouths and wraps tossed over a shoulder to reveal their daggers. As he passed, one called out, "If it's a fight you want, turn left up there. My friend will give you one!" He grinned at them, satisfied—a seasoned ghazi could take them all—and turned off onto the lane on the right.

The stench of the small tannery grew stronger with each turn. When he found the old shop, he was breathing the thick, sickening air and had no idea how they could stand it.

The shop was easy to spot. The lane was not only swept clean but had also been sprinkled with water to keep the dust down. An earnest young man and boy were out front twisting purple, brown, and cream silk thread. A woman draped in layers of expensive bound-dyed silk stood by watching. Her male servant was nearby, eye out and hand on the hilt of his sword. They had not lost all their wealthy clients, then.

He skirted the two twisting the thread to speak to a middle-aged man just inside the shop, peacefully observing the scene. A small tray was set into a stand beside his stool, holding a clay cup and a small bowl of nuts. Embellishers were at work in the shop behind him, sitting cross-legged on pallets, bent over their embroidery and braidwork.

"Assalamu alaykum. I work for Samir az-Zarduzi's family, investigating his death."

"We belong to God and return to him," the man said, peering at him curiously.

"God have mercy on his soul."

But the man did not hold up his hands in prayer or say, "Amin." His refusal signalled that he likely thought Samir had taken his own life. Ammar instantly disliked him, despite so many others making the same assumption.

"Are you Abduljabbar ibn Fadi?" Ammar asked.

"No." He gestured behind him. "He's with the others."

An elderly man sat cross-legged beside a young tailor, holding the edge of a seam, and was speaking gently to him. It was strange, this one sitting as if it were his shop and the owner behind him, guiding an apprentice.

"He seems busy. Maybe you can help me?"

"And who are you?"

"Ghazi Ammar at-Tabbani."

But the man did not offer his own name in return. Ammar did not press, going straight to his questions. "How long did Samir work here?"

"Before my time."

"Which is?"

"Eighteen years."

"Did you know him well?"

"I learned under him."

"But you won't pray for him."

"If you are investigating his death, then you know why."

Ammar wanted to slap the words out of his mouth but said evenly, "I'm investigating because we don't know how he died."

A glimpse of shame crossed his face, and Ammar expected him to ask for God's forgiveness and utter a prayer, but he dug in. "I'll wait and hear the results of your investigation to pray."

"The police say it was a natural death. You aren't willing to go with that?"

"Are you here to argue with me about my religion? What do your Shia Imams say? Probably that suicide is noble. God, glory to Him Most High, said, *Do not kill yourselves.* Yet at Karbala, Husayn threw himself into a battle he could not win."

Ammar reached for a sword that was not there.

The man laughed at him.

The rich woman left with her servant, and, scowling, Ammar went inside to speak to the owner.

Using a cane, Ibn Fadi stood as Ammar approached.

"Assalamu alaykum. I'm Ammar at-Tabbani. I'm investigating Samir az-Zarduzi's death for the family."

"God have mercy on his soul."

"Your man outside wouldn't pray for him."

"He's always been jealous. See that woman who just left? I had to convince her that we could produce the work she expects now that Samir is gone. All our customers are like this. A few have returned since he died, but they want assurances." He gestured to the man outside. "Ibn Latif has good reason. He trained under Samir and then surpassed him, but Samir's work had gained a certain reputation."

"I heard Samir's eyesight was failing, though."

"Yes." He hesitated before speaking, then said, "Toward the end of the time he was with us, Ibn Latif was doing the work, but we told customers it was Samir. I do not like to lie, but the customers demanded it."

"Do you think he would have wanted Samir dead because of it?"

Ibn Fadi took the question seriously. "I don't know."

"The police said it was a natural death, but I keep meeting people who suspect suicide."

He gestured to a pair of high stools and sat. "Samir was in so much pain and too gentle a soul for this world. Of course, no one asked at his funeral prayers how he died. I find it hard to believe still. He was a man of tremendous faith."

Ammar sat beside him. "He died of a convulsion, possibly due to poisoning. It doesn't conclusively point to suicide."

He seemed surprised, even relieved, to hear it. Then asked, "Poisoned over a long time, or immediately?"

Ammar gave him a quizzical look.

Ibn Fadi inclined his head. "My brother is an apothecary."

"If it was poison, he would have ingested it immediately before his death."

"Did he die the day before the funeral prayer, or the morning of?"

"Day before."

"Then it could not have been Ibn Latif's revenge. God help us. Samir was right here with me the day he died. He and I ate together, from the same pot. Ibn Latif stayed away."

"Same jug and cup to drink?"

"Same jug, not cup. I poured Samir's water. I sat with him while he drank."

"Then, I agree. Ibn Latif could not have done it." Ammar winked. "I don't suppose you want to confess?"

Ibn Fadi chuckled, but his laugh released a tear, and he wiped his eye.

"How was he acting when you saw him? His state of mind? Physically?"

"He told us how Sitara had found Bashir again, but this time everything was done correctly. We discussed the trousseau and the preparations for the wedding." He hesitated again.

"Anything you can tell me will help."

"He was proud of his son making such a fine match, but he was carrying a weight. I suppose now that we have heard that the business was failing, that must have been it."

"Was he stumbling, slurring his words?"

"He was as he always was, suffering from his injured hip. But that is all."

"You sure about that? He looked like he was in pain?"

"Yes, why?"

"Your brother would explain it means no medicine had built up over time, soothing his pain but ultimately causing a deadly overdose."

"I see."

"What time did he leave?"

"After our midday meal."

Ammar considered the location of the shop and the distance to the canal landing where Samir died. Given his injury, it was not too far. "Did he have a habit of walking down to the canal when he worked here?"

"Walking? He walked as little as possible. He would pay for a ride on a cart when the pain was unbearable."

A cart, as he thought. The distance to the canal didn't matter so much.

Ibn Fadi asked, "Is that where he died?"

"Yes."

"Why was he there?"

"He never said he went there before?"

"No, but I am glad he had a place where he could enjoy something beautiful. Our eyesight goes, but not always for distance. He must have enjoyed looking out at the water, observing the birds."

The thought of Samir having some respite out on the embankment pleased him. "Thank you," he said. "That answers why very well."

"If he was murdered, I cannot imagine who. He was so gentle. If someone insulted him, he would answer them, 'You do not know the worst of me'."

"That kind of humility could make an arrogant man angry."
He sighed. "It did Ibn Latif."

"How did you react to the inheritance and leaving the shop?"

"We were happy for him but were confused why Samir would be the one to run it. Bashir managed this place with me. His embellishment work was not as highly skilled as his father's, but he had a head for business."

"I'll keep that in mind." But Ammar was thinking more about the coincidence of the bequest just when they needed it. "Did he say anything about the inheritance?"

"Yes." Ibn Fadi nodded slowly. "It was a distant uncle Samir cared for as if he were his son. It was a strange situation, though; the man lived as if he were penniless but had been saving. He could have had servants and nurses and lived in a fine home. Samir only found out when he died."

What about the relationship between father and son?"

"I never saw a harsh word between them."

Even the most dutiful son disagreed with their father at some point. "Never?"

He grimaced. "Only when Bashir forced his father to retire."

"How long ago was that?"

"I hate to recount it. It is embarrassing to his memory. But Samir insisted on working with the silk even when he was making mistakes. We had to undo it, and Ibn Latif had to redo it. Finally, his son had to take the work out of his hands. It was the only time I heard Samir protest."

That must have cost the owner something. "You let that silk get ruined?"

"Bashir paid the price. He refused to let his father be docked."

If Bashir was willing to lose his pay to preserve his father's pride, that tracked with the failing business. He was not going to take work away from him as he had before.

Several young women arrived out front with a male servant lingering behind. He was African and wore silks to rival theirs. His turban even boasted a peacock feather. One of them was bold, eyeing the young man twisting thread with blatant desire.

"I have to ask," Ammar said. "Are the rumours about Bashir and the girl true?"

He cast a glance at the young women. "You see the trouble we face. At first, the girl was circumspect. She made order after order. Soon we realized she was coming with an eye for Bashir. I asked him to work at the back of the shop, where she could no longer approach him. His father and I were concerned for him. He would be held responsible for compromising her despite her nearly throwing herself at him."

There had to be more than a concern for Bashir. It would be a scandal that could ruin his business. "What does that mean, throwing herself at him?"

"Like that one there." He frowned. "Displaying herself and asking questions in a voice meant to promise something more than a sale."

The young woman mooned as the two twisted the thread. How like the rich to come to a neighbourhood like this, throwing their wealth around, and assuming the right to use these people for themselves.

"Walla, in one sense I was glad for the loss of business. But here we are again."

"And Sitara?"

He leaned forward, his voice lowered. "Then, she came without her mother and a servant."

"In this neighbourhood?"

He nodded, equally shocked. "I had to ask her to leave."

"How long was this going on?"

"Not long, but it felt like a lifetime. From her first day to when I asked her to leave, no more than a month. A servant came later to collect all the work she had ordered."

"And there was no sign Bashir ever saw her alone?"

"He was either with me or his father. We were careful."

Not careful enough. No marriage was going forward on the basis of a rich girl slumming by the tannery and a promising glance as *hands brushed over silken knots*. Bashir had lied to him and betrayed his family and this man's trust.

Ammar asked, "Did you know they bought that business only to make Bashir a more acceptable match for Sitara?"

The old man gasped, gripping his cane. "Then they—"

"Yes. It seems they were intimate when you were not looking."

His hands trembled. "I thought Bashir was a dutiful son and employee. I must forgive him. God forgive him. The girl, Sitara, would have been difficult to resist, but I thought he had more respect than that for his father, for me, and for all I had done for him."

"You had no reason to doubt him?"

His shock was settling into grief. "Does one truly know people?"

"Did Samir have any other friends around here?"

"Down the way there." He gestured to the right. "But do not judge our lost friend by those men, please."

Ammar left him, hand over heart in thanks, and walked past Ibn Latif without a word.

21

Yulduz pushed Zaytuna out the door. "Tell 'er, woman. Tell 'er, if you have a backbone!"

"I will tell her. I'll tell her that I'm done."

Kamal Ali stood next to Yulduz. Usually, she would have taken his soft yet unyielding expression as his belief that she could do anything, but now it felt like scolding.

She left for Bint Afshin's home, if only to silence them. If they thought she would change her mind once there—that they could get her back on this case when the mystery of the husband's absence was solved—they were fooling themselves, especially when it was something better left between Gul's parents, and when—warned first by intuition and then by vision —she knew not to touch the thread that bound her past to their present losses.

The hypocrisy of it all. Ammar simmering with resentment over what he saw as her meddling in the work at the office. Him, sitting in the dark on that shabby furniture, feeling sorry for himself. If she did not buy the oil, if she was not there to listen, to prod him, who would? Then her own husband and her beloved Auntie Hakima keeping the news of Layla and Abdulghafur from her so she would not meddle there. She wished she could go back to her morning conversation with her husband and say aloud what she had been thinking: "I was wrong to hurt them. But you are wrong not to intervene." Remembering Yulduz's observation of Layla's clothes that one day, Zaytuna began to imagine she, too, was part of the agreement to keep Zaytuna out of such an important decision regarding her daughter. Yet, here they were, hoping she would do exactly what they criticize in her—get involved where she should not. So yes, Bint Afshin deserved to know, definitively, that she had quit, but no more.

Umm Hurayra was at her stool, and despite not feeling kindness for anyone this morning, she greeted her kindly, then knocked hard on the gate.

Bint Afshin opened it, her eyes red-rimmed and furious. "He's left me! And where have you been?"

"May I come in?"

Bint Afshin stuck her head out into the street.

Umm Hurayra stood with difficulty, putting down the kitten in her hand with its siblings and mother at her feet. "My dear!"

"Don't you look at me! I'll curse your cats!

The mother hissed while kittens scattered, and Umm Hurayra ran inside her home, the gate rattling shut in the quiet street.

Zaytuna slid in past her, saying, "There's nothing more I can do for you."

"You're useless!" The woman shut the door firmly behind her.

She wanted to say, "Your daughter is alive. Maybe your grandchild too. And your husband has been searching for them." Instead, she said, "Your husband needs to tell you himself what he's been doing."

"You know." She grabbed Zaytuna and shook her, her fingers digging into her arms.

Zaytuna held her hands, ready to pry the fingers off if she would not release them. "God ease your pain," she whispered.

The woman threw her hands off. "I don't want your prayers."

"I have your money for you. There will be no charge." Zaytuna took the coins from her pocket and held them out to her.

The woman slapped it out of her hand, and the coins clattered to the ground. She lifted her head so her voice would carry over the walls into the neighbourhood. "I will tell everyone about Zaytuna of that fancy Ammar agency! You refuse to tell a grieving wife where her husband goes at night!"

Zaytuna backed up slowly toward the door, lifted the latch, and slipped out.

"Go! Go!" Bint Afshin shrieked over the wall. "Everyone has left me!"

Umm Hurayra peeked out her gate, then emerged once she saw it was safe. The mother cat and her kittens soon followed. Then another woman joined them from the house beside hers.

She waved Zaytuna over, asking, "Is there news about Gul?"

Of course Umm Hurayra had told her neighbour. She doubted there were any secrets on that lane. Zaytuna answered, "Only that Adnan needs to speak to her himself."

"Yes," the other woman agreed, adjusting her wrap prettily over her ample body. "Like all men, he will come home. They will fight. He will tell her whatever needs telling. It's not for you."

Zaytuna wanted to hug them both. "Do you know where he is?"

"Don't you?" Umm Hurayra asked.

She shook her head.

"There was a beautiful young man pretending to be hungry

and lost. He slept over there." Umm Hurayra pointed to an alcove in the wall of a house two doors down.

"I fed him," the other woman said, her eyes twinkling.

Umm Hurayra said, "We thought you had hired him."

"He was not sleeping," the other woman said. "He was watching the door. But he was gone by this morning."

Ammar said that he wished he had messaged Girgis but had not, so it could not be him. "I don't know who it was."

They looked at each other, not believing her.

Umm Hurayra patted her hand. "We understand if you can't tell us."

"I'm just glad you were kind to a poor boy in need."

"Really not yours?" the other woman asked.

"Not that I know."

"I should have kicked my good-for-nothing sons and husband out and invited that one in. He did not complain about my cooking." She jabbed Umm Hurayra in the ribs. "And I heard no complaints from my eyes."

Umm Hurayra chuckled, then turned to Zaytuna. "Go. We will care for Gul's mother."

The case was still over as far as she was concerned. If somehow it was the young man Ammar had arranged to follow Gul's father, it would only mean paying him and sending him on his way. It was not a turn of events willed by God to tell her to "fix it" somehow.

She refused to open her heart, even by a crack, to the possibility at the risk of feeling her conscience urging her on.

The lane had narrowed, and she had to step aside for an older woman coming up with a basket at her hip.

Her conscience argued with her all the same, and Zaytuna answered it under her breath, "I can no more fix what is between Gul and God than I can restore her to her parents." Her heart clenched back at her, a warning. She said, "What do you expect of me?" But her chest became tight, and she put her hand onto the wall beside her to catch her breath.

The woman approached and put her basket down. "God give you ease, sister."

Up close, Zaytuna saw the woman was not old at all but deeply lined from years in the sun. Her wrap was wound around her waist like an apron and thrown over her head. Her hands were rough, just as hers had been when she worked house to house washing other people's clothes, and her basket was filled with neatly folded linens.

The washerwoman recited, *"God does not burden any soul with more than it can bear."*

"I'm just hot," Zaytuna said, wiping her forehead.

The woman screwed up her face into a teasing smile. "It'll get hotter until you take care of what's hounding you."

Her heart clenched again. She nodded, if only so the woman would go away.

"You have somewhere you can go to get what you need?"

Why would this woman not leave her alone?

"Yes." Zaytuna wished she had a few more moments to pull herself together, but she wanted to get away from this woman more. She walked on, saying, "I'm going there now."

"As long as it's now," the washerwoman called after her.

Zaytuna turned down one alley, then another, until she was at the main road and, without intending, found herself in front of the Shunuziyya cemetery. The long, low walls stretched out before her. The poorest of the poor lived along them, some burrowed in with reed lean-tos covering them, others in makeshift shelters within. Children ran among the graves, and freshly washed clothing dried on lines under the beating sun. Begging pots sat outside the gate. She gave them what she had left. Those nearby greeted Zaytuna, knowing her family for their regular gifts.

She stood at the gate, feeling the love of those buried here—her family, her mother and uncles, Junayd and Nuri, and all those who had guided her—but did not want to enter. If she came any closer, she would feel more than their love. There was a touch of it now, a gentle insistence that she follow the thread to its end.

Taking a few steps back to release that touch, she heard her own voice, the one that never let her run from fear. "Who is this Zaytuna who turns away?" But she answered it back, "We'll see."

Wanting to avoid Yulduz and the inevitable conversation about the case, she left the cemetery to find Saliha. Saliha would tell her that she was right to give up. Saliha would tell her what needed fixing was a night in bed alone with Kamal Ali, not taking on a case that would put her face to face with a young woman carrying the same burden as her mother.

No sooner had the thought entered her mind than she felt her mother's presence. Her chin lifted, her heart opened to the sky, and the words, "I carried no burden," and her mother's endearment, "andudugu: my babies," vibrated through her. Then: "Lift her burden and fix what is between—"

Zaytuna snapped her chin down and closed her heart, then ran until she was out of breath, finding herself in the middle of the road. Passersby went around her or jeered for her to get out of the way. A full dung cart moved past her, pulled by a man with a thick strap over his forehead, trudging slowly forward. Despite the smell, she got behind him and kept his pace.

But at the hospital, instead of reaching out to Saliha, she turned toward to the office.

As she went around the corner, she saw a beautiful young man leaning against the door as if he were made of flowing water. His turban was wrapped carelessly, as if he had dressed hastily after an assignation. His flawless skin was burnished copper, his cheekbones high, his nose long, and his lips full. He was almost womanly, but not one bit of him was anything other than a man. It was his eyes—dark, wide, and long-lashed under eyebrows arched like bows—that captivated. Dumbstruck, she almost laughed at the absurdity of him.

He stood languorously to meet her, placed his hand over his heart, and called out into the street, "Ya Lady, Bright Daughter of the Great Black Lover of God!"

She delighted in the ludicrous hailing, wanting to clap. "Assalamu alaykum, my brother."

"I am Girgis Asqalonaya." He slapped his chest.

How could Ammar think this young man could disappear into the city and follow anyone without being noticed? The women had not only noticed him but hovered around him, hoping for any small favour. She understood them completely and shook her head.

And the battle she had been fighting within herself was lost. Here she had resisted every effort to get her to take back the case; even her mother's presence speaking to her heart could not do it, and so she had been sent this ridiculous young man to disarm her. "God, forgive me."

Girgis heard her and bowed, saying. "Do not ask forgiveness where there is no sin, my lady."

She laughed aloud, letting her "sins" go, and picked up the thread. "I think you followed the old woman's husband. Do you know where he is?"

"I do! Come with me!" And he held his arm out to her to lead her into the market.

22

———————

The call to Friday prayers sounded as Ammar entered a small square. It was no more than a lane, widening enough for the greengrocer to have a few boxes out front and for three old men to pull up stools for the day. The men had the look of grizzled criminals waiting on one last job. Their clothes were out of fashion but bright and neat. Their turbans were wrapped tight, as if they were ready for a scuffle. One even had a long scar across his cheek. The three were leaning in toward each other, deep in chat, until the one wearing bright green pulled back and gave a full-throated laugh that reverberated through the square. Around them, the greengrocer was shuttering for the day and families were leaving for the prayer, yet none gave the old men a second look. Ammar held back for a moment, waiting for them to rise for the mosque, thinking to join them and talk afterwards, but the men did not stir.

He approached with a nod, but they eyed him warily. The acrid odour of wine on their breath hit him. The one with the scar cupped his hand around the dice. Ammar could not imagine why he was hiding it. They were drinking in the street, even on a Friday and during the call to prayer. What do dice matter?

Ah, they suspected him. He said, hand out, "I'm not a marketplace inspector."

"Maybe not," the man with the scar said, "but you walk like police."

"What do police have to do with dice, anyway?" The one in green had hennaed his white beard orange and wore a Turkmen robe with a matching turban and sirwal. The undulating green patterns of his clothes made him look like an old peacock. He nudged the man with the scar. "Throw the dice."

But the man clutched them.

Ammar said, "I am a ghazi, and I was an investigator for Grave Crimes, but now I work cases privately. That's the walk, and I never had anything to do with dice."

The man with the scar bowed his head. "Ghazi, sir."

Ammar took a long look at him. There was something in the way he said ghazi. He drew closer. The man had one of those faces that could hide nothing. Ammar could guess that he had been a soldier, too. "And you, sir." Ammar drew his thumb across his own cheek. "Did you get that on the frontier?"

A look of horror came over him, followed by shame. He pushed the jug of wine behind him, but then his expression hardened into the belligerence born of killing in battle. He drew the jug back out and set it in the middle of the circle, saying nothing.

The third man frowned, lifting his heavy eyes at Ammar, as if daring him to chastise the old ghazi for sullying the honour of the men who sacrificed themselves for the empire.

But Ammar placed his hand over his heart and bowed his head deeply. "Ghazi, sir."

The old peacock slapped his hand on the knee of the ghazi.

"Miqdad, find out what he wants so we can get back to our game."

Ammar answered, "I am investigating the death of your friend, Samir."

Miqdad sat up with some effort. "Don't believe those fools down there saying he took his own life."

Ammar grabbed a stool and sat. "The family doesn't believe it."

"Samir had no reason."

"Most of his friends and colleagues think he did. People say he was in a lot of pain. His eyesight had failed him. He could no longer work the thread. The new business was failing. That's a lot of reasons."

"None he would kill himself over," the old peacock said.

"Tell me why not."

"Listen." Miqdad gestured toward the street leading to the mosque. "What do you hear?"

The neighbourhood was quiet, and the call to stand in prayer lines came from within the mosque.

"Here we are, drinking, gambling. He'd go to pray but join us after. We'd joke with him and say the worst things. We'd insult any man's mother."

"He never chided us," the third man said.

"He go along with it?"

"No. You don't understand," Miqdad said. "He didn't drink. He didn't gamble. He whispered verses of the Quran into every stitch. His customers wore the words of God." The man stifled a sob and lowered his head.

The old peacock put his hand on Miqdad's back. "A man like that does not kill himself."

"He would say, 'God's generosity is greater than any pain', when we asked after his hip."

"How did he come to sit with you?"

"We mocked him coming and going to the mosque," the old peacock said. "He walked right past us every day, that son of his trailing behind."

The third man said, "He always greeted us honourably. No matter how we taunted him, he would agree and pray for us."

"You never fought with the son."

"No," the third man said. "But in the beginning, he stood by his father, giving us the eye that if we touched him, he would handle it. As if he could, but at least he would try."

They chuckled over it as a fond memory and acknowledged Bashir's strength. They were, after all, men who, even in their old age, could have broken Bashir's neck with one hand.

"The son had a kind of courage," the old peacock said.

"The father had the greatest courage," the old ghazi said.

"Did you go to the funeral prayers?"

"Of course," the old peacock said. "Rejep helped carry the bier to the cemetery. Miqdad and I walked alongside. The family could not refuse us."

"So if he did not take his own life, what do you think happened?"

"He just died," Miqdad said. "God takes his favourites and leaves men like us behind."

"No one wanted him dead?"

Miqdad replied, "The son told us he thought he was murdered, but who would have reason?"

"They miss him," Rejep said. "Bashir said he died by the canal, alone and unknown, then without family on the washer's table. If the police had not figured out he was an embellisher, the family might never have known."

Bashir had been there giving the sorry account but neglected to relate that, mother or not, he did not meet his father's body when he had the chance. These men would not give him such grace if they knew.

"They need time," Miqdad said.

"And if he was murdered?"

Miqdad looked at him with renewed grief. "Is it true?"

"I'm going to find out." Ammar stood up. "If I have more questions, can I find you here?"

Rejep asked, "If we hear anything, where do we find you?"

"Ghazi Ammar's Agency of Investigation and Implementation, just behind the Barmakid."

The old ghazi laughed at the name, then challenged him. "Why do you do this? Why were you police? Now this?"

"For justice. We fought, you and I. We fought for the people. Only I don't want to stop fighting for them."

He realized what he had said too late. But Miqdad only looked at him sorrowfully, pricking him into saying even more. "I don't know what front you were on, but I fought Byzantine soldiers who would have marched on to Baghdad if not for us."

The old ghazi asked solemnly, "Did they tell you that you would be like Seyyedina Husayn?"

Ammar touched his dagger, wishing he had left them before wanting to cut this old man for the insult to the Prophet's grandson.

"I'm not insulting Seyyedina Husayn, you fool." He stood with difficulty, his hand on Rejep's shoulder. "I'm insulting you. That you ever believed you did more than serve this filthy empire."

The old ghazi's wounds ran deeper than a gash across his face, and his words struck with the same power as if they were on the battlefield. He could not know it, but he had become Tein sneering at him from the butter churn, reminding him of everything that had gone wrong—their days on the battlefield, policing, that one private case. Tein was always on the high ground, even when he'd been beaten down and drunk like this old man.

But there could be no recompense because nothing was ever enough for him.

Ammar gritted his teeth and walked away.

"Wait!"

He faced them. Rejep was getting Miqdad to sit. The old ghazi's chest was heaving with sobs, but there were no tears. He lowered his head into his hands.

The old peacock said, "If he was murdered. You find the killer. There'll be justice if you can do that."

Miqdad lifted his head. His eyes were glassy. "Seyyedina Husayn would not let it go. Don't you let it go."

23

———————

As they passed the wool and upholstery shops and entered the neighbourhood known for its brothels and gambling houses, even men stared at Girgis. She drew her wrap over her face, exposing only one eye, embarrassed that people might think they were searching for a "daytime marriage," rather than a missing man, his daughter, and her child. She was sick at heart for Gul and could not imagine what it must have been like for her father to find her there.

She expected him to turn off down one lane, then another, but he continued far past where Tein and Saliha had been once on a case, to the point where she could hear the clanging of the coopers and smithies. She prayed the girl was not there, near the heat and noise and, she imagined, the harshest conditions and clients. But when they finally turned, it was into a secluded square shaded by an old tamarisk. Besides a small tavern and several food and juice stalls, there were gated entrances to three buildings, two of which boasted guards out front and long benches for waiting clients—the brothel and the gambling house—and the third was the orphanage.

Girgis held her back.

Children played near the open gate, running in and out, and with raised voices. Two small boys were teasing a man carrying a three-tiered hanging tray loaded with steaming pots of stew and flat bread toward one of the other buildings. He kicked at them, and the tray swayed in his hand. A drunk man outside the tavern, his robe half-open and turban awry, called out in slurred speech, "Leave 'im!" The children backed off long enough for the servant to get beyond their reach. He went past a seated guard with a nod, slipping through the half-open gate. Beside the guard sat an old man swaying, turban gone, head in hand, looking for all the world drunk and waiting it out.

"That is him. There on the bench."

Adnan, Gul's father. Only then did she see the man was not drunk but weeping. The guard had an arm around him and was moaning with him. It could only mean that Gul was dead. He drove her here through his inaction. Now Gul was gone, maybe the child, too. God help him. And she was too late. Tears stung her eyes, but there was no time for grief; she needed confirmation and to know if Gul's child was still alive.

"Was he like this last night?"

"Not that I saw. A boy came and knocked at his gate. Adnan left with him immediately. I followed them here and waited for Adnan to leave the brothel, but he never did. Not even this morning. That's when I came to get you."

"Stay nearby," she said. "I'm going to speak to one of the stall keepers."

She chose the one who had been watching them since they had entered the square.

"Good morning," she said, forcing her composure to meet the task. "A cup of whatever broth you are serving."

He gestured to the stools and a small table. "A bright morning to you. Sit, sister, please."

"With God's permission, I prefer to stand," she said as she

accepted the cup from him and sipped, then pretended to notice the old man weeping. "That poor old man. What could cause such grief?"

"A good man gone wrong."

"He grieves his sins?"

"Perhaps he has finally accepted that giving treats to orphans cannot cover over using women as he does."

She feigned surprise. "You mean that's a brothel?"

"Sister, I did not take you for a fool."

Inclining her head, she responded, "A woman must not seem as if she knows the things of this world."

"What woman would that be?" He gestured to Girgis. "One who brings a beautiful young man to a hard to find square?"

She ignored the comment. "The old man was a regular, I suppose."

The man waved his hand dismissively. "At his age? He only goes to watch."

Zaytuna nearly choked on the broth.

The man grinned.

"How long has he been coming?"

"I am not sure, but several times a week for some time now."

"The house with the children running wild?"

"No fathers to speak of. At least the orphans are close to their mothers. Umm al-Yatama takes good care of them."

"Any among them he favours?"

The man tucked his head back. "And you pretend not to understand the world!"

"It is true that women understand too much."

"There is one. A very young one. Maybe four? She boasts jet curls and a sweet face despite the bluntness of her features."

"Surely all children are beautiful."

"Surely not. And she is better off for it."

Zaytuna frowned at his depiction. "And what does the man want with her?"

"Umm al-Yatama keeps secrets but assured me there is nothing to worry about. I only saw that he kept back extra sweets for her."

"You all watch carefully."

"A bit."

"Do any of them end up in the brothel?"

"Only the very beautiful."

She nodded, understanding. "I see why she is better off for the bluntness of her features."

"Yes."

"How long has he been weeping there?"

"When I came to work today, I noticed him outside in that state you see there."

"All morning?"

"Yes, they've tried to move him on, but he won't go."

"Not good for business."

"It's still early. But they could have men pick him up and force him. I don't understand it."

"It is strange."

"Tell me." He leaned in. "A woman like you, here, with such pointed questions."

Zaytuna said in a mock whisper, "His wife wants to know where that old man spends his money."

He put his stove-scarred hands on the counter. "You are a good friend to her, then."

She reasoned he might be a good resource in the future and decided to tell him the truth. "Not a friend. I am a private investigator. I work for Ghazi Ammar's Agency of Investigation and Implementation."

"The beautiful young man, too?"

"Him, too." She glanced toward the bench. Adnan was still there, but Girgis was nowhere to be seen.

"You gave yourself away to me. How do you expect to do this work?"

"I knew there was no fooling you, so why would I try?"

Pleasure washed over his features. "Abdussamad, at your service."

"I am Zaytuna bint al-Ashiqa as-Sawda."

Girgis emerged from the brothel and caught her attention, questioning whether to approach. She waved him over.

"Abdussamad, this is Girgis. If you do not mind, he may ask for your help in the future."

"You are welcome here." He bowed slightly, his hand over his heart.

"What did you find out?" She asked Girgis.

"Gul had been ill, and a fever took her. Her daughter is still with her body. A woman is watching her. When Adnan arrived last night, Gul was still alive. The three wept together until she passed."

This must have been the weeping she heard in her vision last night. With confirmation of Gul's passing, Zaytuna allowed the grief in; her limbs became heavy, and her eyes welled with tears.

"Ya, Allah!" Abdussamad held out his hands and prayed for her soul. He turned away, wiping his eyes with his sleeve. "He came here only for his daughter and granddaughter, and I thought the worst of him! God forgive me."

Zaytuna touched his sleeve. "We are all guilty of such things."

Girgis waited to speak until Abdussamad had faced them again. "They are expecting a pallet to bring Gul to the corpse washer, but Adnan wants to take his granddaughter with him, and they have refused him. That's why he won't move."

She said, "They want her as a maid-of-all-work?"

Girgis shrugged. "I heard one say it's a loss to their business, but I did not understand why. I heard them mention her looks. She is not pretty enough to"—he paused, seeming ashamed to say it—"Yes, lady. You must be right."

Abdussamad said, "They want payment for her."

Like Layla was as a child, she would be indentured. There was no time for sorrow. Her body came to life. Gul's call was not only for herself, but for the girl. "I heard you," she said to Gul in her heart. "I will protect your child."

"Does the old man have the money?" Girgis asked.

Abdussamad asked in return, "Does the wife you work for want to know about a dead daughter or a living granddaughter?"

"I don't know."

Gul had found her way to Zaytuna when she was delirious with fever and travelling through the realm of dreams and visions. Zaytuna felt at a loss again. She was too late to help Gul. But would she have wanted her daughter to be reunited with her family or kept from them? What would be the best protection? No matter how kind her grandfather was, she would be living with Bint Afshin. Even so, it had to be better than growing up just short of enslaved.

"If I may, if you don't know, it is not your business." Abdussamad gestured to Adnan. "Let him sort it out. No man likes a woman's interference."

He could not know how he had pricked her. Interfere there. Don't interfere here. Everyone had an opinion. "Nothing to be done, then," she said to end the discussion.

Girgis saw her discomfort and gave Abdussamad farewells for the two of them. She was grateful for it, warming to this young man beyond the delight of his beauty.

As they left, she saw something red out of the corner of her eye and followed it. A short, full-figured woman in a red silk wrap came out and spoke to the guard still sitting with Adnan, then went directly back inside. "Allah," she gasped. She could not see her face but was certain it was Fatima. Her shape, the wrap—she even moved like the desperate woman under Auntie Hakima's care. Zaytuna touched Girgis's sleeve. "Can you find out who that woman in the red silk is?"

Girgis ran back to the brothel and spoke to the guard. He returned, nodding that he had it. "Fatouma."

"Is she African? I've only ever heard them use that form of the name Fatima."

"I didn't ask. He just told me the name."

The coincidence was too much. Fatima's anger and sitting to the side at their Sufi gatherings with her red silk wrap over her head took on new meaning. Zaytuna had thought the red silk indicated her family's wealth. Instead, it was meant for this. How could it be that the community had not taken her in? They must not know. Auntie Hakima herself would have moved Fatima into her own home.

She left the woman in red for the time being, second-guessing herself whether she should bring it up with Auntie Hakima at all. She could be anyone, not their Fatima. One more thing to find out. For now, her concern was Gul, especially her daughter, and what, if anything, she should do.

Girgis walked just ahead of her out of the market, drawing stares again, but he seemed to ignore them, even when the crowd parted to admire him.

Once out of the marketplace and on the main road back to the office, he stopped to address her. "Lady, men may not like it, but I have seen a woman's interference be the difference between life and death." Then he spun on his heel and carried on.

24

DAY FIVE

"Aaagh!" Ammar clutched his gut as his knees slowly collapsed underneath him. He fell to his side and rolled over onto his back.

Barely down, Husayn was on top of him, grasping his qamis with his chubby hands, and laughing so hard his threats tumbled out as incomprehensible squeals.

"I—you—can't stop—" Ammar raised his arms sluggishly, then grabbed Husayn and swept him into the air.

"Caw caw!" Husayn yelled, flapping his arms like a crow as they slipped from fighting to flight.

"Come you two," Nasifa said, nudging Ammar's leg with her foot.

"You heard your mother." He put his son down and jumped up.

Nasifa was glowing. He took her into his arms and kissed her cheek, then her neck, hoping again to smell the perfume. But there was nothing but the sweet scent of her skin and the lote leaves used to wash her hair.

"Why aren't you wearing it?"

Her body stiffened, and he pulled back.

"Tell me."

Husayn yelled, "Uncle!" and was off running toward the shared gate to their home.

Before she could answer, his brother was on them, Husayn trailing behind, attacking his leg. Muhsin patted him on the back before shaking him off, sending the boy onto the ground, laughing.

Husayn got up and ran off.

"This boy of yours is just like you."

It was no compliment, and Ammar grew hot, ready to argue.

Nasifa jumped in. "We are more proud of him every day. May God cover him and keep him in good health."

"Amin," Muhsin said impatiently.

"What do you want?" Ammar snapped.

"I thought you'd be glad, not come at me with your usual disrespect."

Nasifa tugged on his sleeve. "I was about to tell you."

"One of you better tell me." He looked between them.

"We got more than a fair price for that bottle of perfume, so you can continue to indulge in your failing business for a while longer."

They took it from her. Ammar did not know whether to punch his brother or fall at his wife's feet. One beautiful thing he had to give to his beloved, she who deserved so much, and they took it from her. His chest opened, his arms relaxed, and his hand ready to become a fist. In less than one breath his brother would be laid flat, but he heard Nasifa stifle a sob. Without looking at her, he stood down and said as evenly as he could manage, for her sake alone, "Alhamdulillah."

Only then did he dare look at his wife. Nasifa was close to tears, and her expression was pleading. He would have preferred to die than know that she feared his response.

Muhsin saw, shook his head at Ammar, and, his news delivered, left.

"Come," he said and took her hand, leading her back to their room.

He sat down on the bed and pulled her close, holding her like a child. "I'm sorry. My perfect wife. I'm sorry."

Slowly, she quieted, but he waited until her breathing was even before speaking again.

"I made you afraid, my love. Never again."

"Your father took it. I only noticed after he had it and went to Muhsin."

"It doesn't matter how it happened. You could have given it to them. Forgive me."

"If I had given it to him?"

"I would trust you had good reason."

She held him and whispered, "I love you."

A knock at the door of their room jarred him alert and off the bed. Ammar controlled his temper only for Nasifa's sake and opened the door. It was his father.

"A message." He seemed to fill the door as he did when Ammar was a child and scowled at him, but when he addressed Nasifa, he smiled kindly. "For our dear daughter-in-law. Zaytuna asks if you would bring Husayn to the butter shop. She is there with Nura."

She answered, "Thank you, Father."

Without a glance at Ammar, he left.

Ammar held out a hand to Nasifa. "I have to interview the family this morning. If you can leave soon, I can walk with you there."

"You go on. I still have a few chores, then I'll speak with Mother to make sure she does not need me."

He was sorry to miss the walk with her but relieved not to have to face Tein when he left her at the butter shop. The answer he got from the family today would turn the case one way or another, and he needed a clear mind.

"I'll go now, then." He kissed her goodbye, then looked for Husayn outside, but he was already out with the goats.

His mother came out and took his hand.

Her wrap was tossed over one shoulder. The thin white cotton was sprinkled with tiny flowers, the picture of his mother in spring; soon her hands would be working the soil in their garden. A breeze caught its edge, and she adjusted it with grace. If there was a person with courage in this household, it was her, navigating his father's moods and drinking, yet still loving her children and grandchildren with a generous heart and hand.

"I was coming to say I'm off," he said.

"Don't be hard on yourself, son."

Who knew a man's heart more than his mother? He took her hand and kissed it. "Walla. She will never have reason to fear me again."

"Then it's done. She will not."

"But she did in the first place," he said. "She did because of me."

"You have a temper, son."

"But never with her," he said, hoping that was enough.

"When you show your temper to others, you show your temper to your wife. You teach her where to walk, what to say, and how to act by showing her what you expect—and what you will tolerate—from others."

She knew this from his father, and he choked on the thought that he had become the same. "God forgive me."

His mother hesitated, examining his face, perhaps judging how much more he could hear.

"Say it."

"Be happy in your work."

It was not what he expected, and there was more to it than

that, but she kept her peace. He kissed her hand again and held it to his cheek. "Inshallah."

She smiled. "Is that the 'God willing' of doubt, polite refusal, sarcasm, or sincere intention?"

"You know me too well."

"You are my baby, always."

"I know it may mean more work for you, but let Nasifa go to Zaytuna today."

"Of course." She squeezed his hand.

He left her, weighing the horror that he had acted like his father, that he put Nasifa in the position of having to learn the patience of his mother, or that Husayn might ever come to fear him. He was nearly out of Buratha before he could begin to put his thoughts together for the interview with Bashir's family when a man came out ahead of him wearing a fine wool shawl draped over his turban with embroidered edges spelling out a prayer, and he wished he could have a piece of Samir's work and with it some of his gentleness.

Today, he would ask Bashir about the inheritance and the financial losses at the shop. It was a strange thing not to disclose when anyone could see that their father's death might be related. If he were still police, he would have considered it to be a willful misdirection, but these people had hired him, forcing a case that they could have left buried. They were covering something else, something embarrassing, but he had to know.

As he neared their neighbourhood, the walls and gates of the houses grew in size, and fruit and palm trees swayed from inner and outer courtyards. He had on fresh clothes and had used Nasifa's alum stone but sniffed himself all the same. To his nose, he was good, but he would find out when he saw their faces. The same servant let him in, this time leading him to the main room for guests.

This was where the money was spent. The low couches were

covered in gold and cream velvet brocade with matching back pillows and bolsters to lean on. Everything had a tassel. Hammered copper trays were set out on wood inlay stands, and all on rugs layered to cover the room.

He did not dare sit on anything and was still standing when Bashir joined him.

"Good morning. Please sit."

Bashir did not react badly to him and even sat on the nearest couch. His scent must have been deemed acceptable. Their servant followed with a tray of nuts and delicate cookies, glasses, and a long-necked copper pitcher.

"I should get my mother and sister," Bashir said.

Ammar stopped him. "I'd rather speak to you alone. There may be things you don't want them to hear."

"My God, what could that be?" Bashir stopped short.

"Only private matters—what you might not want to say in front of them."

Bashir sat down, concerned.

Ammar asked, "I'm curious about the inheritance. Ibn Fadi said it was a distant uncle?"

"Yes, he died over a year ago, but his estate was held up in court. He had no legal inheritors, so most of it went to the poor. The bequest was only just released to us."

"It must have come as a surprise."

"It did. We had no idea about any of it until the bequest was released. Father did not want us to get our hopes up. You know how these things can go. But I don't see why this would upset my mother."

"Not that. This. I need to understand why the business was failing."

His back straightened. "You are turning the case toward suicide again."

"The failure of the business might be why he was murdered. But you haven't been giving me the full story."

"Forgive me." He let out a resigned breath.

"When you hold back, it makes it harder for me to find out what happened."

"It is only out of respect for my father's memory. He has already suffered so much. Must he suffer, too, in his passing?"

"Will justice for his death make him suffer?"

Bashir took a moment, then answered reluctantly, "We were losing money from the start, but I did not know," he said. "My father handled all the transactions and gave me my share of profits each week, exactly what I expected we would make. I only found out when my mother came to me and told me the truth."

"How did she know?"

"She found him weeping, and he admitted it to her."

"Everyone says that you were the one with a mind for business. Why did he handle it?"

"He insisted," he said, frustrated. "Ibn Hisham was bringing me into his business, more appropriate for Sitara's social station. The shop was to be for my father's dignity. It was my intention to run it for him behind the scenes. He refused, saying he must take it on himself."

"And when you confronted him?"

"I looked at the books. They were badly kept but showed he was paying too much for thread, including exorbitant costs for the gold and silver. And he was much too generous to our employees."

"And his sight was failing. They told me at the old place they had to undo his work."

"Yes." He winced. "Ibn Latif was happy to see us leave, and with good reason."

"I also heard you and your father fought when you insisted he retire."

He offered only a clipped nod.

Ammar leaned in. "Do you want to tell me about that?"

His eyes hardened. "Back at suicide? Or do you suspect me of murder?"

They were accusations, not questions, and Ammar didn't understand it. Respect for his father demanded an answer, not this. But then he saw Nasifa's face when she feared him. His mother's hesitation to speak before he left. Ammar shifted uncomfortably. "What makes you think I'm not on your side?"

"Your manner. Your tone." Bashir stared at him. "You want me to fear you."

If he had been standing, he would have stumbled from the slap.

Bashir challenged, "Is this what you were like as police?"

The question righted him. It was wrong for his wife, his mother, and his son to hear him use the voice reserved for warfare and the streets. But he would not give in to clients who wanted him to look the other way rather than have their case solved. They may have been paying him, but he was not their servant.

"It must have been effective," Bashir continued. "But now I understand why your office is so shabby. Who would refer you to their friends, knowing they themselves would be interrogated?"

The last question came with a flourish, and Ammar met it with silence. He knew the damage a little quiet could do, and he let it grow between them.

Finally, Bashir stood. "I see I hired you in error."

"If you want someone else, hire him. If you want a man who solved murders in Baghdad rather than passed them off as natural deaths, then sit."

Bashir sat slowly but on the edge of the couch, ready to dismiss him.

"Tell me about the fight with your father."

He did not like it but answered, "I took what little he had left in life."

The son was making his own case for suicide now.

"When I found out the business was in jeopardy and took over, I ruined him for good."

"Did he say that?"

"No. He acquiesced, making apologies for being an old man. I wanted the receipts, but he said he burnt them out of shame."

"What did you do about it?"

"I spoke with the employees, reducing their pay. One left us, which was fewer than I expected. But I was furious with the supplier that he should be so unscrupulous as to overcharge a failing old man. I challenged him directly. He denied it. He even accused my father of covering up his own incapacity. I threatened to bring a marketplace inspector to his door. But he defied me and welcomed the inspector's adjudication, so I left, calling him a thief."

"Did you find a new one?"

His cheeks flushed. "I had to go to another market entirely. Word had spread that I had accused him, and no one would work with us. What could he do but smear our name to cover his own?"

"I need to speak to him. Would you be willing to take me?"

Bashir shook his head. "I will not face that thief again."

"He won't talk to me without you there. You'll need to act like you are sorry."

Bashir sputtered an objection. Ammar thought he would walk out. But then he said, "I will come. There will be no apologies. I will leave it to 'your manner' to make them talk."

25

———

His churning put aside, Tein chased Nura and Husayn around the square. Husayn slipped between the two and ran after her, who turned on him mid-step and tumbled with him to the ground.

Zaytuna and Nasifa enjoyed the play from a distance, sipping their buttermilk and nibbling on halva mounded on a hammered copper plate.

"I never thought I would be the type of mother to say this," Zaytuna said, stretching her legs out on the low couch. "But if she does not marry Husayn, who will have her?"

"The two of them would start a crime syndicate!"

"Don't say that in front of your husband."

"I don't say much to him these days."

Zaytuna reached for her friend's hand. "That's not like you two."

"It's the family. They are pressuring him to give up investigating. Every day, they make him feel like a failure, and it makes him think he should give me a life I've never had and do not want." She kissed Zaytuna's hand and let it go. "He brought home an expensive bottle of perfume that a man he interviewed had given him."

"Someone he interviewed gave him a bottle of perfume? Did he say why?"

"Stop investigating, Zaytuna. The point is that he gave this bottle to me, but his father sold it for the money they expect from him."

"He must have been angry."

"The more he feels like a failure, the more his temper flares. It scared me."

Zaytuna had seen his temper more than once, directed at her, others, and Tein. She could easily imagine it scaring Nasifa. "Did you tell him?"

"His mother did. I will not see that side of him again. Walla, I trust him. But his unhappiness will come out in other ways."

Tein was on all fours, the children on his back, and was swaying like a camel, threatening to tumble them off. Nura fell onto his neck, holding tight, while Husayn held onto Nura. Their laughter and screams drowned out the poor camel's grunts and filled the square.

"At work," Zaytuna said, "he complains about Tein not coming back. He has it in his head that he could do more with Tein than me. The cases I bring in are not to his taste."

"His heroism."

"He misses Tein."

"Three years those two have been avoiding each other and barely speaking when they do meet." Nasifa frowned. "What is to be done about it?"

"Something must be done about all of it," Zaytuna said. "It cannot be easy for you."

"You have met his father and brother."

Zaytuna nodded knowingly. "How is Umm Ammar doing?"

"She has perfected bearing up under the men in the family."

She paused, watching the children, then said, "I had another offer of marriage when I met Ammar. A garbage picker. Haider's family was known to be honest and even-tempered. He was gentle and kind but also ambitious. He started with one cart, then bought more and hired men to do the work. He hoped to have contracts for the best homes in Buratha."

Zaytuna watched her, waiting to hear if she wished things had been different.

"But I would not trade my life for that one. I love my Ammar for the dangers he has faced and the courage he has shown—he would have been among the brave men who fought at Karbala. And he will be happy only when the fear of herding goats is well behind him." Nasifa gave her a sly look. "I only wish to get out of the house more. Remember when we worked together on a case? I could be useful again."

Zaytuna could not answer except to say, "Inshallah." If she knew Nasifa at all, she would not act without her husband's approval, and that was unlikely.

"Enough of that," Nasifa said, smiling at the children playing. "I love when you tell me about your cases. Maybe I'll have some insight that will solve this one."

They often sat like this, watching the children play while Zaytuna talked about tracking down foolish husbands or lost valuables, Nasifa sharing observations worth considering. After filling her in, Nasifa prayed for the family and for their heartache to be healed. Finally, they held out their hands and prayed for Gul's soul.

"The child. What can be done?" Nasifa asked.

Just as the children were tiring, Kamal Ali came out of his office to take over for Tein. Husayn had stolen Tein's turban and was stalking around the square, expecting to be chased. Tein had endless patience for the children, but as he held out his hand for his turban, even the boy noticed he had gone too far and sheepishly returned it to him.

Tein passed them, brushing off his clothes. "I just need to wash up. Can I join you after?"

She was about to shake her head so she and Nasifa could have more time alone together, but Nasifa had already welcomed him, saying, "Ahlan."

"I have been thinking about the child," Zaytuna said hurriedly, as Tein went off to wash. "I want to ask Kamal Ali to pay for her release. The family does not have to know."

Nasifa shook her head. "You cannot act without the family's knowledge. But if you did, you would only call attention to their poverty."

The answer irritated her. It would be an act of private charity. The grandfather would simply come one day to find the girl released. Zaytuna could swear them all to secrecy. Maybe she would have Girgis drop the money off anonymously. It would work. How else was she to answer Gul's plea? As if the case did not have enough resonance, leaving the girl there was like leaving Layla behind, and she would not do it.

"I know that face," Nasifa said. "He needs to tell his wife. She will be consumed with guilt. The only way out is for her to stick her own hand into that money jar. If not, Bint Afshin will make her granddaughter suffer for being a constant reminder of not having saved her daughter."

Nasifa was right as far as it went, but she did not know on what grounds Zaytuna was making her decision. "I had a vision of the daughter begging me to 'fix it'."

Nasifa considered her seriously. "What does 'fix it' mean to you?"

"My mother told me after she had been raped—"

Nasifa gently took her hand.

"—that she had fixed what was between her and God."

"What do you think your great mother—may God be pleased with her—meant by that?"

"That she was protected by God," Zaytuna said, "no matter the brutalities of this world."

"Protected, meaning not necessarily in body."

"Protected in soul. Whatever this world did to her, her soul was at peace with God's will."

Nasifa did not respond immediately but sat with Zaytuna, hand in hand, as they watched Kamal Ali try, and fail, to corral the children.

"When I was a child," Nasifa finally said, "I told my grandmother about a dream I had of a girl taunting me for my over-mended clothes. In the dream, the girl said horrible things to me, much worse than I faced during the day. My grandmother said those dream words were not the girl's words but what I believed about myself after the girl's daily insults. She advised me to release those words and accept the dignity God gave me."

She let what Nasifa said sit a moment, then said, "You think it was not Gul in my vision, but my inability to be at peace with God over the injustices of this world."

"I believe so."

It was good advice, except Zaytuna had learned to trust her visions. It was Gul. Nasifa could not know what it felt like to hear a dying woman beg for her help. The vision could not mean standing by and doing nothing, and, frankly, she was surprised Nasifa would suggest it. Her temper sparked, and without thinking, Zaytuna snapped at her, "Odd advice coming from a woman in the tradition of Lady Zaynab, who stood up to the tyrant Yazid himself. I thought justice mattered to the Shia."

"That is not what I advised." Nasifa straightened at Zaytuna's tone.

"Help me understand, then."

"Since you took a tone with me, I'll take a tone with you.

When you are angry or sorrowful at this world, you rush in when you should wait."

The message was to stay out of their business and attend to her own. There was no point in arguing further, and she let Nasifa have the last word, but Zaytuna did not welcome another person telling her she was guilty of interfering.

Kamal Ali waved to the boy in the back to bring out more food as he herded the dirty and tired children over to them. Nura was already rubbing her eyes. She might not even stay awake long enough to eat.

"I have to take care of some business in back," he said, then disappeared into the shop.

Tein emerged in fresh clothes, his turban dusted off.

"Assalamu alaykum, Tein," Nasifa said, as she took the sleepy Husayn in her arms. "I hear you'll join our family for lunch soon."

"Inshallah. I have been a bad friend." He poured himself a cup of buttermilk from the jug and drank it in three gulps.

"Never. You are always our good friend. We only long for your company."

He raised an eyebrow. "Ammar would not say so."

Zaytuna wanted to jump in, but Nasifa's advice still stung. Gratefully, Nura was whining from exhaustion and near tears, forcing Zaytuna out of the conversation. If anything went wrong, at least it would not be put down to her meddling.

"Ammar thinks you are angry with him over something long past."

"Oh?" Tein looked away into the square.

"Why won't you work with him?"

Still staring into the distance, he said, "I've had enough of violence."

"Are you worried you'll become violent again?"

Zaytuna prayed that neither child would begin crying.

He faced her, the grief in his expression telling of the times he had killed, the time when he had held a man by his throat, and more. "On our last case, I nearly beat a woman."

"The Prophet advised that the true jihad is the battle for the soul's goodness. How do you battle for the soul by churning butter and taking care of children?"

Nasifa had gone too far, and Zaytuna nearly spoke up in defence of her brother.

But Tein glanced at her to say he had it in hand and answered Nasifa gently, "That's what I'm doing, even if you cannot see it. I won't go back."

Kamal Ali joined them, sitting next to Zaytuna and holding out his hands for the now sleeping Nura. But Zaytuna shook her head at him. She asked her brother, "When you did me the favour of asking questions at Adnan's workplace, how did you feel?"

"As if I did not know if I was doing wrong or right."

Her heart broke for him, and she vowed never to ask for help again.

Tein turned his attention to Nasifa. "Every time I see Ammar, he wants us back together as if we could return to the good old days on the frontier or on the streets of Baghdad. But there were no good old days for me."

"He thinks you still blame him for how he wronged that poor girl, Mu'mina."

It was what Kamal Ali had earlier hinted at, along with the insistence that she not ask herself. Yet, Kamal Ali made no move to keep Nasifa from meddling. Worse, his thigh was pressed against hers, begging her silence, as he waited for Tein's answer.

"He faced those mistakes like a man," Tein said. "Ammar showed as much, if not more, bravery in admitting what he had done wrong and setting it right than he ever had to show in battle. This is not about him. It is about me." He asked, "Will you tell him that?"

"You should when you are ready."

She was grateful that Tein finally shared what he had been feeling, but it irked her that Ammar, Nasifa, Kamal Ali, and even Tein had censured her—all of them telling her to wait, to be more thoughtful—while they meddled in each other's lives. They had no grounds to criticize her, especially because they did not hear Gul's call. She touched the sleeping Nura's hair. She would fix this situation with the granddaughter. No matter what they thought.

26

———————

"We will not speak to that one."

The thread supplier glared, pressing his hand flat on the counter to mark the division between Bashir and the shop where he was no longer welcome. The establishment was vast. Rows upon rows of diamond-shaped boxes held spools of thread organized by colour and type. Tables were set out in the centre to examine the thread and sample embroidery and braidwork. At the end, there stood a large cabinet, secured by bands of iron and three padlocks, no doubt holding the gold and silver thread.

"He's only here to tell you to talk to me," Ammar said. "Talk to me. Not him."

"How is that any different? You're his representative!"

Ammar leaned in close. "I don't think you stole from Samir. I think he made it up to cover over his losses."

"Finally, a man with some sense!" He gave Bashir a dirty look. "How will you convince him?"

"Samir said he burnt his receipts out of shame. I'm guessing you didn't burn yours?"

His eyes lit up. "Stay right there."

Bashir had fumed on the way over and was now pacing the

street, obviously wishing to leave. If Ammar was right, though, he was going to have to eat his words in front of the very man he accused of taking advantage of his father.

Several men were in the back with employees who unspooled sample thread and demonstrated their quality.

The supplier finally returned. Another man followed with a large bound volume. He was slim and wore the robe and turban of a Quran teacher and an expression that said he was ready to beat his pupil for dropping a word. He gripped a bamboo pen as if it were a small knife.

"My bookkeeper," the supplier said.

The bookkeeper used the pen to point to a number in the large volume before them. "See!" He turned the pages to another number. "And there!"

It did not mean anything to Ammar. He turned around to call Bashir over, but he was now pacing at the end of the street. "How do I know if those numbers are right?"

"Look here." The supplier took his time, showing him line after line of sales to other shops for similar weights and types of thread.

Ammar looked for Bashir again, but he had vanished. He had insulted Ammar for being too rough, yet here he was lacking the courage to face the men he had accused.

"You see?" the bookkeeper demanded.

It took some time for him to make sense of it, but Ammar did see. They had not charged him any more than they had charged any other customer. He had no idea whether that was a fair price or not, but they did not overcharge him.

Ammar asked, "And the difference he accused you of taking?"

The supplier stood back, cheeks flushed. "Enough to support a family. It was an absurd accusation on the face of it, let alone on our reputation."

"I'll apologize for Samir's son. He seems to have left in shame."

"God enjoins us to forgive," the bookkeeper said, but his face was saying it might be a long time coming.

"In Bashir's defence," Ammar said, "not everyone in the market is trustworthy, and he is inexperienced."

"Ghazi, sir. We price by type, which is clearly marked. Then, by weight."

With pronunciation worthy of one of the great mosques, the bookkeeper recited from the Quran: "*And give full measure when you measure, and weigh with a true balance. That is better and fairest in the end.*"

Ammar nearly laughed. The man was a Quran teacher when not at work on the books.

"Even unscrupulous men will not break God's command and falsify the scales," the supplier said.

He was correct. No one escaped being tricked in the market, but never that way.

"It would be a help if you would share what you thought of Samir."

The supplier said, "Other than he looked like a man lost in the desert?"

Ammar wished people would stop describing Samir as a man ready to take his own life.

The Quran teacher added with scorn, "If Samir did as people say, then it is no surprise. The whole family is marked by iniquity. That one there allowed his betrothed to be the subject of gossip." He leaned in, saying, "She is Karim ibn Hisham al-Baghdadi's daughter."

"Hush," the supplier said, gesturing at him to lower his voice.

"Why hush?" Ammar asked.

Looking around first, he said quietly, "Take care. He is a man of great stature."

Ammar suddenly realized he had never asked about Bashir's future father-in-law's business. "And how did he get that stature?"

"He owns Qafilat fi Himayati'l-Muhaymin. Our silk thread arrives on his caravan from China and Bukhara. Our cotton from his purchasers in Sind."

A customer came up beside Ammar. The supplier bowed to him and waved an employee to take him to the back.

"I do not imagine you deal directly with Ibn Hisham," Ammar said.

"Of course not. Only his representatives."

"The tailors and embellishment men in Suq at-Tarrazun, they all buy from you?"

"Yes, all but Abu Fidda."

"Does Abu Fidda buy directly from them?"

"It is likely. The city is vast, and Ibn Hisham is not the only importer in Baghdad. Yet he maintains a significant hold in Karkh."

"How do you think Ibn Hisham feels about the gossip?"

The supplier shot the bookkeeper a look to keep quiet, but he scowled in reply and spoke anyway. "The better question is why Bashir never met with an accident."

The question that kept coming back. "I told my colleague that the girl's father reminded me of a man who commanded armies. We couldn't understand why he did not marry his daughter off to someone more appropriate."

The supplier said, his voice low, "Men like that, you see them sometimes; they cannot deny their daughters' wishes."

"Every man must have a weakness," Ammar said, shrugging.

Now he needed to identify Samir's weakness. Find out why he was falsifying his books. Where was the money going? What could ruin a man who had the world before him? Typically, he would say a woman was giving him trouble. Like the supplier said, the loss could support another family. Maybe, like Zaytuna said, she was a servant in one of the estates near the canal. With men, it was women or gambling. But Samir's drunk comrades would deny both. No matter, he had to follow it up. And he had to ask, why was Samir sympathetic to those men? Did he see himself in them? Was he a secret gambler?

The supplier suddenly straightened, and the bookkeeper's frown became even deeper. Bashir must have returned.

Ammar faced him. "I've seen the books. Your father paid the same price as everyone else."

"Did you ask if that price was inflated?"

The bookkeeper pointed to Samir's account, demanding, "How do these prices compare to what you are paying now?"

He leaned over, squinting at the tiny but neat hand of the bookkeeper, then righted himself. His expression said it all. He was paying more now than his father was then.

"I," he stammered, "I owe you an apology."

The supplier put a hand on the Quran teacher's arm, who was gripping his bamboo pen tightly, and said, "We accept your apology."

Ammar bowed his head and took Bashir's arm to lead him away. There was no telling how long the supplier's goodwill would last or how long the bookkeeper could restrain himself from stabbing Bashir. Ammar got him far enough away, then pulled him aside.

Bashir looked like he was about to be sick. From the lies of his father or the humiliation of having to apologize, Ammar did not know.

"Some water?"

"Please. Water." Bashir panted lightly.

Ammar guided him to a nearby street where he heard the clang of the water seller. The man bowed to pour from the long-spouted copper jug strapped to his back, first rinsing the cup, then filling it. He handed Bashir the cup, and Ammar paid him. Bashir took small sips until the cup was empty, then handed it back, wiping his mouth with his very expensive sleeve.

The polite thing to do would be to wait before questioning him. But the right thing to do was to push Bashir to talk while his defences were down. Ammar crowded him enough to make him uncomfortable, but not enough to make him want to escape.

"Now listen, you made a mistake. But that mistake tells us something. Your father was spending money and not getting any happier from it." He thumbed behind him. "That one said he looked like a man without hope."

"He showed a face to those people he never showed his family, then."

"Where do you think he was spending the money?"

"At his age," his voice was tinged with disgust, "I refuse to believe there was another woman."

"We have to consider it," Ammar said.

Bashir grabbed his arm tightly. "He was devoted to my mother."

"Men have been known to be devoted to more than one."

He looked Ammar up and down. "And you? Are you married? Could you? Even the Prophet Muhammad—salla Allahu alayhi wassalam—spoke of its difficulties and advised against it. Yet, you think my aged father could have done the same?"

"All right. Maybe not a wife or family, but an expensive woman."

Bashir's mouth gaped.

"Gambling, then?"

"You filthy man, what depths is your mind!"

"The depths that have seen why men are murdered. So tell me."

"All those years with those drunk men in the square, and he never threw the dice once?" He stared down Ammar. "You are grasping."

Men have secrets, sometimes from everyone, and maybe the secrets had become too much. He decided he would track down the gambling first, and he knew exactly who to ask—his and Tein's old friend, Khalil.

27

Khalil was leaning against a wall in the bustling market street, chewing suggestively on a toothstick. A length of turban wound under his chin fell across his face. It was not to hide his identity. Everyone in this neighbourhood knew him. The women liked it, that and his wide brown eyes lined with kohl and the soft waves of his thick, oiled beard. As he got closer, he saw Khalil's blue and cream Turkmen robe was long and trailing open, exposing a brown and red striped qamis and loose pants tucked into supple boots. It was an absurd costume, making him look even more like a man waiting to draw a woman into an alcove than an enforcer.

"Assalamu alaykum, Khalil."

"Brother!" He pulled Ammar into an embrace meant to check him for hidden weapons.

Ammar barked out a laugh. "My wife doesn't know me that well!"

"Pity for you," he said, turning to watch a woman with a generous body walk by. She had adjusted her wrap so that everyone could see three rolls of fat leading to her ample behind.

"She'll be back."

"You seem pretty confident."

"This is not the first time she's walked by, and it will not be the first time I've had her flesh in my hands."

"God protect us," Ammar said under his breath.

"I welcome His lack of protection when it comes to women."

"While you wait for her, I need to know if a dead man had a gambling debt."

"Mabruk! You got a case with a dead man!" He slapped Ammar's shoulder. "Money in that!"

Ammar fell into Khalil's good humour. "Murder at least takes some time to investigate."

"How many days' pay do you have now?"

"Fifth day."

"How long do you think you can stretch it?"

"I'm not sure. I keep running into people who think he killed himself."

"Did he?"

"Maybe."

"You've got to hold out. Questioning looks. Pull on that thick beard of yours." He peered at Ammar. "Do you even oil that beard, man? Is this what happens when you marry?"

"Listen. He was an elderly embellishment man who was losing his sight and in a lot of pain from an accident. Lots of money flowing out of his business. Maybe gambling. Maybe a woman. Something else. His family insists he was killed, but nearly everyone I meet thinks he did it himself."

He inclined his head. "Are you sure you want to talk to the boss? There will be a favour in payment."

"In kind?"

"As always."

Ammar nodded. Information in kind he could manage.

"Let's talk to the boss, then. See if his name is on the rolls."

Khalil led him to an alley just after a shop selling raw wool for stuffing. It was as Ammar remembered—the reed awning was shabbier than the others, and broken slats let in more light but also more rain. This time, there was also a quarter barrel on its side with garbage spilling out.

"Nice ambiance, as always."

"As always, it keeps out the curious."

There were no toughs standing on either side of the door as there were last time. Probably away shaking down debtors. Abu Sa'id was working his prayer beads, seated on a low couch facing the door as if he were waiting for them. He wore a trim turban of simple cloth and, unlike his enforcer, the short qamis and robe of a fighting man, with a dagger at his belt. He was getting on in years, but no one would try him. A door to his right led to a room where a scribe sat at a low desk. The scribe looked up, nodded at Khalil, then returned to writing in a large volume.

Ammar said, "Assalamu alaykum, Abu Sa'id, sir."

"I remember you. You were police, and then you were not."

"Still not."

"Where's your Nubian friend?"

"Churning butter."

Abu Sa'id put aside his prayer beads. "Good. There was a look in his eyes. I see it with some of the men who want to work for me. I send them away. They hate what they have in them." He tipped his chin at Khalil with a smile. "Not like this one here."

"You forget I know Khalil from our ghazi days," Ammar said.

Abu Sa'id smiled. "He must have been a sight."

"He was like one of those far northern men the storytellers use to scare people." He asked Khalil, "What are they called?"

"Berserkers," Khalil answered with quiet pride.

In those days, Ammar had kept his distance from Khalil and warned Tein off him. Baghdad and age had softened him, but not by much.

"Tell me what you need," Abu Sa'id said.

"I've got a dead man. Maybe murdered. Maybe killed himself. Consensus is suicide or a natural death. But the family believes it was murder. I'm checking off the obvious first: gambling, then women."

"You know we are not the only debt collectors in Baghdad."

He bowed his head slightly. "But you are the most respected."

Abu Sa'id chuckled. "Flatterer."

"What's the name?"

"Samir Abu Bashir az-Zarduzi."

He called into the next room. "Butrus, check our records."

The scribe turned back page after page, finally calling out, "No."

Abu Sa'id said, "You'll have to find someone less respected to ask."

"Thanks, boss," Khalil said, turning to duck out the door.

Ammar had put his hand over his heart in thanks when Abu Sa'id asked, "Out of curiosity, why does the family think he was killed when the consensus is otherwise?"

Khalil seemed surprised his boss was still talking and came back into the room.

"The police called it a natural death, from a convulsion. They wouldn't believe it."

Abu Sa'id knocked his ring on the table. "There's a story here."

Ammar asked politely, hoping this was the payment for looking through the books. "Would you like to hear it?"

The boss nodded, sat back, and crossed his arms. Khalil

settled into his usual leaning-against-a-wall pose, leaving Ammar awkwardly standing in the middle of the room.

"Samir and his son, Bashir, were reputable embellishers, but poor. They worked in the Tanners' District."

"No money there," said Abu Sa'id.

"But their work was so well regarded that the wealthy braved the neighbourhood for his work. It became a point of pride to go there."

The boss said, "They love to slum it, the rich."

Khalil nodded sagely.

Ammar relaxed. They may be men on the edge of the criminal world, but at least he understood them.

He continued, "A rich young woman went there one day and fell in love at first sight."

"With the old man!" Khalil exclaimed. "There's your reason for the convulsion. Too much for him."

"Wait until you are an old man," his boss said. "You'll find nothing is too much if you have slow hands for it. You young men don't know how to please a woman."

"Boss," Khalil started to boast, but one look from Abu Sa'id and he shut his mouth.

Ammar coughed uncomfortably.

Abu Sa'id waved him to continue.

"She fell in love with the son, Bashir, not the father. She kept returning."

"Bold girl."

"Supposedly Bashir is chaste and never meets her."

Abu Sa'id smiled. "I love where this is going."

"Eventually, the shop owner forbade her from returning. In the meantime, Samir inherits money. They leave that shop to buy their own in Suq at-Tarrazun."

Abu Sa'id leaned forward. "You lost momentum with those

last lines, Ammar. Don't try this at a tavern. Did the girl go to the new market and find him again?"

"This time the father of the girl agrees to let her marry him."

Abu Sa'id asked, "How long between when they first met and this?"

"A little over three months."

"Ah, here is the 'supposedly'. The young man was not so chaste after all."

"Ha!" Khalil said, "Bet you can't ask the family about that!"

"No. But it's the only thing that makes sense. The point is that the family thinks the father was so happy about the wedding and the rise in their status, too, he would not kill himself."

"No chance he died of happiness?" The boss asked.

"The people at the Barmakid say it was an overdose of medicine, accidental or not, or someone poisoned him."

"And the police missed that?"

"The family says on purpose, and I'm inclined to believe them."

Butrus cleared his throat.

"Yes?" Abu Sa'id asked.

"If he owed money in that neighbourhood, Yusuf al-Multani would have the account."

Abu Sa'id did not seem bothered that Butrus brought it up.

"Khalil, tell him where." He addressed Ammar, "To be clear, you know we don't kill debtors."

"I remember—the dead don't pay." He did not add that breaking the knees might make a debtor wish they were dead. Ammar suddenly realized, the hip. "That reminds me. Samir had a painful hip injury. Everyone says it was from an accident with a cart. Could it have been persuasion to pay up?"

The boss shrugged. "Again, not us. We do knees. But I can't

say what others might do. Sometimes the collectors get a bit out of hand. Not everyone has our restraint."

Ammar knew full well.

"Why are they pursuing this? It's going to taint the wedding," the boss said with a dismissive wave of the hand.

"They can't give the case up, boss! Not until Ammar has made his money."

Abu Sa'id held his hands out in prayer. "Not until Ammar has made his money. Ya Rabb!"

He laughed with Khalil and said, "Amin," but felt a fool. So much turned on the wedding, yet he had not pressed Bashir on it like Zaytuna had advised him.

"You have not given us all the gossip," Abu Sa'id said, twisting his ring around his finger. "Who is the family they are marrying into?"

"Karim ibn Hisham al-Baghdadi. Apparently a big name in imports."

Khalil scoffed. "You don't—"

The boss gave Khalil an imperceptible look, silencing him.

The mood had turned. Ammar kept his stance easy but was on alert.

Khalil offered carefully, "Important family, then. Lots of blessings."

The boss said to Ammar, "Not a family you want to cross."

Ammar was glad he came. "Criminal?"

"The way the man does his business, it should be criminal. He would give his daughter the world, or that boy would be dead and the girl shipped off to a village to have the baby. The father's death cannot be related."

The very mention of Ibn Hisham had raised the spectre of the marriage and death being related, even for Abu Sa'id. Ammar prodded casually, "Oh?"

Abu Sa'id blinked.

Ammar never imagined Abu Sa'id as a man who would let anything slip. Trying to put him at ease, Ammar said, "It sounds like I should advise them to drop the case, then."

"They are pushing their luck. Even a man who dotes on his daughter can be pushed too far."

Ammar wanted to know how Samir might have pushed him too far.

"When is the wedding?" Abu Sa'id asked.

Another question Zaytuna had instructed him to ask that he had not. Ammar hesitated, not wanting to admit he did not know. "Still in discussion."

The boss asked, "I think Ibn Hisham has a son who is his right hand man?"

These questions were going somewhere. Abu Sa'id was about to give him a real lead. He answered, "A son, yes. I don't know about the rest."

"They should hurry the wedding up, then."

"I'm a discreet man. If there is anything that could help—" Ammar said carefully.

He shook his head, laughing. "Come now. I am saying there is a limit to how big a baby can be presented as premature to family and friends."

But that was not it. "I'll suggest they drop the case and push up the wedding."

"There goes your payday," Khalil said, sadly.

"Maybe not." Abu Sa'id said with conspiratorial pleasure.

Khalil grinned hungrily. "What, boss?"

"Nothing like that, Khalil." He tapped his ring on the table three times. "I am thinking of Ammar here and how to make sure he gets a few more workdays in. Take him to check out the other debt collectors. Make sure and introduce him as our dear friend. Drag it out. Then, Ammar, go to the family with a full picture. They'll feel like your investigation was thorough and be more willing to let it go."

Ammar bowed his head, wondering what this generosity would cost him in favours.

Abu Sa'id continued, "No shame in taking their money. If the son is going to be working with Ibn Hisham, he's got enough in his change purse to feed your family for a year."

28

———————

"What's with the long robe, Khalil?" Ammar asked. "You don't have to fight anymore?"

"I can reach my dagger and fight in this robe better than a man whose sword is already in his hand." Khalil slapped his chest. "But I'm in charge now. I train the men. No more kneecapping or threatening debtors for me."

"You miss it?"

He gazed at him with tender longing. "A bit. I do. Thank you for asking."

Ammar placed a hand on his back and reminded himself never to get on his bad side.

"Take over from the boss someday?"

A shadow crossed Khalil's face. "Don't talk like that. You could get me killed."

"No one is listening." But Ammar checked anyway. They were on a busy street in the market, passersby walking with purpose, shopkeepers and customers haggling over cones of pungent spices and baskets of dried herbs.

"Abu Sa'id has his ways."

There was little chance Abu Sa'id would let Khalil take over.

Khalil's mind went to killing, not the politics of the criminal classes and keeping the books.

They turned a corner. "There." Khalil gestured to a juice stall that took up the space of two shops and even had tables and low couches inside.

Ammar had expected a similar shabby alley designed to avert scrutiny, but Yusuf al-Multani's office was out in the open. Several men sat inside, deep in conversation, while a guard kept watch in the street.

Khalil bowed his head slightly to the guard. "Abu Sa'id sends his warmest greetings to Yusuf al-Multani. We're here to ask about a man who may be under your care."

He gestured to them to go in, then went back to observing the street.

A stout Sindi man sat like a caliph on a long couch at the back. Even in the half light, the colours of his densely patterned silk robe shone, most of all purple set against cream. He wore it open, exposing a cream silk qamis bound with a matching purple waist wrap. There were thick silver rings with large inset stones on most of his fingers. A wide vase of red roses was next to him. Their scent permeated the back of the shop, fighting for attention with al-Multani's jasmine and musk perfume. Ammar did not see anyone likely to be a secretary. If al-Multani had a "Butrus," he did not work here, and Ammar doubted if he would get what he needed.

"Abu Sa'id sends his warmest greetings, sir." Khalil bowed his head deeply with his hand over his heart.

Ammar did the same.

The little caliph asked, "And how is his family?"

"Alhamdulillah, sir. May I ask after your family to share the news with Abu Sa'id?"

"Alhamdulillah, likewise."

"He asked if you would help our good friend with a question." He gestured to Ammar. "Ghazi Ammar at-Tabbani is a private investigator who is looking into the death of the father of his client."

Ammar suddenly realized the risk in suggesting that Samir might have been killed by this man's overeager enforcers and said carefully, "We believe he committed suicide. But the family would like to know why. I suggested he may have fallen into debt and could not live with the shame."

With a sigh, al-Multani said, "Weak men do not pay their debts, and no prayers need be said for the one who succumbs to his weakness in this manner."

Ammar kept his expression steady. "If one of your men knew of him, I could take the news home to the family and settle the case."

"All my men are not here." He gestured toward the couches lining the walls. The three men who had been deep in conversation before now observed Ammar. "How can I give you an answer with any certainty?"

"May I ask?"

"You have my permission." He gestured to his men. "Answer our respected ghazi."

"Did any of you come into contact with a man by the name of Samir az-Zarduzi? An older man, an embellisher by trade. His shop was in Suq at-Tarrazun. He had a significant hip injury and walked with a limp."

The men gazed at him with expressions of boredom verging on violence. One of them, a Sindi man like the little caliph, had the brutal body of a killer and a nose flattened to the side. Debtors would only have to look at him to find a way to pay up.

"My men here do not seem to have met the father of your client," al-Multani said. "But if he is in Suq at-Tarrazun, why not go there? We are quite a distance."

They were the closest, according to Butrus.

Khalil said, hand over heart. "We came to you first out of respect."

"The name, though, is familiar." He plucked a rose from the vase and paused to smell it. "Some gossip about a marriage with an important family."

Ammar said, "Yes, that is him."

"The story is worthy of the taverns." He gave Khalil a knowing look. "If there is nothing else, as you can see, we are quite busy."

Khalil said, "Abu Sa'id is grateful for your assistance."

"If he tires of you, come and see me," he said to Khalil. "There is a hunger in your eyes, and I am always on the lookout for good men."

Khalil bowed his head deeply. "If Abu Sa'id should ever release me from his service, you will find my cheek on your doorstep."

Ammar almost swung his head around to gape at Khalil's manner and guessed the berserker had tamed himself enough to manage the politics of the job, after all.

"You, Ghazi," al-Multani said.

Ammar stood at attention.

"This is a lot of effort for nothing."

He did not answer "nothing for pay," but that was what it was starting to feel like. As much as he wanted to drag it out, he knew he would not let himself. One more day to cover the woman angle. If nothing came of that, he would end the case.

Once dismissed, they left, walking sideways so as not to show their backs to al-Multani. Nearly out, the guard intentionally bumped into Ammar's shoulder. Ammar pretended it did not happen. The debt collector was the caliph of this neighbourhood, and his subjects should expect to be corrected on a whim.

Once well out of earshot, Khalil said, "He's an ass."

Ammar barked, "Ha!"

"Abu Sa'id could have him killed and take over his territory with the snap of his fingers, and everyone would thank him for it."

"The thing is," Ammar said, "al-Multani's place is closest to the gambling halls around Suq at-Tarrazun."

"And their house?"

"Yes. They live near the market."

"We'll ask around a few more, especially near their old tailor shop. He may have been street gambling—dice, cards, that kind of thing."

Not likely, but he was not going to stop Khalil from helping him.

Khalil paused, tugging on Ammar to stop. The street had become crowded, and people spilled around them heading to the square ahead. "You said he was in a lot of pain and could have had an overdose of medicine. Why are we looking for something that didn't happen? No one was going to kill him over a debt. Not even that ass back there."

"What about the hip injury?" Ammar asked. "It could have been a threat to pay."

"When did it happen?"

"The corpse washer said within the last few years."

"Does the timing work?"

"He didn't even have an inheritance to lose back then." But Ammar pushed the point. "A gambling habit doesn't come from nowhere. It was an old warning. Now he crossed the line again."

"How did it happen?"

"They say he pushed a man out of the way of a cart but got hit."

"I've never heard of a debt collector pushing someone in front of a cart to send a message. There's a code of conduct, Ammar."

"You don't know."

"You're making things up now." Khalil crossed his arms, taking a comical stance.

Ammar relented. "He was spending money. So much that he nearly ran his family business into the ground. What are the options? It's always women or gambling."

"Or a boy, or some rich food he likes, trips along the canal instead of walking, or even charity."

"I thought you were here to help me earn a few more days' pay?" Ammar was joking, but Khalil was right, and he wanted to kick himself for not considering basic expenses adding up, like the apothecary and riding in carts, but most of all charity, especially given how everyone spoke of Samir's gentle nature. When he poked around about lovers, he would ask about charity, too.

"You work these cases all alone now?"

"You remember Tein's sister?"

"She's your partner?" Khalil's eyes widened. "She carries herself like those great Sufis down in Tutha. I saw her at the market recently and hid from her. She sees everything."

Great Sufis? Ammar was with Zaytuna day to day and would differ. But she could probably get a favour out of Khalil without having to pay for it, if that's what he thought of her. He wondered what Zaytuna would think of the characterization. Certainly, she would like to be thought of as a partner, but Ammar corrected him there. "Not a partner. She works her own cases—family crises, small matters. I take cases like these."

"Hmm. I can't see her being happy doing that. She is a great woman."

His attitude toward Zaytuna was starting to irritate him. "She's married and has a child."

"God bless her and her family, then. May she enjoy her little cases."

Ammar winced as he said "amin" to his prayer, even though he thought her cases were little, too. He would pull her in tomorrow and get her opinion, especially to discuss the conversation about Ibn Hisham.

They drew closer to the small square ahead. It was nearly full. Those at the centre were clapping their hands, and women ululated. He thought he heard a lone drum.

The excitement of the crowd was rising. Ammar looked for watchmen. "Where's the best exit out of the square?"

Khalil leaned in. "You're not police anymore. Let them riot."

"I want to know how we are getting out of this, if they do."

"Liar. You are standing like Ghazi Ammar, Soldier of Justice."

Ammar had to laugh. "Okay, what's happening?"

Khalil's eyes sparkled mischievously. "You aren't going to find anything of use for your case, so let's go waste some time."

"Like the old days!"

"You should come by more often," Khalil said as they waded into the crowd.

Ammar felt the old bonds of friendship in the sincerity of his voice and the expression on his face. But he also felt the heat and crush of the crowd and had located their exit if they needed one. The lone drum was clearer now, and he even heard the rhythmic tinkle of small bells. Khalil towered over the crowd, but Ammar could only see the backs of their heads. "What is it?" he asked.

"Ho! A young Ghuraba fellow is dancing with bells on his ankles and wrists. More grace than a woman. They are throwing coins at him!" Khalil looked down at Ammar. "Maybe there's the boy your dead man spent all his money on."

29

DAY SIX

They never got close enough for Ammar to see the dancer, but Khalil had enjoyed watching from his superior view and afterward threw himself into taking Ammar to every debt collector and gambling house in Karkh. Khalil showed him off at each like a prize camel with a declaration that he was Abu Sa'id's "good friend," making him feel more of a man than he had in some time.

Samir's name sparked a flicker of recognition in some, but only to tie him to the gossip. All but one were reluctant to say Ibn Hisham's name. Ammar took a chance and asked that man why he thought Ibn Hisham let the gossip go unanswered. He replied, "Gossip is for us down here on earth. He and his like live among the stars." But Ammar doubted that very much.

It was dark when he began the walk home. Night watchmen had questioned him along the way, shoving their torches too close to his face, and he had to explain who he was and where he was going. By the time he fell into bed next to Nasifa, he should have been exhausted, but his time with Khalil had brought him to life. It was like being with Tein again. They had discussed the case through and through, eaten together, laughed, and even stopped for another street performer. By the call to prayer this morning, he had barely slept and mumbled to Nasifa that he would not wake for it.

But he only returned to half-sleep. One question kept coming back to him until, finally, he was ready to consider that Ibn Hisham had killed Samir. Khalil had waved off any connection, but Ammar could not move past it. Yesterday, they had agreed he would look into women and charity and track down the Christian girl by the canal. If the business loss and witness did not pan out—and if he put suicide out of the discussion for the moment—the question of Ibn Hisham remained to be answered.

Now, walking back to question the shopkeepers at the location of the family's new shop in the Suq at-Tarrazun, he turned the matter over in his mind.

From one angle it made no sense—killing Samir did not solve any of his problems. Ibn Hisham could have sent his daughter away or killed Bashir. On that count, a man of his stature could have had Bashir's whole family killed and gotten away with it. But there was no need. It was expected that Ibn Hisham would have to take the family on as his own—that the weak old man, out of place in that world, would be treated as his own brother—and their presence in Ibn Hisham's household would be seen as a display of his benevolent power.

From another angle, killing Samir did solve a problem—just not one he had considered until his day out with Khalil had made him feel like his own man again. The gossip had to be eating at Ibn Hisham. The man who commands it all could not control his own house. How must it feel to have to sacrifice so much for his bold daughter? Killing Samir was something he could do just for himself. Ammar understood that impulse, at least.

Most of the embellishment shops in Suq at-Tarrazun were

still shuttered, including Abu Fidda's. Just as well. He did not want to answer any questions about how his wife had liked the perfume. The man who had interrupted him and Abu Fidda last time was there but doing everything he could to ignore Ammar. He went to the only one not avoiding his eye—a man with a long-suffering face, the type who might give Ammar the information he needed, if only by way of complaint.

"Good morning."

"May your morning be bright," he replied, but his expression said the opposite.

"I have a few questions about Samir az-Zarduzi."

He came out in front of the shop to see if anyone else would take the task on, then shrugged at him to continue.

"I know Samir ran the business into the ground. The question is, with all those customers, how did he lose so much money? I can say with certainty it was not gambling."

"I could have told you that. He was ill-suited for business but had a cautious temper."

"What do you think about other women?"

"Uff. Samir was feeble. The pain he was in. How could he manage that?"

"He needed the distraction and could not get it at home?"

"Never."

"You never saw him with a woman here?"

The man shook his head at Ammar as if he were an idiot. "If he had an illicit woman or a secret family, do you believe he would bring her to his place of business?"

A boy, maybe fourteen or fifteen years old, walked up behind him and leaned over the shop counter. "Father. The crazy woman. Remember her?"

"Did I invite you into this conversation?" One look and his son picked up a rag and pretended to polish the counter but never stopped listening.

"The woman?" Ammar asked.

"Fine," he said reluctantly. "There was a woman who came here for charity each Friday."

"Might as well tell me." Ammar put his thumbs in his belt, settling in.

"She wore her wrap like a streetwalker."

The son piped up, "Lighting the lamp."

It must be some new slang. Even so, he understood the meaning well enough: she had opened her wrap to brighten a dark day.

The shopkeeper frowned at his son but nodded. "She wore a face veil, but her eyes were wild. I took her for one the world has harmed and will never be right. She would go to him and hold her hand out. I never saw him place more than a coin or two in it, but I was not paying close attention."

"Did she ask for money from any of you?"

"No, she would come to him and go."

"Father," the son said from behind the counter. "She had a boy with her, remember?"

He lowered his head and said through gritted teeth. "God forgive me for what I did to deserve this son."

Ammar saw himself in the boy and wanted to slap the father for himself and all the sons who did not measure up to their father's designs for them.

"Yes. A boy, no more than a toddler, was with her at times."

"And Samir never let on anything about her?"

"No, but I cannot imagine she was his wife."

"A woman he wronged? His son?"

"Wrong a woman? Deny a son? Samir was not the kind of man who would shirk a moral duty."

Ammar could not keep the accusatory tone out of his voice. "I've seen enough to know that no one is above anything."

The man's back stiffened. "We are through here."

"And last Friday. Did she come then?"

The man gasped. "How could she know not to come? You do not think—?"

Ammar took satisfaction in his reaction. "You never heard a name?"

He turned to his son. "Come and be of some use for once and tell him what you know."

The boy put down the cloth and joined them. His expression was open, almost playful, everything his father was not, and he did not care what his father said or did to him. No wonder the boy vexed him. Nothing could be done once a man loses the respect of his child. This one would outlast him and take control of the shop.

He said, "I think her name was Salma."

"How well do you think he knew her?"

"Oh, they knew each other. When she showed up the first time, he was surprised. And, get this, he used her name first. She did not have to tell him."

The father observed his son with concern.

"Did she come regularly?"

"Never missed a Friday."

"Never missed, except right after he died."

"She would wait until Bashir left." The young man pointed out an alcove just out of view. "She'd hide there."

"Anything else?"

"Sometimes he handed her a fat purse, rather than a few coins in her hand. That's it."

Ammar gave the tailor a look. It was impossible he missed all this.

"Tell me, what do you think? Was she here for charity, or was there more to it?"

The boy smiled broadly. "More to it. She even threatened to tell his family once."

"Tell me about the threats."

"I didn't hear anything specific, but it sounded ugly to me."

This was too much. Ammar took a step back and said loud enough for the shopkeepers to hear. "I'm trying to find out if someone killed Samir, and you all decided not to tell me about the woman threatening him?"

A customer walked into the square and stopped, nervously touched his turban, and walked slowly out. One shopkeeper stared Ammar down, while the others carried on as if he had not spoken.

The shopkeeper grabbed his arm. "We did not tell you because he killed himself, and it may be her threats that led him to it. Let it go." He addressed his son. "You must at least agree with that."

"Bashir should leave it." The boy said, chuckling. "That fancy girl he caught? If I were him, I'd be trying to erase my father's past!"

He lifted a hand to slap his son, but the boy casually ducked and went back to the shop.

"Thanks for your help," Ammar said. "If there is anything else, make a note of it."

"I would think that was enough," the shopkeeper said, stepping away from the counter.

Ammar called out to the son, "I'll return if you remember anything."

He would have to talk to Abu Fidda. If anyone here got details about this woman, he did. More, he wanted to know why the man who told him so much did not tell him about the woman. He called over the shopkeeper again to ask when he arrived.

But it was the son who came forward, eyes bright, answering, "He comes and goes at his own pleasure."

So that was what the boy wanted, not his father's place, but to be in Abu Fidda's position. Ammar had little doubt he would get there. He bowed his head in farewell.

There was a woman, and the boy was his son. If Samir was surprised to see her, then he had hoped he had gotten away when they moved shops. The son was two or three? Where did he keep her all that time? Once she found him again and saw what he could afford, she probably demanded a better place and more. That and weekly payouts accounted for the money. Like the supplier had said, it was enough to support a family. Ammar guessed that he tried to cut her off and she killed him. The next stop was back to the old tailor shop and his tough old friends. They knew all along, and they were going to tell him.

30

The men were on their stools, jug of wine out. Watching Ammar approach, Miqdad let the dice in his hand clack, sending cracks across the quiet square.

"Good morning."

Rejep said, "Yet everything about you says no good is coming."

"I have a sensitive issue to ask you about. But you'll do your friend no harm by telling the truth."

"You accusing us of lying?" Miqdad grasped the dice, making a fist.

"Only that you knew something useful and did not tell me." Ammar measured his words. "When you put it all together, though, you might not like it."

"Proving he committed suicide?" Rejep asked. "Leave."

"The opposite." Ammar held a hand out. "Walla, it may prove he was murdered."

The old peacock gestured at a stool but did not pull it up despite it being within arm's reach. Ammar took it, saying, "There was another woman, a son. He would have owed her support."

"He was besotted with his wife," the old peacock objected. "Talked about her and blushed!"

"We teased him for it," Rejep said, nodding.

"Would he have told you if there were another woman?"

"If he did have a woman," Rejep said, "he did not tell us, so that should answer you."

"A woman and her son came by his new shop every Friday and demanded money."

"You saying she came here, too?" Miqdad asked.

"Yes, she probably did."

Rejep answered for all of them. "I've never seen a woman like that."

"I've not even described her."

"Doesn't matter," Rejep said.

"Even if she murdered him?"

There was a shift in them, torn between preserving Samir's memory and justice.

The old peacock chose a middle way. "If a woman like that were here, those tailors down there would know. Ask them."

Ammar got up and put the stool back against the wall. They were good friends, if misguided. He put his hand over his heart. "I appreciate your loyalty to Samir. May he rest in peace."

They held up their hands and prayed for Samir's soul.

Ammar only hoped that Ibn Latif was working. That bitter man would not mind sullying Samir's memory. But why hadn't Ibn Latif told him in the first place?

The earnest young man was out front twisting thread, but this time he was with an older man. They were working a deep blue-green. A plainly dressed older woman was watching, basket of bread beside her.

Ammar was drawn to the rhythm and flow of their work and stopped for a moment.

She nodded to him, saying, "Like the Tigris rushing on a bright morning."

"In miniature, yes." The older man said, smiling.

Ibn Latif came out of the shop and leaned in the doorway, waiting for Ammar to speak.

But he addressed himself to all three men, just as he had with the old men, telling them it was no betrayal of Samir to help him find the killer.

Ibn Latif sniggered.

But the young man answered gravely, "I understand."

"Mind the thread, Hamza, not that business," the older man said.

Hamza's eyes were on the thread as it twisted, and he wound it over and under his hands, but he was still listening.

"Did a woman come here with a boy, maybe two or three years old?"

"You mean his bit on the side?" Ibn Latif asked, taking obvious pleasure in the expression.

The man could be counted on. "Was she his wife, or was it an affair?"

"I did not take her for a wife. Either way, he got a son out of it."

"What makes you think she was his woman?"

"She flirted with him, tugging at her wrap, batting her eyelashes over her face veil. She had spent some time on her eyebrows the way women do."

Ammar asked, "How old was she?"

"By her eyes, late twenties at most."

"That's young for him."

"Who knows the minds of women?"

Ammar glanced at Hamza to see if he had anything to add. He was bursting with it, but the older man kept him from speaking.

"And Bashir never saw her?" Ammar asked Ibn Latif.

"She came only on Saturday mornings when Bashir was out with the boss to pick thread from the suppliers."

"As much as you hate Samir, you never told his son?"

Ibn Latif smiled mischievously. "Samir always wondered when I might expose him."

"You liked that."

He did not reply immediately. Anyone could see that the implication that he might be morally in the wrong was eating at him. Ammar gave him the time he needed to defend himself and say what he wished he had not. But the man was in greater control of himself than Ammar gave him credit for. Ibn Latif only said, "And here everyone thought he was the best of men."

But Hamza could not take it. "I heard her thank him for his kindness. It was charity, no more!" His face had turned red, and he looked like he might cry.

"You dropped a loop!" The man fastened his end of skein and put it back in the silk-lined basket, then stood, hands out to take the thread from him.

Free of the thread, Hamza yelled at Ibn Latif, spittle flying. "May God disgrace you!" More followed. It came out half-choked, but his meaning was clear: Ibn Latif was the scoundrel, not Samir.

Ibn Latif threw his hand out. "I am the evil man? It was my work, and I was supposed to sit here and smile, hand over heart, and say, 'Alhamdulillah, we are grateful to have the master among us' while you all lied?"

Ammar stood back, watching it unfold and waiting for Hamza's reaction.

"Like a whore," Ibn Latif continued, "she called to your precious master, and he went to her. If there was nothing to it, then why did he lead her down that alley there to talk? You know what happens in that abandoned house."

The boy began to blubber. The older man gave Ibn Latif a dirty look and tried to lead Hamza away, but the young man shook him off. Hamza wiped his face with his sleeve. "He was kind to me and brought me here and got the boss to hire me!"

"Still a filthy whoremonger." Ibn Latif crossed his arms.

"The boy called him father!" Hamza yelled. "They were married! There was no sin!"

Ibn Latif slowly smiled. "If it was a secret from his first wife, it was a sin, boy." He addressed Ammar, "I heard the child call him 'Baba'."

"I can't believe Bashir never found out," Ammar remarked.

"I agree," Ibn Latif said. "Perhaps Bashir knew and chose to keep his father's secret."

If he did, he was going to have to answer to Ammar. Bashir's evasions made no sense. This could be his father's murderer.

"I wish I could be there to watch when you confront him," Ibn Latif said with pleasure.

"Why didn't you tell me this before if it pleases you so much?"

He crossed his arms. "I decide when I speak."

The boy burst out. "You're jealous! For what? You had to help an old man and this business? Now he is dead. Maybe you killed him!"

Wide-eyed, Ibn Latif turned toward the men in the shop. They had been watching the scene unfold and stared back at him in silence. Only then did Ammar notice the boss sitting cross-legged at the far end of the shop, work left in his lap, hand over his face. No help was coming.

The boss had already confirmed that Ibn Latif could not have poisoned Samir, but Ammar allowed the silence around his panic to grow.

"Ask them!" Ibn Latif finally yelled, pointing to the men in the shop who were now watching in horror. "Ask any of them what happened after he left. The woman came here with their son. No one would tell her where he went!"

Hamza hung his head. "She screamed, tearing at her clothes. Said she'd find him. That he would pay for abandoning her and their son, and not just in money."

Ibn Latif nodded with satisfaction.

Ammar was getting angry himself. "No one thought to tell me this? You all were happy to call it suicide."

He stared at the men in the shop. The boss was shuddering while the rest looked guilty. These men—taking it on themselves to decide which was worse for Samir's family: the woman or his suicide.

"But why not?" Ibn Latif closed in on Ammar. "I hear his family far and wide whisper it is suicide and refuse to pray for him. I knew Bashir would go mad from the shame. I never suspected he would hire an investigator, but how perfect! All this questioning. Raking up the dirty secrets. Exposing his lies. Bashir'll lose that rich bride in the end. All to save his dear father's name from the stain of taking his own life."

He expected Ibn Latif to clap like a child who got what he wanted, but Ammar took a menacing step toward him, and it wiped the gloating off his face. "You told her about the new shop."

"Eventually."

"How long ago?" Ammar demanded.

"She came back. I don't remember."

"You lie," Hamza said. "She never came back."

"True," he said, giving it up with a shrug. "I found her and told her."

Ammar put a hand flat on his chest, pushing him back. "You just as good as killed him."

Ibn Latif raised his hands in surrender, saying, "I only hoped to expose him to his new friends."

"You better tell me where she lives."

31

"I need you," Ammar said urgently.

"What is it?" Zaytuna opened the gate, waving him in, and called out, "It's Ammar."

Tein came out of his room, Saliha behind him. Fresh from the bath, they glowed. Her brother's beauty was like their mother in her most luminous moments. His high cheekbones and broad nose, his perfect chin—even the battle scar that snaked up to his throat enhanced it. Saliha had put him in the long indigo and black robe she favoured and a matching turban shot through with red and gold threads. She was wearing a gossamer Chinese silk with a spill of multicoloured birds flying through swirling clouds. The two of them challenged the birds in beauty and grace.

"Assalamu alaykum, ya, Ammar," Tein said, grinning.

He arranged his face to meet Tein's smile. "Wa alaykum assalam. I've finally caught a break in the case and came to get Zaytuna." He addressed her, "It's to do with a woman. I think you should be there."

Saliha came around to Tein's side. "So you need her for woman things."

"Yes," Ammar said, obviously confused by Saliha's tone. He looked around. "Where's Nura?"

"With Qambar and Yulduz across the river. Layla, too. One of Maryam's cousins is getting married. They'll come back tomorrow."

"You two look fit for the wedding," he said to Tein and Saliha.

"Not us," Saliha answered. "I have a day off, and Tein used his special relationship with his boss to get a day with me."

Zaytuna said, "It seems that I am free."

The courtyard was quiet for just a moment too long. The leaves of the pomegranate tree rustled, and a child ran through the lane outside, singing to himself. Tein and Ammar stared at each other, as if daring the other to speak—Tein smiling, Ammar strained—but neither would act.

She took charge. "Saliha, come with me. I could use your eye on a bit of mending."

Saliha restrained a smile and followed Zaytuna into her room. They shut the door behind them and leaned against it, each with an ear to a gap in the slatted door.

"Mending?" Saliha pinched her lightly, pleased. "Do you mean meddling?"

Zaytuna whispered, "I keep getting told not to meddle."

"Not by me. Now quiet. I can't hear."

Ears to the gaps, they caught Ammar saying, "I did a bit of investigating with Khalil the other day."

Tein asked, surprised, "You went to Abu Sa'id?"

"Yes, but the old man wasn't one of theirs. Abu Sa'id sent Khalil out with me to question the other debt collectors and gambling houses. We even stopped for food and saw some street performances."

"Oh, poor Ammar," Saliha whispered to Zaytuna. "He sounds so lonely."

"I hope Tein understands that and doesn't react badly."

They put their ears to the gaps again.

"Let me guess," Tein said. "No one knew anything."

"No. Our man isn't a gambler."

"I would gamble that Abu Sa'id sent Khalil with you to make sure they told you nothing."

Saliha grasped Zaytuna's hand, and they put their eyes to the gaps.

Ammar was standing with his chest out and chin up.

"You just wish you were with us," Ammar said. "It was like old times."

"You never had old times with Khalil. You never trusted him. Not on the frontier, and not when we were police. You were right about that. It took me longer to learn."

"He's changed. He's in charge of the men now. Maybe he'll take over from Abu Sa'id."

"God protect the debtors."

Ammar stepped back, incredulous. "You were going to work for him when I met you that day."

"I was desperate. You saved me from it." Tein's voice was thick with emotion.

"So you came to work with me at Grave Crimes because you were desperate?" Ammar's body was relaxed but alert, ready to fight. "You left once your life was set up here with Kamal Ali's money. You go with whoever feeds you."

Saliha took her hand again, squeezing it tightly, but let it go when she saw Tein's shoulders slump. Zaytuna could have told her. Tein's fighting days were done. She knew it from the day Nura was born and he held her fragile body in his great hands. But Saliha's reaction showed she still wondered if Tein's pain would spark into violence again. Zaytuna wished she could reassure her with more than a twin's certainty.

"I was grateful you found me," Tein said, putting his hands

behind his back, so he almost bowed to Ammar. "You changed my life. You changed my sister's life. If we enjoy a good life now, those blessings were set in play by you."

He challenged, "And now?"

Tein waited before answering him, then said finally, "Come to me in the future, not Khalil. I won't work cases anymore, but I'll have your back if things get dangerous."

There was a moment of profound silence. Tein was offering what he said he never would, and Ammar accepted it, a smile warming his face.

Saliha gestured for them to leave the room, but Zaytuna wanted to wait a moment longer, hoping for more—an embrace from Tein, a hand on the shoulder, but Saliha had already jerked the door open.

"I think that seam will do nicely," she said on her way out.

Ammar swung around. The moment was broken.

"Tein says he'll come out with me," Ammar said with a nodding acknowledgment to him. "That is, if things get rough."

"Oh?" Zaytuna quipped, "Taking my work from me, brother?"

Tein put on a smile and said with playful gravity, "You can't handle the streets, woman."

"What!" Saliha slapped his arm, playing along.

Zaytuna came back at her brother, imitating the voice of a pious scholar. "Not at night, of course. A married lady is not to be seen out at night. God, Glory to Him Most High, says—"

"Now this one!" Saliha said to Ammar meaningfully, "Never marry a twin."

"Nasifa would not allow it." Ammar was now grinning. "A twin or otherwise."

"And she's not a twin?"

"No."

"Then you're safe."

They laughed, more than the moment called for, but it broke the tension, and Zaytuna had what she needed.

Ammar asked her, "How is your case?"

"My case?" she asked, having forgotten in the moment. "It only needs wrapping up and a few negotiations, and all will be as well as it can be."

"You found the girl?"

"Didn't Nasifa tell you?"

His face fell.

"I forgot," she lied. "I remember now that I asked her not to share the news. We found the father and Gul at a brothel. Gul's daughter lives at an orphanage just across the square. The money was going to them."

"How did you find him?"

She reached out and touched his sleeve. "I have to thank you for that. Your young man from the canal. Girgis followed him, then found me at the office."

"Girgis! I didn't call for him. How did he know?"

"Really?" Girgis was even more impressive to her now. "He has initiative, that one."

"We should use him again," Ammar said.

"But Ammar." She reached out to him. "Gul died. The morning we got there, the father was out front mourning her, and the daughter was still with her mother's body."

"Allah!" He held out his hands in prayer. When he faced her again, his eyes were glistening with tears. It was unlike him, and she suspected the tension of his moment with Tein had released into grief for Gul.

"I don't know if Gul's father has told his wife yet," Zaytuna said.

"Don't you think she figured it out when he came home with her granddaughter?"

"That's just it. The brothel won't release her without payment. They hope to use her."

"Not—" Tein burst out.

"Cleaning."

"God protect her," Saliha said, but she was as relieved as they all were.

Ammar said, "He probably rushed home and told his wife."

"You do not know his wife," Zaytuna said.

"Are you going to tell her?"

"I took myself off the case. I even returned the money."

"Then you're done."

"That's what everyone says. I'm done." She thought of the girl, so like Layla. Her voice cracked. "Where is the justice in it?"

Ammar touched her sleeve. "He will tell his wife. They'll get the girl together."

"That's what Nasifa said, too."

He smiled softly. "She has good judgment and does not meddle."

At the word, Zaytuna took a step back. The intimacy between them gone.

Saliha crossed to stand beside Zaytuna. "You call it meddling in a woman but seeking justice in a man."

Ammar flushed, from embarrassment or temper, she did not know.

Tein came around to her other side.

She wanted to kiss them both but did not want Tein to lose what gains he had made with his old friend.

Ammar started to speak, then let out a short breath and started again, saying, "You're right. I would storm in and take the girl by force."

"You could have done that when you were police, Ammar. But not now," Tein said quietly. "Now, what would you do?"

He took a moment. "I'd want to know if the old woman wants the girl."

"It's a good question," Zaytuna said, releasing him from her own temper. "I wanted to pay out of pocket for her, an act of secret charity, but Nasifa said that if the old woman did not pay for the girl herself, she would resent her own granddaughter."

Saliha nodded understanding. "Her granddaughter will only be a reminder of how she failed her daughter."

Ammar asked, "So why are you wondering whether to go?"

Zaytuna did not answer. She had gotten up in the middle of the night to pray and sit with the vision, but she still did not understand what was required of her, only that she had to honour Gul's call.

The four stood in the silence of the question for a moment. Then Saliha embraced her, whispering in her ear, "We have to go, but I trust you. You decide. Not them."

An idea came to her, a way to help her answer what she should or should not do and find out more about Fatouma. She kissed Saliha's cheek in return and whispered, "I could use your help getting into the brothel."

"Yes, please." Saliha released her with a squeeze of her shoulder and a conspiratorial smile.

Zaytuna stood back, admiring her brother and her friend. "So, where are you two going in your finery?"

Tein coughed uncomfortably, but Saliha ignored it, saying with a note of naughtiness in her voice, "We're going to visit our old spot."

Zaytuna had some idea and nearly gasped at the risk. The days before they married were not chaste, and they took their privacy where they could get it.

"All right, that's enough." Tein drew Saliha toward the gate.

Poor Ammar, missing Saliha's innuendo and Tein's discomfort, asked, "Where's that?"

"There's an alley not far from your office," Saliha answered. "A rotted building with an alcove that has always been just for us."

Ammar blushed deeply as he desperately searched for something to say but only sputtered.

"She's joking, Ammar," Tein said as they walked by.

But Saliha's playful expression told him she was not, and his blush spread from his beard to the edge of his turban. Zaytuna had to bite her tongue to keep from laughing.

They left the gate open, and Zaytuna went to it, saying to Ammar. "Let me get you a drink of water, then we'll go. You can tell me about this crack in the case and whatever 'womanly thing' I'm supposed to do on the way."

32

"Tein's wrong about Khalil."

Zaytuna did not answer him, and it set him on edge.

"Everyone can change," Ammar said.

"You don't have to convince me of that."

He grunted. She would know. Zaytuna had changed more in the years since they met than most people do in their whole lives. When Tein brought her to Grave Crimes to share her theories on the death of a boy from her neighbourhood, Zaytuna was an angry, brittle twig of a woman, railing at the world—men especially. She had been reckless and defiant, but she had grown, and she should give Khalil the same concession.

"You'd think Tein should know people can change, too," Zaytuna said.

"Why doesn't he?"

"Tein doesn't believe he's changed."

Ammar pulled her out of the way of foot and cart traffic. "What do you mean?"

"It was a sacrifice, that offer he made to you. I hope you understand that. He worries he'll drop back into the old violence, maybe even start drinking again."

His gut pitched with the memory of Tein grabbing a man by the neck and letting him hang from his hand during a street riot.

She said in answer to his silence, "I understand."

"How could you?"

"He loves you."

The words landed like a sucker punch. Ammar bent over, wanting to throw up.

"He said you showed more courage facing what you did to Mu'mina than you had to in battle."

He panted into the sickness.

"Come now," she said, tugging on him to stand.

He did as he was told and stared at her, still panting. Her face had that light on it he never understood, but his breathing eased enough to let her words in, although he did not know what to do with them.

They stood quietly for a moment longer. Then she asked, "Do you want to carry on?" she asked after a moment. "We can go tomorrow."

The thought of quitting shot through him, lifting him out of his confusion and into anger that she would take advantage of him like that, suggesting he was too weak for the work. He left her, storming ahead.

Ammar walked through the clamour of the street without looking back. When she fell in beside him, he willed her not to speak. For once, she followed his lead and kept her mouth shut as they neared the turnoff for Salma's neighbourhood.

"Tell me about this woman," she said.

He touched his dagger to steady himself before speaking.

"If we are going," she pressed, "I need to know now."

"Likely an affair," he answered tersely. "Secret second wife? He'd been supporting her for years. She went to the old tailor shop for the money and went wild when he left, threatening revenge."

"That sounds like the affair or the marriage was long over."

"Yes."

"She's not someone he took pity on, and it became a manipulation? You know there are those who take advantage of kind people like him."

He did know. For some it was their employment, and they were not above threats to get it, but this was not that. "They had a son."

She stopped him. "Everyone knew and did not say?"

"The boy called him 'Baba'."

"But it could be any man's son. Samir could have paid for her once, and now she begs money from him for the child. She could be doing this with any number of men."

"They were certain he recognized the child as his own."

"Bashir didn't know?"

"I need to find out," Ammar said. "We turn here."

The alley became narrow, with lanes branching out here and there in a warren of one-story homes, some with thin reed mats hung up for a door, others only tattered curtains. But the streets were busy with working folk—a man in dusty clothes walked by carrying a leather pail of tools as a woman came out of a doorway, drying her hands and calling to a boy with a sack slung over his back—poor but proud, and he respected them but was losing his respect for Samir if this is where he put the mother of his child.

Zaytuna asked, "All that money given to her, and this is where she lived?"

"If he'd honoured her out in the open, it would have been better," he said.

"Money enough to ruin a business, Ammar. Does this account for it?"

"No, and we're going to find out why."

They found the passage Ibn Latif described. It led to a sliver of a courtyard with three doors. The sun was beating down, and the courtyard was empty.

He called out, "Assalamu alaykum, we are looking for Salma, the wife of Samir az-Zarduzi, and her son."

A boy maybe ten or eleven years old stuck his head out one of the curtained doors, then ducked back in.

When it opened again, a broken woman appeared. Maybe she was twenty or thirty like they said, but she seemed much older. Her head was uncovered, and her hair was cut short as if she had gone at it with a knife. There was something strange about her face. It was lopsided. Then he saw the abrasion that she must have hidden with her face veil.

"My sister," Zaytuna went to her and took her hand.

But the woman jerked it away, cackling strangely. "I don't need your pity."

"We're here because you were wronged," Ammar said, taking a step toward her.

Her expression changed in an instant from pride to calculated hunger. Ammar shivered, feeling like a gazelle who knows the hunter will soon have it roasting on the spit.

The boy came out and stood beside her. Ammar knew the look on his face. Baghdad was filled with bareheaded, barefooted children with worn-thin clothes who had seen too much. This one was already carrying himself like a man. But where was the toddler who called Samir "Baba"?

"Bashir send you?" She held out her hand. "There better be money coming, and more than Samir gave over."

"Samir had been giving you a lot." Zaytuna asked, "Where did it go?"

"Tavern," the boy said plainly.

She hit him on the back of the head, but he barely moved despite the obvious force. "Don't lie! Don't I feed you and Sumayr? Don't I pay the rent on this palace?"

Sumayr. So "Little Samir" was here, sleeping, he hoped.

"She's not always like this," the boy said.

"Like what?" She dug into her sleeve and pulled out a coin. "Go!"

He snatched it from her and ran out through the passage. No doubt there would be a jug of wine with him when he returned. But no matter what Samir had been paying her or what she was paying out in drink, it did not account for the money that was bleeding out of that shop. Maybe she was gambling, too. Entertaining men who did not mind her face?

"Bashir going to pay me for what he did?"

"Bashir?" Ammar asked, shocked. What had he done?

Zaytuna cut him off. "Can we sit?"

"If you don't mind dirt on that wrap of yours."

"My wrap has seen plenty of dirt on its ass."

"Ha!" The woman smiled crookedly and sat just inside the doorway, taking the shade for herself.

Zaytuna sat down, holding the edge of her wrap out against the sun.

Ammar settled across from them, getting the full brunt of the heat. "I suspect the family may not have told us the truth."

"That family knows the truth! I told Bashir. I pushed my Sumayr right in front of him. 'There's your brother! What are you going to do about it?'"

"What did he do?"

"Denied it. Called me a thief. Me!" She slapped her chest, then broke out into a cough so hard her body spasmed, then went right back at it. "Samir should have let me die. Kill me and my boy right there, rather than live with this." She ran her finger along the abrasion on her face.

He asked, "Let you die? What happened?"

"Him, thinking he was doing me a favour by pushing me out of the way of that cart."

Another thing Bashir had lied about! He said his father had saved the life of a young man from Jerusalem. Even that the family still sent letters in gratitude for the old man and had performed the pilgrimage to Mecca on his behalf. "The cart accident where he was run over—it was you he pushed out of the way?"

She jutted out her chin, displaying her sagging cheek and hideous scar. "You call this pushed out of the way? I was dragged!"

Zaytuna asked, "When was the accident?"

"A few years." She shrugged.

"How old is Sumayr?"

"You got it all wrong," she said, understanding. "I was just pregnant with Sumayr when I was hit." She pulled back, frowning in disgust. "When my man saw my face, torn up like meat, he took his belt and left."

"Men!" Zaytuna exclaimed.

"You know. You know." Salma nodded.

Ammar said, "You said Samir was the father."

"When I went to him like this"—she held her hand out in front of her belly—"and told him what he did to me by saving my life, he vowed my child would be his child. He would raise him as his own."

"What happened?"

"That snake, Bashir, threatened me. Said he could get the police to come and put me and my children in prison for some crime he would make up." Her expression turned dark with fear. "We'd never see daylight again!"

"He threatened you at the tailor shop?" Ammar asked.

"Bashir came here, dragging his father along."

"How you must have felt when you saw them!"

"The fire in me, girl! The fire!" She slapped Zaytuna's thigh. "Samir stayed true to his word, though. He came back alone with money but told me he couldn't come again on his own because of his hip. I could come by the shop when his son was out, and he'd pay for what he'd done."

"But he did not take your son in as his son," Zaytuna said.

Shut nodded briskly. "That boy's been raised to know who is his father."

Ammar imagined the old man's bind and understood why Bashir had lied about the accident and this woman. He was protecting his father then, just as he was now by pursuing this case. Miqdad and the others with their dice and wine had called Bashir courageous for watching to make sure they did not take advantage of him. Ibn Latif knew Bashir would go mad with any insult to his father's memory. Bashir could not have known it would have been better to support her openly, for once cut off, she had killed the father he meant to protect.

"God protect us from evil things!" Zaytuna exclaimed. "The insult to you and your son when he moved shops and didn't tell you."

She grabbed Zaytuna's hand. "You know! You know what men are like!"

"I do," Zaytuna said, with a kind of disgust that Ammar knew came out of her encounters with the worst of them. "When you found Samir again, I hope you told him what needed saying!"

"More than that! I told him what would need doing if he did not pay up."

"Good!"

Ammar asked, "Did he pay?"

She tucked her head back as if she had forgotten who he was, then spat on the ground before him. "He paid, but less and less. Finally, he told me not to come back."

"He deserved what he got, then," Zaytuna said with force.

"Bashir will too if he doesn't pay what his father owes me."

She pointed at Ammar. "You tell him! You tell him that what happened to his father will happen to him if I don't see the money."

They had her. He willed Zaytuna to push her to confess it all. In all her suffering, he wished they could let her go, but this would never end. She would threaten another. She would kill again.

Zaytuna's eyes lit up. "How did you do it?"

"Me?" She asked, her eye on Ammar. Her expression became suddenly thoughtful. "He killed himself, and that son will, too. God is the Judge and drives sinners to die in sin."

She was smart enough not to say it aloud. She knew what the prisons were like and knew how you got there. But she was the one who gave him that poison.

"Tell me how—" Ammar started, hoping to get her to admit to the murder, but Zaytuna cut him off.

"We'll tell Bashir. You can be sure there will be a change." She kissed the woman's hand and stood, indicating to Ammar he should go.

But Ammar did not rise. Was she out of her mind?

"Come," she said sharply.

A child cried in the room. Salma did not get up but crawled in, the curtain dragging along her back.

Zaytuna was already out of the passage and into the alley.

He hurried after her. "You just cut off her confession!"

"You think she killed him?" She stepped aside for a passing man.

"Yes! She got him the poison. She drove him to it!"

The boy returned, coming around the corner with a small clay jug in his hand, taking his time.

Zaytuna stopped him. "Boy, who is your father?"

"The man who seeded me? Who knows? But me and

Sumayr have a handful of fathers on the go right now. It's a fair business."

Ammar stared at him. "Why would you admit that?"

"You aren't bringing us more money. She's crazy and can't tell. I can."

The boy sauntered past them to bring his mother her wine.

"See?" Ammar said.

"No. I do not see. Just because she is using other men like she used Samir doesn't mean she killed him when he cut her off. Listen to her son! So many men; the loss of one did not seem to matter. You saw her face in there—why risk prison by killing him?"

"You're wrong," he said. "And I'm taking this to Grave Crimes."

33

"I'm not following you there."

"Don't," Ammar said, rudely pointing the way back. "Go home."

But Zaytuna did not move. "That woman will be questioned, maybe even arrested, then wrongfully convicted, or let go. I am surprised you would act so impulsively on the suspicion of a vulnerable woman's guilt again."

This was not the same as Mu'mina. He had been wrong there. Wrong from the start. Mu'mina scared him for reasons that still shamed him. But this woman had nearly confessed. She was threatening to kill Bashir. She was using her sons to extort money.

Zaytuna went on, her tone cutting, "If you think she procured that poison, you need to go to every apothecary in this cursed city or find a witness who saw her do it if you are going to damn her to prison."

He stood back from the force of it, but she was mistaken if she thought she could stop him.

"Did it seem to you that she had been spending money

amounting to the business loss?" She took a step forward. "Did it?"

He had let her go on for too long.

"Is that woman here?" He thrust out his arm violently, mimicking taking Salma into custody. "Do I have her?"

She sucked in a breath at the force of his response.

"I'm going to go to Shabib and Ahab and talk it through with them. I'm not going to throw her at their feet. I want to hear what evidence they have. They'll want to hear mine. We'll go from there. And, yes, I'll start by questioning the apothecaries in this neighbourhood. But her threats to that family will not go unanswered."

"How do you imagine she would kill the family? Get that boy to trip Bashir in the street?"

"My God, woman! Stop!" He walked away from her to keep from saying worse, then turned around and came right back at her. "You push and push, just like you want to buy that little girl's freedom. You think you know it all!"

She grabbed his arm, her fingers digging in. "I want Kamal Ali to buy the girl's freedom only if the family won't or can't."

"Have you considered she might be happier in the orphanage? What will taking her solve? She'll be torn away from the only people she has known? For grandparents she doesn't know?" He cocked his head. "And if you free her? And if they won't take her, is she coming to live with you?"

Her expression took on a disturbing intensity. "If she wants to stay in the orphanage, she can. Kamal Ali can pay for all of it. She won't be indentured, at least. He could find a husband for her when she is old enough."

"You've got it all solved, have you?"

She said, choking on her words, "I have to fix it."

"Fix it, then. I'm going to fix this." He left her and turned at the next street.

She ran after him. "Ammar, stop! At your best—at your best, Ammar—you are meticulous. This is not like you."

The comment hit him. "Come with me then. See for yourself who I am."

"I'm going home. Think first before you accuse her."

"I told you what I'm going to do," he shot back.

"So that's the end of it?"

He said, "I've taken this case as far as I can."

"No," she said. "You haven't questioned Sitara's family."

"What do they have to do with Salma?"

"Not her. How does Samir's death serve Ibn Hisham?"

He started to tell her his suspicion, a suspicion he had dropped when Salma's guilt came into view, but she cut him off before he could speak.

"Think of how Ibn Hisham is feeling having to take this family on. Simple, weak Samir."

"I have thought this through," he said, declining to share the rest.

"Bashir said his and Sitara's father were like brothers. But he's lied to you over and over in this case. Did Bashir do this? What's really going on?"

She was right that the implication had to be considered, but then it would be dismissed. "Bashir would not have killed his own father to secure his marriage to Sitara and then hire me to investigate it."

"I agree. It makes no sense. But you have not even explored it."

"You're the one spinning tales now," Ammar said. "All his lies can be explained by him wanting to preserve his father's reputation."

"He can't stand people thinking his father took his own life."

"No, he can't," Ammar said. "That's why he hired me. That's why he lied."

"But if the gossip hadn't come up, would he have left it alone?" Zaytuna put a hand to her forehead. "Have you seen this before? Have you seen killers trip themselves up because of their pride? He never thought you would catch him. He only thought your investigation would make people doubt Samir had killed himself."

Ammar crossed his arms. He had seen it. Plenty of times. Most murders were down to fights or petty crimes. If there were witnesses or a distinctive weapon left behind, the killers were easy to catch. Others were down to ill-thought plans they thought a few lies could cover. Some even presented themselves to the police, thinking they were invincible. But a few were tripped up because they had not counted on the mess that murder makes in the lives of the victims and found themselves exposed. She was right. He whistled. "I'll tell Shabib and Ahab that, too."

"If you are going to give them this case, then give them all the possibilities."

They walked together in silence out of the poor neighbourhood and through the surrounding estates to the Basra Gate High Road. She was the one who was agitated this time, but he did not have the power to put her at ease and, right now, did not have the patience to worry about her.

The high road was crowded. Carts moved ahead slowly, pulled by plodding donkeys. Camels burdened with heavy sacks swayed as they walked. And two horse guardsmen went past side by side, their staves high.

She stopped him before she turned south to Tutha and he toward the Round City and the offices of Grave Crimes. "Tell them everything. Don't put it all at the feet of that awful woman."

He reassured her, then let her go. As he walked, he began putting out all the evidence before him so he could present each point logically, with its evidence. Once laid out in his mind, he was ready to confront them. They would take him seriously. They were nothing but watchmen when Ammar got Ibn Marwan to hire them as his and Tein's replacements. They owed it to him to listen.

Despite the din of the city, he could hear the slapping of the moat water against the walls of the Round City before he got there. The pride he had taken in his work at Grave Crimes filled his chest. This great city—Baghdad, the centre of the Abbasid Empire—and he had been its most effective investigator of grave crimes. Two guards stood resolutely on either side of the ramp up to the Basra Gate House and another two at its arched entrance, but there were armies in the barracks below who could be mustered in a moment. A hot wind howled through the gatehouse, drying his sweat. He tugged at his robe and adjusted his belt as he passed with the throngs over the ramparts. Some stopped to touch the Solomon Gates, saying a prayer. Ammar paused with them, hoping to muster the prophet Solomon's keen mind for justice in the conversation ahead.

Shabib and Ahab slouched on the low couches, tossing an apple back and forth.

"No one died in Karkh today?" Ammar joked from the doorway.

Ahab jumped up and crossed the room to embrace him. "Brother!"

"We heard you've been investigating Samir az-Zarduzi's death," Shabib said, standing.

Ammar sat down but leaned forward intently. "I need to talk to you about that."

They sat with him. Shabib picked up the apple and took a bite out of it.

Ammar asked, "Why didn't you bring the body to the Barmakid?"

"Because the old man killed himself," Ahab said. "God forgive him."

Shabib chewed his bite of apple and murmured a prayer.

Their reverence did not answer the matter. "That corpse washer didn't have the expertise to call it."

"There was a girl at the canal," Ahab said.

"The Christian girl. I still have to question her but didn't know how to find her."

"Turned out she's a Muslim girl pretending to be Christian," Shabib said, gesturing with the apple in hand. "You know. So no one would connect her to her family."

He knew—she was there for her tryst with Girgis.

"What did she see?"

"From where she was on the road, everything. Him weeping and going down to the clearing. Him breaking the seal on a small jug. Him drinking its contents. She saw him fall to the ground, then the body when she and Girgis got there. If she weren't in a state, I don't think she would have waited there for us to question her," Ahab said. "She ran as soon as she could find her feet."

The suddenness of the evidence confused him. He pressed on, unwilling to believe it. "Samir was alone when he came down and drank it?"

"Alone," Shabib answered.

"I talked to the boy she was meeting. He never said she saw it."

"She thought God made her witness Samir's death as a warning. Wouldn't let Girgis near her to tell him anything." Shabib added, "We made her go over it a few times to see if she would change her story. It was the same."

Despite not wanting to, he trusted that they had interviewed her properly but asked, "You got the jug?"

"We did, and we got rid of it," Ahab said. "Then we took him to a corpse washer who wouldn't know what he was dealing with, although he had a good eye for the rest."

"I don't know if I would have done that," he said carefully. In fact, he knew he would not have. He and Tein would have taken the jug and the body to the Barmakid. They would have had the contents of the jug tested. They would have had the body examined. They would have found who prepared the poison for him and arrested him. They would have told the family the truth and let them decide what stayed a secret and what did not. Tein complained about the corruption of the police, but now he saw it was more than payouts and favours—these men called it a natural death to spare the feelings of the family, spurring on his investigation, resulting in harmful secrets being revealed and threatening a marriage. Who were they to see themselves as dispensers of mercy like this? Justice was taking a case to its end. The only concession was that now he had an idea of who had prepared the poison and could tell Ibn Ali.

"So, can we assume your case is closed?" Shabib asked.

"Are you certain?"

He had no idea what he looked like in that moment, let alone an idea of what he was feeling. But whatever it was, it made Ahab get up and sit beside him and take his hand. "My brother. Yes. We are certain."

What was left? He said, "My case is closed."

34

———————

DAY SEVEN

It was early yet, but the brothel seemed busy. The guard was seated on the bench, coolly watching men stagger out as if they did not know what hit them, except for one who rubbed his belly, having eaten the meal of his life.

Saliha started toward it, but Zaytuna held her back. "The food stall first."

A pot was simmering behind him. Zaytuna smelled the tang of meat braising in date syrup and soured with vinegar. She greeted Abdussamad with a compliment to his cooking, "Delicious. Sikbaj."

"A favourite of the people and the caliphs." He bowed slightly. "You're back?"

"Yes. Alhamdulillah."

He took Saliha in, saying, "Who is this gracious woman you have brought to this most unladylike corner of the market?"

Saliha did not reply with equal flirtation but presented herself as a professional. "Not a lady, a corpse washer. I advise my colleague on her cases."

His tone flattened with disappointment. "You're too late for the body."

"Not too late to question people at that gracious establishment about the nature of her death."

"Why not just ask her father? I hear he was with her to the end." He tugged on his beard. "Why ask at all?"

They were there to determine if the woman in red was Fatima before going to Auntie Hakima. But this man was not owed an answer, and Saliha simply stared him down.

He sucked his teeth at her, then turned to Zaytuna, gesturing at the orphanage. "They've already got Gul's daughter sweeping."

There were children playing in front of the orphanage, while the matron of the place watched, leaning against the open gate. She was a tall, broad-shouldered Sindi woman with a plain, gentle face. She wore her wrap like an apron and tied up her hair in a bright kerchief.

"Only four," Zaytuna said with worry.

"How old when you began?"

The question surprised her. No one took her for a woman of poverty anymore, and she felt she had lost some of herself since she had learned how to hold a delicate spoon.

"Once one of us, always one of us." He bowed his head slightly.

She did not know whether to thank the man for seeing her for who she was or deny that her life had been as she imagined. Even when she and Tein had wandered from town to town with her mother, she had never had to work like Layla. They never had to endure what this child would face.

"Have you seen the grandfather recently?"

"He visits the girl every day now."

Zaytuna considered if she wanted to run into him or not.

"Already left for the day."

That answered that question, at least. But it raised the idea that she should speak to him alone. All this time following him, knowing his business, knowing he was a good man. He deserved the chance to speak for himself.

"That must mean the grandparents haven't the money," Saliha remarked to Zaytuna. "Or the brothel has decided not to release the girl."

Knowing Saliha would not advise her against herself, she said, "Tell me what to do."

She screwed up her face as if she were thinking hard, then Saliha opened her eyes wide as she found the answer. "Meddle."

Abdussamad laughed, then leaned over the counter. "What were you thinking?"

"We need to speak to the woman who runs the orphanage," Zaytuna said.

Saliha asked, "What is her name?"

Zaytuna answered, but with a questioning glance for Abdussamad, "Umm al-Yatama?"

"Yes, Shivani by birth, but no one calls her that."

"Mother of the orphans," Saliha said as they walked away. "What will we ask her?"

"I want to find out how the girl is doing, but also how much it costs to release her."

The matron had gone back inside, so they entered the gate. The courtyard was wide and clean. There were low couches with plenty of pillows under the second-floor arcades. Flowering plants were set out around a basin of water at the centre. Small birds flitted in and out, bathing and sipping water. Children were learning the Quran by rote in a nearby room.

The teacher called out, "*Wa duha, wa layli idha sajja—*"

"*Wa duha,*" they repeated in tiny, high voices.

Zaytuna nodded, hand to her heart, answering the sign of the verse, accepting its reminder—God's declaration to Muhammad when he thought all was lost that He would never abandon him.

A boy came around from the back, maybe twelve years old, carrying a sack with tools. He seemed well-fed and content. Even his work clothes were soundly made and cared for. But if he were one of them, he would still not be free.

She stopped him. "Assalamu alaykum."

"Wa alaykum assalam, Aunties."

"We're looking for Gul's daughter. God have mercy on Gul's soul."

"Amin. Yasmin's in Quran class. Do you want me to get Umm al-Yatama?"

"Please."

The boy went back the way he came, rather than yell for her.

None of this was what she had expected. Had she imagined they would be tortured? The girl would be in the kitchen scrubbing the grate while her peers were playing? That they would be roughly hewn, like Layla and the children who used to run up and down her old street?

The matron came out to them with a welcoming posture, but Zaytuna saw the fierce protectiveness of a mother in her large, expressive eyes. Her clothes carried the scent of an incense she did not know, but it was comforting, and she imagined the children in her arms.

"Assalamu alaykum," she said. "How can I help you?"

Zaytuna hesitated, unsure now how to proceed, and Saliha stepped into the breach.

"Wa alaykum assalam." I am the women and children's corpse washer for the Barmakid Hospital. We advise the police on cases."

"There's no case here. There's been no police." Her eyes narrowed, not out of hostility, but concern. "Do you mean poor Gul? She died of fever."

"Did you see her yourself?"

"God raise her up. The fever visited everyone. We kept

away. I went to Gul's bedside at the end when she asked to see her daughter, when we all knew she was not coming back from it."

"Heartbreaking," Saliha said, her voice catching. "The sweet child. The mother saying farewell."

Tears welled in Umm al-Yatama's eyes, and she wiped them with the back of her hand. "Yasmin's only calm comes when she is reciting God's words. I hold her until she falls asleep, then her bedmate curls up next to her, taking care of her until morning. She won't play, so we try to keep her busy other ways." She smiled sadly. "I gave her a hand broom, and she seems to like sweeping the dust around."

So they did not have her cleaning after all. Zaytuna wished she could kiss the woman's cheek in thanks.

"Has she no other family?" Saliha asked.

"Her grandfather comes. A good man. He treats all the children as his own. We'll miss the both of them when they go."

Zaytuna touched Saliha's hand in excitement. "She's going to live with her grandparents?"

"Not yet. If you work with the police, you know how this goes. Them over there do not let the children stay for free, and they won't let them go for free. He can't afford to take her yet, but I know the man. He'll find a way."

Zaytuna nodded to Saliha to let her know she had all she needed. She said to the matron, "Alhamdulillah, these children have you to care for them."

"I was one of them," she said. "I'll stand by them to the end of my days."

They left, and the sound of the children's voices reciting the same chapter of the Quran carried them out. "*Alam yajiduka yatiman fa'awa.*"

Saliha said, "Did you hear that?"

Moved, she put her hand over her heart to hold God's love

closer to her, repeating the line: "*And did God not find you an orphan and shelter you?*"

Saliha leaned into her, wiping her eyes.

As they crossed the small square, Abdussamad called out to them. "What did you find?"

They ignored him. Zaytuna was unwilling to give him anything after having so wrongly characterized the life of the orphanage and Yasmin's fate and went to the brothel.

The same young man sat on the bench in front of the building. He stood as they approached.

"Good morning. How can I help you?"

"Bright morning to you," Saliha said. "We are from the Barmakid Hospital. We work with the police to confirm the cause of death in women and children."

"I never heard of that before."

Without missing a beat, Saliha said, "It is a study by the esteemed Dr. ar-Razi into causes of death in the city."

His eyes narrowed, but this one did so with skepticism. "The city is crawling with corpse washers asking after the dead?"

"Only where there has been a sweep of illness."

He relented, at least a little. "It was a hard time. A few are still sick in there."

"We were given the name of one woman in particular to interview." She turned toward Zaytuna as if she could not remember her name.

"Fatouma," Zaytuna piped up. "An African woman?"

"African? No, you got that wrong. She's an Arab through and through." He shook his head at the thought of her. "When she's not on her back, she's praying or crawled under the stairwell, rocking back and forth, muttering something. It's putting off the customers. I can't see her working here much longer."

It had to be Fatima. She tugged on Saliha's hand so they could leave.

But Saliha asked, "Can we speak to her?"

Zaytuna jumped in. "That won't be necessary—"

"You couldn't, anyway. She's got the fever."

"Not too bad?" Saliha asked.

"She'll live." He stood back, reassessing them. "Not like Gul."

Saliha remarked dryly, "So you do have news of the dead."

"I'd say you already knew about her," he said suspiciously.

"As I said," she answered plainly. "The corpse washer reported the death to the Barmakid, alerting us to come to you."

"May God heal them all." Zaytuna held out her hands in prayer.

"Amin," he and Saliha answered her prayer.

They thanked him and went, but he called after them, "Why Fatouma? Who told you to ask after her by name?"

Zaytuna grabbed Saliha's elbow and hurried her out of the square.

"Is that your Fatima?"

"Yes. He described a certain practice we do under the stairs. It must be her."

"She won't be working there long, especially now we've asked after her."

Maybe Ammar and Nasifa would judge her harshly, as she now had to prepare Auntie Hakima for Fatima's expulsion from the brothel, but she did not care.

"You did not ask about the cost to release Yasmin. What will you do?"

Zaytuna looked at her seriously. "Meddle."

35

Bashir and the rest of the family were not home. Their servant directed him to Ibn Hisham's estate. When Ammar objected to bothering them there, the man said Bashir had insisted. The walk was a fair distance, outside of Karkh and past the northern bridge crossing the Tigris. It was midday by the time he arrived. He expected Bashir and Basma's reaction to the evidence that their father had killed himself to be volatile but their mother to be relieved it was over. For their sakes, he hoped he could get them alone.

As he neared Ibn Hisham's neighbourhood, the estates became grander, the walls taller, and the houses set back behind large outer courtyards, no doubt matching private inner courtyards set aside for women and guests. No expense was spared. The wide-arched gates to these homes were intricately tiled, and their walls were dripping with jasmine and other vining plants. When he found the estate, he walked past the gate to the servants' entrance, hoping he would have better luck getting Bashir alone that way.

A maid answered almost immediately. She was a red-haired Syrian with creamy skin set off by shades of blue in her uniform and seemed proud of her beauty. He hoped the housekeeper kept an eye on her; there was no trusting men of this class with their servants.

"I am Ghazi Ammar at-Tabbani. Bashir ibn Samir az-Zarduzi asked me to come to deliver an important message. He and his family are guests of Ibn Hisham. But I need to see him privately."

"Come in."

As he passed her in the doorway, she wrinkled her nose. His temper flared. He had bathed before he left. He had used Nasifa's alum stone. But he had to work. He had to walk nearly out of Baghdad itself to come here. Was he supposed to rent a horse or donkey, pay to be taken in the back of a cart, or maybe they would prefer he be carried in a litter with servants rubbing him down with musk?

He followed her into a hallway that led to several rooms, each used to store household items: fuel for the kitchen, bags of grain and legumes, fresh fruits, and jars upon jars of preserved fruits and vegetables. The excess was more than he cared to imagine.

She paused before a room, opening the door for him. "If you would like to use our room for ablutions."

He went in without thanking her. The room had high windows. The floor was stone, with a sluice leading out under the wall. There was a tap over a low basin with soap and a bench beside it with a bottle of orange flower water and folded towels. He undressed down to his underclothes and let the cold water run over his head. It was a shock, but he washed, dried off, doused his clothes with orange flower water, and came out as quickly as he could.

When he came out, the girl was gone, and a male servant was waiting for him.

"The families have gathered and are waiting for you."

"Both? My message was to see Bashir Ibn Samir privately."

"Nevertheless, they insist."

The servant led him to a vast room. Carpets covered the floors from end to end. In the centre of the room, a tray table wider than his arm span held the detritus of a meal. Two servants came in and carried it away. Low couches hugged the walls, each upholstered in gold brocade with thick tassels. Small tables were set out. He would have expected the extended family to be there before a wedding, but it was only Ibn Hisham, his wife, and son, and Sitara on one couch, while Bashir, his mother, and Basma were on the other. None moved to greet him.

"Assalamu alaykum. Ibn Samir, if I could speak to you privately?"

His back was straight. "Anything you have to say, you should say to all of us."

Ibn Hisham inclined his head. "We are family."

He gave Bashir a hard look to say he would not like it, but he waved him on.

"Please," Ibn Hisham gestured for him to sit.

He did, but with enough distance that he would not have to endure their comments over any lingering scent. The news would be shocking enough.

Ammar placed his hands flat on his knees and came out with it. "I have compelling evidence that your father took his own life."

The women gasped, and Bashir's mother shrieked, "I told you. We should never have prayed for him," and then fainted into her daughter's arms.

Never should have prayed for him. Now he understood why she would not let Bashir take the body with the porters or go to the hospital that morning. Why she resisted the case. Then it hit him. That's why Samir killed himself out at the canal. It was where he went to watch the birds and have some peace, and where he thought no one would know how to find his family. Ammar hated to admit it, but unknown to them, Shabib and Ahab had respected Samir's dying wish. He had hoped to disappear for good and save his wife exactly this.

Ibn Hisham's wife and daughter rushed to her. The servant left the room. But Ibn Hisham's son seemed strangely vindicated and turned to his father, who nodded curtly in reply. Ibn Hisham got up, indicating for the men to follow him.

"I tried to warn you," Ibn Hisham said to Bashir.

"Ghazi, how do you know?" Bashir demanded of Ammar.

Ammar joined the men. "Do you want me to tell everyone or just you?"

The servant returned with an older woman who hurried to attend to Umm Bashir.

Sitara left the women and stood beside Bashir.

Her father turned to her, saying gently. "My dear, this conversation is for the men."

Sitara's expression and stance were firm. She was not leaving.

He expected some back and forth, but Ibn Hisham gave in immediately. He saw exactly how this ill-matched marriage was going forward. Sitara had him wrapped around her finger. But not her brother. He glanced at his father with disgust. No doubt, if he had had his way, his sister would have been sent away.

"An eyewitness saw Samir walk down to the canal with a small, sealed jug, break the seal, drink the poison, and die."

"No one forced him?" Bashir said, hoping still.

"Not at the scene, no."

"What does that mean?" Ibn Hisham asked.

"By all accounts, Samir was suffering physically, but he was also suffering under other pressures." Ammar gave Bashir a look, offering him the opportunity to stop the discussion now. But he gazed at him as if he had no idea what was coming. "As you know, he had made a mess of the finances of the new shop, which caused him distress."

"We warned you," Ibn Hisham's son said, mirroring his father.

But his father held out a hand to silence him. "Yes, Keyvan, we did. But obviously he had to hear it from this little, ill-kempt man."

Ammar wished he could see Ibn Hisham in battle—there he would find out what mattered in the stench of bodies and blood.

"Please," Bashir said to Ibn Hisham, then addressed Ammar. "Have you found out where the money was going?"

Bashir knew about Salma. What was he thinking? Ammar went ahead, staring right at him as he answered. "The woman he tried to push out of the way of the cart was badly injured and blamed your father. There's more to it than that, but she had been extorting him for weekly sums."

Keyvan gestured questioningly at Bashir. "You told us it was a man. A man from Jerusalem."

Bashir put his hand on his heart, shaking his head, as if this were the first he was hearing it. "That is what my father told me. My poor father, he tried to protect us to the last."

The man was a good liar. Ammar began looking at him with new eyes. "It doesn't account for all his losses, but it does at least point to additional reasons that he took his own life."

Bashir pressed, "Did she give him the poison?"

He wished it were not so, but Zaytuna might be right. Bashir's behaviour began to point to his wanting his father out of the way of this marriage. Did he give his father the poison? It seemed insane, but as Zaytuna pointed out, his desire to protect his father's reputation outstripped the logic of self-preservation.

"We have no evidence of that," Ammar answered. "I spoke to Grave Crimes. They knew he had killed himself and withheld the information to make things easier for the family. If anyone provided him with the poison, they are not going to look into it. It's done."

"No!" Bashir took a step toward him. "You must! There must be justice!"

The man was mad. What if new evidence pointed to him? "I can question the apothecary who I believe made the poison, but that's all."

"You must find out!"

Ibn Hisham said to Bashir, nodding to Ammar. "Consider your mother, Bashir. There is no need to take this any further. I suggest you accept the conclusions of Grave Crimes."

Sitara had been watching the conversation intently, especially her father and brother. She finally spoke, and with finality. "This news, as tragic as it is, will not delay the marriage."

"Dear, it is too soon," Ibn Hisham said, his hand out.

Keyvan ignored them both and directed his comments to Bashir. "You have stirred up talk everywhere. I have been forced to defend you and your family in my own circles. It is an insult to have to answer any gossip whatsoever."

"Bashir and I will marry as planned," Sitara said, shoulders thrown back. "It was going to be a small celebration. Now, we will limit it to our guardians alone." She turned to her father. "You will sign the marriage contract."

Ibn Hisham's lips trembled slightly. What hold could a daughter have over her father?

But Keyvan stepped in. "And the gossip from that?"

She hissed, "Curse the gossip!"

Her outburst brought Ibn Hisham back to life, reminding him perhaps that he was her father, not her servant. "Sitara!" He took hold of her wrist. "I give you too much rein, but this is beyond all scope. We will wait and allow the gossip about his death and your hurried celebrations to be forgotten." He addressed Ammar with a tone that meant he wished he did not have to say it. "You understand me."

Ammar did. A small, hurried ceremony would suggest to all that she was pregnant.

"We wait, and months later"—she nearly spat at him—"months later when they see there is no child and they are left with nothing but their ugly suppositions?"

So she was not pregnant after all.

Keyvan glanced scathingly at his father. "If I were her guardian, there would be no marriage at all. But it is too late now. There is no way out of the ruin of your reputation and the stain on ours, as everyone will assume you lost your child."

"Reputation!" In one swift movement she took Bashir's face in her hands and kissed him.

"Sir! I—" Bashir stumbled backwards.

Ibn Hisham exclaimed, "Bashir! Now is your chance to free yourself from this terror!"

Instead, Bashir righted himself and addressed Sitara. "I will be your husband still, if you will have me."

Sitara launched herself at Bashir again, but he held up both hands, and she backed down. Not meekly in the least, but as if she were containing her fire only to please him.

Ammar watched the scene, astonished. She was spoiled, and marriage to her would be a trial. Her father's warning to Bashir was a good one, but it wasn't Ammar's place to say so.

"Bashir, you are a fool." Ibn Hisham turned to his daughter. "I am to blame for your behaviour. Your mother is weak, but I was weaker. I have ruined you. But now I will protect you."

Keyvan smiled. He took a breath to speak, but his father stopped him.

"You assured us that your father could not have committed suicide," Ibn Hisham said to Bashir. "I permitted this engagement to continue on that assumption. Yet he has killed himself as everyone suspected, and with toad on his tongue. My daughter has likewise poisoned this family with your association. I cannot permit her to marry into a family in which the disease of taking one's life lies within them."

Bashir reached out and grasped Sitara's hand, pulling her beside him and holding her close.

It was a shocking declaration of feeling and would get him nowhere.

"Walla. I will never sign your marriage contract." Ibn Hisham raised a hand to drive home his point. "Sitara, you cannot marry without your guardian's release, and I will never release you!"

Sitara finally broke, wailing, her body twisting with her scream. Bashir tried to comfort her, but she was consumed. Keyvan stepped into the chaos and pulled her away from Bashir, who could only stand aghast as his love was dragged away from him.

Sitara's mother rushed to her. "My daughter!"

Ammar reached out to Bashir. But he brushed him off, yelling, "Go! Go! You'll have your cursed money for ruining her only chance!"

There was nothing more he could do for these people. The turmoil of their lives, and they are the ones who sneer at him for how he smells and dresses? Worse, he suspected he would never see a fals in payment.

A servant led him out through the front door, the lush outer courtyard, and into the street. He stopped, turned around, and stared blankly at the shut gate. It had all happened so fast; he could barely pull together everything that had been said and done.

"Ho!"

Ammar flinched, turning toward the voice.

Khalil was grinning. "What are you doing here?"

"What?" He stood back at the surprise, then gestured to the house. "Giving those people I was working for some bad news."

"Well met, then!"

It took him a moment to shift his attention to Khalil, then he noticed how he was dressed. He could not imagine the cost. "You look like the people I just left."

He spun around on his heel. "Just the robe. My clothes are underneath. Abu Sa'id trusts me to collect at the big houses, and I must look my best."

"It's good to see you." Ammar put a hand on Khalil's shoulder. "That was—"

"Say no more. I just finished. I need to change out of this robe, then let's get back to the market, find a storyteller, and get a kabab."

Ammar, agreed, shaking his head at it all.

They walked arm in arm away from the house.

"A hard day. Tell me everything," Khalil said.

"Wait." Ammar stopped, pulling away from Khalil, a current of shock overtaking him. "The father said something. 'Toad on his tongue'."

"Toad?" Khalil shook his head, not understanding.

"It's a medicine. A poison." He grabbed Khalil's arm. "How could Ibn Hisham have known!"

Ammar took off and ran for the house, Khalil right behind him. He pounded on the gate. But before the servant could open it, Khalil threw both arms around him and dragged him away.

36

———————

Struggling under Khalil's grasp, Ammar yelled, "Ibn Hisham killed their father!"

Khalil had dragged him to the end of the street before releasing his hold and pushing Ammar up against a wall. "Come on, now!"

"Toad!" Ammar yelled, trying to force Khalil to listen. "Samir drank toad poison!"

"Crazy talk!"

"Listen, and I'll explain." Ammar grunted. "For God's sake."

Khalil stood close to Ammar with his hands at his sides, but his stance showed he could have Ammar under control as he liked. "Let me get this straight. You going to accuse Ibn Hisham of murder?"

"Yes!"

"It makes sense in your head, I'm sure. It won't once you say it. Trust me."

Ammar was puzzled, questioning why Khalil had dragged him from the house and now looked like he was waiting to wrestle him to the ground. He explained, but only to get Khalil to drop his guard, "Ibn Hisham revealed he knew Samir drank toad poison."

"You know for a fact that toad killed him?"

Bilge, the apothecary, put it in his poultice. Ibn Ali confirmed toad poison could kill him. Then Ibn Hisham said it, and that turned a possibility into a fact. But Ammar was not going to argue his logic with Khalil and answered, "Yes. Certainly. A fact."

"A slip of the tongue, Ammar. That makes him the killer?" Khalil addressed him as if he were a child who should not believe such silliness. "Who could have told him?"

"Does he know anyone at the Barmakid? Grave Crimes didn't even know. They never tested the contents of the jar. They threw it out." He continued, watching Khalil for any break in his stance. "This man is used to taking charge of everything. He might have been tracking his whole investigation."

"Ammar, you don't know how this sounds."

"I have to go back to the house." Ammar watched him for a break in his stance, but he was firm.

"Maybe he knew," Khalil allowed, "but what does that prove?"

"I have to question him."

"You could never let anything go." Khalil put a hand on his arm. "It's not a good trait, Ammar."

Ammar fell into the stillness of battle. His body relaxed instead of struggling, he turned in toward Khalil and threw his fist up toward Khalil's chin. It never landed. Khalil was ready for him, dodging the blow. He grabbed Ammar's arm and dragged him around the corner, throwing him up against a stopped donkey cart, saying, "Give it up. You're getting paid."

The donkey screeched, and the driver yelled.

Ammar dropped to the ground, sliding out of Khalil's grip,

and rolled under the cart. As Khalil reached for him, he scrambled out the far side and ran back toward the house.

Khalil called after him over the donkey's brays, "Don't go back in!" Then, "Ammar!"

Ammar ran smoothly, his breath even, listening for Khalil behind him. At the gate, he checked over his shoulder. Khalil had not followed. He pounded on the gate, but it opened under his fist. Before he could enter, a watchman ran past him and into the house, a servant right behind him. He followed them into the great room.

Ibn Hisham was on the floor. A dagger was shoved up and into his chest at the perfect angle to avoid his ribs and go straight into the heart. There was little blood. It would be trapped in his chest until the dagger was removed.

Keyvan had hold of Sitara. She was thrashing in his grasp. Bashir was trying to wrest her away from her brother. Ibn Hisham's wife and Bashir's mother were in a heap on the floor, wailing.

"Someone move those women to another room!" Ammar commanded, gesturing to the servants huddling in the doorway, staring.

"Are you mad!" Keyvan yelled, shoving his sister at Bashir.

He did not know if Keyvan meant him or Bashir, but it did not matter. The servants did not move, and Ammar was stuck having to think around the wailing. He approached the body to make sure of the angle of the blade. If either Bashir or Sitara had killed Ibn Hisham, it was a lucky thrust. But he did not need a witness to tell him they did not do it. Khalil's presence confirmed it was a hit.

He got up to get the watchman, who was standing in the archway, gaping.

Ammar took hold of him. "Go to Grave Crimes, but for

Karkh. The Basra Gate office. Tell them Ammar at-Tabbani said to come." He shook the watchman. "Listen! Not here. Karkh."

He nodded, his eyes filled with terror, and ran off.

"Who did this?" Ammar demanded.

"A man came in from the street," Keyvan said, struggling to control his shock.

"Don't lie to me. The police are going to be here soon. No one just walks into a house like this and stabs its master to death."

The servant who guarded the gate said, "We let him in. He was dressed as you are and said he was your partner."

"My partner—my partner is a woman. What did he look like?"

The servant was scared but reported his features like he had been a watchman once. "Large. Muscular. A Sindi. Nose flattened to the side."

It had to be the little caliph's man. The one on the couch. They don't kill debtors. That could only mean Ibn Hisham had a debt that had crossed a line. But what had al-Multani said before Ammar left? "This is a lot of work for nothing." Ammar recalled he had only told al-Multani he was investigating the reasons for Samir's suicide. Not murder. And he had not truly considered Ibn Hisham for it yet. Was he reading too much into it? Unless—Ammar allowed himself—unless al-Multani knew Ibn Hisham killed Samir and was warning Ammar not to bother looking for the killer because he would be dead soon anyway for what he owed. Who would believe him if he recounted it? But this was not spinning tales.

Sitara let go of Bashir, recovered enough to stand on her own, and answered, "A man used to violence." She was still trembling, but unlike her brother, there was no grief. Ammar watched as her expression transformed sickeningly from shock to exultation before his eyes. She was happy to see her father dead. This family—he only hoped Bashir would get free of them now.

Tein was right. Khalil was there to distract him from the case, to make sure no one talked to him. And he was on the spot today to drag Ammar away from the house so he would not be there for the hit. Ammar left, going out into the street to see if Khalil was waiting.

No one was outside other than normal passersby. A man pulled a dung cart with a shovel to clean the street. No one gathered out front of these estates, sitting on stools in front of their houses, chatting, or observing the comings and goings. The neighbourhood was quiet and empty, but the news of the killing would travel through it soon enough.

Back inside, Sitara was trying to move her mother out of the room with the help of a female servant, but she broke free of them and threw herself on her husband's body and pulled out the dagger. The blood seeped out of the wound in Ibn Hisham's chest. With a great wail that shook her body, she held the dagger above her as if to take her own life. Her son snatched it from her but did not offer her any comfort. She fell onto her husband's body again, pressing her hands on the wound. Sitara stood rigidly beside her. Bashir's mother and daughter joined Ibn Hisham's wife on the floor, answering her cries with their own.

Bashir stepped forward, finally sensible. "Ghazi, what are you going to do?"

Keyvan waved him off. "This is not your family. Take your women and leave."

In the time that Ammar had gone to the street and come back, Keyvan had gotten himself under control. More than that, Ammar realized, he was determined. There was work to do. It was more than a family member realizing that someone had to be responsible in the moment. The son had taken the helm.

Ammar recognized it. It was the face of the father. Keyvan was now the commander.

But commander of what? An import-export business that had taken a loan so great his father was killed for it? The message was clear: the debt had to be paid. Ammar did not care how Keyvan would do it or that it meant this family was about to see the end of their sumptuous life and the reputation he had been protecting.

Ammar said to Keyvan, "I need to talk to you."

"Why are you still here?"

"I was the lead investigator for Grave Crimes in Karkh. You want me here."

"I will wait for the real police to arrive." He went into the adjoining room, and Ammar followed him.

There was a writing desk set out on the floor with a bejewelled inkwell and fine pens. Keyvan opened a large inlaid cabinet, then turned toward Ammar, his hand in a large casket. He called out to Bashir in the other room. "How much do you owe this man?"

Bashir either could not hear him or chose not to answer.

He filled a purse with coins. "The tribulations I have inherited from my father. I will not be so weak."

"I don't want your money."

"Bashir can repay me once he gets hold of his senses," he said disdainfully, holding out the purse to him.

Ammar crossed his arms instead of taking it. "Your father said that Samir died with 'toad on his tongue'. What did he mean?"

Keyvan snapped his fingers, and a servant entered. "Help him out."

Ammar left without help or the coins. No matter what anyone wanted, this case was not closed. Ammar was going to confront Khalil's boss, Abu Sa'id, and get the truth out of him.

37

Ammar walked back to Karkh using the route the investigators for Grave Crimes were likely to take from the Round City. It was not long before he saw them walking briskly and no doubt raising a stink in the midday heat. He snorted, hoping they knocked Keyvan to the floor with it.

"Assalamu alaykum!" Ammar called out.

"Wa alaykum assalam. Why aren't you at the house?" Ahab asked.

"They kicked me out."

Shabib raised an eyebrow. "Oh?"

This time Ammar did not hold back, the tension of the day releasing in a tirade. "You were wrong to bury the evidence. Samir may have drunk that poison on his own, but Ibn Hisham made it happen. He knew what was in it."

"How do you know?" Shabib asked. He was concerned but calm, despite Ammar coming at him.

"Because I was doing your job for you! I questioned the apothecaries. One was giving him toad venom for his pain. The body—the signs were there!"

"What signs?" Ahab blanched, realizing their error.

"The boat hand told me about the vomit. The evidence you wiped away."

Shabib said, "Tell us what Ibn Hisham said."

"He said that Samir died with toad on his tongue."

Shabib shook his head. "Samir could have told him what was in his medicine."

In the scuffle with Khalil and the chaos of the hit, the simple truth did not occur to him. It was the most obvious answer, and he hated it because it veered away from his assumptions and gave those two an out. He objected lamely, "And Ibn Hisham did not try to stop him?"

"There is no crime in that," Shabib answered.

"He wanted that man dead."

"There is no crime in that either."

But Ahab cut in, hand out in declaration. "None. Except before God."

He meant it to calm Ammar down, but it was not working.

Ahab continued. "What happened? We could not get much from the watchman."

Feeling caught out, he said too much. "I was there to speak to Bashir. Ibn Hisham mentioned the toad, but it didn't hit me until I left. I ran back, and Ibn Hisham was already dead."

"Ammar. The killing. What did you see?" Shabib asked.

"It was a hit. A man said he was my partner to gain entrance, then stabbed Ibn Hisham in the heart, up through the ribs."

"Whoever wanted him dead knew you were there," Ahab said.

"Why is that?" Shabib asked.

Ammar did not want Khalil brought into it yet—let alone raise what al-Multani had said pointing towards a debt owed—not until he had followed every line of inquiry himself. He hedged, "I wasn't making a secret of the fact that I was investigating the death."

Shabib looked at Ahab. "Ibn Marwan needs to be brought in on this immediately. We both don't need to be at the scene. One of us should go back to the office."

There it was. Ibn Marwan was being brought in. Whoever ordered the hit was going to request a favour, and it would be honoured. There would be silence. The case was out of his hands if he could not get what he could before their sergeant got involved. He needed an excuse to keep them both on the scene. "The son, Keyvan, he's acting strangely. He knows something about why Ibn Hisham was killed. I would have wanted a partner to work the questioning effectively and capture what he has to say."

Shabib took it in, then agreed. "Better we bring a full picture to Ibn Marwan."

"I remember too well," Ammar said. "You got that right."

"Anything else?" Ahab asked.

"I don't want to colour your interpretation of the case. Let's meet later today or tomorrow to discuss what we all saw."

Shabib's face told it all. He did not want Ammar involved, and for good reason. The last time the two of them were in front of Ibn Marwan, the sergeant had offered to fire them to get Ammar back. In the past few years they had established themselves as reliable investigators, but some humiliations never go away. Shabib answered in the only way he could, "Inshallah." Meaning, only if God wills it, because certainly Shabib would not.

Ammar left them to it, turning off on a side road and heading straight to Abu Sa'id's office.

There was a guard in the alley this time. He was as big as Khalil but dressed like a soldier fresh from the frontier. This one's cuirass had been proudly beaten in battle.

"Ghazi, I'm a friend of Khalil, and your boss knows me."

He smiled slightly at the recognition of his status. "Name, Ghazi, sir?"

"Ammar at-Tabbani."

The guard stuck his head into the office, announced him, then waved him on.

The boss was sitting behind his desk, as usual. Butrus was scratching away at his books.

"Assalamu alaykum, sir."

"Wa alaykum assalam. If you are looking for Khalil, he is off on business today."

Ammar stood uncomfortably in the centre of the small room. "I know. I met him."

Abu Sa'id inclined his head. "Did he get you away in time?"

"I thought you did not kill debtors."

"Did he get you away?"

"Yes."

"You can thank him for that. Although I appreciated his reasoning."

"Which was?"

"That if you were there, you would follow it up, and that would lead to more heartbreak. But here you are. So, I can only assume he did not get you away far enough."

"It wasn't Khalil's fault. He tried. Ibn Hisham said something before I left that made me want to question him again. I had to fight Khalil to get back, so you know. But I got there just after the killer had left."

"Are you going to follow it up?"

"I'm a private investigator now. I do what I'm paid to do."

"And has someone paid you to investigate Ibn Hisham's death?"

"No."

"Then why are you here?"

"I have to know."

He shook his head slightly. "I told Khalil this would happen. I will say what I can."

"I thought you did not kill debtors," he said again.

"Then you may surmise that he was not in debt."

"No?" Ammar did not understand. Why would a man working for the little caliph be hired to kill him? Why would Abu Sa'id know at all, if not?

"The word was out on him. That's all I will say. When you told us about your case and I realized you might get mixed up in this, I told Khalil to go around with you so your name did not become attached to Ibn Hisham's fate."

He took a step forward. "It wasn't to keep them from talking to me?"

"No. It was to demonstrate that you were under our protection."

Ammar's chest tightened. He had no idea how close he had come to leaving his wife a widow and his son an orphan.

"I hope you are smart enough to know that your curiosity should end here."

"I don't know about that," he said through his fear.

"What do you think you are going to get out of it?"

"Answers."

"Answers are overrated."

"Fine. Justice, then."

"For whom? Samir az-Zarduzi? Justice was done."

Abu Sa'id's answer could only point to Ibn Hisham's guilt. He let go of the sensible explanation that Samir had told Ibn Hisham about his poultice. Just like al-Multani had said, Ammar's case was "a lot of work for nothing." But why would debt collectors seek justice over the death of an embellisher? Ammar almost laughed, considering that Samir's work was the favourite of one of them—maybe al-Multani—and this was their revenge. He asked straight out, "Why do you want justice for Samir? What did Ibn Hisham do?"

"I can't answer. But you need to accept that what you want is done."

"The police will be asking questions."

"We would expect nothing less, but Ibn Marwan has already been apprised."

"Before?"

"In negotiation with," Abu Sa'id said.

Another man would have smiled patronizingly at Ammar or given a knowing shrug. Telling him was a kind of honour from Abu Sa'id. But Ammar still felt like a fool for thinking favours were only done after the fact, not in collusion with the police. And he felt more the fool because Tein had warned him about this, too. But he refused to believe that Shabib and Ahab were in on it. Their weakness was mercy clouding their judgment, not a desire for power. They would never accept what their sergeant had done.

"You must stand down," Abu Sa'id said. He knocked his ring against the table and took up his prayer beads to seal it.

If Ammar had any sense at all, he would listen. But his sense did not extend as far as backing down. He felt a fool because he should have known, not because he got involved. "Sir," he said, "I am grateful for your protection." Ammar put his hand over his heart and bowed his head, pausing for a moment to drive home that he understood what the man had done for him and to cover what he suspected Abu Sa'id could see—that he was a man who did not know how to give up. There was also what he did not see —Nasifa would rather have him dead than a coward, and Ammar would never give his son reason to be ashamed. It was time to call in Tein's favour.

38

————————

Ammar had to bang on Zaytuna's gate to be heard over the din inside. The children were screaming. Everything he had seen and heard and what he needed to do next turned their play into raw, senseless noise. Zaytuna opened the gate, hiding behind it. She was smiling, out of breath, and dressed for home, her hair wrapped high.

Her face fell when she saw him, and she waved him in. "What happened?"

Tein was watching the children intently and had not noticed Ammar arrive. Nasifa was seated next to Saliha, chatting, and she only looked up once he was well inside—then she was beside him in an instant, her hand on his cheek, looking him over for injuries. How must he seem that she would do that?

Ammar took her hand and kissed it. "I'm good."

"You are not. Sit," she said in a voice reserved for Husayn.

Zaytuna was already out of the kitchen with a cup for him by the time he was seated.

"Honey and vinegar water."

He did not notice that the children were quiet until everyone had gathered around him. The only ones missing were Yulduz and Qambar. Tein had Husayn on one hip and Nura on the other. Only then did he see that Husayn was scared. Ammar held out his arms. Tein handed over Husayn. Ammar took his son into his arms, kissed his cheek, and then buried his nose in his soft hair, the scent of his son like medicine.

"I don't want to speak in front of the children," he said, looking up.

Tein put Nura down and said, "There's a ball in my room."

She ran for it, and Husayn, now reassured, squirmed out of his father's arms to follow her, and Layla went after them both.

He asked Nasifa, "Did you tell them?"

"As you requested. They know Samir took his own life." She moved closer to him, her shoulder touching his, and he felt reassured.

"Today, I found out it was more than that. I don't understand all of it yet."

Zaytuna said, "We're listening."

Kamal Ali gestured for him to speak but said nothing.

"I was forced to tell the family at Ibn Hisham's home, in front of all of them. Bashir resisted the news, as I expected. But Ibn Hisham declared he would not sign the marriage contract releasing Sitara from his guardianship."

"That's why you're so shaken?" asked Zaytuna.

"No." He glanced at Tein. "I left, and Khalil was waiting outside, playing it like it was a coincidence."

Tein kneeled in front of him, placing a steadying hand on his knee instead of shooting the look of vindication Ammar would have expected from any other man.

"Khalil tried to lead me away from the house, but I realized Ibn Hisham had let slip he knew what poison had killed Samir."

Alarmed, Nasifa asked, "How could he know that?"

"I ran back, and Khalil tried to stop me."

Tein leaned in, lowering his voice. "He was distracting you, after all."

"Protecting me," Ammar said. He took a sip of the honey and vinegar water. It was cold and reviving, and he drank the rest as the others silently waited, except Zaytuna, who tapped her foot, sharpening her impatience.

The children squealed.

He began again. "When I got back to the house, Ibn Hisham had been killed." Ammar rolled the cup between his palms. "A dagger to the heart."

Zaytuna stopped tapping her foot. The others stared. Nasifa became very still.

"I called in Grave Crimes. The family dismissed me. Then I faced Abu Sa'id."

In the moment it took him to take a breath, Zaytuna prompted, "And?"

"I had been walking all over their hit. Khalil took me around on Abu Sa'id's orders so I wouldn't be targeted. He was at the house to make sure I wouldn't intervene and get myself killed."

Beside him, Nasifa's stillness deepened.

"Did you see the police?" Tein asked.

"I talked to Karkh Grave Crimes on my way back. They told me that Ibn Marwan would handle the fallout. But Abu Sa'id told me that Ibn Marwan had been involved, negotiating the hit with whoever called it."

Tein squeezed his knee. "Nothing changes, brother."

"What are you going to do?" Zaytuna asked.

"I want to know why Ibn Hisham was killed. I want to know if he had anything to do with Samir's death."

Kamal Ali finally spoke. "Is that wise?"

"I want to ask the same," said Saliha. She came and stood by Tein, placing a hand on his shoulder.

He nearly came back at them, astonished, but Zaytuna interrupted him. "You think Samir did not kill himself after all?"

"He was alone when he took the poison. But maybe the commander helped him along."

Zaytuna drew back. "How?"

"I'm not sure yet."

Kamal Ali asked, "Does Bashir want you to continue?"

Before he could answer, Tein interjected, "Why do you need to follow it up?"

"Justice."

Tein asked, "And knowing will give you justice?"

"There's something left, Tein. Something unanswered. I can't leave it."

Glancing quickly at Nasifa, Kamal Ali said, "Ammar, if this Abu Sa'id had to protect you, perhaps you should consider letting it go. Your family."

Instead of agreeing with Kamal Ali and demanding Ammar withdraw, Nasifa emerged from her stillness to press her shoulder against his in support.

But Tein was firm. "Your case is closed."

"Tein, wait," said Zaytuna. "The question of how Samir died is still open."

"You're taking his side because you can't let go of your case," Tein shot back.

"Not true—"

"Oh?" Tein looked at her with disgust. "If he pays the cost, how will you feel? How will you face his family?"

He could sense Nasifa wanting to speak for herself, but Kamal Ali cut her off, challenging Tein, "Zaytuna will speak."

Zaytuna answered her brother's demands. "Do you think we are mere servants to our clients? Both our cases require us to do more than our clients have asked if justice will be served."

Ammar wanted to embrace her.

"Neither one of you grasps what is at stake." Tein dragged a hand down his face and got up, moving to sit just outside their circle.

Taking her side, Ammar said, "Tell us, then. Your case. What did you decide, Zaytuna?"

She looked worriedly at Tein but answered. "We will not hurry to release the girl. I saw how she lives. She is safe there. The grandfather visits every day. But I will speak to her grandfather first, then the two together to see what they want. I will offer help from an unknown benefactor if they need it."

"Or want it," Tein scolded from his spot against the wall.

Kamal Ali cleared his throat in warning to Tein.

He bowed his head slightly in apology, but it was out of deference, not because he thought Kamal Ali was right.

"Yes, Tein. Or want it." Zaytuna said, taking her husband's arm.

She spoke as though she meant it, but her expression betrayed there would be no doubt they would accept her help. He and Zaytuna were more alike than he had considered. Neither one of them was willing to give up on setting things right, and for a moment he was glad it was her with him at the office and not Tein. But he had come to ask Tein to honour his promise.

Ammar got up to sit closer to him. His shoulders were tense, anticipating Tein's reaction. "Would you take me to meet Razba?"

Kamal Ali asked, "Who?"

Tein swung his head around. "He is Ghuraba. A leader. A dangerous man."

"He is an acquaintance of YingYue's father," Zaytuna explained. "They have a mutual interest in printing, but he also joins Tein and the other men when they discuss philosophy."

Tein ignored her, still staring at Ammar in disbelief. "What could you want from him?"

"If anyone can tell me why Ibn Hisham was hit, it's him."

"He gave us information before out of respect for Abu Ying-Yue. If you go to him now, you'll be the one owing him a favour. It's not like owing Abu Sa'id."

Zaytuna turned to Nasifa. "What do you have to say?"

Nasifa answered her evenly, "I trust my husband's judgment."

His perfect wife. Ammar gazed at her with pride, and she nodded to him in encouragement.

Tein stood to get away from Ammar. "You don't even want to be seen at their mastaba without invitation."

But Ammar followed him. "Take me to Abu YingYue's paper shop and speak for me."

Saliha rushed to Tein's side. "This is not what he offered."

Tein took her hand, pulling her close as if he needed her for strength.

"Take me," Ammar said.

Tein said with warning, "You want Abu YingYue to ask him to help you so you won't have to pay him back. But Abu YingYue may have to pay back Razba. You may not care, but I won't endanger him."

"Is this true?" Zaytuna touched Ammar's sleeve. "You cannot put Abu YingYue at risk."

She was not what he thought after all, and he turned on her. "You of all people—you who cannot leave one cursed thing alone in the name of justice—say this to me?"

Kamal Ali stepped forward, his expression threatening, but Zaytuna ended it before her husband had to get into a fight he could not win, saying, "We can continue this discussion later." She turned to Nasifa. "The children are tired."

Nasifa got up. "I agree." She went to collect Husayn.

Out of nowhere, Zaytuna grasped Ammar's arm, whispering, "I had a vision of this. I haven't told you. It was warning that you would push against a door that could be opened by other means, and it would not end well for you. Please, Ammar. Trust me."

So this was why she decided not to stand with him. A vision. He had no time for it and said sharply, "You tell me the other means, then."

She started to object, but Kamal Ali stood beside her. "My wife does not speak lightly. If she is giving you a warning, I suggest you heed it. Still, you will do as you must. But I tell you now, do not involve this family in your plans. Nothing you do will harm a member of this household."

First the threatening look, ready to fight. Now this. He had always been the kind man who overpaid everyone to churn his butter and did whatever his wife asked of him. His courage for the sake of his family soothed Ammar's temper enough to clasp his hand and vow, "Never."

Nasifa returned, settling Husayn in his arms. She said to Kamal Ali, "My husband stands for justice, just like your wife. But with a difference. My husband is a man of the battlefield. I welcomed it and the dangers it brings when I married him. I could never love a man who could be otherwise."

Zaytuna said encouragingly, "Not a goat herder."

Nasifa smiled at Ammar. "I will not leave you should you choose to herd goats, but do not test me."

He could take down armies with her by his side. They left to mumbled and cold farewells, and when the gate shut behind them, he said, "My Zaynab."

She glowed under the honour of the name and asked as they walked away, "How will you find this Razba, then?"

"Tein will help in the end. He promised."

39

DAY EIGHT

"I need to get ready," Zaytuna said. "Girgis should be here soon."

Still shocked by Ammar's recklessness, Tein said, "I don't think Nasifa understands what it will mean for her husband to owe Razba."

"Do not underestimate her. I know that speech was exactly what he needed to hear. He has been fretting over not being the husband she wanted, so she told him yesterday, and, if I can read his face, he believed her."

"Oh, he believed her," Tein said. "She may have told him what he needed to hear, but she also told him to go find Razba."

"We don't know what she's said since. But it's true. She will support him."

Saliha emerged from the bedroom, tucking the end of her wrap at her waist as she crossed the courtyard. "You two look as if you are planning something."

"Discussing Ammar." But she had it half-right—Zaytuna was wondering how to ask Tein to protect Ammar but not compromise himself as he had on the simplest job he had done for her.

Yulduz came out of the kitchen, wiping her hands on her apron. "Where's the girl?"

"Layla? Ate breakfast and left with Farhana."

"Now?"

Zaytuna shared her concern. It was still early. She expected Abdulghafur was waiting for Layla on the banks of the canal to watch the birds fishing for their breakfast. But her friend was with her, so at least they would not be alone.

"And the little one?"

"In our room with Kamal Ali. What is it, Yulduz?"

"You can't leave that girl in the orphanage. I know you said it's a good place, and the matron is kind, but it's not the same as being with 'er family. I tell you, it's not the money. That man is afraid of 'is wife." She nudged her. "You have to speak to them."

She glanced at her bedroom door, wondering if Kamal Ali had heard Yulduz. He must have; the old woman's voice could carry across the clanging at the Seffarine Market.

"I understand," Zaytuna said. "It feels as if we have left Layla behind."

"My point." Yulduz jabbed her arm. "Let's go tell that old biddy ourselves."

Qambar limped out of their room, and Yulduz gestured for him to speak up. "Come now. Tell her what you told me last night."

"Huh?" He shook his head, then remembered. "Sometimes a man needs a push, Zaytuna."

Zaytuna deflected. "Is that how you fell in love with Yulduz?"

He still gazed at her as if she were the wild Turkmen girl he had met when they were barely older than Layla now.

"Meddling," Saliha said, passing them. "I support it."

Tein retreated to his room, sucking his teeth at them.

"You know we're right," Saliha called after him.

Kamal Ali came out, Nura sound asleep in his arms. "She was awake and ready a moment ago."

Zaytuna longed to hold Nura but left the little girl resting on her father's chest.

"Do you want to know what I think?" Kamal Ali asked.

"Mmm," she answered, then kissed Nura's little hand, whispering, "I love you, kitten."

"Talk to her husband alone. Not her. Give him a chance." Kamal Ali gave her an indulgent smile. "I suspect he needs another woman to give him the courage to speak to his wife."

She kissed his cheek in thanks, and he gazed at her lovingly.

"When you two are done," Yulduz said, "let's go."

Tein came out, tightening his belt, ready to leave for work with Kamal Ali. "I heard."

"And?" Zaytuna asked.

"It's a good idea," he said reluctantly.

"Where is Saliha?" She wished her friend had witnessed the men telling her to meddle.

Tein shrugged. "Must have left for work."

"But she was just here."

Kamal Ali said, "We're taking Nura with us to work."

"Budder," Nura said dreamily, eyes half open.

"You might as well go ahead and ask me," Tein said, facing her.

"Is there a way you can watch out for Ammar and not—"

He held up his hand, understanding. "I was up all night thinking about how to do it. I'll take him to the paper shop, not the mastaba. I can't protect him there. And I won't let Abu YingYue be dragged in."

It sounded fair, but she searched his expression for any doubt.

"I'm good. Trust me."

"I appreciate it, then. And I think you can be certain that Nasifa would, too."

Kamal Ali and Tein went to the gate.

She followed them and kissed her sleepy daughter and husband farewell, then shut the gate behind them.

Yulduz and Qambar had gone to their room to dress, and she sighed loudly, having the peace of the courtyard to herself for a moment. She reached to a lower branch of the pomegranate tree, touched the young fruit, and said a prayer for Layla and Abdulghafur. "May their tender hearts be protected, God. Those two have been through so much."

"Amin," Saliha said.

Zaytuna jumped, thinking she was alone. "You should be at work!"

But Saliha was lingering at the door to Layla's room, holding a scarf the girl had borrowed. "Girgis will be here soon?"

"God forgive you!" She smiled. "You are waiting for him? He is not as beautiful as all that."

"I will be the judge." She went to the gate to look for him, asking her, "Have you hired him yet?"

"You mean, as a regular? No."

Looking down the lane, she let out a delighted laugh. "I think your man Girgis is here."

He followed Saliha's welcome into the courtyard, saying, "Good morning, my esteemed ladies!"

"Bright morning to you, young man," Zaytuna answered.

He flashed them a winning smile with the power to unwind knots in Zaytuna's shoulders. But Girgis was more than a beautiful distraction. The heaviness of these cases, even the easy ones, pressed on her and he lightened her spirits. If Ammar refused, she would hire Girgis herself.

"So this is the one who says you should meddle?" Saliha asked, still taking him in.

"I am at your service," he bowed comically.

Yulduz emerged from the room, took one look at him, and her eyes sparkled.

Zaytuna restrained a laugh. "You need to find Adnan, the grandfather, for us again. We need to speak to him without his wife around."

Saliha gave Girgis a long look before turning her satisfied eyes on Zaytuna. "Hire him."

40

———————

When Ammar first met Razba, he had been sitting in the back of Abu YingYue's shop observing men block-printing prayers. He wore deceptively simple clothes but with the grace of a caliph pretending to be a commoner. The man who spent his free time with YingYue's father discussing developments in printing was the headman of the Ghuraba. His people were everywhere and everyone: scholars and businessmen, street healers and talisman sellers, ballad singers and the pickpockets who followed them. Razba ibn Salim's influence stretched into every corner of Baghdad's corridors of power, legal and criminal. But that day, Ammar had been brash with him and suspicious.

"Watch your manner with him this time," Tein said as they entered the Stationer's market.

He had hoped being with Tein would offer some sense of the old days with good banter and talk of theories and next steps. Aside from that one warning, Tein had led the way with his mouth shut—that is, until they neared Abu YingYue's shop. There, the warmth he had denied Ammar was shared with the market folk as he greeted clerks and shopkeepers by name and asked after their families.

Ammar knew Tein was a regular, but the familiarity still irked him. Zaytuna would say it was his own fault for not meeting Tein halfway, for wanting more from him than he could give. Years ago, Tein had invited Ammar to one of his philosopher's meetings, but he had been bored out of his head and vowed never to return. Now, seeing the life Tein had built without him and the camaraderie he shared with others, not him, stirred up a kind of resentment that turned into blaming Tein's cautiousness on a safe life of simple labour, children, and endless talk that did nothing.

"Ya, Tein! Ya, Ammar! Ahlan!" Abu YingYue was standing outside his shop chatting with a customer and had seen them coming. He bowed slightly to the customer and came to meet them. Ammar respected the man. As always, he was dressed to suit the modesty of his character in his usual undyed linen turban and robe. "What a pleasure, my brothers. Sit, sit." He gestured to a cluster of stools outside the shop.

Ammar looked in the back. Razba was not there.

"We can't stop for long, my apologies." Tein put a hand on Ammar's shoulder. "Ammar is on a case and needs to speak to Razba. I hoped he would be here."

"I have not seen him for several weeks." He looked at Ammar with concern. "Do you mind my asking why?"

"I think it is better left unsaid," Ammar answered.

"So much is better left unsaid in this life. Perhaps you should heed it."

Ammar took a step back. Abu YingYue had always been excessively polite. Yet here he was, passing on a warning and in a tone that bordered on rude.

Tein frowned at Ammar to punctuate Abu YingYue's words.

Ammar ignored them both. "I understand the risk of debt to Razba."

"I was hoping if Ammar met him here," Tein said, "it might be a friendly inquiry."

"Will my friendship with Razba be complicated by your request?"

Ammar said, "No. I will make sure of it."

"No," Tein said, correcting Ammar, "I will make sure of it."

Abu YingYue seemed reassured but asked tentatively, "Should I send word?"

"Please," Ammar said.

Abu YingYue went to the back to compose a message. Tein watched him rather than speak to Ammar, making him want to force a conversation. But Abu YingYue returned quickly, folded paper in hand.

"He gave me a location where I could send a message." Abu YingYue glanced at Ammar. "For all Razba's openness with me, he is a private man, and I do not press him for details."

"Like you," Tein said. "I do not think Ammar should take this step. But, as he said, he is willing to take on the risk. He was in the police for a long time before you met him. He understands."

"Yes, I remember that about you, Ghazi, sir." Abu YingYue inclined his head respectfully, but it was clear he still did not like it. He called over a boy who was waiting for work. "Son, take this to Ishaq al-Habashi, Bookbinder's Lane."

The boy ran off, and Abu YingYue gestured again to the stools. "Now, you must stop with me for some juice."

With the wave of a hand, another boy was there with a tray of glasses and a pitcher. The last time Ammar was here, he had a pomegranate juice that reminded him of days on the road to the frontier, stealing fruit off trees and carving out a full mouth of seeds with his teeth. He sat and watched the boy pour the juice out of the long-necked pitcher. It was apple ginger, hot and sweet on his tongue. It was a common enough mixture, but this was uncommonly good. He thought he might bring a small jar home to Nasifa. He had today's expenses to use, and he wanted to use them on her. She was as much the reason he was here, still on the case, as his own determination.

"Where do you get your juice?"

Abu YingYue smiled. "We have a man who does not serve the public, only the shops. He handpicks the fruit and is the master of blends that would make the caliph's court jealous."

Ammar sat back, sorry she could not enjoy it, too, and eyed Tein over his glass.

"I hear YingYue has had a letter from Mustafa with good news," Tein said.

"Yes." He sat down with them. "She has already sent her letter agreeing to Mustafa taking a second wife. We only hope that they will visit us soon. I miss my son-in-law, even if my daughter's marriage was not willed to be a typical one."

"Good morning, fellows!" It was Razba.

The three of them stood, returning his greeting.

He joined them, smiling through his trim beard, slightly out of breath, but somehow still graceful. "I came as soon as I got our dear Abu YingYue's note. I was with al-Habashi." He addressed Abu YingYue. "Beautiful binding on that manuscript."

Ammar waited, prepared to offer the deference Tein expected and that he hoped would get him the information he wanted. If he imagined Razba would treat him badly given how Ammar had been the last time they met, Ammar was wrong. The man appeared to have nothing but goodwill mixed with the acute interest he remembered.

"Abu YingYue tempted me with a mystery. I love a mystery." His eyes widened with pleasure. "Do you need me to solve the riddle of a talisman? Or do you no longer help out 'friends' with their troubles?"

Tein answered, "Ammar has opened a private investigations office near the Barmakid Hospital. I came with him only for the pleasure of meeting you again. It has been too long. While Ammar needs your help, I had hoped to hear about any further developments in printing that employs punch die letters to press on tin."

Ammar stared at Tein. He talked as if he had not just warned Ammar never to speak to Razba but, worse, like he grew up among the scholarly classes and had never seen a day on the battlefield. Was this the way he was now with Baraqan, Ibn Ali, and the others? How far apart had he and Tein grown? And Zaytuna? Her courage put her brother to shame.

"Let's talk about printing another day. I suspect Ammar here has more pressing matters on his mind." He chuckled at his own pun as he took the stool offered by Abu YingYue. "What can I do for you?"

"Have you heard of Karim Ibn Hisham al-Baghdadi?"

He crossed one leg over the other, revealing a densely patterned silk lining to his linen robe. "Yes, he was murdered in his home last night. A clean, if brutal, killing by someone who knew their craft."

"I want to know why he was hit."

"And why would I know?" He took a glass of juice offered by Abu YingYue. "The Ghuraba keep themselves to less deadly encounters with the public."

"I only want to understand why he died. I was at the house just before it happened, reporting to his future son-in-law on the death of his father."

"Maybe if you help me, it will bring something to mind?"

It was a request for an exchange of information. He glanced at Tein, who seemed hopeful. Maybe this is all that would be required of him? Ammar gave Razba as much as he could, recounting every detail that came to mind, even Suwayd's curses.

The man asked leading questions, trying to tease out secrets about the families and the tailor shops, but Razba was especially interested in Salma and the con game she was running.

"So she had several fathers on the hook for payments?" He raised an eyebrow. "Like the boy said, it is a fair business. All the same, I would not allow this in our community." He leaned in. "But tell me more about the young lovers."

Ammar tried to remember everything the Jewish apothecary had told him, even reciting her love poem, which delighted him.

Razba turned to Abu YingYue. "I am glad you called for me. This is fine entertainment."

But Ammar was there for more than this and hoped what he shared was payment enough. "I have reason to believe Ibn Hisham was involved in Samir's suicide."

"Interesting."

"May I discuss this part of the case?"

"If it is equally entertaining."

"Compelling, I hope." Ammar raised the objection he had from the start: "If Ibn Hisham did not want his daughter to marry Bashir, no matter Sitara's demands, he could have arranged for him to meet with an accident."

"It would have been simpler, I agree." He frowned. "But some men are not simple, and they enjoy the slow destruction of another."

"And you think Ibn Hisham was one?"

"I know he was one."

This was it. Ammar waited.

"I will tell you, because I want you to know, as a former member of the police and a man committed to justice, that justice comes in different forms and you are not the master of it."

Ammar felt his first real fear speaking to the man. He glanced at Tein, whose expression was rigid with expectation.

Abu YingYue recited, "*And never think that Allah is unaware of what the wrongdoers do. He only delays them until a Day when eyes will stare in horror.*"

"God most surely tells the truth." But then Razba recited, "*God is the Actor for whatever He desires.* And in this world, God's justice is delivered by means of the acts of His creatures."

"*They do not precede Him in speech or action, and they work by His command,*" Abu YingYue recited in response.

It felt like some kind of theological debate, but Ammar did not understand and did not ask, afraid of never getting the answer he needed.

Razba turned his attention to Ammar while keeping an eye on Abu YingYue. "Ibn Hisham was the head of a criminal organization. Yes, his import-export business is legitimate, but it is a cover for other, illegal endeavours about which I will not speak here so as not to endanger any of you or your families."

"Please, Razba, my friend," Abu YingYue said. "Say as little as possible." He looked at Tein with concern. "Perhaps you and I should leave so we do not hear anything further?"

Tein stood. "With our families mentioned, Ammar has gone further than I am willing to go. You have my word. I swear on God's name. Walla, I will not repeat what little I have heard already." Tein gave Ammar a look of warning and left with Abu YingYue in the direction of Baraqan's shop.

41

———————

"Shall we continue?"

Ammar asked, "Will my family be safe?"

"This is the line you draw?"

"Yes."

"Then I shall tell you as little as possible." He winked, sending a cold spike down Ammar's spine. "It was my plan, but I thought it was best if those two left. I do not want them involved in my business. My relationship with Abu YingYue is inviolable, and I have come to treasure my time with Tein and his friends."

"How often do you sit with them?"

"From time to time. I enjoy the debates and have made myself useful by procuring a manuscript they desired by al-Kindi." Razba slapped his thighs. "Back to Ibn Hisham."

"Please."

"What I am going to say is known only to the leaders of organizations with whom I share certain interests and a few of our trusted allies. You may never speak of it."

Ammar took a few shallow breaths, considering what such a secret might mean for him and his family, then reminded himself of Nasifa's courage and the courage she expected from him, and nodded for him to continue.

You may have noticed his daughter is uncontrollable, yet she is the delight of his eye."

"Yes."

"This is not her first time falling wildly in love. I hear there was a particularly handsome ostler at one point, and she had to be pulled from the bushes with her lover."

"What?" Ammar sat back.

"Shocking, I know, to see the upper classes behaving like the lower ones. But high or low, the soul is an animal if not tamed. Bushes and alcoves are enjoyed by the poor, hidden courtyards spilling with roses for the rich."

"Is she pregnant?"

"My sources say no. Your young man was chaste, not for her lack of trying."

"Why didn't Ibn Hisham marry her off ages ago?"

"You can imagine after the scene in the bushes, she has no reputation."

"But they said there was an engagement in the works, but when she fell for Bashir—"

He shook his head. "A story the family tells from time to time."

"Then why would he not marry her off to Bashir, since he is willing? It would seem like their social class and a suicide in the family are hardly barriers in this case."

Razba leaned in, a look of disgust on his face. "Because her father dotes on her."

"You mean he wants to keep his daughter near him. I've seen this in some families. They keep their daughters from marrying so that they will be constant company for them in their old age."

"Not that. No." He said slowly, so Ammar fully grasped his

meaning, "That she has not become pregnant with her own sibling is God's mercy."

A deep wave of sickness rolled through him. "How do you know?"

"She told the daughter of one of my allies in desperation once. The daughter told her mother, she told her husband, and the whispering spread among us. Ibn Hisham shut it down by claiming Sitara was mentally fragile, and given her behaviour, everyone believed him."

"But you believe what she said."

"Not only me. But I've seen it before. To me, her behaviour proved it was true."

God protect us from evil things!"

"Those abused sometimes act out recklessly, like Sitara, or retreat within themselves."

"But I saw them together. He had no control over her," he objected, not wanting to believe it. "How could he have forced her?"

"Ibn Hisham was obsessed with her. The effects of his crime on her bound her to him in turn." A ripple of anger crossed his expression that would make any man fear for his life.

It was true.

Razba gave Ammar a questioning glance. "Shall we move on to God's justice?"

But Ammar was remembering Sitara's pleasure with her father's death as if he were back in that room last night and how she stood rigidly beside her mother. "Did her mother know?"

"When mothers do not know, it is often because they have chosen ignorance over their children's safety. I have faith that God holds them to account."

The revelation sickened him further, but he took refuge in the mention of God's justice.

"Was Ibn Hisham killed for this?"

"Yes."

"Why did they let her suffer for so long, then? Why only now?"

"There is a code of what can be done and when. No one could act without deadly censure or anathema."

His back was up. "And raping his own daughter does not break the code!"

Razba put a hand on his thigh. "Quiet. Few believed her."

"Why didn't you do anything? Who could censure you?"

"We do what is in our power without starting a war. If it helps, in my community, I cast out those like Ibn Hisham—into the Tigris."

Ammar wished he had taken the dagger out of Ibn Hisham's chest and opened him up like the Arab warriors of old to throw his liver to the dogs.

The boy came by for the glasses, but Razba waved him off.

"For those of us who believed her, there was hope that Ibn Hisham would allow her to be married to the young embellisher. But then Bashir's father passed, and we became aware of Ibn Hisham's scheme to destroy the family. Those who previously denied Ibn Hisham's abuse of Sitara came to our side."

Ammar listened, hand on the hilt of his dagger.

"Despite one of us insisting that it was not suicide to all who would listen, those innocents in Grave Crimes covered up Samir's murder."

He wanted to shake Shabib and Ahab and tell them exactly what they had done, but he could never say it, and never would.

"Their compassion threatened the girl's escape."

"The one who insisted—Abu Fidda in Suq at-Tarrazun?" He had done everything in his power to push the case forward, unable to say why, and supported Bashir in hiring an investigator.

"Yes."

What had Abu Fidda said to him? He remembered, and a chill ran through him: "I am certain of God's justice. The killer will taste it, if not by your hand, then another's." Ammar muttered, "God help me," realizing he had been caught in other people's plans from the start. "Was it a coincidence that Bashir hired me? Or was it one of you?"

"As far as I know, it was the watchman's doing."

Ammar stood. "This is—"

"Take a moment." Razba leaned back against the shop wall, the glass of juice balanced between his fingers, and took small sips as Ammar stood before him trembling.

Ammar dug his thumbnail into his finger, hoping the pain would bring him around. It worked, but not before he drew blood.

"May we continue?"

He shook his head, not wanting to hear more, but sat again and said, "You said some men enjoy the slow destruction of another human being."

"Yes. The marriage to Bashir was never going ahead. Sitara had to remain ready to her father's hand. But instead of simply killing Bashir in an accident, as you suggested, Ibn Hisham chose to destroy the family. As we see it, he wanted their lives ruined, their business destroyed, their spirits crushed, and Sitara chastened. Would she try to leave him again when she saw what he could do to the man she loved, his family? He approached the father and told him that he had arranged for him to buy a particular shop to raise their status in order for the marriage to go ahead."

"What the family claimed was an inheritance?"

"Is that what they called it?"

"It seems so."

He frowned. "It was not a gift. It was a loan designed to destroy Samir. Repayment was meant to be a portion of the profits of the shop, but then Ibn Hisham charged exorbitant interest that the father could not pay."

"Bashir did not know."

"No."

"And Samir thought he had ruined his son's prospects and his family's future."

"Yes."

"All these details. You knew everything."

He paused before answering, "Not everything."

"The injured woman, Salma—was she involved?"

"I only heard of her today, from you. Perhaps a coincidence."

"The physical pain Samir suffered. Salma extorting him. The loan. Suwayd's curses. When Bashir finally took the business out of his hands, he must have been even more desperate."

"All was lost," Razba said. "Samir drank the poison."

"Ibn Hisham let slip he knew what kind of poison Samir had taken."

"I know nothing about that. It's possible Samir informed him that he planned to kill himself and how, and Ibn Hisham did nothing to stop him. But by all accounts, he presented himself as a brother to Samir and advised him closely. Who knows what he whispered in his ear? I can only say for certain that Ibn Hisham had finally gone too far, and the decision was made."

Ammar remembered Ibn Hisham's son, Keyvan, and his unsettling calm, slipping into his father's role so soon after he was killed. "May I ask if the son knows?"

"No, you may not. But justice is done. The girl is finally free of her father, and Bashir's family has justice, even if they will never know it."

"You consider it a murder, not a suicide."

"He was driven to it. I do."

"As do I." He looked at the simple embellishment on Razba's sleeve. "His friends said Samir recited Quran into every stitch."

Razba's face fell in a moment of unguarded sorrow. "What will you do now?"

"Find the man who made the poison."

"Good man."

"Thank you for your help." Ammar stood.

"Alhamdulillah." Razba said, standing with him to offer his farewell. "I hope you will be able to help me someday."

The price was more than the information he had already shared. Time slowed as he answered, "I am at your service."

42

"He's at the orphanage now, Lady," Girgis said.

Zaytuna gestured to Yulduz. "Let's go."

"Will 'e be there long?" Yulduz asked Girgis from where she and Qambar were sitting.

"I watch him off and on. He is at the brickworks from afternoon to sundown. He will not leave until after the midday meal."

"Sounds like you've been watching him nonstop," Zaytuna said.

"I will work hard for you. Harder than this if you hire me."

"Girgis, consider yourself a full-time and valued employee of Ghazi Ammar's Agency of Investigation and Implementation."

"And how much do you pay for such value?"

"We'll discuss it later with the boss, but I will not stint you."

"Lady Daughter of the Great Black Lover of God, I am yours!"

She gestured to Yulduz. "Do you hear that?"

"I'll not tell Kamal Ali," she quipped.

Qambar said to Yulduz, "As long as he does not pledge

himself to you, my love." It should have been a joke, and he tried to laugh, but his eyes welled with tears.

"Now, you." Yulduz blushed and got up, swatting at him as he tugged on her sleeve.

Qambar got up after her, but with difficulty, and groaned under his breath. Zaytuna reminded herself to speak to Ibn Ali about a stronger poultice for Qambar. Couches would be easier on him to get up and down, too.

"Maryam will prefer that one to 'er cousin," Yulduz said, taking her wrap off the peg.

"Her cousin!" Zaytuna had forgotten. "Is she still angry we did not hire him?"

"Only because she has to hear his complaints."

"We'll hire him when we have a case on that side of the city," Zaytuna said.

"Is it true?" Yulduz gave her a hard look. "I'll not lie to 'er."

Caught out, she smiled. "If you remind me when the time comes, it will be true."

Yulduz adjusted her wrap. "Let's go talk to this man, then."

Girgis said, "If you do not need me, I will walk with you part of the way. I must let them know at the canal I will not be returning."

He practically danced down the street in front of them. So far Girgis had been more than helpful, but, watching him walk so gaily, she worried that he could also not help but be noticed. Then his gait changed, shifting his shoulders forward and plodding heavily like a labourer, such that if she had not been watching the transformation, she would have thought it was a different man. He would work out just fine. When he finally disappeared into a crowd, she missed it entirely.

At the square, Zaytuna nodded to Abdussamad as he was placing small clay pots with steaming stew on a hanging tray for a waiting brothel worker. He gave her a quick nod, and she replied with a hand to her heart.

"There," Yulduz said.

Adnan was sitting in front of the orphanage. She had not gotten a good look at him before, when he was grieving on the brothel bench. Now she saw that Gul's father had a long face with a blunt nose and strangely long eyelashes, reminding her of a donkey. She half expected the children to demand rides from him, and his gentle demeanour told he would give them. Yasmin was running with the others in the dusty square but always kept him within sight. She watched them approach her grandfather with worried eyes. Zaytuna wanted to reassure her but left it to the people who loved her.

Adnan noticed them coming, sighed deeply, and then stood to greet them.

"I suppose it's time we meet." He gestured to Yulduz. "I saw this one and her friend. I'm sorry, but you were easy to lose."

Yulduz stiffened. It was just embarrassment, but sharp comments would soon follow.

"And me?" Zaytuna asked.

"Umm Hurayra told me about you."

Of course, she did. The Mother of Kittens only wanted to help.

Yulduz was close to making her case, and Zaytuna put a hand on her arm to silence her.

It was no good. Yulduz nearly spat at him. "See us or not! As if that's a crime? You lost your daughter. Now are you going to take that girl home to 'er family or not?"

Zaytuna closed her eyes with irritation.

The old woman carried on. "You! Lying to your wife all that time. Your wife, unwilling to do for that girl what needed doing and more worried you're cheating on 'er than if 'er daughter is still alive."

Given his wife's temper, Zaytuna assumed he was used to this from old women and knew to wait them out. And he did, stroking his beard and looking for all the world as if Yulduz were discoursing on the fineness of the weather.

When Yulduz had said all she had in her, Adnan spoke. "You got it all wrong. She knew I was looking for our girl. I'd been looking for Gul since the day she left. My wife insisted Gul would come home once the baby came close to being born. But Gul didn't. That day came and went. I kept looking, just kept it secret."

Zaytuna said, "She only suspected once you were taking out money."

"That's right."

"She never thought it was another woman?" Zaytuna asked.

"Never. Like I said, I knew my wife had hired you from our neighbour. So I was careful, watching out for that one and her friend," he said, gesturing to Yulduz. "I'd have missed that young man, but Umm Hurayra told me about him, too." He smiled. "Blushed, she did."

Zaytuna said, "He's the one who followed you here."

"I didn't notice. I guess you keep him on the rolls, then."

"Done." Zaytuna smiled.

He sighed again, this time as the weight of hiding had fallen from him, and sat down heavily.

"Does your wife know your daughter has passed?" Zaytuna asked. "God have mercy on her soul."

"Amin." He wiped new tears away. "No, not yet."

"What're going to do?" Yulduz demanded, stomping her foot.

"I'm bringing Yasmin home with me as soon as I can pay for her."

"When?" she asked with another, less forceful, stomp.

"When I have the money."

Zaytuna liked him. He was a quiet donkey of a man. No

braying, just plodding, stubborn steps that no berating woman could sway.

Yulduz gave up stomping and sat down beside him.

She pulled up a nearby stool. It was for a child, and Zaytuna's knees were almost up to her ears. "I look a fool."

"Not a fool to care about us," he said. "I'm thinking you disagree with my plan."

"Only because I worry you cannot afford to free her."

He heaved one sob, then quieted, and finally said, "I cannot."

"You alone? Or you and your wife?"

"Come. You've been following me. I shape mud into bricks. Even less now that I found Gul and Yasmin. My wife is good with little coin, but I know what we've got. All I can do is come here each day and make sure Yasmin knows her grandparents love her."

"So you'll tell your wife about her?"

"Didn't I just say so?" He looked out at Yasmin, who still had her eye on them. His face screwed up again with tears, and he covered it with his sleeve.

When it passed, she said, "There is a benefactor who would like to help you. But you and your wife must be ready, together, to take Yasmin home."

His back got up. "She is our girl. We must pay."

"People wiser than me said you would say the same. More, that if you did not pay, your wife would see the girl as a reminder of all she had done wrong."

"Treat her badly. I know it. She's a loving woman, but her ways are hard."

"What will you do?" Zaytuna asked.

"I could take on another job," he said, resigned to do whatever he can. "At night, so I don't miss my mornings with Yasmin."

"What if that benefactor could sway these people to lower the price of Yasmin's release?"

His face brightened with hope. "We would accept that with gratitude."

"I'll take care of it for you, inshallah."

Zaytuna got up clumsily from the tiny stool, laughing at herself and making them laugh. Then, she held her hand out to Yulduz. As she did, she saw a flash of red disappear into the brothel. Fatima. She would go speak to Auntie Hakima about her next. But now, she went inside the orphanage to see Umm al-Yatama and tell her that a benefactor would pay whatever the old couple could not.

43

———

The charge of his meeting with Razba had worn off, leaving Ammar in a state of simmering fury. The market was a blur as he made his way to confront Bilge al-Attar. His ears thumped. His breath was rough. When he arrived, a few of the apothecaries had already closed for midday, but most were still busy. Mazal had two customers, one waiting on a stool while she worked with the other. She wore the same honey-yellow and blue striped turban with sprigs of dried flowers sticking out of the folds. He wished his errand were with her. The sickness of Ibn Hisham's crime could not be healed by his death, and he needed her bright spirit, even a few lines of bad poetry. Instead, he found an alcove near Bilge's shop and hid within it, waiting for his last customer to leave.

Ammar had no plan. He could not arrest him. Grave Crimes had no interest. But he would have the truth. He left the alcove for the shop. Ammar could see his certificate in Chinese was no longer hanging in the shop.

"You are back," Bilge said, coming to the front.

Ammar smiled, arms outstretched. "This is my welcome?"

"What do you want?"

He put a hand on the counter between them. "Was anyone with Samir?"

A shadow of guilt settled into Bilge's expression, and he frowned.

"Tell me who."

"He's dead now. They are both dead," Bilge said. "Leave it."

"Say his name."

Bilge said, chin out, "The caring father of the bold daughter who threw herself at the son of a pitiable embellisher."

"And?"

"And nothing," he said coldly.

"I cannot arrest you."

"No, but you can continue to ruin me. After you left, Firdaws Ibn Ali came here with a marketplace inspector. They raided me! They went through my medicines and took what they liked. They stole my certificate saying I studied in the tradition of Sun Simiao." His voice rose as he gestured to where the certificate had once been. "Gone!"

Ammar nodded slowly. "I am certain they will return it as soon as it can be verified."

He leaned across the counter, full of pride. "This is how you know I have the truth! The authorities are after me! They are afraid of my knowledge. I will take their power and hand it to the people!"

"But they did not shut you down," Ammar replied.

"It was you who did this to me." He spat on the ground before Ammar.

Ammar answered him with the literal truth. "I did not ask them to come."

"They tried to stop me from prescribing my most potent remedies, but their conspiracy against me will not hold." He went to the back and brought out an opaque glass jar, carefully sealed with clay. "This"—he placed it reverently on the counter between them—"is toad venom. You tell them. They will never stop me from using it where necessary. I will never keep this remedy from the people."

"Your Chinese medicine?"

"Gone. This venom I procured from a woman who collects it from our marsh toads. I prepared it in the manner I was taught, in the tradition of Sun Simiao, which I am permitted to prescribe under my certificate. Sun Simiao. Do you hear me?"

He repeated the Chinese name as if it would put the calligraphy back on his wall.

"And Ibn Hisham came with Samir to get the toad venom?"

"No. He introduced Samir to me as a client." He said, gloating, "Ibn Hisham has been my client for years."

"I thought Samir had wandered across because Mazal's medicine was not strong enough."

"Yes." He paused. "No." Bilge seemed like he was trying to remember what lie he had told before.

"You prescribed the poultice for Samir with the toad venom and the opium and all that?"

"As I said."

"What else?" Ammar demanded.

"That is all."

"But he died."

"Where are you going with this?"

He shrugged. "Maybe I was wrong about you."

Bilge's expression betrayed a spark of hope. "Will you defend me to Ibn Ali? End this persecution?"

"I can tell him about this, yes."

"Tell him that Ibn Hisham's own doctor asked for my preparation of Samir's poultice."

"That's impressive."

"Yes! He had been treating Samir and saw its effects himself."

"Ibn Hisham brought Samir to you," Ammar said, nodding

in appreciation. "Got his own doctor to treat him? Ibn Hisham was concerned for Samir's health like family."

"Were they not to be family? Ibn Hisham even came to pick up what would be his last treatment so that Samir would not have to suffer the walk."

Here it was. Ammar exclaimed, "A great man like that!"

"God have mercy on his soul. It was my honour to have him as a client."

Ammar backed away from the counter and paced slowly, head down.

In the silence, Bilge continued to press his case. "His own doctor spoke of its benefits! Like nothing he has ever seen. You hear me?"

Ammar stopped pacing and faced him.

Bilge became frustrated and came around outside the shop. "Tell Ibn Ali what I have said. He will know I have been wronged. The best physicians in Baghdad know my name. They will restore my reputation!"

Ibn Hisham had procured the poison from Bilge. He had ruined Samir's life and convinced him suicide was the best thing to do for his family. No doubt, Ibn Hisham had promised Samir he would take care of his wife and children as his own. Ammar wondered whether he should tell Bilge but was stopped by an ugly thought.

He asked it as if he were preparing a case to defend him. "Let me get it straight for Ibn Ali. When did Ibn Hisham start seeing you?"

"Many years ago." Bilge jutted out his chin. "He first came to me for a sleeping potion and has been my satisfied client ever since."

"A sleeping potion? He did not seem like a man who had trouble sleeping."

"His young daughter was having difficulty."

Ammar took a step toward him, hands behind his back, and repeated, "His young daughter."

"The one betrothed now. I believe she was four or five at the time."

"And you prescribed it?"

"Yes. He was happy with the results and came back for it regularly."

"Did you ever see the girl or her doctor, or have any evidence at all that she needed it?"

He sputtered, "He—he described her symptoms to me! I prescribed as I would in any case."

"For a child."

"Yes, even a child." Bilge trembled and put a hand on the counter. "I thought you were here to defend me!"

Ammar squared himself, arms relaxed at his side. "I am. I know what Ibn Ali would ask. He'd want to know how long you prescribed it."

"She grew out of her sleeping troubles just a few years ago."

He choked back the vomit rising from his gut and asked with a low growl at the back of his throat, "Was there poppy seed or opium in it?"

"What do you think of me?"

Ammar forced himself not to say what he thought: Bilge al-Attar was a man who abetted another in raping his daughter and killing a vulnerable old man.

"What did you prescribe if not that?"

"A syrup of valerian and violet." He took a step back, a look of terror coming over his face. "That only."

Ammar had to know, even though knowing would torture him. "How deeply would she have slept?"

"I was justified in this. Ibn Ali would agree!" He took another step back, his hand now on the door to get back inside and put the counter between them.

Ammar held up his hands. "I just need to know."

"At—at that dosage, she would be very drowsy, but nothing like poppy. Ibn Hisham said she fussed and was afraid to sleep at night."

The first thing Ammar felt was his fist crushing Bilge's cheekbone. Then he was on top of him, punching him again and again. Then he felt hands on him, pulling him away. After, he saw the sky. A yellow and blue turban sprigged with flowers. And Mazal's face.

Then he heard her voice: "Ghazi, sir, I would have let you beat him longer, but the others pulled you off. You have protected the people of Baghdad. I will compose a poem about your heroism. Now, let me care for your poor hand. You have skinned your knuckles on his bones."

44

———————

"Fatima and I sit together at times." YingYue took Zaytuna's hand. "She pleads for God to forgive her, but she never opened up to me beyond that. I do what I can to reassure her, but Auntie Hakima asked us not to pry."

They were sitting in the courtyard arcade, alongside Auntie Hakima, shaded from the hot midday sun. From there, she could see the stairwell. A young man was gently rocking back and forth, whispering prayers. Others sat under reed awnings, chatting quietly, while another tapped absentmindedly on a drum.

Auntie Hakima said to them both, "You did right. We do not pry into the soul of a seeker without invitation, by them or by God."

That surprised Zaytuna, but she left it, asking, "What should we do?"

YingYue said, "If Auntie Hakima agrees, I have a room available in my home. My father and I will care for her."

"Yes, alhamdulillah," Auntie Hakima said, smiling.

"The guard said she will lose her job soon."

"The timing is as God willed it." Auntie Hakima touched Zaytuna's arm. "You did well to notice and bring it to us."

Zaytuna was relieved, wondering at God's will that allowed her to hear Gul's call, leading not only to Yasmin's grandparents bringing her home but also to Fatima's safety—but wondering, too, at Auntie Hakima's claim that they do not peer into a person's soul without invitation. It was not true, and Fatima could have been helped long before this. These people had pried into her own soul. All that time when she had been in so much pain—a woman acting out like a troubled child—the Sufis of this community had seen her and known how to heal her.

She remembered the first time she had seen her uncle Junayd again after having stayed away for so long. The greatest of the masters had thrust her head into the ocean of divine oneness until she drowned in it for just one moment, passing away from herself, forcing her onto the path to peace. If they had not looked without invitation, what then?

Auntie Hakima coughed, calling her to attention. "Tell me about the girl at the orphanage. Tell me about the fixing."

There it was; the old woman had been looking. She had never mentioned the vision, nor would Kamal Ali tell Auntie Hakima without her express permission. "I did not invite you," she teased, but it sounded petulant.

"The moment you came to us as a child, forlorn, your hand in your mother's and Tein in the other, you were begging us to see you."

"Every child begs to be seen."

"Here is the difference." She poked her finger into Zaytuna's thigh. "You begged to be seen every minute of every day, in your childhood and after; even when you were hiding from us, your heart called out to us. We never left you. Your uncles followed you in heart and in person. This old aunt never took her eye off you."

The revelation touched her. She twisted the strands of wool

on the sheepskin underneath her as gratitude expanded beyond her body to God and to this community for holding onto her.

YingYue asked, "Fatima does not want to be seen?"

"It's the shame she carries. Shame traps a heart. But she is here. She wants to release it, and we will not abandon her. When she opens her heart to us, we will help her unravel her troubles."

"I wonder how she got there," YingYue said sadly.

"Some women choose that life, but I can say with certainty Fatima did not."

"How do you know?" Zaytuna asked. "If you have not been invited into her heart?"

"The shame. There is no shame in those who choose it"—she paused—"and I will not judge them."

YingYue seemed shocked.

"Oh!" She waved her off. "I would not choose it for them, but God knows the paths of His servants, not me. Remember the Prophet's account of the brothel woman in the desert who gave a thirsty dog water before she drank herself? And what he said about the pious woman who tortured the kitten? One was rewarded with paradise; the other promised hell."

Zaytuna remembered and said, "God is truly the Just."

"Now, woman. Answer me. What about this case?"

Auntie Hakima was not asking about the details of her investigation. Zaytuna let the question sit for a moment before saying, "I did not want to help at first because Gul's life was too close to my mother's. That her child's life was too close to my own and Tein's. It grieved me, and I did not want to touch that grief."

"What did you grieve about for your mother?"

"That my mother had suffered. That she carried a burden."

"That you and Tein were her burden?"

"She loved us with the love of mothers. I do not doubt that.

Not anymore. It was her suffering." Zaytuna shuddered at the image of her mother under the olive tree and the night Zaytuna lay beside her as she was raped.

"And what did your mother say about herself?"

She saw herself standing in the street, feeling her mother's presence, hearing her words, and answered, "She carried no burden. But how can I believe that?"

"Your mother was like Prophet Abraham in the fire. She was not burned."

"Not even in body?" Zaytuna stared, not understanding. "Fixing what was between God and her—I thought she meant she trusted God so wholly that her soul was protected no matter what happened to her body."

Auntie Hakima laughed lightly. "Your mother is not like you and me. She trusted God, accepted His will, and was accepted by Him, then perfected. That was her fixing."

She felt relief wash through her like a gentle wave. But she knew the grief would return and she would have to remind herself again and again until it settled into her heart: *My mother was like Abraham in the fire. She was not burned.* The vastness of her mother's station with God was beyond her. She asked, "If that is 'fixing', how can any of us?"

"Fixing has levels. We are invited to fix at our level; our level is what we can bear—remember, *God does not burden any soul with more than it can bear*—and God does not take us to task beyond that."

The washerwoman who checked on her when she was running from Bint Afshin's home had recited that same verse to her. What else has she said? Zaytuna remembered, and her heart clenched: "It'll get hotter until you take care of what's hounding you." But she did not know how to take care of the rest. She pleaded, "My mother told me to lift Gul's burden—"

"Yes?"

But she could not answer because she did not know what else her mother had said. She had run and had not heard the rest. "How could I fix what is between God and Gul? Gul died."

The old woman became quiet for a moment, and then she let out a deep humming sigh. Taking Zaytuna's hand, she said. "You did not hear what your mother said."

"No, not all of it."

"Not Gul. Not Gul." She closed her eyes and sighed again. "Oh, how I missed your mother."

Then Zaytuna felt a bead in her fingers where there was none and knew. "Not Gul. Me. Fix what is between God and me."

"What went wrong?"

The first touch of awareness opened up to her. "I ran from what my mother said, then I ran at it, desperately, and nearly ruined everything."

Eyes bright, YingYue said, "Tell us."

She let her thoughts unravel before the two women. "It's about more than this case. I think that without me everything will fall to pieces. So I rush at wrongs to right them and sometimes hurt people. I nearly hurt Gul's daughter. I did hurt Layla, I ignored my brother's pain, I insulted Nasifa, and I unmanned Ammar." Ammar—she winced at how she had made him feel incapable of the most basic things. "I ignored their needs, belittled their strengths, and shamed them."

Auntie Hakima asked, "How is knowing that fixing what is between God and you?"

Zaytuna focused on the young man tapping the drum and let its beat slowly move her forward in understanding. "When my mind is rushing, I have difficulty even seeing what God has willed for me: what He has put before me—what to do, when to do it, and how. And I have difficulty hearing others' wisdom or even their own wishes."

"You see and hear now more than you did, but you'll be learning this lesson for some time."

"Some time." A spark of frustration lit within her. Zaytuna closed her eyes for a moment. She was doing it again. She even wanted to rush at growing into trusting God. "I don't trust that what is meant for me now is already with me and what is meant for me in the future will come to me."

Auntie Hakima nodded. "I was chatting about trust with a friend, a Jewish woman who makes medicine. She recited from one of their books: *To everything there is a season and a time to every purpose under the heaven.*"

It was beautiful, but she still felt like a fool who would never learn.

YingYue swayed, her eyes far off, and said, "Do not be hard on yourself, my sister. The signs of God are in the turning of the heart: its movement is between remembering and forgetting." Her eyes glistened. "Mustafa taught me that our prophet Muhammad—God bless him and peace—said, 'The hearts of the children of Adam are between two fingers of the All Merciful; He turns them as He wills'."

Auntie Hakima held her hands open in prayer. "Can we raise this need to rush up to God now?"

Her mother's presence became an embrace, and Zaytuna answered, "Yes."

Auntie Hakima recited the Prophet's prayer, "'O Turner of Hearts, make my heart firm upon Your way'."

Zaytuna released herself into it and felt as if a long-nagging question had been answered. Where she expected such an answer would tell her what to do, this one told her not to do anything at all. She wept with relief as the sense that she was required to tend to every fire—any fire at all—fell away.

"Now, my daughter. How are you?"

"In truth"—she paused, breathing easy—"as if I had a thousand and one nights' sleep, and all of them in my husband's arms."

"Now," she lowered her voice, tipping her head toward the kitchen where Abdulghafur was working with Hilal. "Have you talked to Kamal Ali?"

"He thinks we should let it go, and she will tire of him. I know he can find her a suitable man when she is old enough."

"What do you think?"

Zaytuna took a moment, settling into herself, trusting that a door would open. "She is too young to even think of marriage, let alone know what she wants—but what she wants is correct for any age: love and a home."

"Yes."

She started, "I wanted more for her than him, because—" She stopped, not wanting to say it in front of YingYue.

Auntie Hakima pressed, "Tell us your true worry."

She looked at YingYue, begging for understanding. "That she loves him the way I loved Mustafa, a childhood attachment borne of having only each other, an attachment that made sense as children but not as adults."

YingYue's eyes softened, and she squeezed Zaytuna's hand.

"You and Mustafa did not share the same character," Auntie Hakima said. "YingYue and Mustafa were right for each other; it was only that she was meant for God alone—"

She wanted to kiss Auntie Hakima for honouring YingYue and Mustafa's love.

"—but Layla and Abdulghafur."

"Layla has found an oasis with us," Zaytuna said, "with this community, and she does not want more. In that, she is very much like Abdulghafur; they only want a life of peace in their small world."

As if they had conjured her, Layla came running through the courtyard toward the kitchen but stopped short when she saw them. Her sweet girl blushed to her ears and then frowned angrily at being caught.

Zaytuna shot up and hurried to her, taking her hands. "I was wrong. I haven't been listening. I haven't been seeing what you truly want. If you love him, we welcome him."

Layla jerked her hands away, then drew her wrap over her eyes, stifling tears. Zaytuna pulled her into an embrace, and Layla fell into it as she used to, holding on as if she might be torn away.

When she quieted, Zaytuna lifted Layla's face and kissed her cheeks. But then her mind raced ahead of her, past everything she had just realized, straight to the risks she imagined Layla was taking with Abdulghafur, and said, lightly scolding, "We will do this right. No more hiding or sneaking off to the canal with your girlfriend to cover for you."

A look of horror came over Layla's face.

Only a moment before, Zaytuna had felt free of rushing at everything, and here she was doing it and hurting her sweet daughter again. She took Layla's hands before the girl could run away and kissed them. "I am sorry, my sweet. I am the clumsy woman love turned into a mother. God forgive me. Have him come and speak to us formally. If he wants to marry you—"

"He wants," she said, her eyes pleading.

She gave herself a moment to trust, to find a touch of ease before she spoke, then said, "A long engagement, for all our sakes. He is our family now. We will work it out with Hilal and your father. Will you do that?"

Eyes wide, she exclaimed, "Anything! Yes!" And she ran off to the kitchen.

Auntie Hakima joined Zaytuna. "You rushed. You stopped. You trusted. As YingYue said, forgetting and remembering, over and over, but always forward. This is fixing. And you meddled wisely."

45

Bloodied fist salved and bandaged by Mazal, Ammar stalked off like an animal with the taste of blood in its mouth and headed to Ibn Hisham's estate. People gaped and scattered. By the time he reached the estate, he looked wild and stank. He knew the truth and wanted to shove it in their faces.

A servant opened the gate. Ammar pushed him aside, other servants stepping back as he stormed through the courtyard and into the great room where Ibn Hisham had been killed.

Keyvan, Sitara, and their mother were there with the men from Grave Crimes. Keyvan was holding court as Shabib and Ahab were no doubt trying to explain why there would be no investigation. Sitara sat away from them all, wrapped in black, staring into the distance, and had not noticed him come in.

"What is the meaning of this!" Keyvan stood up.

Shabib and Ahab watched him guardedly, then Ahab stood ready to intervene.

But Ammar walked past their stares to Sitara. "I know what your father did to you. Does Bashir know?"

Her vacant stare transformed into pleading. "Yes. He hated

lying to you. But he did it to protect me. To protect his father. He is an honourable man."

"I'll take you to him, if you want."

She gaped at Ammar for only a moment, then stood, taking hold of him. Keyvan stood but held an arm out, stopping Ahab and Shabib from rising. He only heard a strangled gasp from her mother.

No one moved but he and Sitara.

Ammar did not have to drag her along. Sitara kept pace with him as they rushed out of the house and across the courtyard. A servant opened the gate for them, begging them to hurry. Out of the gate, she broke free of Ammar and ran ahead, her black wrap billowing behind her. A man pulling a dung cart laughed as she passed.

Had it happened so fast that no one had followed? They were well away and still running when he finally heard footsteps behind him. She did not stop. He yelled to her, roaring, "Don't stop! Find Bashir!"

Ammar watched until she had turned the corner and was out of reach, then faced them, not knowing who to expect. He was surprised to find only her brother.

Keyvan stood before him, gasping for air yet commanding, his father resurrected. "How dare you!"

"One way or another, she's not coming back," Ammar said, breathing hard.

"I will have Grave Crimes arrest you for abduction."

He said it with the certainty of a man who knows his connections, but Ammar did not care.

"Promise me you'll sign their marriage contract," Ammar said.

"You think she'll last? She'll be fucking that dung collector in a month."

Ammar pressed his stinging knuckles against the palm of

the other hand, begging himself not to fall into unseeing rage and tear this man to pieces. He said through gritted teeth, "Sign the contract."

"I am the guardian of this household." He seemed to take strength from Ammar's barely controlled fury. "She belongs to me, and no one takes what is mine."

Ammar took a step towards him, ready to ask if he felt safe from the men who had killed his father. But Keyvan was looking over Ammar's shoulder, and his composure cracked.

Khalil drew up beside Ammar. "Brother, need a hand?"

Keyvan took several steps back. "You! You were outside the house that day."

"I am sure you did not tell those police that. Not that it would matter. They have their instructions." He turned to Ammar. "What's happening here?"

It should have been a relief. Instead, he was trapped on both sides and could not answer.

"What was our good friend Keyvan saying?" Khalil asked again into his silence.

Ammar found his voice. "He was praising God for his sister's coming marriage."

Keyvan took another step backwards.

"He said he would give up his rights as Sitara's guardian to me."

"I like this plan," Khalil said, drawing close to Keyvan with menacing ease. "That way, Sitara will marry well and live in the sunlight of good society."

"I, uh—" Keyvan stammered.

"You must be a very busy man, what with your father's tragic demise. Wise to give up your rights over her."

Keyvan glanced behind him as if he hoped to run, then said quickly, "The ghazi is her guardian now."

A man was hurrying past, skirting wide around them. Khalil

called out to him, "You heard him, right? Keyvan ibn Karim ibn Hisham al-Baghdadi has made this man, Ghazi Ammar at-Tabbani, his sister's guardian."

The man nodded fearfully, grasped the edge of his long robe, and ran.

Servants from neighbouring estates had come into the street, pretending to be on errands, but were taking in the scene. Keyvan noticed and tried to restore his dignity, standing straight and saying formally, "By God, I vow I will not challenge it."

But Khalil took one bursting step toward him and yelled, "Go!"

Keyvan nearly tripped over himself as he ran back to the estate.

"You going to make sure the lovers marry?" Khalil said as he sauntered back. "That's sweet."

Ammar swayed. The world was swimming before him.

Khalil put a hand on his shoulder. "I got you, brother."

He bent over, hands on his knees, as much to get Khalil off him as to get his bearings. "Keyvan can still take it back," Ammar said heavily. "The part about the guardian. He can still stop her."

"No, he can't. You know there are people who will make sure he keeps his vow."

Khalil would put the word up the ladder. It was done. She would be free.

"I've never seen you like this." Khalil sized him up. "And what happened to your hand?"

What could he say? That he had gone so far for the truth he had compromised himself to men like Abu Sa'id and Razba? That he may never be free of them? That he would do it again, if only to honour Samir's death with the truth and release Sitara? Ammar had no choice but to act a part and put Khalil at ease.

He stood unsteadily and shrugged. "All this for what? A fine romance? I probably won't even get paid. Bashir's business is ruined." He smiled crookedly. "I'll be herding goats this time tomorrow."

"Not at all, brother." Khalil put his arm around Ammar, pulling him in close. "Their business has been restored. And I have been assured that you are to be paid handsomely for your efforts. Where now, friend? Food? A street performer?"

"Get me to the bridge to Buratha. I need my wife. I need my son."

"Don't say we can't find some justice in this world, Ammar." He led Ammar away. "Never say that."

AFTERWORD

I plotted this novel before I wrote *Disgraced*, my first contemporary thriller written under the pen name Jayne Green, and only picked up writing *Some Justice* again recently. As a result, I misplaced my early notes of acknowledgement. I tend to ask offhand questions and request assistance and keep a list of everyone's names. My sincere apologies to all.

My gratitude goes to Murat Coskun, whose guidance influenced my characterization of Zaytuna's experience on the Sufi path for a contemporary audience. To Fatima Khan, a therapist and social worker, who advised me on writing about suicide with contemporary readers in mind. Emily Silkaitis, who shared her work and that of others on suicide in early Islam. Jibril Stevenson, who came up with the name "Ghazi Ammar's Agency of Investigation and Implementation." Jess Tat for her incredible map. Abu Noor Abdul-Malik Ryan, Ahmad Aburayya, Omar Anchassi, Nazila Isgandarova, Carool Kersten, Nassima Neggaz, and Arin Salamah Qudsi, who answered questions and helped me with resources. All those on Facebook who advised on cover design. Tracy Shirvill for a much needed beta read and vote of confidence. Karen Heenan and James

Thompson for conversations about writing. Oliver Coffee Bar (and its cheering section), where I plotted and edited most of this book. Finally, Karen Heenan and Michael Quinsey for detailed notes and edits.

This novel could not exist without the extensive assistance of those who shared resources and answered questions for the books in The Sufi Mysteries Quartet. For detailed accounts of the historical sources that inspired my medieval Baghdad novels and my long list of acknowledgements, see The Sufi Mysteries Quartet. For reflections on writing historical fiction, see the blog section of my website. www.llsilvers.com

———

As always, independent authors need your support. We do not have the promotional tools enjoyed by authors who are traditionally published. We cannot even get our books reviewed by big media or go up for significant awards. We need you, the reader, to help us out by leaving reviews on your favourite online platforms. Even just a few words are a tremendous help. Also, word-of-mouth matters. If you enjoy our books, tell a friend, make a post on social media. Thank you!

ABOUT THE AUTHOR

Laury Silvers is a North American Muslim, retired historian of early Islam, and activist in the gender-justice movement, now writing novels inspired by her research, her advocacy, and her wild imagination. She writes contemporary thrillers set in Toronto under the pen name "Jayne Green."

Visit www.llsilvers.com to find out more, including details about her first series, *The Sufi Mysteries Quartet*, murder mysteries set in tenth-century Baghdad with historical and mystical backstories; "Rat City," her alt-medieval noir novella in the collection *Revenge in Three;* and *Disgraced*, the first Toronto Thriller published under the pen name Jayne Green.

All social media platforms @laurylsilvers

A HARD WOMAN

THE SECOND GHAZI AMMAR
MEDIEVAL MYSTERY • COMING 2027

Yusuf al-Multani is worried his favourite wife is up to no good.

Private investigator Ghazi Ammar at-Tabbani is not eager to take the case. No man wants to hear his wife is unfaithful, but bringing the truth to an underworld boss like al-Multani could prove dangerous—for his wife, Rayhana, and for Ammar himself. Ammar's partner, Zaytuna, wants him to take the job, if only to find a way to warn Rayhana off her lover.

Ammar is determined to stay out of it until a mysterious message arrives through Abu YingYue asking him to take the job as a personal favour. He knows who sent it and knows he cannot refuse.

Working with Zaytuna, Ammar believes he can find a way to protect al-Multani's wife and perhaps even save their marriage. But the deeper he digs, the more he discovers Rayhana is in too far over her head to be saved—not just from her husband's suspicions, but from the very people she thought would protect her.

A SMALL TOWN

A TORONTO THRILLER • COMING 2026

From Jayne Green

Denora Dunne has a secret no one knows, not even her estranged daughter. When hints arrive on scribbled bits of paper through her mailbox, Denora wants to know who sent them and how they found out. A retired life of spy novels, trips to the local coffee shop, and losing the fight with her messy garden did not prepare her for neighbours turned into secret police, peering through doorbell cameras and sharing tips on the Small Town app. But she'll do anything to protect herself and her daughter, and if she's learned anything from all the novels she's read, it's how to isolate an enemy spy and plug a leak, even if that means murder.

OUT NOW BY LAURY SILVERS
AND HER AKA JAYNE GREEN

THE SUFI MYSTERIES QUARTET • LAURY SILVERS

THE LOVER • THE JEALOUS • THE UNSEEN • THE PEACE

Enter into the world of medieval Baghdad as Zaytuna and Tein solve mysteries and come to terms with the legacy of their mother and the violence that has consigned them to lives without love. Widely used in university courses, each mystery uncovers a different aspect of medieval Islamic history.

"Completely engrossing and richly atmospheric. Tenth century Baghdad comes alive through the eyes of a dazzling cast of characters." —Ausma Zehanat Khan, critically acclaimed author of Blackwater Falls, A Deadly Divide from The Getty-Khattak Mysteries, and The Khorasan Archives

RAT CITY in REVENGE IN THREE • LAURY SILVERS

Love, money, power, betrayal... revenge. The Count of Monte Cristo has enthralled generations of readers the world over. Now three Muslim authors offer their interpretations of this classic tale. From the seedy underbelly of a medieval plague fortress, to the lawless borderlands of the Wild West, to the darkest depths of outer space, each novella delivers a full dose of adventure and excitement while exploring different aspects of society, politics and religion.

Rat City • Alt-Medieval Noir • Laury Silvers

In the walled city of Aman Kala, the grisly murder of a sacred Rat Keeper pulls Detective Derya Mack into an investigation that threatens to expose the power struggles that guarantee the very safety the fortress offers from the plague world.

The Pasha of Texas • Western • Jibril Stevenson

A botched robbery lands Eddie Dawson in a Mexican prison. His friendship with a Muslim prisoner opens the door to repentance and faith, if he could only let go of the ghosts of his past.

The Spatial Condition • Science Fiction • J. Austin Yoshino

Mohsin Dawoud, 3rd mate on the interstellar cargo freighter "Nightshade", has been preparing for life in space with his betrothed, Solmaz. When the Nightshade is attacked, it draws him into a conspiracy of jealousy and greed among Earth's most powerful that could destroy the life he spent years building.

DISGRACED • A TORONTO THRILLER • JAYNE GREEN

When cybersecurity expert Nick Barnes targets the payday loan company that ruined his mother's life, those in his path are forced into desperate and compromising actions. From a young journalist who sacrifices her integrity to a lonely man caught in the cult behind it all, Nick's vigilantism triggers redemption for some and self-destruction for those unwilling to confront their own twisted desire for justice.

A tenacious journalist • A predatory loan company • A hacker out for vengeance • A secretive cult

A young journalist, Tomoko Abrams, stumbles onto her first big story—a professor and his graduate student are on the run after exposing a predatory loan giant. But the anonymous data behind Martin and Parisa's analysis is tainted, sent to them by Nick Barnes, a cyber-security guru bent on revenge. Little does Nick know that his plot to take down Wellington Payday Loans is caught up in the prophecies of a secretive religious cult, a cult involving Martin's brother, Conor, and a mysterious man who seems to be controlling it all.

———

My novels are available through all online booksellers, large and small, and on order from your local Bookseller.

CONTENT NOTICE

The novel addresses sexual violence against a female child, suicide, psychological manipulation, and women and children living in vulnerable conditions, including sex work.

On suicide, some readers may find the novel disturbing. It depicts a spectrum of medieval attitudes towards suicide, some supportive, others not. Ibn Ali's view, stated with clarity, is grounded in classical perspectives and leans into my own. Please see the terms page, which has a section on medieval views of suicide.

If you have experienced loss or thoughts of self-harm, you are not alone. Support is available through local services, or you can reach out to:

- In the U.S.: National Suicide Prevention Lifeline—call or text **988**
- In Canada: Talk Suicide Canada—**1-833-456-4566 (24/7)**
- If outside North America, visit **findahelpline.com** for international resources.